# HIDING IN THE DARK

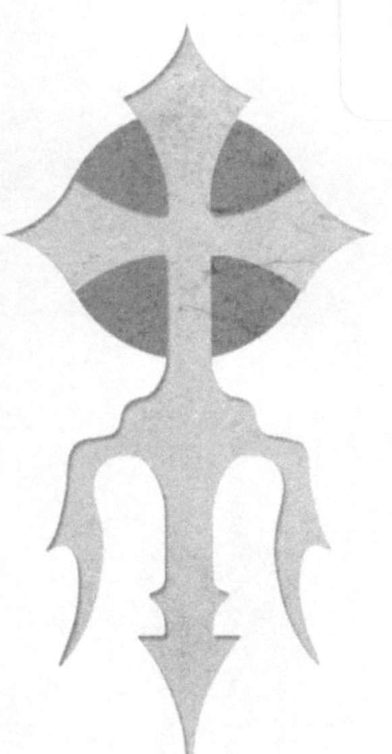

THE RIGHTEOUS SERIES BOOK 4

## BROOKLYN CROSS

RINGO

MEL
SCOOTER
PEREZ

SPECIAL DEDICATION
TO ALL THOSE THAT
RISK THEIR LIVES SO WE CAN
LIVE FREE AND TO THE FRIENDS AND
FAMILY THAT SUPPORT THEM.
Thank You

# ALSO BY BROOKLYN CROSS

The Righteous Series

(Vigilante/Ex Military Romance - Dark 3-4 Spice 3-4)

Dark Side of the Cloth

Ravaged by the Dark

Sleeping with the Dark

Hiding in the Dark

Redemption in the Dark

Crucified by the Dark

Dark Reunion (Coming 2023)


The Consumed Trilogy

(Suspense/Thriller/Anti-Hero Romance - Dark 4-5 Spice 3-4)

Burn for Me

Burn with Me

Burn me Down (Coming 2023)


The Buchanan Brother's Duet

(Serial Killer/Captive Horror Romance - Dark 4-5 Spice 3-5)

Unhinged Cain by Brooklyn

Twisted Abel by T.L Hodel


Lost Souls Series - World Crossover with T.L. Hodel's World

(Motorcycle Club/Enemies to Lovers/Friends to Lovers/Revenge/Redemption/Strong MFC/Possessive MMC - Dark 3.5-4.5 Spice 3-4.5)

Malice - Releases March 28, 2023

Surrender - Releases May 16, 2023

Showbiz - (Coming Soon)


The Battered Souls World

(Standalone Books Shared World Romance/Dramatic/Women's Fiction/All The Feels- Dark 2-3 Spice 2-3)

The Girl That Would Be Lost

The Boy That Learned To Swim (Coming Soon)

The Girl That Would Not Break (Coming Soon)


The Brothers of Shadow and Death Series

(Dystopian/Cult/Occult/Poly MMF Romance - Dark 3-4 Spice 3-4)

Anywhere Book 1 of 3

Backfire Book 1 of 3 by T.L. Hodel


Seven Sin Series

(Multi Author/PNR/Angel and Demons/Redemption - Dark 2-5 Spice 3-5)

Greed by Brooklyn Cross

Lust by Drethi Anis

Envy by Dylan Page

Gluttony by Marissa Honeycutt

Wrath by Billie Blue

Sloth by Talli Wyndham

Pride by T.L. Hodel

# AKNOWLEDGEMENTS

It is with love
that I would like to thank my
'Fluffy', Good Girl
friend for spending hours of her precious
time letting me interview her.
She took the time to share her private life
and the intimate details of her
daily struggles. I not only appreciate
her trust in me to share these difficult
moments of her life, but that she
trusted me enough to use parts of
her story in my book.
Thank You

# *Playlist*

Battle Lines - Bob Moses (Series Anthem)
No Roots - Alice Merson
Ride The Lightning - Warren Zeiders
Heathens - Twenty One Piolets
Phobia - Nothing But Thieves
Dog Days Are Over - Florence + The Machine
Zen - X Ambassadors, K.Flay & grandson
23 - Chayce Beckham
Beggin - Maneskin
Something To Lose - Landon Twers
Stronger - Kanye West
Die A Happy Man - Thomas Rhett
Stay - Rihanna
Bells - The Unlikely Candidates
Ironic - Alanis Morissette
Thunderstruck - AC/DC
Kryptonite - 3 Doors Down
Thinking Out Loud - Ed Sheeran

# READ AT YOUR OWN RISK

This is a Dark Romance novel
and is intended for mature audiences only.
This book is for sale to adults ONLY, as defined
by the country's laws in which you made your purchase.
This book may contain violence,
graphic scences that include non-consensual
and dubious consensual sexual scenes,
alcohol and tobacco use, strong language,
bully themes, and scenes that some readers
may find disturbing.
Like most other content rating systems this is
only used as a guide.

# PROLOGUE

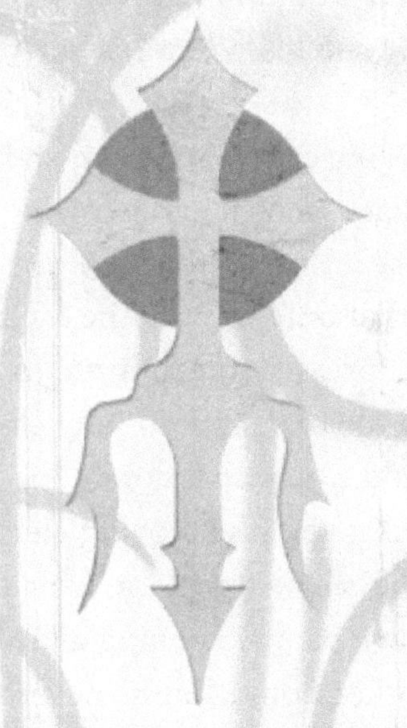

*Twenty-two years ago.*

Kes hated the stupid plaid tie he had to wear for school. He yanked on the knot that felt like it was choking him and undid the top button of his dress shirt. Why did he have to wear a stupid uniform?

He looked out the window as the large town car made a turn, and he groaned.

"Did you say something, Kestrel?" the driver asked.

He pulled his Spiderman backpack up on his lap and dug around until he found his sketch pad and pencil. "No. Why are you taking me to my dad's office? I thought I was going home," he sulked as he worked on his latest masterpiece. He was really proud of this one. It had taken days to get the shading right, but the tall skyscrapers looked amazing, and so did the shocked looks on the people below as Spiderman sailed from one web to the next above them.

"I'm sorry, I didn't ask. You know the drill."

"I know, I know. Dad wouldn't tell you why he does anything. I just kinda hoped. I hate going to his work. It's boring, and all he does is talk on the phone."

The large shiny building came into view, and a few minutes later, Kes was hopping out the back and being escorted inside. His dad's driver handed him off to the security guard like a bag of lunch, who took him to the private elevator that only went to the top floor.

The security guard pressed the button to take him up and then stepped out and waited for the doors to fully close. Like he was going to run anywhere, what good would that do?

His stomach lurched as the fast-moving elevator came to a stop, and he stepped out onto the silent top floor. You'd think that a big, fancy place like this would have people running all over the place, and maybe it was like that on the other floors, but he never went to see those. It was always the same on the top floor.

He passed two executive offices that had titles he didn't really understand, but no one was inside. At the end of the hallway was his dad's office, but the girl who normally sat there waiting for him wasn't around either.

Annoyed, he pushed his way through the door to the outer area of his dad's office and stopped as the sound of a scream reached his ears. His heart beat faster as he neared the mostly closed door to his dad's office. More screams, softer this time. There were more sounds as he got closer —grunting like an animal, and moans that ended with really bad swear words.

Kes peeked through the crack in the door, and his eyes went wide as he saw his dad doing something the other boys talked about and passed around pictures of from dirty magazines. He might only be eight, but some of the older boys loved to show off their collections, and he was curious, so he'd looked. His dad's naked butt flexed as he was screwing the secretary, at least that's what his friends called it. His hand was wrapped in her hair, yanking her head back. That was all he could see of her other than her legs, which were spread around his Dad's, but it was enough to know that his dad was cheating on his mom.

"Oh fuck, Mr. Reynolds! Yes!"

Tears of anger welled up in his eyes as he backed away from the door and went to sit out in the waiting area. He was livid. He pressed the pencil hard into the next picture he started to draw and broke off the lead of his pencil. Kes dug around in his backpack until he found the sharpener. He angrily twisted the pencil around the little whole trying to drown out the moans with the grinding noise. The pencil sharp once more, he worked on the image of Venom. The thought of his dad and what he was doing and the stupid noises faded away. That's how he saw his dad—a villain just like Venom in Spiderman, someone he couldn't trust. His dad lied to his mom. Lied to him. Their whole family was a *lie*.

The door opened, and the secretary and his dad stopped talking as they saw him sitting in the waiting room. He glared at them, wanting to say something, but kept his mouth shut.

"Oh, Kestrel. I'm sorry I wasn't out here to greet you. Your father and I were finishing up a meeting," the secretary said, smiling as she continued to smooth down her skirt.

He didn't say anything—he just continued to glare until his dad spoke. "It's not polite to ignore people, Son."

His stare fixed on his dad, who he was *so* mad with.

*He hated him.*

He wanted to yell and scream and pick up the stupid decorative statues and toss them at his dad's head. Instead, he bit his tongue and looked down to finish his drawing.

His dad marched over and snatched the doodle pad from his hands. "Hey, that's mine!"

He jumped up from the seat and grabbed for the book, but his dad held it up so he couldn't reach it. "Oh, so you can speak and haven't suddenly gone mute?"

Kes jumped, trying to reach his precious book, but his dad walked away with it in his hands. "Give it back! Those are mine!"

"They are garbage and a waste of time. I've told you to stop scribbling down that crap, and you chose not to listen, but now...." His dad walked over to the shredder, and panic gripped Kes's chest. "As punishment for your impolite behavior, the garbage is exactly where they are going."

"No, Dad!" he yelled as his dad put his entire sketch pad into the shredder. Tears streamed down his face as he reached for the pad that was being eaten by the mechanical beast. His dad grabbed him around the waist and dragged him away from the shredder and into his office.

"Remember, Son. I control everything you do. Don't make me destroy anything else."

*He hated him. He hated him. He hated him.*

# CHAPTER 1

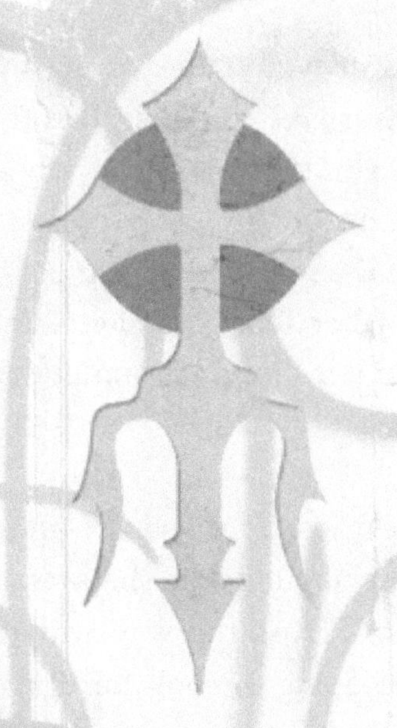

Ashley stared at the circular glowing buttons as she made the agonizingly slow descent to the ground floor of the medical building. "Ashley, you must understand that you will only ever get worse. We can do our best to keep the symptoms from progressing any further, but there is no cure," the doctor had said. Those words were now running on a continuous loop through her head like a broken record. She was purposely taking slow deep breaths to try and control the emotional breakdown that was threatening to consume her.

Was she in shock? She didn't know. How could she? She'd never been in shock before to know.

"So, what you're saying is that there is a chance I won't get any worse?" she'd hedged. She pinched the bridge of her nose as she remembered the doctor's expression, the pressure building behind her eyes.

"It is a very slim possibility, but theoretically, it is possible with the right medication and if you take all the steps I've laid out for you to follow."

The elevator dinged. It was at the wrong floor, the growing panic was making her hands shake and her breathing quicken. She was tempted to get out and run the rest of the way down the staircase, but she missed her chance. Too many people made their way through the sliding silver doors, and she squished herself into the corner. The man in front of her stepped on her foot, and she glared at his back when he didn't notice. She jerked her foot out from under his, and he still didn't apologize.

*Rude.*

Didn't he know she'd just received life-altering news? Did any of these people give a shit about what she was going through? No, of course not. The woman across the way was too busy on the phone discussing what she was going to cook for dinner while the guy in the middle was annoyingly humming some stupid song.

Her heart fluttered with a wild burst of emotion that shifted between annoyance and desperation. She sucked in a deep breath and gripped the silver railing to help hold the semblance of her emotional state together.

As soon as the doors opened, she pushed her way out through the throng of people and speed-walked for the exit. Bursting outside, she lifted her hand to block the bright glare of the setting sun. She had to get out of there.

Waving like a wild woman, she flagged down a passing taxi and yanked open the door, slamming it behind her.

"Where to?" the driver asked.

Ashley just stared at him in the rear-view mirror, unsure what to say. She didn't want to go back to her apartment and sit there alone.

"Lady, I'm sorry, but you need to pick a location or I have to take the next customer."

"Salvation Place, take me there, please." The driver gave her a once-over, and normally, she would feel compelled to explain that she wasn't going there for a free meal or a place to stay. People seemed to want to believe the worst of others, as if just because she was going to a shelter, it meant she was scamming the system.

It was windy that evening. The palm trees' leaves billowed out like bright green flags as the tops of the trees swayed. The sun's reflection rippled like bright orange and pink waves off of the glass buildings. Ashley dug around in the small green backpack she carried and pulled out her phone. The problem was she didn't know who to call.

She stared at the dark screen, her own image staring back at her on the shiny surface. Her mother and father would mean well, but she could already hear that conversation, and it was not one she wanted to have right now. It would be all about positive thinking and for her to keep her chin up—that she should've started meditation sooner and that she needed to move back home so they could help take care of her.

She didn't need taking care of, she didn't need to be more positive, and she sure as heck didn't need to have her feelings dusted aside with a simple 'keep your chin up' when she was entitled to her feelings. Giving up on the idea, she put the phone back into the bag and pulled out her wallet as they neared her destination.

"Thanks," she said, and as the car came to a halt, she handed over more money than she needed to. She just wanted to get out of the car, keep moving, and not think too much right now. Thinking led to feelings, and feelings were going to lead to a breakdown.

"Hey, lady, this is way too much!"

She closed the door, ignoring the driver and jogging toward the big old church that had been converted a few years earlier.

"Hey, Charlie," she called out, waving to the elderly man that had worked there as a caretaker longer than it had been a shelter.

"You're early." Charlie leaned against the mop he was using to clean the floor. His weathered face, with the distinct smile lines around his eyes, crinkled as he gave her a scrutinizing look.

"Yeah, I got off work early. Is Dennis in yet?" She continued toward the door to the back, not wanting to get into a heart-to-heart. Right about now, she wished she'd stayed in drama class. Maybe then she would've learned not to wear her heart on her sleeve like a neon sign.

"He's in his office. Ashley?" She paused, hand on the wooden door, and plastered a smile on her face as she looked over her shoulder at Charlie. "Are you okay, girl? I don't mean to pry, but you seem off."

She waved her hand in the air and made a goofy face, sure that Charlie saw right through her ploy. "Oh yeah, I'm fine. Just work stuff, family stuff, you know how it is."

"Mmhmm." Charlie lifted a brow at her but started whistling as he continued to mop the floor.

Sighing, she pushed through the door and nodded to the few homeless folks that were already there for the night, or maybe they hadn't left. Beds were hard to come by, and some of those that stayed there regularly rarely left their bed and the small space that was given to them to stay in.

The open space looked like it was set up for an office building. Dennis, who managed the place, had wanted to give people some privacy and found old cubicle partitions tossed away by a large corporation. The setup didn't allow for as many beds, but she had to admit that if she were living here, she'd want some small space to call her own.

Ashley passed the dining hall and waved to those that were already setting up the long table for food service, but she continued down the hall to the lone office in the back. Dennis's door was closed, and she paused, going over the lie she planned on telling for as long as she could get away with it.

Stupid or not, Ashley couldn't face what her new reality was going to be, couldn't even think the words. Plastering a smile on her face, she knocked on the office door.

"It's open," Dennis called back.

She opened the door to find him pacing the room on the phone—he held up a finger. "What do you want me to do? We are a not-for-profit organization. We rely on donations to keep our doors open to those that need us most…what? That's completely unreasonable. How are we supposed to raise that much money that quickly?" There was a long pause as Dennis listened to whoever was on the other end, his face growing redder by the second. Ashley worried he was going to have a stroke. "Oh yeah? Happy fucking Thanksgiving to you too." He went to slam his phone down and then realized it was a cell and hit the end button japing his finger violently onto the screen like he was trying to the same effect.

"The building owner again?" she asked, closing the door behind her.

"That man doesn't have a heart. He has millions, and this place is nothing more than a tax write-off, but now he wants to sell it to a developer unless we can come up with the rent money that's past due. ." Dennis flopped down into the rolling desk chair, which complained at the added weight. "That would mean he's going to kick us out before the new year. Merry fucking Christmas." Dennis sighed. Tossing the phone on the desk, he stared up at her. "It is a problem for another day and not one you should have to worry about, but if you have some magic fairy dust, I would sell my soul for some of that right about now."

"Sorry, no magic fairy dust, but I was coming to say that I can volunteer the whole day for the next couple weeks."

"What about your work?"

As much as she hated to lie to Dennis, Ashley swallowed hard and stuck with her lie. "I have some vacation time coming to me, and this is how I would like to use it."

"You do know most people actually take time off from work, right?

Go somewhere tropical or kick their feet up and read a book. How about you spend time with your friends or go visit your family?"

She crossed her arms over her chest. "Do you not want me here volunteering, Dennis?"

"No, it's just—" He waved his hands like he was swatting away a fly and closed his eyes. "You know we can always use the extra help. If this is the place you want to spend your vacation, who am I to tell you otherwise?"

A weight that she wasn't even aware had been pressing in on her lifted as he agreed to let her come there. Sitting alone in her apartment with her terrified thoughts for the next couple of weeks would not have been healthy for her sanity. She was already struggling to hold it together.

"Thanks, Dennis. I will head out and help with dinner prep. Other than fairy dust, if you need anything else, let me know." Ashley turned and opened the door but paused as Dennis called her name. She looked over her shoulder at Dennis.

"Thank you, I do appreciate the extra set of hands, and you know you are welcome here."

A small, genuine smile lifted the corners of her mouth as she nodded and saw herself out. One battle was done, the rest of her life—well, that would have to wait for now.

# CHAPTER 2

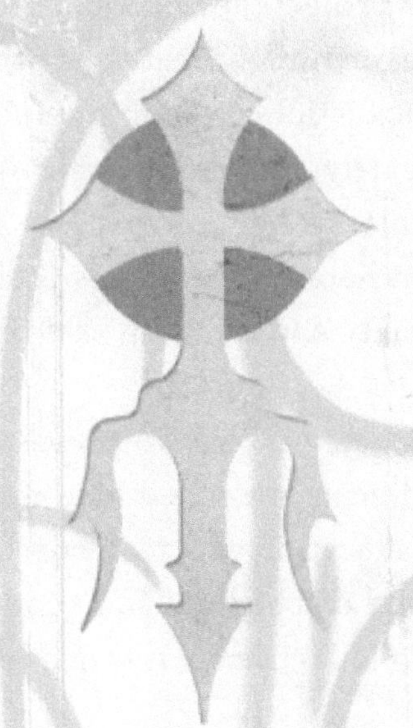

Kes pushed his grocery cart along the wharf, hood up and head down, but he was very aware of everything going on around him in the darkness. A large ship was slowly venturing in to dock on the far side of the port—the massive hull was silent other than the soft sloshing of water that could only be heard if you were a good listener and bothered to pay attention. A loud horn sounded in the distance, a ship announcing its departure—that lone sound always made his heart ache.

He turned his focus on Greta, the homeless woman heading in his direction. As she neared, he slowed to a stop, and her cart brushed his slightly as she drew alongside him.

"Saint Nick," Greta greeted, making the sign of the cross over her chest.

He was used to this. She had this thing where she thought he was a saint or an angel sent to protect the homeless. He'd tried to convince her many times that he was definitely neither of those things and that, in fact, he was probably the dictionary definition of a fucking dick.

Greta had unfortunately suffered a brain injury in a car accident which made it impossible for her to work. No family to speak of—she eventually ended up out here on the streets pushing a cart like himself. She drifted between reality and a false world that only her mind could unravel.

"Momma G, you have news?" His voice was barely above a whisper, but he knew she would hear. She hated loud noises and moved around according to how busy a location was at any particular time of the day.

Her frail-looking hand reached out and gently squeezed his forearm. "The rat you seek has his tail in a trap. A trap of string and tape."

"Where?"

"555."

Those that lived on the street would help him from time to time with his missions. Especially when his target happened to be hiding among those on the streets. He suspected that his target had taken to hiding among those on the streets while he laid low. This normally brilliant idea was hampered by the fact that Kes ruled the streets on this side of town. He was a dark shadow nobody ever saw coming.

Reaching into his pocket, he pulled out a twenty and held it in his open palm for her to take. Greta made a scoffing noise, her lips pursing as she shook her head no. Her hood fell back, revealing the wild braid of unwashed grey hair that made her look out of control.

"No money."

"Food, Momma G, for you and Big Dave. Take it. It is a trade, not a handout." There was a misconception that those who lived on the streets were literally bums—didn't want to work, worthless non-contributors to society. What he'd found since he returned from the Sandbox was the opposite. The majority of them were simply unable to fit into the confines of society as it was structured. This was something he understood better than most.

"Not a handout?"

"No, this is a trade. Words for money, yes?"

Greta slowly nodded and pulled up the hood on her long coat before taking the offering. "Saint Nick, our savior."

Kes bit the inside of his cheek. He really hated to be seen like he was anything more than what he was, and that was a useless, walking mass of destruction. Saviour—those words should be saved for those that deserved them.

Greta's cart rattled, the one wheel not turning properly as she moved on. He'd fix that one night when she was asleep. Resuming the pushing of his own cart, he focused his gaze on his destination, which was the fifth building, and then the fifth alley. He passed it to find the fifth cargo container. It had taken some time to learn the unusual way Greta would relay locations, but he'd become an expert over the years.

The dark reddish-colored cargo container was the only one with a giant five painted on the front in white paint like an X marks the spot. He parked his cart off to the side before making sure no one was watching, and then he opened the container. The tiny bit of light that was reflecting off of the building into the container only revealed to him a pair of booted feet tied up.

Muffled yells reached his ears, and he smiled wide as he picked out the swear words in the continuous sentence. Pulling the small flashlight out of his pocket, he clicked it on, blinding his prisoner. The man blinked and tried to turn his face away from the bright beam of light, but that didn't hide the fact that it was the man he'd been looking for.

Clenching the little flashlight between his teeth, he turned to his cart and lifted up the few bags on top to pull out a black body bag. He gave the thing a shakeout and then unzipped the side before turning toward the man in the container.

"Oooo aaa uuu?"

"Who am I?" Kes shrugged. "Does it really matter?"

The eyes staring back didn't seem to agree, but he asked a different question. "Wwaa aaaee ooh oooing?" Came the muffled question.

This was one of those stupid questions that he often wondered why people bothered to ask. Kes looked at the black body bag and then up again to the wide, terrified eyes.

"Well, Spike, what does it look like I'm doing?"

"Geet aaay ohm meee." Spike tried to inchworm away, his legs pulling up and pushing against the metal.

"Keep it up." Kes squatted down next to Spike's body. "I like it when you struggle." His voice was soft and soothing, but the threat echoed around the container. Spike froze, his chest rising and falling quickly, creating a soft wheezing sound around the tape over his mouth. "You have two choices. Get in willingly to go for a ride and a chat, or…I'm sure I can come up with some creative ideas for how to make you get in.

Spike swallowed hard, his Adam's apple bobbing exaggeratedly as he did so.

"You have information that I want. So, we're going to go for a little ride and you're going to tell me what I want to know."

Spike shook his head back and forth. "I noooo ooothing."

"I think you do. Are we doing this the easy way?" Spike slowly began to nod, and Kes sighed, a little disappointed that there wasn't going to be more of a fight.

Ten minutes later, he was pushing his cart along the wharf toward a glistening white yacht. His cargo was folded up like a book, his legs hanging over the end of the cart with more bags piled on top. Every now and then, the cart would jerk, and he smirked at the obvious discomfort as a moan or grunt reached his ears.

It was his parent's boat. Well, more accurately, it was their company boat for private events, but his parents were still the majority shareholders. He'd purposely chosen to move the boat to this camera-less end of the marina, and so far, no one had even noticed. He had to give his heavy cart a hard run up the ramp to get over the edge of the boat. He unceremoniously dumped the contents onto the deck. The black body bag rolled around and wriggled back and forth like a large snake.

Ignoring the struggling man, he set about to prepare the boat for launch. As soon as all systems were a go, he backed the boat out of the slip to slowly cruise out of the marina, no one ever the wiser about his unhappy cargo.

The further he got, the darker the surrounding landscape became until the marina behind him was nothing more than a few glittering dots. The breeze was strong, rocking the boat just enough that it was a good thing he wasn't prone to becoming seasick.

As he cut the engines, the yacht drifted to a stop, and he took a deep breath of the intoxicating sea air. This was why he needed to live near water. There was nothing like this feeling. Nothing so peaceful—or at least, that was until the thumping started. Rolling his eyes in annoyance, he made his way along the side of the boat and prepped the rigging for what he had planned. Now was the fun part.

K es looked at the old-school watch on his wrist and smiled. It had only taken him twenty minutes to get his bait out on the line. That was a new personal best.

Bending over, he stared into the small bar fridge that held a wide assortment of snacks and drinks, but Kes instead grabbed a bottle of V8 juice. His stomach had growled endlessly since arriving at the marina, and he had to keep his strength up.

He dropped down onto the observation bench and kicked his booted feet up on the armrest as he took in the night sky. The stars were stunning—everything felt cleaner and blissfully void of all other humans. All humans other than the one currently dangling from his rigging, that is.

It wasn't your standard fishing rig, mind you. Instead, he'd chosen to string up and tie his worm to the end of a chain.

"Come on, man, don't do this," Spike begged. The chains rattled as he pulled his feet up from the overly interested sharks that were starting to gather. He'd freed Spike's hands once he had him strung up—it was more entertaining than watching him suffocate to death with the chain slowly tightening like a vice.

Expectedly, Spike held onto the chain above his head like he was on a zip line. All he needed was a tropical shirt and a camera around his neck to complete the image.

He stretched and slowly pushed himself up to his feet, rolling his shoulders out. Picking up another bucket of chum, he poured it over the side of the boat, the water making plopping sounds as the diced-up fish parts splashed. He used the back of his sleeve to wipe some of the concoction off of his face as the water stirred and swirled, tails and fins slicing through the dark surface.

Putting the empty bucket aside, he proceeded to lean on the railing and took in the gently swaying man. "You ready to talk?" He pulled a toothpick from his pocket and gripped it between his teeth.

"I don't have the information you want," he yelled, his frustration obvious. "It was true back in the container, and it is still true now. Fuck, I can't feel my legs!" The chains rattling as he shifted position.

"All the better for you, I guess, when the sharks start biting."

The man stilled and comically looked towards the dark water that his toes were inches from touching.

Kes smirked as he pictured the look on his parents' faces if they knew what their fancy boat was being used for. It was almost worth sending them a picture.

"You're not really planning on lowering me down, right? You're not that crazy?"

Kes physically shook his head and blinked as he processed the stupid question. "Just when I thought humanity couldn't get any stupider, you ask me that. Here I thought you were a smart man Spike, a true opponent."

"I'm not the fucking idiot not listening. I don't know who is calling the shots. I'm just like everyone else. I get my orders through text messages. My men work for me and get their orders through text."

Kes smirked. "I'd watch your tone." Spike swallowed hard but was smart enough not to talk back. "You were contacted by someone to become the face of the Golden Dragons, but you never met them? Never had any phone conversations? Never even asked why *you*, of all people?"

"I was already in the business of dealing and had a substantial network. When the first message arrived, it said they were impressed and wanted to offer me a deal I couldn't pass up. That I would be making triple what I was before with only half the headaches. How do you not say yes to that?"

"You do know what they say about deals that look too good to be true?"

A tail smacked the water beside Spike's feet, and he gave a high-pitched yell and drew his knees up as much as he was able.

"And what of the warehouse and the Ice Man? How did that happen?"

"Some dude approached me at the races and said that I'm making a mistake with Ice Man, and goes into this whole thing about who he really is along with the lawyer. I'm not a stupid man. I knew there had to be more to the story that was being spun about Tyson and Alejandro. I sent some of my men out to find those in Ice Man's crew and made large cash donations to those that were willing to double-cross him."

"That simple?"

"Yes, it was that simple. Why the hell do you even give a shit anyway?"

Kes didn't answer the question. In reality, he didn't care what happened to anyone most of the time. But his brothers?

"Look, just bring me aboard, and if you want to, hand me over to the cops. Just please, bring me aboard!"

Kes ran his chain and dog tags through his fingers as he thought. "Not quite yet. I have one more question."

"Fuck, I'll answer whatever you want, just get me back on the damn boat." Spike yelped as a more daring predator lifted its head to investigate the dangling feet and nudged his toes with its head. By a quick glimpse, he guessed it was an oceanic whitetip, and by the very alive waters, he could only assume there were a number of them below the churning waves surrounding them.

"No, now answer this for me. Why did you run?"

"I got a text saying shit was going down, and I needed to lay low for a few weeks. I assumed it had to do with the police or with Ice Man since I knew he'd escaped. I'm not the type to hide, but I am the type to listen to my employer."

Kes straightened to his full height and stared at his prey. "You have not been very helpful, Spike."

"I can't tell you something that I don't know, but I can make you a deal."

Kes pulled the toothpick he'd been sucking on out of his mouth and flicked it into the water. "What kind of deal?"

"You let me live, and give me my phone and I will set up a text meet and greet or whatever else you want."

Kes slipped his hand into his pocket and pulled out the cell phone in question. He held up Spike's phone up from him to see. He almost felt bad when Spike's face lit up.

"Yes, that phone, let me get the answers you need, let me set something up." He nodded furiously, like that would somehow superpower Kes into agreeing.

"It's useless." He tossed the phone into the water, and Spike yelled and reached for the black piece of electronics before it disappeared.

"What have you done?" His eyes stared at the spot where the phone had gone under the water.

"I already unlocked it and had all the data downloaded, but it appears your employer was done with you. You'd become too much of a liability, and they told you good luck, which is code for watch your back. They will be coming for you."

"This can't be happening," Spike muttered, his voice was soft as his body sagged limply from the chain. His eyes snapped up to meet his own. "You always planned on killing me."

The corner of Kes's lip curled up before he put his lips together and whistled the first tune that came to him. He slowly wandered over to the controls for the winch and gripped the handle.

"Forward is down, back is up, or is it the other way around?" He pushed it forward, and the chain jerked down slightly, drawing a terri-fied wail from Spike. Up to this point, he hadn't screamed for help, as some of his other kills did, but he did so now.

"Please don't do this. Please, I'll do anything. I'm loyal, and I have skills. I'll do whatever you want." Kes pulled back on the handle, and Spike slowly rose away from the water. "Thank you, oh God, thank you, you won't regret this."

"I know I won't." The look in his eye must have said it all, as Spike went feral on the end of the chain and desperately tried to haul himself up the last bit of chain to the winch's arm, the only safety to be had. He waited for Spike to get a grip on the arm and then released the chain. Loud rattling ensued as it slipped from the winch and fell into the water. With a sick glee, he watched each and every link slip below the dark surface. The weight would be heavier with every passing second, dragging down Spike's waist.

"No, no, no!" Spike yelled as he tried to maintain his grip as the large coil of chain on the deck now unfurled and followed the rest into the water. Arm's shaking, sweat dripping from his brow, Spike stared at him, terror in his wide eyes.

"I don't save men that deal in human trafficking, Spike. The only question you have to answer now is will your choices see you in heaven or see you in hell?" Shock registered on Spike's face as he realized there really wasn't a secret left to be unearthed. Other than who his employer was, of course, but he was useless in that regard.

With a final scream, the man's hands slowly slipped off the arm of the winch. With a comedic display of flailing arms, he fell into the waiting water and disappeared just as his phone had. Kes watched the final bit of chain snake its way up the arm and off the winch to disappear as well. He couldn't help but wonder as the fins slipped silently below the surface if the sharks chased Spike down and had the meal they'd waited patiently for before he drowned. It didn't matter, dead was dead.

"I used to see the light in the dark," he whispered.

Kes scanned the softly rolling waves and smiled at the water as all returned to an eerie quiet broken only by the rhythmic sloshing against the hull.

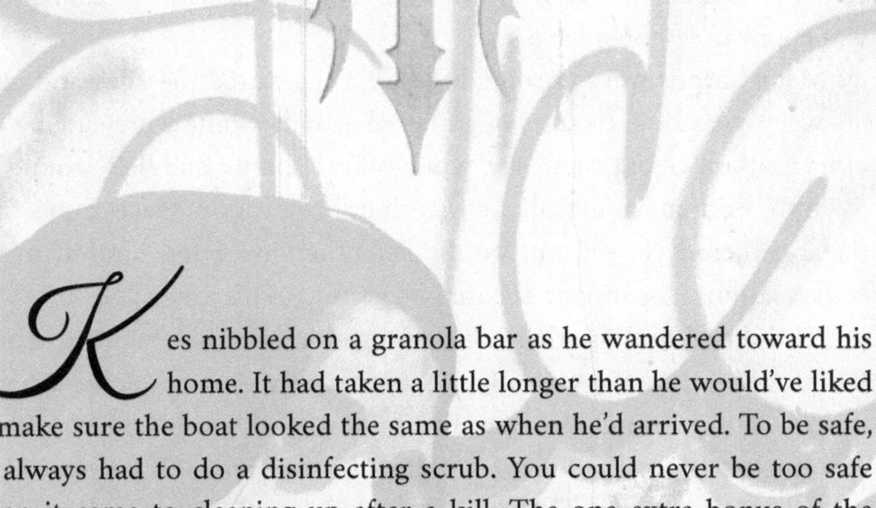

Kes nibbled on a granola bar as he wandered toward his home. It had taken a little longer than he would've liked to make sure the boat looked the same as when he'd arrived. To be safe, he always had to do a disinfecting scrub. You could never be too safe when it came to cleaning up after a kill. The one extra bonus of the yacht was the ability to have a shower. Chum was a tough smell to get rid of otherwise.

He wrapped the other half of the granola bar up for later and traded it for a toothpick, choosing to twirl it around with his tongue as he thought. Spike may have proven useless when it came to the Golden Dragon's true identity, but he did have a very detailed list of buyers and sellers. Everything from drugs to women was on his list.

A couple walking in his direction scooted as far away as they could get from him on the sidewalk. The man wrapped his arm protectively around the woman and glared as they passed. The man watched Kes out of the corner of his eye but didn't slow down. Kes avoided the Dwellers as much as they avoided him. He took the long way back, weaving his way through the various allies that most wouldn't dare look down, let alone walk. For Kes, though they were as comforting to him as a warm cup of cocoa with a shot of Irish Cream on a cold day.

The overpass was quiet this time of night, but it was loud during the day as people went about their lives running around like lines of ants on a mission. The Dwellers were sheep. Nothing more than an itty bitty cogs in the giant wheel of father time—a rat race with no end, and he was happy to let them have it.

Metal barrels were burning brightly as he exited the alley and made his way toward the clusters of gathered groups. Some were singing and others talking about their day, while others simply huddled around the warmth. Soft murmurs about the church Salvation Place came from those gathered closest, but he didn't bother involving himself in any conversations. Kes instead focused on getting to his own spot.

He did nod to those that acknowledged him as they huddled around the glowing fires for warmth. He averted his eyes from the dancing flames. Flames brought screams like a ghostly echo to his mind. His tent was furthest from the fenced entrance to the area, and he weaved his way through the small clusters of people, each one a collection of different stories that should be written in a book. Instead, they were lost to those who loved them. Like a family heirloom that had been stolen, their memories and stories would forever be adrift in a sea of forgettable faces.

Unzipping his faded tent, Kes ducked inside and sat down on his makeshift bed. Unsheathing a knife from the strap across his back, he gripped the handle until he could feel every little contour imprinted on his palm. The knife brought him as much comfort as any lover ever had but with far less hassle. He'd just laid down to sleep, holding the knife over his heart, when he heard the shuffle of feet nearing his tent. Kes looked toward the tent opening and waited.

"Kes?" Came a small voice.

"Yes, Nezumi?"

"Can I come in?"

All he wanted to do was sleep, but he couldn't tell the kid that. "Yeah, come in."

Kes spun the knife in his hand and hid it behind his back as the zipper opened just enough for the young girl to crawl inside. She was nine now, but if you didn't know any better, you'd think she was six or seven. Being born and raised on the streets didn't exactly provide the best nutrition before or after birth, and the brown-eyed girl had ended up born prematurely with an addict for a mother. Nezumi had already had two heart surgeries, both before he even met her, which had been provided for by an 'anonymous' financial donor. You'd expect someone that had been kicked in the teeth from the time they were born to be leery of the world, but instead, she was the epitome of optimism, which blew his fucking mind.

"It's a little late for you to be awake, isn't it?" He lowered the hood of his sweater as Nezumi, or as everyone liked to call her, Zumi, crawled across the mostly barren space to sit on a red milk crate. He didn't need much in there other than a small table he'd made out of old skids, the cot he'd picked up at the Army surplus store and the red crate to park his ass. Zumi looked tiny sitting on top of the crate. He could see her shadow as she turned and looked at the guitar he kept at the foot of the bed. Reaching out, she ran her hand down the wood like it was a pet.

"You ever going to sing a song?"

"You going to tell me why you're in here?" he shot back.

She shrugged her shoulders, her black, shoulder-length hair bouncing with the motion. "I saw you sneakin' in. I just wanted to say hi." Zumi played with a string on her sweater, her small hands weaving around the thread much like he'd done earlier with his dog tags.

"I wasn't sneaking. And saying hi couldn't wait till morning?"

Again with the shoulder shrug. She bit her lip and looked away, her normally bubbly personality nonexistent. "I didn't want to be alone," she mumbled as she drew her knees up onto the small box.

"Where is your mom, Zumi?"

"I don't know. I mean, I could probably find her, but why would I want to?"

He sighed and rubbed his eyes. "Turn on the lantern." He watched her shadow reach out and click the small lantern hanging near her head. "Have you eaten?" She shook her head no, and he instantly reached into his pocket to produce the other half of his granola bar. "Here, you can have this. I already had something else to eat." He held out the small treasure, and Zumi's face lit up as she reached for the wrapper.

"You sure?" she asked, her hand pausing just as her fingertips touched the colorful foil.

"Yes, now take it." There was only a moment of hesitation before she took the offering and then moaned as she bit into the chewy little delight.

"Thank you," she said as she wrapped up the rest to put in her pocket.

"No, you eat that now." Zumi paused, and he could see the wariness in her eyes. Tonight was only one meal, and there was an entire day to get through tomorrow, and another the day after that. "If your mom is not back with something to eat by morning, we'll go to that all-you-can-eat buffet down the street."

Her eyes grew as big as saucers. "The one with the waffles? You only ever take me there for special occasions."

"Yeah, that one, and I know, but who says we can't make up our own special occasions?"

"Thanks, but you don't have to do that." She nibbled on the granola bar again, not missing a single crumb.

"Don't be stupid, Kid. If I didn't want to feed you, I wouldn't feed you. Now be useful and pull over the small table. If you're going to sit in here, you can at least let me kick your ass at Rummy."

"Pfft, you wish, you're terrible."

An hour later, he peeked over his cards and smiled at the top of Zumi's head. Her small back softly rose and fell as she breathed. Setting the cards aside, he went to reach for the extra sleeping bag to wrap around her shoulders when he heard a loud crash, and multiple voices began swearing.

"Hey, watch where you're going!"

"Fuck off," came Chelsea's slurred voice.

*Great, just fucking great.*

"Zuummii? Where the fuck are you?"

Kes stood and made his way to the tent opening. His patience was too thin for dealing with this shit again tonight.

"Mom?" Zumi stirred as he opened the tent flap and slipped outside. Chelsea was stumbling over the camp area, lifting flaps and earning yells from everyone she was disturbing. Marching toward her, he decided that it was for the best that he'd left his knife in the tent, or he'd be tempted to slit her throat.

"Chelsea, she is over here with me," Kes called out to stop the rash of home disturbances before someone got pissed off enough to do more than yell.

As the woman looked his way, he took in her disheveled appearance and the smeared makeup that made her look more like a clown than the prostitute she was. With one shoe on and the other in her hand, she stumbled in his direction, her eyes narrowed into slits.

"What was she doing with you in your tent?" she yelled, drawing eyes from all directions like raccoons poking their heads out of trees to watch the drama unfold.

"What exactly are you insinuating?" His voice came out as a low growl, his knuckles cracking as he clenched his fists into tight fists. Female or not, he would lay her out if the next words out of her mouth were that he was doing something disgusting like taking advantage of Zumi.

"Kes, don't." Small hands clasped onto his arm, and he looked down into Zumi's scared face. "She's drunk. She doesn't mean it."

"I meean its…its…it," Chelsea argued as she swayed on her one shoed foot. He could picture his hand wrapping around her throat and ending this bullshit right now. He didn't give a fuck that she was a street walker, but he did care that she treated her kid like crap. A personal trigger that made the blood boil in his veins.

"You know Kes wouldn't hurt me, Mom. Come on, let's get you to bed." Zumi switched arms and began herding her mother away. As they turned away from him, he could hear Chelsea already babbling about something else. Zumi looked over her shoulder at him and mouthed that she was sorry.

Annoyed more than ever, Kes stomped back to his tent and pulled the flap shut. Getting back on his cot, he flicked off the lantern and gripped the knife to his chest. He stared at the dark nylon ceiling, listening for any more signs that Chelsea was going to be an issue tonight. Maybe the issue was that he saw too much of himself in Zumi and the way she struggled to please a parent that never put her first. His father wouldn't know the meaning of putting his son first if it bit him in the ass.

If Chelsea ever put Zumi in danger, he'd end her. He'd bury her alive, six feet under, and Kes wouldn't lose a wink of sleep. Chelsea needed to watch her back—there were monsters in these streets, and he was one of them.

# CHAPTER 4

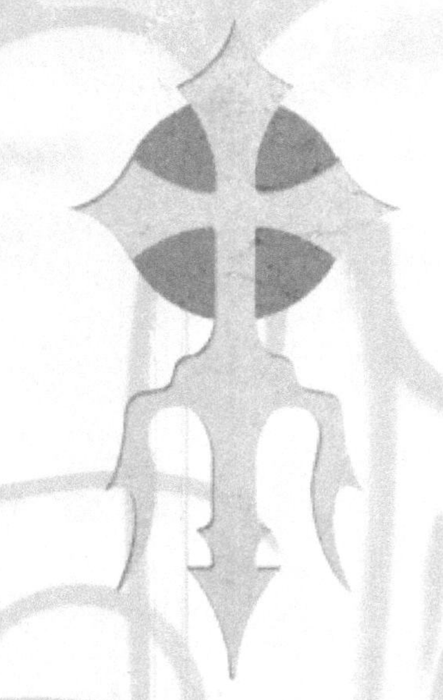

Ashley reached over and groaned as she smacked at the stupid alarm on her phone. It was still dark. Why had she set her alarm so early? It wasn't like she had anywhere to be.

Her mind immediately went to yesterday, and she laid her arm over her eyes as she tried to block out the thoughts that kept trying to plague her. Like worms, the thoughts were burrowing holes into her brain, and no matter how many times she told herself to stop thinking about it, the worries only got worse.

"I'm not doing this. I'm not lying here and making myself crazy." Ashley threw the comforter off and swung her legs over the side of the bed. She made her way to the closet to get changed into her workout gear and clipped the doorframe hard with her shoulder.

"Ouch." She jerked with the sudden impact and almost collided face-first with the door. Reaching out, she gripped the clothing rack to keep herself from becoming more off-balance.

Heart pounding, she slowly straightened. *It was nothing.* Even as she thought the words, the sting of tears pricked at her eyes. Blinking them away, she made it the rest of the way into the walk-in space and picked out an outfit before heading to the bathroom.

She felt like she was in a fog. All her movements were on autopilot as her mind floated around in the midst of what-ifs—everything from getting dressed, to the yoga workout, and even to walking down the hall to the kitchen to make the drink she was now sipping.

Ashley pulled her legs up under her as she stared out of her sitting room window. She swirled around the magic green elixir that was supposed to be the cure-all, at least according to her mother. Taking another mouthful of the disgusting-looking green drink, which was oddly tasty, she had to admit she felt better after a workout and shower. Focusing on her body helped to relax and calm her mind, which was always in a state of panic. Lately, the panic attacks ranged from bearable to full emotional breakdown.

"One thing is clear, being alone with your own thoughts is not always healthy," she grumbled as she stood and put her empty glass in the dishwasher before heading to the door.

Slipping on her shoes and a light jacket, she strapped on a small shoulder pack, ready to tackle the day. The elevator ride down was blissfully quiet, and even the bus stop only had a few people waiting. Things were definitely trending in the right direction.

Her cellphone rang, and she stared at the doctor's office number, swallowing hard. Her thumb shook over the answer button, unsure if she wanted to know what they had to say.

Taking a steadying breath, she hit talk. "Hello, this is Ashley."

"Good morning, Ashley. I'm Lindsay a nurse from Doctor Matheson's office."

Ashley swallowed hard even though the nurse's voice was cheery. "Good morning. Did I forget something yesterday?"

"No, not at all. I'm just calling to let you know that all of your new medications will be ready for pickup from the pharmacy on the lower level of our medical building at four o'clock today. They close at five, so I wanted to give you lots of notice."

A buzzing like-white noise started in Ashley's ears. She knew she was panicking and couldn't hear the rest of what the nurse's instructions were. It was as if the woman's voice had been reduced to squawking on the other end of the line.

"It is very important that you speak to the pharmacist and set up a proper regiment that you can stick with. If you have any questions or unusual side effects, give us a call. We are always happy to help." The last word was far too chipper. There was no help, that was a lie. As if she actually meant that there was any real help, but of course they would do their best to lie.

"Thank you, I will pick everything up at four," she heard herself say before the line ended.

A woman waiting with her small son looked over and smiled, and heat flushed throughout her body. Did everyone hear? It didn't matter. There were only six people standing around—the thought of any of them knowing anything set off another round of panic.

Taking slow breaths, she focused on counting backward from a thousand until her brain cooled its freak-out. No one had heard, and if they had, she could've been picking up something far more boring—no need to be embarrassed.

Luckily, the bus arrived a moment later, and the remnants of her irrational fear dissipated. Letting everyone else on first, she climbed the stairs and swiped her bus pass. "Good morning, Sarah," Ashley said, smiling at the woman who had become a staple in her daily routine.

"Well hello there, Honey. I missed you yesterday. Was everything alright?"

That should've been an odd question coming from a city bus driver, but she'd been riding the exact same bus for the past three years. Sarah, the driver, had been with the route at least as long. They weren't exactly friends, but they were friendly. She knew that Sarah was divorced and had two girls, and that she loved seafood and God. "I'm good, Sarah. I just had a few appointments, so no work."

"Alright then, Honey. You grab your seat. I made sure your favorite is still open."

As she stared into Sarah's warm and caring eyes, Ashley wondered why she'd never made a point of making more close friends. She kept everyone on the periphery of her life. It was the safe zone—friendly, but not friends. It made her wonder what else she'd been pushing to the side all these years. What else had she missed out on and now may not ever have the chance to enjoy?

Ashley smiled wide. "You're the best," she said before grabbing her usual seat near the front. Ashley opened her phone and scrolled through the massive to-be-read list on her Kindle app, which she'd been collecting but never seemed to get through.

The cover of *Dark Light* by Billie Blue caught her attention, and she ran her finger over the screen as she stared at the angel wings. She could use an angel right about now. Clicking on the book, she flicked to the first chapter and settled in to get some quality reading time done on the way to the shelter.

She'd been so immersed in the pages of the beautifully written fictional world that it felt like the blink of an eye when the bus rolled to a stop and she had to get off.

"Thanks, Sarah."

"See ya later, Honey."

Marching the final distance to the former church, she slowed to a stopped to stare up at the large church that at one time would've been a pinnacle of the community. The rainbow of stained glass glistened in the bright morning light. The once stunning structure now showed its age. Bricks were chipped and falling away, while the decorative moldings and panels were broken or missing altogether. The building looked the way she felt inside and not in a good way.

This would be her new mission. She needed to find a way to save this place. It was the one spot where she felt like herself.

Life had a nasty habit of kicking her in the teeth, but she'd always been a fighter. All the other times she'd gotten knocked to the ground she wouldn't lie down and stay there. Her hand clenched around the strap of her pack as a flare of anger filled her and made her gut burn with determination. If the last twenty-nine years had taught her anything, it was that life could be cruel, but you were never given more than you could handle. She would handle this.

# CHAPTER 5

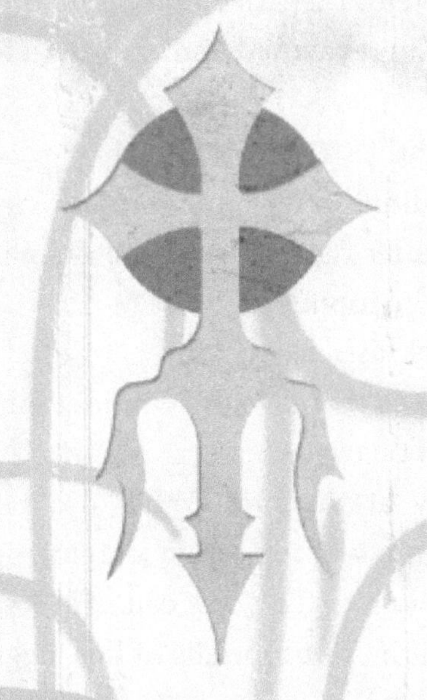

Kes stepped out of his tent and yawned as he stretched—his side mildly barked with the movement. He rubbed at his side and the scar that would forever remind him that there were worse things than the pointless crap the majority of the world worried about. Who gave a fuck about who wore it best and who was fucking who when bombs were landing on your home and you were being shot in the streets. It was just another reason why he hated spending time with the Dwellers. They had no idea how good they had it. They didn't think twice about the roof over their heads, the schools they got to attend, or the freedom they blatantly abused.

The rustling sound of a tarp caught his ears, and he looked up to see Zumi slip from the spot where she and her mother slept.

He nodded as she looked up and spotted him. A small smile lifted the corner of her mouth. She tucked herself into her sweater like a turtle and tiptoed lightly and sprightly like a pixie around the tents and random sleeping bags with their sleeping occupants.

"Hey," Kes said as Zumi yawned and stopped a few feet away.

"Hey."

"Is your mom alright?"

Zumi nodded but didn't offer any more information, and he was the sort of asshole that didn't really care if the woman lived or died, so he didn't bother to push the topic.

"You still want breakfast?"

Those big brown eyes that always reminded him of a deer looked up at him. "You really don't have to."

He cocked a brow at the kid. "What did I tell you about being stupid?" He turned and walked away, digging into his pocket for a smoke. "Come. Don't come. It's your call." He knew she would follow and smiled as he heard the soft footfalls of her jogging to catch up.

"What about my mom?"

"What about her?"

"Should I just leave her?"

He took a drag on the smoke and glanced at the kid. "Will she notice you're gone?"

"Harsh, even for you." Zumi crossed her arms over her small frame. "You shouldn't smoke. It'll kill you."

Kes laughed hard. He then promptly started choking on the smoke.

"Serves you right. That shit stinks."

"You're one to talk. When was the last time you showered?"

"Shut up. That's rude."

"And how would you know what is rude, Kid?"

Her lips pursed as her eyes narrowed up at him. If she wasn't the size of an overgrown six-year-old, she might actually be scary. "I may not go to school on the regular, but I pay attention, and unlike you, I actually have social skills."

"Ouch, that one stung." He took another drag from the little cancer stick and then butted it out on the palm of his hand, putting the rest in his pocket for later. "Better?"

"Not really. You're just putting off what you plan on doing later."

Kes stared at her as they wandered along the still quiet sidewalk to the diner. "You should really be in school, Kid. You're smart, smarter than most."

"Yeah, like that's ever going to happen. Every time I get caught sneaking into classrooms, there's another teacher that knows my face to kick me back out. I'm running out of schools to sneak into. Doesn't that seem stupid? I mean, they want kids to learn, and I want to learn, but I'm not allowed in because my mother's a bit—." Zumi crossed her arms over her chest.

She didn't finish the sentence, but Kes knew what she was going to say.

"Face it. The world has me destined to be a nothing forever, an insignificant bug that no one sees and those that do wish they hadn't."

He grabbed her arm and gave it a squeeze as he brought them both to a halt. "Don't you ever say that—you're not a nothing. I see you." He let go of her arm but continued to give her a hard stare. Zumi played with the cuffs on her sweater but kept her eyes on the ground. "I mean it, Kid. Don't you let your mother or anyone else tell you differently. You hear me?" Kes bent over so that she was forced to look at him.

"Yeah, I hear ya."

"Good, now come on. I hate crowds and want to get a seat before anyone else." The rest of the walk was silent aside from the sounds of the city waking up. Metal security shutters rattled as they were lifted up on storefronts while the rumble of cars slowly filled the street. The odd whiff of sewage from the grates reached his nose, but the stench was nothing in comparison to the stink of the Dwellers or the lies that rolled off of his father's silver devil's tongue.

The diner was as old as the city and looked it. The sign that once proudly displayed the name, The Piccolo, no longer glowed and hung at an odd angle, but the food was some of the best in town. Every generation had elected to keep the original recipes—they left them the fuck alone, unlike a lot of failed businesses that constantly changed. The Piccolo had stood through war, riots, and one natural disaster after another.

The little bell over the door announced their arrival.

Larry's voice boomed from the back. "Take a seat, and I'll be with you in a minute."

He led the way to a booth in the back and loved the fact they were the first customers. It meant the coffee would be fresh and the food would arrive fast. His stomach gave a loud growl as they sat, and Zumi giggled at the unsightly sound.

"How can I help you?" Larry rounded the corner, head down and pen and pad in hand. He lifted his head, and when he did, he smiled wide. "Kes, you son of a bitch. How the hell are you?"

"Good, Larry, hanging in there. You know how it goes."

"Yeah, I do. Who is this?" Larry eyed up Zumi and then looked back at Kes like he had a secret to tell.

"Zumi here is a friend. We are both in need of your all-you-can-eat buffet. I don't see it set up." Kes looked around, realizing that the entire area that used to hold the mass of metal trays was missing.

"Sorry, Kes. Business has been slow." Larry lifted a large shoulder, his face showing the stress of his words. "We had to stop doing the buffet. We were throwing too much out."

"I'm sorry to hear that."

"It is what it is, you know. Everyone has had a tough go of it lately—we'll get through this bad patch, we always do. So enough about my sad story, what can I get the two of you?"

"Do you have waffles?" Zumi asked, her voice soft.

"Sure do, and since you're a friend of Kes here, I will do them up with the fruit explosion topping."

Zumi's eyes lit up, and as hard as she was trying to hide it, she was excited. "Like real fruit?"

Larry laughed, his baritone voice booming in the confines of the four walls. "Yes, real fruit, and I'll bring you both milk and juice."

"The usual for me, and get her a side of bacon. She needs the protein." Kes leaned his forearms on the table as Larry retreated to the kitchen.

"Kes, can I ask you a question?" Zumi mimicked his pose so it looked like they were in serious negotiations. Heck, maybe they were.

"What kind of serious question?"

Her small shoulders lifted and fell, her raven curls framing her face. "I wanna know how you ended up out here. Like, you just don't seem…." She stopped and sighed. "I guess I don't see you as one of us, you know? You just seem like you're just be hanging with us."

Kes turned so he could lean his back against the wall and lift a foot onto the bench. He busied himself with tracing the pattern on the plastic tablecloth as he thought about what Zumi had said. The images that he tried hard not to think about bubbled under the surface of his mind.

"Sometimes, Kid, there is ugly in this world, and sometimes there is this whole other fucking level. One that rips out your soul if you let it."

Eyes that were far wiser than eyes in a nine-year-old's face should be blinked at him. "I live that every day."

Their eyes locked. Her calm and yet oddly challenging expression made him want to squirm in his seat.

"Here we go," Larry said, saving him from having to try and explain himself to a kid that couldn't understand the horrors that he'd seen. He prayed that she never would.

"Oh my god," Zumi squealed and stared at the mountain that had been placed before her—golden waffles and piles of chopped fruit topped with strawberry sauce and whipped cream. Kes and Larry both laughed at the expression on her face.

"Now *that* is the face I like to see on my customers. If you need anything else, just holler."

Kes nodded as he picked up his fork and knife to dig into the steak and eggs, trucker-style breakfast, but it was the kid across the table and her unbridled enthusiasm over a waffle that made him smile.

His phone vibrated in his coat, and he was tempted not to answer, but he yanked it out of his pocket to see the word "Crosshairs" glowing back at him.

"Shit, be right back." Kes stood, not even sure if Zumi heard him over her loud moaning with each bite. He stepped out onto the street and hit talk but didn't bother to say anything. He had to give Trev credit—he waited a whole three minutes before his annoyed voice came through the line.

"Kes, I can hear you breathing. Why are you not saying anything?" Trev asked, and Kes could easily picture the exasperated face Trev was undoubtedly making on the other end. It was way too much fun getting under his skin.

"'Cause I didn't have anything to say." He smirked, loving to poke the bear.

"A 'hello' or a 'hi there, old friend.' I'd even have settled for a grunt since it's you."

Kes smirked. "You still knew I'd answer, didn't you?" he asked, listening as the breathing on the other end of the phone got louder. Back in the Sandbox, he would've had his ass in so much trouble for that kind of backtalk. He would've been scrubbing a latrine, polishing boots, or doing a thousand burpees by now. Being able to snap back was one of the very few great things about being back.

"For the love—just give me a fucking update," Trev said, the annoyance clear in his tone.

"No new information, which is why I hadn't called."

A woman pushing a baby carriage gave him a wide berth and a side-eyed glance like he might suddenly leap on top of her as she passed.

"You do remember we are on a timeline? Maeve's verdict could happen at any time, and the more information we have about who we are dealing with, the better."

"I haven't forgotten. Are we still going forward with the plan regardless?" Kes was pretty certain he already knew the answer, and that he'd need to be ready at a moment's notice.

"Of course, we do not leave a man behind."

"But she's a woman."

Kes smirked as Trev started swearing and hung up on him. That seriously just made his morning. Smiling, he stuffed the phone into his pocket and wandered back inside toward his seat.

Larry had pulled up a chair and was chatting with Zumi. Whatever she was saying made the large man laugh.

Zumi had a way of getting under your skin and sticking with you. Like a bur, but in the best way possible. He hadn't met anyone with more natural sweetness mixed with charisma. She smiled wide and then tossed a berry into the air to catch with her mouth. Larry, of course, cheered and tried to mimic her, but the little piece of fruit bounced off his face and rolled away to a chorus of laughter.

Kes slid into the booth and watched as they performed the trick again for him, which of course, ended up with the same result.

Zumi practically glowed from the other side of the table, and he had to wonder if she was an angel of hope for everyone—or maybe just for him.

# CHAPTER 6

"Shoot." Ashley looked up at the large clock on the wall. Where the heck had the day gone? She was officially running late. She hated running late. She blamed her parents for that since they were always late. She'd showed up for events late more times than she could count including her graduation. She'd barely made it to the stage as they were calling her name. She'd had to run across the parking lot as everyone stared at her. It didn't help that she was the valedictorian and was supposed to be giving a speech.

"Sorry, Dennis. I have to run." She grabbed her purse as she passed the manager. "Tomorrow, I want to go over some fundraising ideas I have if you have a few minutes."

Dennis looked up from lining up the silver-colored trays for serving and wiped his hands on his apron. "It's almost serving time."

"I know, and I'm sorry, but I have to go pick something up, and I can't be late."

He looked at the trays, and she couldn't stand the despondent look on his face. "I can come back later if you want?"

"No, no, you have done enough. I'm just overthinking it. Have a night off for a change."

"You sure?"

"Yes, now get out of here before you're any later." Dennis waved as if shooing her away.

"Okay, see you tomorrow." She speed-walked like she was in a race for the door, the entire time digging around in her small pack trying to find her phone. "It has to be in here somewhere," she mumbled as she made her way through the open door into the front foyer and walked into what she was sure was a wall.

Her small pack went flying. The contents, including the phone she'd been searching for, crashed to the floor. Ashley stumbled backward and surprisingly didn't end up on her ass. The wall turned out to be a human —a tall, very solid male whose face was hidden by a grey hood.

"Oh my god, I'm so sorry." She didn't bother to look at his face as she went to her knees to gather her things.

"Here you go," a young girl said, holding out a runaway lip gloss and her house keys.

"Thanks so much." She smiled at the young girl and took the items she was holding.

"You should watch where you're going," the hooded man said.

She looked up at the imposing figure, his hands firmly stuffed in his pockets. On any other day, she would've given him a piece of her mind, but she didn't want to make a scene in front of his daughter.

"Thanks, I'll try and remember that life-altering piece of advice." Ashley stood in a rush as she stuffed the last of the runaway items into her bag. Her mistake was not noticing that the mystery man had removed his hood, and as she turned her head to fix him with a parting glare, she froze in her tracks.

Her heart pounded hard as she stared into the amber-colored eyes she'd never thought she'd see again. Her mind was blank. She had no idea how long she stood there as her thoughts whirled, trying to catch up to her racing heart, but she needed to get the hell out of there and fast.

"Nice bag," he said casually.

She looked down at the Army green-colored pack, confused as to what he was talking about—her bag? An old need licked up her spine with the sound of his voice. She needed to get away from him.

"Sorry I bumped into you, but I have to go." In the most awkward moment possible, she managed to walk directly into the locked door as she tried to make her escape outside.

*Yup, it was official. God hated her.*

Willing herself not to look back, she moved to the open door and practically ran out. There was no mistaking who that was: Kestrel freaking Reynolds and his stupid, arrogant face, not to mention those unique amber eyes. Was it really fair that he still looked that good? If anything, he'd gotten better looking since high school.

Pulling up her Uber app, she checked to see if anyone was in the area and clicked for a car that was a minute out. Her foot wouldn't stop tapping as she waited for what felt like forever. A silver sedan pulled up with a bright, smiley woman in bright pink, who could've been the cover model for *Sickeningly Sweet Magazine*, in the driver's seat.

"Hello sugar, you hop right on in." The pink lady smiled as she patted the passenger seat, and Ashley was tempted to pick a different car. Just then, the heavy wooden door of the church squeaked as it was opened.

Determined not to discover who was coming out, she jumped into the front seat.

After she relayed the address of the medical building, Pink Lady began talking, and Ashley would've sworn that she didn't take a breath as she smoothly moved from one topic to the next and back again. Her mind drifted away from the car and spiraled backward in time.

*shley finished setting up the locker the way she'd pictured in her mind. She was finally a freshman at a competitive private school, and she'd been envisioning what this moment would be like for so long. Closing her locker, she smiled at the girl with the locker beside hers as she built up the courage to ask her name.*

*"Well, well, well, what do we have here?" Ashley turned toward the sound and was surprised to see a tall, athletic boy, with a crowd of his friends behind him, talking to her. Her hand clutched her backpack strap tighter. The boy, who had seemed to spring from nowhere, had stopped a few feet in front of her. His eyes roamed up and down her, and a strange nervousness mixed with curiosity spread throughout her body. Unsure what the correct answer was, she cleared her throat and held out her hand while the girl beside her seemed to turn into a Medusa statue.*

*"I'm Ashley," she managed to whisper. "I'm new," she stupidly added.*

*"A pair of freshmen are in our area, boys, at our lockers, and this one has the nerve to introduce itself." He looked at the outstretched hand that was visibly shaking, and Ashley jerked it back like she'd been bitten.*

*In a comedic horror fashion, she looked at the assigned locker and then back again, confused as to what he meant. "I was assigned this locker," she said, holding up the map with the locker number on it for him to see.*

*He didn't even glance at the paper, a smirk lifting up one corner of his lips.*

*"Maybe, but you just donated it to me, so clear your shit out." The leader's amber-colored eyes were like lasers and pierced right through her body. He stepped, she was forced to take a step back as he proceeded to lean a shoulder*

*against the locker in question. He crossed his arms over his chest, which accentuated just how hot he was as he loomed over her. The group he was with fanned out, blocking any way out for both her and the girl she hadn't yet learned the name of—nervousness rolled around her stomach, making her feel ill.*

*A quick glance at the girl had Ashley wondering if she was still breathing. She had the urge to reach out and poke her to see what would happen.*

*"What locker should I use, then?" Ashley turned her eyes back up to meet the unnerving amber ones.*

*"None. I need both. So, get your shit and scram before I make you."*

*"But...." Before she could finish her sentence, he leaned down so his face was right in front of hers. He smelt so good, and his eyes—she wanted to stare at them all day. He was the cutest boy she'd ever seen. The scariest as well, but holy hell, was he hot. Her knees shook at his sudden closeness, and she could feel the heat racing up her neck to her cheeks and knew they would be bright red.*

*"You see that girl over there. The pretty brunette that is glaring at you?" He nodded toward the other side of the hall. Swallowing hard, she managed to follow his stare. "That's my girlfriend," he whispered like it was a secret. She wiggled her fingers at the boy in question and then blew him a kiss. "She's a cheerleader. Super jealous type, and really popular. What do you think would happen if I told her you came on to me and that you were saying dirty things that you wanted to do to me?"*

*"What? But I didn't. I...."*

*He leaned in closer, his arm sliding along the lockers so it looked like he was moving in for a kiss. Ashley was rooted to the spot—fear laced with twinges of something else she couldn't really explain made her blood run hot and was a potent combination keeping her in place.*

*"Oh, but you did. Your big blue eyes say it all. This bright red blush you have going on definitely says it all. You want me to kiss you." He ran his finger down her cheek discreetly so no one else would notice. "I'll make you a deal, say the words 'I want you,' and I will let you keep your locker."*

*She opened her mouth to speak, but no words would come out. He leaned in a little closer so their cheeks were almost touching. The heat from his body was pressing in on her, making it hard to breathe.*

*His lips hovered so close to her ear she could feel their gentle touch. "Say it, and I'll give you your first kiss and the locker," he whispered. "You're pretty adorable."*

*Body shaking, she said the first word that came to mind. "Yes."*

*"Yes, what?"*

*"I want you."*

*The boy stood straight and smiled wide. "Told you I could make her say it in less than five minutes."*

*"Fuck, Kes. You're like a panty-dropping God," one of his friends said as he handed over a small stack of cash.*

*Blinking, she watched the exchange, and then the boy now identified as Kes walked over to the brunette he'd mentioned and pushed her up against the lockers to devour her mouth. He glanced over his shoulder and smiled, but it was a mean look. It was like he hated her for no reason, she suddenly felt a flush of heat run through her body. She had the feeling this was just the beginning.*

*"What? You didn't think I'd actually want you, did you?"*

*"I think she did, Baby," the brunette purred as she ran her hand through Kes's hair. Ashley was disgusted by how she stared up at him, like he was some sort of god and she would do whatever he asked.*

*"Sad, Newbie, but on the plus side, I did mean it when I said you could keep the locker. This is the loser side of the school. Why would I want your dumb locker?" The group laughed, and anger settled in her stomach like a tiny pit of rage.*

*Wrapping his arm around the cheerleader's shoulders, he wandered away with the group he'd arrived with—the rest of the students in the hallway who had played witness to the humiliating event smirked and laughed as they stared. Great, just great.*

*Fucking Kes Reynolds.*

# CHAPTER 7

"*She* totally likes you," Zumi said in a sing-song voice.

Kes stared at the closed door through which the stunning blonde had just disappeared. He didn't think she'd recognized him, but he'd never forgotten her. Those big blue eyes were the only thing he'd dreamed about until death and destruction had taken their place. It had been so long since he even thought about seeing Ashley Hartley that she'd become a phantom in his mind. An intangible ghost that he'd never see or have.

The instant he'd heard her voice, he'd known it was her, but when she'd looked at him, his heart had stilled. Was it wrong that his first thought was to check her hand for a ring?

"Earth to Kes," Zumi waved her hand at him. "And you like her too, huh?"

"Huh?" Kes looked down at Zumi, who was smiling as if she'd just won a pony.

"I said she likes you, and you definitely like her back. You're all googly-eyed." She fluttered her lashes while making a silly face. "You know, like in that old cartoon movie you got for me to watch when I was sick—the one with the deer, skunk, and bunny."

"Don't be ridiculous."

The problem was, the kid wasn't far off the mark. He'd always been all 'googly-eyed' over Ashley, but she hated him, and with good reason. He'd been such a dick to her for years, and then, in his one shining moment where he could have written away their dark past, he'd ruined it all over again.

The pulse in his neck was pounding hard as he marched across the floor to the donated clothing section. Zumi was skipping beside him, her hair bouncing with the motion like it was trying to fly.

"I bet you could make her your girlfriend," Zumi practically sang. "She is really pretty."

"Yes, I'm sure she would be all hot for a guy living in a tent under a bridge."

Zumi pulled on his arm, and he groaned as he stopped and stared down at his pint-sized interrogator. "I thought you always told me that we could do and be whatever we want—that I could have a future and become more than just a girl living on the street. Do you believe that, or were you lying to me?"

His mouth fell open. "Umm, I meant you, not me."

"If you meant just me, then you're still a liar. I'm no different than you. In fact, I would say you could walk away from the tents tomorrow if you wanted. You could get any job you want. You try to hide it, but you're super smart and have mad skills." She held up her finger like his mother used to do when giving him shit. "And you have enough money to buy me breakfast, and now a new jacket. If you can find a way to make that much money, then you can find a way out from under the bridge." She crossed her arms and gripped her elbow with one hand, tapping her chin as she stared at him. "I think you already have, but you choose to stay. Why? I don't know, but I will."

"You spend way too much time paying attention to me. Maybe your mother was right, and you should stop visiting my spot."

She narrowed her eyes at him, and he swallowed hard.

"Now who is the one being stupid?" she mocked. She poked him in the arm. "You're scared, and I'm going to find out why even if you don't tell me."

His blood pressure was rising, and he had no one to blame other than himself. Luckily, the promise of a second good meal for the day intervened.

"Do you smell that?" Zumi made a little moaning sound as her eyes zeroed in on a long table filled with metal serving trays of food. "Do you think we could stay for a meal? I know I'm being greedy, wanting two in one day, but I just…."

"Yes, we can stay, but only if you stop harassing me and pick out a jacket."

"You love to barter way too much, but fine, I accept." Zumi wandered toward the area that had a *clothing* sign over the door, and he could've sworn he heard her whisper under her breath, "At least for now."

The food tasted like ash in his mouth, but at least Zumi seemed to be having a good time. He leaned back against the wall and watched as she did impressions for some of the people staying there. She certainly had a flair for the dramatic. He could see her on television or Broadway—hell, he could see her singing on stage with a million screaming fans if she wanted.

He ran his hand through his short hair as he looked up at the high roof of the church with its ornately carved wood. How many weddings and funerals had this place seen? How many tears had been shed inside these walls?

Kes pulled his hood up into place and let out his signature whistle. Zumi turned in his direction and then waved at everyone, saying goodbye as she ran to catch up.

"Aren't you forgetting something?" He paused with his hand on the door.

"Oh shoot, the food and jacket. One second." The manager of the place smiled and held out the items that had been set aside for her. She ran back, her eyes the happiest he'd seen, but she was out of breath, her hand darting to her chest.

"Are you okay?" he asked, worry creeping into his tone.

She rubbed at the spot over her heart that he knew held a long scar. "I will be—too much excitement for one day. Come on. My mom will be worried by now."

He doubted that, but he held his tongue. He shouldn't be angry at Chelsea. She was just like everyone else out there doing what they could to survive, but he couldn't stand the thought of Zumi following in her footsteps. Prostituting her body to men and being hooked on alcohol and drugs to make it through the day was not what he wanted for her. She deserved better than that, and she deserved a chance to live her dreams to the fullest.

As he predicted, Chelsea hadn't noticed Zumi was gone all day, but she sure did scarf down the brown paper bag of food they'd brought from the shelter without a thank you. He left mother and daughter to argue over what to save for the next day.

Flopping down on his cot, he closed his eyes and tried to sleep, but all he saw was a stunning smile framed by hair that looked like spun gold. After all this time, he never thought he'd see her again, and certainly not at Salvation Place. What had she been doing there? Was she a volunteer? Was she there fixing something, or maybe checking it out to move in? That last thought was ridiculous, and there was no way she was living there. For all he knew, he'd never see her again, and their one chance moment to reconnect had run out the door as quickly as she had.

Grabbing his knife, he crossed his arms over his chest and wondered what her lips tasted like—he smirked as he remembered she always wore strawberry lip gloss. It was her signature scent. His cock stirred as he pictured ravaging that sweet mouth. He fell asleep with her blue eyes vivid in his mind.

*The fire danced in the confines of the makeshift bonfire rings somebody had crafted together. It was brilliant, really—they'd taken metal barrels and cut them into thirds. He loved the camping vibe the simple act had created. The flames cast shadows on the faces of those he trusted most in this world sitting around, boots on the rims, beers in hand.*

*"Alright, Ringo, your turn. What's the first thing you're going to do when you get home?" Morry asked.*

*"You mean besides fuck my girlfriend to death while eating a cheeseburger with bacon?"*

*"That's a given," she countered as the group laughed.*

*"I can tell you what I am not going to do. I'm never going to a fucking beach again. I never want to see sand again for as long as I live. I don't want to feel the shit down my pants or have the fucking stuff squish between my toes. That, ladies and gents, is what I don't want."*

*"I will second that," Trev said, his arm wrapped around Mel's shoulders.*

*"I will third that. Amen to a hot fucking shower and no sand." TK raised his beer and clinked bottles with Morry. The rest of the group followed suit like it was a bad omen not to.*

*"Aww, and here I was going to take you out on my boat when we got back, show you a real California party." Kes smiled at his friend.*

*"Oh, I can handle the boat and the water, just as long as I don't have to walk across any motherfucking sand to get to it." Ringo took a swig of his beer.*

"Wait a minute. Why are we not invited to this boat?" Arek asked. "I want to party."

Kes leaned forward, his elbows on his knees as he hit Arek with a deadpan stare. "Honestly, man, you're just not pretty enough."

The group erupted into another round of laughter as Arek stood. "You think so?" Kes watched in horror as Arek pulled the green T-shirt off over his head and flexed for the group like a WWE wrestler. The entire group was officially in hysterics as Arek kissed first one bicep and then the other. "Look at these guns, and you can't say no to these abs. I'm a fucking chick magnet." He pointed to the washboard abs. "The bat signal has nothing on these babies." Arek tapped his abs with his fingers like he was playing a baby grand piano.

"For the love of God, tell him he's pretty so he can go and put his shirt back on before I go blind." Ringo held his hand up like he was blocking out the sun.

"Fine, you can come, Arek. You all know it's an open invitation—if we make it back, that is." A somber silence washed over the group as the reality of the deadly mission they were going to be undertaking in a few days settled over them. "Sorry, I didn't mean to bring the mood down." Reaching out, he nudged Ringo's arm. "Why don't you sing us a song?"

Kes leaned down and grabbed his acoustic guitar, running his thumb down the strings to make sure his girl was still in tune.

"I don't know." Ringo downed the rest of his beer, the plain brown glass bottle dangling between his fingertips.

"Come on, man. You're like a legend. Let's hear this gift from the gods." Morry tipped her beer bottle in Ringo's direction.

"Okay, fine, but only 'cause I can't say no to that pout. Kes, give me an E." Ringo stood as a flash that was wholly unnatural lit up the night sky in the distance. They all turned to look in the direction of the flash as targets, one-by-one, were taken out by drone strikes. The bright flashes were easily seen even from miles away.

Kes restarted the song, "Ride the Lightning," and this time, Ringo sang the song that had become their anthem. It was the song the two of them sang every *time they flew into danger and every time they made it out again with their dicks still intact.*

*"I was born on the wild side," he sang out.*

*A rumble in the distance announced another target had been hit.*

*"Ride the lightning, feel the thunder."*

*Kes stood and tossed the guitar strap around his neck as he let the music flow out of him. A soft breeze swirled around them, the flames of the bonfire dancing higher and raising goosebumps along his arms.*

*"Fly on wings of fire."*

*For just a moment, he wasn't in a desert. He wasn't about to go on a mission that was the most dangerous he'd ever attempted. For just a moment, he wasn't the pretty boy that was born with a silver spoon in his mouth and insurmountably high expectations. For a moment, he was just a guy singing around a fire with his friends, and he never wanted the feeling to end.*

*"When they call me home."*

*Ringo's voice trailed off, sounding so much like Warren Zeiders that he would have sworn it was him singing. As the last note faded into the night, so too did the rumbling and flashes in the distance, blanketing them in an eerie calm.*

Kes woke to a dark tent and sweat dripping off his brow. Using the back of his hand, he wiped away the tears that were sliding down his cheeks.

"When they call me home," he whispered into the darkness.

# CHAPTER 8

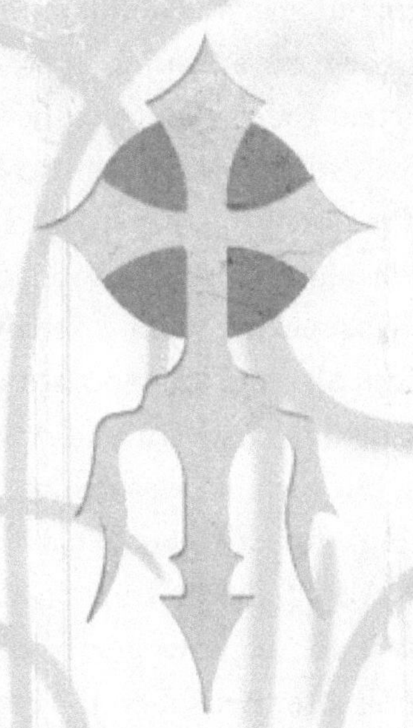

Seven days and six nights—that was how long it had been since Ashley's crazy chance encounter with Kes Reynolds. She tripped over what she should call him. Her bully, her crush, her nemesis, her lost love…there were too many choices. She didn't really know what he was to her. What did you call the person that tormented you all through high school only to confess that they loved you, then showed their true colors when they disappeared from your life without warning? He certainly wasn't a friend. He'd never been a lover for longer than a couple of kisses. It didn't matter what he was or wasn't, at this point. In fact, the entire moment seemed like a dream, something her mind had concocted. That was certainly possible these days.

"Here you go. I hope you raise enough money. It would be sad to see this old church go, even if it is used for street folk and delinquents." Ashley started to smile and then stopped. She opened her mouth to tell this woman where to go, but she was holding out a hundred-dollar bill. Far more than the ten they were asking for the car wash. Saving the church was more important than what this one woman thought. In her own ignorant way, she was still helping these 'street folk.'

Nodding, she took the green bill, hating herself a little for caving in on her beliefs for cash. Straightening, she rubbed at her lower back and sides, the uncomfortable squeezing feeling getting a little worse despite the fancy new medication. She had an appointment coming up, and not only was the idea of sitting in a chair with a drip attached to her arm for hours on end terrifying, but the cost was insane. Her insurance through work would cover the bulk for now, but what would happen when she could no longer work? Would she end up on the streets slowly dying alone, or would she have to swallow her pride and go home to her parents so they could look after her when they should be enjoying their retirement?

She shivered despite the hot sun beating down from a cloudless sky. Nope, she wasn't going to go there. She would enjoy the day. Stuffing the money in the small pouch she had strapped around her waist, she waved over the next car in line.

"Hey, baby." Ashley leaned down to look in the car and was even more tempted to hit this guy than the previous woman. "Ten dollars is a bit expensive for no skin." He not-so-subtly leaned over enough to look her over like she'd just offered him a sexual service instead of a car wash.

"It's a church fundraiser, sir. If you want that kind of a show, may I suggest the Golden Rail, which is just down the road?" She smiled while the thought of leaping through his window and choking the shit out of him ran through her mind.

"Aww, come on, don't be like that." He revved the engine of the fancy car she had no name for—she lifted a brow at the guy as he blatantly stared at her chest. "You know you want to go for a ride. I'll make it worth your while."

"Do you want a car wash, sir? If not, you're going to need to move along." She took a step back from the car and crossed her arms over her chest. Her skin was crawling just being near this creep.

"I can pay a lot more than ten dollars for the right kind of buff job."

Was this scumbag for real? Ashley dropped her arms and clenched her fists, ready to give him a piece of her mind, when a voice that rooted her to the spot beat her to the punch line.

"The lady said she's not interested. Move along before I make you."

"Fuck this. I can find hotter ass for far less hassle." Slamming the car into gear, he sped out of the parking lot, almost hitting a car parked on the street as he did so.

Ashley swallowed hard as she debated whether she should turn around or pretend she didn't know who Kes was or that he was standing right behind her. Ignoring him was the cheap way out, but she was in a cheap mood.

"Thanks, but I can handle myself," she said waving over the next car in line.

"A thank you would suffice."

She could feel that arrogant smile burning a hole into her back, and she was so tempted to turn around and punch him in the face. She'd certainly had that fantasy more than once. She felt her fingers clench into a tight fist.

"Do it," he said softly. Her eyes flicked up to the reflection in the window of the car that had just pulled up. His hooded figure stood looming behind her like the Grim Reaper had come to take her early. She couldn't see Kes's eyes, and yet, she could feel them staring back at her from the shadow of the hood. "You know you want to hit me, so do it."

Heat flushed through her body with those softly spoken words that did all the right things to her body even though she fought it. "I don't know what you're talking about. I don't even know who you are." Bending over, she leaned on the car door and smiled at the little old lady.

"Give 'er a good scrubbin', dear, and I'll give ya a twenty."

"Will do." She smiled at the feisty woman and straightened up to retrieve her hose, but she backed up into a wall of heat and muscle. Swallowing hard, her mind screamed at her to run while her body ceased to remember how to work at all.

"Don't lie to me, Ashley. I hate it when people lie."

"Shocking, considering it comes so second nature to you." She glared over her shoulder, her pulse ratcheting up with just that glance. "I have a car to wash, so you can either help or move along, but I'm not having this conversation with you. Not now, not ever. You had your chance."

"You do recognize me."

Ashley bit her lip, the anger simmering to a dangerous level that brimmed with a darker desire. She had no intention of giving him the satisfaction of upsetting her again. "Of course I do, you tend to remember assholes, but I can't say I'm happy about it," she whispered harshly.

"You okay, dear?" The older woman asked as she leaned across the seat.

Ashley turned her attention back to the little grey-haired woman that was so tiny behind the wheel she wondered how she saw over it to see the road at all. "I'm great. Sorry about the delay."

Masking her expression into one of serene calm, she turned to tell the man in question to go away, but he was gone. Like a fucking magician, he'd disappeared and stolen her moment. History loved to repeat itself.

Confused, she turned to look up and down the parking lot to the adjoining street but couldn't see his grey-hooded form anywhere. The sidewalk was full of people, but not one of them was the imposing figure of Kes. His disappearance was unsettling, and she was tempted to ask the woman if there had been a man behind her a moment ago.

Maybe the brain issues were further along than she thought. Maybe her doctor was wrong, and she had less time than he thought. Maybe, she was simply going insane, and her mind was playing tricks on her because she was secretly hoping to see him again.

*Nope, nope, nope, she was not going there again, no emotional freakouts. This was a breakdown-free space on a breakdown-free day. He'd been there. Her flushed body told her he'd definitely been there.*

Picking up the hose, she squeezed the handle and tried as hard as humanly possible to put the annoying man from her mind.

For six freaking nights, he'd lurked in the shadows. For six nights, he had followed her home. And for six nights, he hadn't slept as he imagined pushing her down and stealing the anger away from her body as she screamed his name.

He'd turned into a predator, stalking Ashley like those he usually hunted stalked their prey. He knew she was in bed by no later than eleven each night, that she liked souvlaki from the same place he did, and that she used straw-fucking-berry shampoo and body wash along with the lip gloss. He'd never be able to smell a strawberry again and not think of her while wanting to lick the taste off her body.

He cracked his neck, the tension building in his head. "Fuck, what the hell was I thinking?"

He'd had no intention of speaking to her again. He'd tried to convince himself that he was content to watch from a distance, but when that piece of shit drove up, he couldn't stay out of it. Ashley was his. She'd always been his, and the claws of a need he'd thought was long dormant had resurfaced. As hard as he tried, that fucking needy demon was not laying back down.

Fuck, she'd smelled good, her sweet berry scent calling to him like a siren. When she'd bent over in front of him, he'd come dangerously close to grabbing her hips. With just one look, she'd flipped a switch, and he felt more like his old self, the self before his life turned upside down. The self that pictured a future where she played the starring role.

His hands could almost feel her soft skin and the silky strands of her hair running through his fingers. Red flags were waving in his brain, reminding him that he'd never be content with just watching her from a distance. He'd craved her since the first moment he'd laid eyes on her, and he would happily rot in hell if it meant he got a taste.

He marched down the narrow alley to get as far away as possible before he could march back out there, drag her into a dark corner of the church, and fuck her up against the nearest available wall. If he were a crack addict, she was his crack, and he was jonesing bad. Muscles tight, cock hard, he felt crazy. Like a wild animal driven by instinct, he was hyper-focused on what he wanted—his body was a carnal mess of lust.

Letting out a grunt, he kicked the metal trash can he was about to pass and sent it and its contents flying as a stray cat took off at the loud bang.

His chest rose and fell with rage, his breathing as fast as his racing pulse. He clenched his fists and was tempted to make them bleed against the reddish brick.

Closing his eyes, he took a slow, shuddering breath as he reined in the beast of need that was riding him. He focused on nothing, pushing aside all thought so he could recalibrate his emotions.

Calmer, his eyes snapped open.

There was work to be done tonight. He needed to get his sex-riddled mind back on the tracks before the train ran into a wall. Taking one last deep breath, he marched toward his destination. Ashley was a fantasy of the past, but the fucker he'd been sat in the back of his mind and laughed at his resistance.

Tonight's menu consisted of a fat, bearded fuck who always smelled like garlic sausage. His lip curled up as imaginings of what he was going to do to his next prey danced along the stage of his mind, like the Black Swan herself.

The lights and cameras were already set. All he needed was his newest cast member.

# CHAPTER 9

Ashley flopped down in the chair across from Dennis feeling waterlogged. There was not an inch of her that was not damp to varying degrees. Her shoes squished with every step like she had permanent fish bowls attached to her feet—it was her new most hated sensation, and she couldn't wait to get home, showered, and into dry clothes.

Dennis was still counting the money from the car wash, so she took a moment to rub at the muscles in her legs that were quivering uncontrollably. It wasn't the quivering that was unnerving, it was the fact that she could barely feel her hands rubbing at her legs. It was like the muscles or skin were numb—it was like they were asleep and yet not at the same time.

"You okay, Ashley?"

She stopped and looked up to see Dennis giving her a curious look. "Muscles are twitching, I need to drink more water. You'd think that after being soaked all day, I wouldn't need to drink that much water." She smiled, hoping he didn't see through the bluff. "How did we do?"

He rubbed at his eyes and sat back in the badly beaten-up leather chair. "Considering it is a car wash, we did well, but at best we have an eighth of the needed money, or I can put this toward food since we are low on donations this month."

"Are you sure?"

Dennis nodded. "I counted it twice."

Placing the money in a bank deposit envelope, he stood up from the desk and grabbed his coat. "I'm sorry, Ashley, but it looks like this place will be closed in a few weeks." He paused by the door—she'd never seen him look so dejected, and they'd seen some tough times there lately. "Maybe start praying for a miracle. I'm going home, maybe I'll get to eat my dinner hot and see my wife for a change."

Ashley slowly stood as Dennis disappeared, and as she tried to take a step, her leg didn't pull forward properly, and she caught herself on the chair to hold herself upright. With a shove, she got herself back onto the seat.

"You pushed yourself too hard, that's all it is," she said softly, but it did nothing to convince the panic forming in her chest.

Ashley rubbed at her arms, but this cold was deeper, something she couldn't rub at. She turned and looked around the room to the coat rack, and sure enough, there was an old wooden cane. She just needed to get across the room, but it felt like it was ten football fields away.

She could drag herself across the floor, but then what if she couldn't stand? Ashley's bottom lip shook, and she bit it as she held back the waterworks.

*No, I'm not giving up.*

Ready this time, she pushed herself up and tested out her steadiness. Her feet still had the odd numbing sensation, but her legs seemed to be working as she took a tentative step forward. Each step toward her goal was a small victory.

Reaching the coat rack, she gripped the knobby end of the cane, which looked more like a small wizard's staff, and leaned on it for support.

*You can do this.*

It was slow going, and Ashley figured Dennis would be back for morning by the time she made it out of the church. She cringed at hearing Charlie whistling his usual tune in the front foyer. The door was thankfully open and she stepped out, earning a gasp from the older man.

Ashley held up her hand to stop him from rushing over. "I twisted my ankle, but I'm okay." She winced a little with her next step.

"Do you want someone to take you to the hospital?" Charlie made his way over, and how pitiful did she feel that this arthritic man that was more than twice her age was asking if she needed help.

"No, I'm all good. I just need to ice it and I've got some pain meds at home."

Charlie offered, "Are you sure? I could go with you."

"Positive, but could you see me to the bus stop? Would be nice to have the company."

He pointed a finger at her. "You are one stubborn lady."

"That is something you and my mother would certainly agree on," She laughed, but Charlie didn't seem to be as amused by her joke.

He wrapped an arm around her waist, and she hated to admit it, but it was much easier to walk with his help, and as luck would have it, the bus was pulling up just as they arrived.

"Thank you, Charlie, you have a good night and don't work too hard."

"Don't you worry about me." He gave her shoulder a little squeeze as she stepped up into the bus.

Thankfully, a little more of her mobility had returned, and what she'd assumed would feel like climbing Mount Everest she tackled with minimal issue. It was the sudden lurch of the bus's motion before she was seated that almost had her face-first in the aisle. She glared at the driver in his rear-view mirror as she got herself situated in a seat.

By the time she got home and inside she was ready to collapse. It was amazing what she'd taken for granted all these years—it was eye opening and emotionally draining.

She was toweling off her hair when her cell rang. Grabbing it, she smiled at the silly picture of her best friend, Trish, that came up on the screen. She had eventually learned the name of the girl who had been paralyzed by fear that first day of her freshman year. Mind you, as good of a friend as Trish was, she was terrible at helping her with anything to do with Kes and his friends. Trish would turn and walk the other way if she saw them coming in school and leave her to fend for herself. What did that say? Not much, other than Trish was not the person she'd pick as backup in a zombie apocalypse.

Ashley answered, not able to keep the grin off her face. "Hey stranger. How's Africa?"

"Stunning, amazing, hot as hell and heart breaking all at the same time. I am getting stunning photos though, and the locals are the best now that they have gotten to know me. How about you, how's my bestie?"

Ashley was tempted to tell Trish about her diagnosis, but Trish would want to fly home—it was in her nature—and there was no way in hell that was happening. "Good, but it looks like Salvation Place will have to close. I just got in from an all-day fundraiser, and we're not even close to having enough money."

"That does sound bad. Can I do anything to help?"

"I don't think so, unless you have magic money-fairy dust up your sleeve?"

"Noooo, but I can donate one of my photos to sell. They catch a good price, and don't you dare say no." A horn blew in the background, and Ashley could hear a group of people yelling to 'look at the giraffes.'

"Well, in that case, how can a girl say no?"

"What else is new? I've been gone two months. There has to be more than that going on." A heavy sigh followed, and Ashley couldn't help but laugh.

"What, the wild animals not enough to keep you entertained?" Ashley laid the phone down on speaker as she rummaged around in the drawer to find the cork opener. This was a glass-of-wine kind of night.

"It's not the animals that are entertaining." Trish broke out into hysterical laughter.

"You dirty dog." Ashley grabbed a glass off the top shelf and glared at her hand as it slightly shook. "You get it girl, you deserve it."

"I do, don't I?" They laughed again as Ashley got herself seated with the bottle in hand, glass left behind on the counter. She wasn't letting a shaky hand ruin her night or her couch. "Alright, now enough about me, you were about to tell me what's new."

Ashley groaned and took a long swig from the bottle. "Well, if you must know, I ran into Kes Reynolds again, like literally ran into him and dropped my stuff all over the ground."

"No shit! That's, that's…."

"Fucked up, yeah I know." Ashley could picture the shocked look on her friend's face.

"Is he still as good-looking? Is he still as big of an asshole? Oh, and more importantly, is he still filthy stinking rich?"

"Short answer—the hottest, better than high school, totally not fair. He's like a fucking fine wine, only getting better. I'm not sure about the jerk part, but considering who I'm talking about, I'd say yes, just seemed toned down a little. As for rich—I don't know, I think he's homeless, actually, which is weird."

"What? Kes is homeless? How does that even happen, his parents were like multi-multi-multi millionaires."

"I don't know, Trish, it's only a guess. I've seen him twice now at Salvation Place and both times he was in the same outfit. All I know is I can't go back to the way things were. I need to steer clear of him." She took another gulp of the delightful red wine. "I've worked too hard to move past the hurt to tumble backward."

"I need to sit down, I'm blown away. Kes homeless, it's like a 'karma is a bitch' kind of thing, I'm seriously apologizing for any shit I've done now." There was a distinct thump sound as she obviously found a seat. "Homeless or not, he better not treat you the way he did then."

Ashley smirked. "Oh, are you planning on kicking his ass if he does?"

"Hell no, I'm still terrified of him and his eerily intense stare. I'd probably run the other way, like you should."

"So, nothing much has changed, is what you're saying?"

"No, but now I have friends that have friends and I will call the cops if I have to," Trish practically growled into the phone, and it only made her laugh harder. "Seriously though, Ash, you've grown and he's—well, who knows with him, but you won't take his shit anymore."

"I'd prefer not to have to deal with him at all."

"L.I.A.R." They erupted into a fit of giggles until tears ran down Ashley's cheeks.

It felt good to laugh, to forget for a little while that her life was turned upside down, that her future was still a big question mark.

wo hours and three-quarters of a bottle of wine later, she hung up and determined it would be a bad idea to try and stand. Sleeping on the couch it was, and hopefully there wouldn't be anymore annoying dreams about Mr. Kes Reynolds.

# CHAPTER 10

The library had become her only reprieve from the endless teasing. She was officially known as Kes's Pet Project, and no matter what she did or where she went, the students would call her that, or worse.

She sighed as she stared at the algebra in the textbook. She'd figured that once she was no longer a freshman and came back as a sophomore, the bullying would stop, but it had only seemed to escalate. If it weren't for the fact she'd earned her spot there with excellent grades and a crazy amount of hard work, she would've dropped out by now. Any other school had to be better than this, but it was the principle of the thing. Why should she be chased off?

"There you are. I've been looking all over for you," Kes's voice rang out from *behind her making her cringe, clenching her eyes shut. He was everywhere, and she couldn't escape. Another part of her never wanted to. Just that one sentence and her heart had picked up the pace. It was the most fucked up combination of emotions.*

*"What do you want, Kes. I'm busy." She didn't bother to look up even as his tall shadow cast across her text, making it hard to read. Kes pulled out a chair and proceeded to sit down.*

*Unable to focus, she looked up at her tormentor and crossed her arms over her chest. "What is it, Kes? No puppies around for you to kick?"*

*Reaching out, he snatched her backpack, and she stood up in a rush to jump for the bag. Her chair slammed backward onto the floor, and the librarian gave her a stern glare.*

*"Sorry," she called out as she fixed her chair. She sat back down and growled at the annoying boy across from her. "Give me back my backpack."*

*"I just want to see if you have anything good in here." Kes grinned as he shamelessly went through her bag.*

*"What the hell would I have that you'd want?"*

*He pulled out her chewy granola bar and dropped the backpack on the floor. She bit her lip, so tempted to leap across the table.*

*"See, I found something."*

*"Good for you. You've resorted to stealing food from a younger student. Must make you feel like a big man." If her words bothered him, he didn't show it. Instead, he calmly reached over and flipped her books onto the floor.*

*"You should really watch your mouth."*

*"Real mature." She reached down and picked up the books. "And what could you possibly do that you haven't already done?" As soon as the words left her mouth, she knew she shouldn't have waved a red flag in front of the bull.*

*Kes grinned wickedly before dramatically gasping loud enough to get everyone's attention. "No, Ashley. I told you I don't want to sleep with you," he yelled. "How many times do I have to tell you, I'm a respectable student that doesn't like their cock sucked. Such a mouth on you!"*

*Her mouth fell open as she stared around the room at the tables of students that could've been deaf and still heard him yell. Heat and embarrassment tag-team raced through her body as she scrambled to figure out how to stop him from making things worse.*

*Leaning forward, she glared daggers that she wished could kill. "Have you lost your mind," she whispered. "You could get me kicked out."*

*"Ms. Hartley, how dare you proposition another student, and in my library, no less." The librarian stood to glare at her, and panic gripped her throat. She couldn't be expelled. He may have really done it this time, but she needed this school.*

*"But, I didn't," she called out as she snatched her discarded bag off the floor. The woman had picked up the desk phone to call the principal. Ashley hastily stuffed her books inside all while Kes sat and ate the granola bar he'd stolen from her, looking as annoyingly relaxed as he always did. She wanted to shove that fucking bar down his throat and make him choke on it.*

*"Busy, I guess I will have to go there myself." Those sharp eyes swung her way as she zipped up her bag. "You can run away all you want—I'm going to write you up and notify the principal of your disturbing behavior." The librarian made her way toward the door, and Ashley panicked to correct the situation that jerkface had caused. She made a dash past Kes.*

*He stuck out his leg at the last second, and she went flying, landing hard on the old, carpeted floor, which instantly created rug burns on her bare knees and palms. She'd already learned the hard way to wear shorts under her school kilt, or she would have given him quite the show as the kilt pulled up her waist with the momentum. Everything jarred, and she sucked in a breath as the sting of the fall registered.*

*"Get off your knees, Ash. This is simply sad. Throwing yourself at me like this? I have never wanted you to touch me, and you're making me feel objectified." She glared over her shoulder at Kes. "Maybe I'll file for sexual harassment charges against you."*

*"You wouldn't right?" Ashley grabbed her bag and held it against her chest like a shield.*

*Kes stood from the table, his tall form seeming even larger as he closed the distance. He knelt as he reached her side, and she bit the inside of her cheek to stop from crying in front of him. That's what he wanted, what he got off on, and she wouldn't give him that.*

*"Keep up the snotty attitude, Doll, and I'll make sure no school will ever take you in again. Who would want a troublemaking sexual deviant that was already caught cheating?"*

*"You know I didn't do any of those things." Her bottom lip quivered as she tried to hold back the tears. "Why are you doing this to me?" Her voice cracked slightly, and she hated that she was so weak. Even as he stared at her like she was less than the dirt on his shoe, she couldn't deny that she still wanted him. Even though she knew better, she kept hoping that like some stupid movie, he would wake up and be different. Kes would protect her instead of treating her like she was worthless—tell her he loved her instead of tormenting her. That was how screwed up her brain was.*

*Reaching out, he ran a piece of her hair through his fingers. "Because I can. I don't know why you won't leave the school. No one wants you here." He shrugged. "You don't belong with the rest of us."*

*Standing, he dropped the empty wrapper in front of her and walked away, leaving her there with pain inside that went far beyond a skinned knee or bruised ego. The students who had silently watched burst into laughter, forcing the tears to make an appearance.*

*I hate you, Kes Reynolds. I really hate you.*

# CHAPTER 11

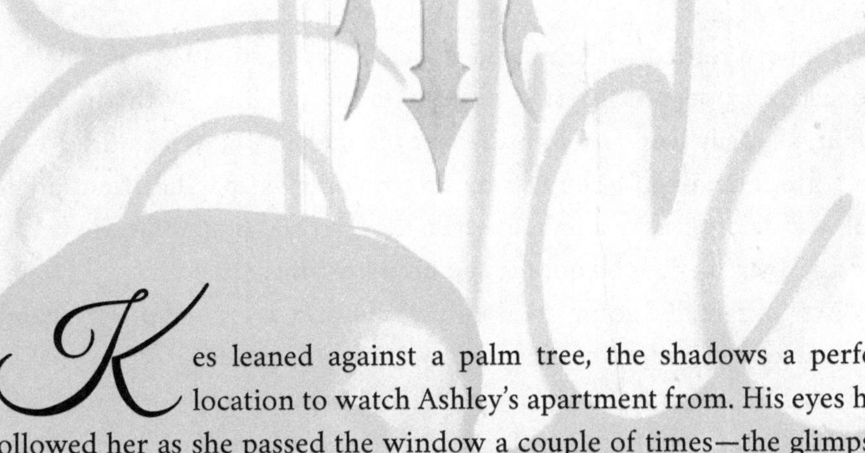

Kes leaned against a palm tree, the shadows a perfect location to watch Ashley's apartment from. His eyes had followed her as she passed the window a couple of times—the glimpses were brief, but she looked happy. She was smiling and laughing, and he was suffering a serious case of the green monster.

She was beautiful and sweet and smart, and—the chance of her being single was somewhere between slim and none. Although, he hadn't seen a man come to her apartment. He wasn't sure what he would do if one showed up. The thought didn't sit well with him. His mind shifted to murderous even though he had no right.

The breeze picked up, and unlike the people who passed by around him, all bundled up for the unseasonably low temps, he relished in the cooler air and breathed the refreshing stuff deep into his lungs. He took a drag on the cigarette he was smoking and then looked at the thing, Zumi's disappointed face coming to mind.

"Shit." Dropping it on the ground, he stomped it out. "I'm going soft."

Ashley's light turned off, and he waited a moment longer before taking a step along the sidewalk to leave but then he stopped and looked up at the darkened windows. Veering off course, he casually walked across the street and between the twin five-story apartment buildings. The back alley was unsurprisingly quiet, not that it would've mattered. The streets and its residents were his home and his family. The fire escape was too high to leap to, even for him. Spotting a large dumpster on wheels, he sent a few rats scurrying as he put his back into moving the bulky weight.

It loudly rattled as he moved it below his destination, and he was shocked no one was peering out a window at him. With the added height, he easily launched himself over the metal railing to land softly on the bottom landing. When he was sure no one was paying attention, he took the stairs three at a time to reach the fifth and final floor. He peered into the apartment as he questioned his own sanity.

"Are you really going to do this?" he asked out loud. His hands reached for the bottom of the window. "Guess you are."

It was locked, but the style was old, and with a few expert yanks with the right amount of twist, the lock popped free. He pushed it open at the bottom like his own personal dog door and, like a shadow, slipped into the darkness. Living on the streets taught you its own unique skill set—lying, stealing, and breaking and entering were commonplace. You learned what you needed to survive.

It was a shallow step to the kitchen floor, and he suddenly hoped she didn't have a dog. He'd never seen one, but this would be a terrible way to find out.

He gave a soft, low whistle and waited to see if anything came running. When nothing did, he moved through the room toward the hallway. It felt odd and yet comforting to be in her space. Everything smelled like her, and although the place wasn't large, it gave the feeling of a warm hug.

He stepped into the living room area and walked over to the bay window to look down at the spot he'd occupied. He glanced around the homey space, the pictures hanging on the wall drawing his attention. There were no smiling wedding photos. In fact, there were no men at all, other than a picture of her and her father.

A longing that still cut like a knife ached in his chest. This could've been his life, here with her, but instead, it was stolen from him.

Turning away from the photos, he spotted a wine bottle on the coffee table and started heading over for it, but when he realized Ashley was on the couch behind it, he froze. Ashley was balled up on one of the couch cushions, and she was shivering, the only sign of movement. Making sure to be silent, he stepped closer and picked up the wine bottle to inspect the contents. It was mostly gone.

He looked between the bottle and the woman on the couch. "Naughty girl." He put the bottle to his lips and chugged the remaining bit of the tasty red liquid. "Not bad."

He licked the remaining liquid off his lips as he sat the bottle down. He was going to need liquid courage for this. Bending down, he moved a piece of hair away from her face, but she didn't flinch.

"You have always made me feel insane, do you know that?" Kes whispered as he traced the back of his knuckle down the side of her face.

She murmured something incoherent, but it was not hard to picture it being a few choice words.

As carefully as he could, he slipped his arms under her adorable sleeping form—the thin T-shirt and boy shorts not providing much protection against a chill. But lord, her skin was soft. He gently rolled her toward him and then stood with her in his arms, Ash's head leaning against his shoulder, and his heart beat faster under her ear.

She murmured a little.

"Shhh, you're okay." His lips brushed her temple, and he closed his eyes, breathing her in.

"Kes."

"Go back to sleep," he whispered, but he didn't think she was actually awake—her eyes were still closed, and she wasn't screaming or smacking him, which would definitely be her response to him in her home.

Ash mumbled, "Why do you hate me?"

He stopped moving and stared at her beautiful sleeping form. "I don't hate you. I never hated you," he whispered in her ear. She shivered in his hold, and he smirked as she moaned slightly.

Kes looked around the hallway. He was pressing his luck—he needed to get her to bed. The first door was a bathroom, and the next one looked like a small spare room made up like an art studio, but lucky number three was what he was searching for, the bedroom. Pulling down the blankets with one hand, he laid his little doll down and tucked her in.

She sighed softly, and unable to resist, he laid his lips against her temple. "You've always owned my heart." The words were barely a whisper, but she mumbled his name again, and an ache formed inside his chest.

The temptation to curl in beside her was strong. Kes's fingers twitched along with his cock at the thought of curling up to that adorable ass, his hand cupping a breast as he held her body close to his.

Before he did something even crazier, he stepped away until he blended with the shadows and slipped back out into the night.

# Chapter 12

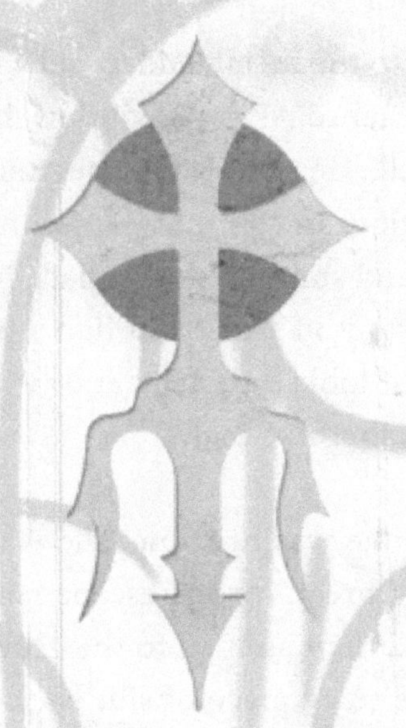

The sun was just starting to rise, the shimmering light bathing the world in a mysterious mix of orange and grey shadows. Kes sat on the roof of Ashley's apartment building, feet up on the ledge and ass seated on a discarded construction bucket, as he watched the great orange ball rise.

Something you learned very quickly in the Sandbox was you don't take anything for granted. Not your life, not the food you put in your gullet, and certainly not a sunrise. It meant you'd made it through another night alive and hoped to live through the day to dance all over again.

Unfortunately, he had to get going before the sun made it impossible to sneak down the fire escape. His side tweaked as he stood, making him wince for a moment, but it was nothing more than a phantom pain. It would pass. The first year after his injury had been the worst, but now it was just another reminder that he was alive, whether he wanted to be or not.

Kes wandered over to the metal ladder and slipped down as stealthily as possible, but as he reached Ashley's window, he had to jump back and lay flat against the wall. He could hear her moving around the small kitchen, her footsteps slow and stumbly. Kneeling, he took the chance to peer around the brick and smirked as she made her way to the coffee pot with her sunglasses firmly in place and hair up in a wild mess on her head. She somehow still looked perfect, and yet she'd push his ass right off the escape for seeing her like that.

*Head hurting, Doll?*

Once the pot of coffee was brewing, she wandered back out of the kitchen, and he made a break for his escape route. Kes dropped to the closed dumpster lid and then jumped to the ground with a soft thud. He took a step to push the rusty piece of shit back to where it was rotting away before and then shrugged and left it alone.

*Why make life difficult?*

Kes shrunk into his long coat and sweater, letting them swallow him as the sun got higher in the sky. He yawned as he strolled up the alley toward his home, his eyes scanning the members of the homeless camp that were still sleeping or sitting outside of their small makeshift homes. He protected the people that lived out here, and since he had arrived, the crime and abuse had dwindled. He smirked to himself as he remembered his first round of punishments vividly. His pocket vibrated, and he pulled it out, expecting Trev to be on the other end.

"I told you I don't know anything yet," he growled into the phone.

"I have no idea what you are talking about, Son."

Kes's stride faltered at the sound of his father's voice. "How the hell did you get my number?"

"Son, you forget who I am. I know everything. I know you've been sleeping in that shitty tent under the bridge, and I also know that you like to take my boat out for joy rides from time to time, although you still refuse to come home. I also know that you are breaking your mother's heart by not calling her since you've been back in town."

The shot about his mother hurt, and yet, she'd stood by his father's side when the man blew up his world. Why would he call or visit? And for fuck's sake, how much did his father know about his extracurricular activities? Maybe this would give him an excuse to kill the asshole after all. Not that he needed any more of a reason.

"What of it?" Kes drawled.

His father sighed, and Kes could picture the look of annoyance on his face as he sat behind his enormous mahogany desk in his glass palace downtown. The thought made him smile. Anything that annoyed his father was a good thing.

"I want you to stop this nonsense and come home. You should be learning how to take the reins of the business, not wasting your life away on the streets like the rest of the garbage."

"Are you referring to the people or the actual bags of garbage?"

"Is there really a difference?"

Kes visualized reaching through the phone and choking his father. "The answer is no."

"Why are you so goddamn stubborn? You know this is where you belong. Don't make me cut you off."

Kes barked out a laugh, the sound of annoyance thick in his tone. "First off, I don't need nor want your money. Second, the trust fund has already been issued, so you can't take it back. Maybe you shouldn't have set it up for me to receive it at twenty-five. It seems to me you're a few years too late to be making this threat."

"I meant the entire company. Not settling for the meager amount in your trust."

"I have no use for lavish things, Father, not like you. It will last me a lifetime, so I guess thanks for that."

There was the sound of a door slamming in the distance, and Kes smiled wide as he pictured the office door slamming shut. An evil sliver of foolish pleasure coursed through his body.

"Ungrateful, that's what you are. Now come home, or I will send someone to come get you," his father snarled.

Kes wanted to growl into the phone, his patience slipping over the edge and sliding fast down the other side. Bad things happened when his patience disappeared. "You're planning on trying to kidnap me, your adult son because you don't like my choices? Choices, I might add, you forced upon me. Choices that would never have occurred if you'd simply let me live my life."

"I did what I had to then, and I will do what I have to now to make sure that you don't continue down this road. I'm your father, and if that means I have to force you to get help for your issues, then that is what I will do."

The threat was evident. To anyone else, it might seem like his father was simply concerned for his troubled son, but that was not the case with his father. Daddy Dearest just couldn't handle not being in control. If there was a spot in the dictionary for control-freak on steroids, his father would be the poster boy, and when he'd finally grown sick of it and stood up for himself, he'd been punished.

"Try it, and I promise you, it will be your biggest mistake and the last one you ever make," he whispered into the phone menacingly like he was Lucifer himself.

He could hear his father's breathing pick up. Good, he'd better be nervous. He didn't toss around idle threats. "What exactly are you saying, Son?"

"Don't play dumb, Father. We both know what I mean."

"How did we get here, Son? How is it that I tried to help you, and you ended up hating me? All I have ever wanted was for you to make good choices and be happy in this life."

Kes snorted. The concept of 'happy' was foreign to the man. He didn't know the meaning of real happiness, and he certainly never wished it on anyone other than himself.

"You know how we got here, and I will never forgive you. I will never come work for you either. You and mother and the board can all kiss my lily-white homeless ass."

"Son, please listen to reason. You are going to die out there."

Kes paused and looked off at the sliver of ocean that he could just see in the distance. "See, that's where you're wrong. I already died, and even the devil didn't want me. Don't call me again, and if you try to force me...." Kes hit the button and ended the call, not finishing the threat again. There was no point. His position had been made clear. He was going to need Baby Doll, to do some hacking. The onboard AI was the best there was in the world. He really did love that freaking Hummer and the high-tech AI. If his father had any incriminating evidence, it needed to be destroyed. He'd never let that man have control over his life again, not ever.

"Let go of my arm, Mom. You're hurting me." Zumi's voice reached his ears on the soft breeze, her distress obvious. He turned in the direction of her small tarp-covered home, where he found Chelsea jerking on the young girl's arm. Really bad fucking timing, Chelsea. The anger from his call was spilling over into every stride he took toward his target.

*Fucking piece of trash. He might make good on his fantasy to slit her throat yet.*

Stuffing the phone in his pocket, he marched up to the scene of the woman and the upset girl. "Give it back! I know you took it, you little bitch," Chelsea yelled as she shook Zumi hard.

Kes could clearly see the tears running down Zumi's reddened cheeks, and his temper flared. "I'd let her go, Chelsea." He stepped up behind the woman and gripped her arm the same way she had a hold of Zumi, but he suspected his hold was much firmer.

"Ouch. What the fucking business is it of yours?"

"Let your daughter go, now." Giving the woman's arm a jerk, he dared to get close to her face and her wild, bloodshot eyes. "Or you don't want to know what I will do next." Like magic, Chelsea released Zumi, and the girl rubbed at her arm, her bottom lip shaking.

"The little bitch stole my last baggie. I had one left, and she took it for herself," Chelsea pointed at Zumi.

Zumi shook her head back and forth. "I didn't take it. I don't do drugs, Mom."

"You're a liar. You stole it so I couldn't have it. Maybe to sell, but you took it from me." Chelsea glared up at him. "Let me go."

"Or what? Are you gonna call the cops on me? What are you going to tell them? That you were abusing your nine-year-old daughter because you think she took your coke and I stopped you? Do it. I need a good laugh today."

"This is none of your business," she spat back.

"I don't give a fuck about anything else you do in your life." Kes released the woman's arm before he broke it for fun. "But if you hurt Zumi again, I'll make sure there is nothing left of you for anyone to find."

He watched the skeletal woman blink as she processed his words. "You're an asshole."

"And I like it."

Stepping around Chelsea, he placed a hand on Zumi's shoulder and guided her away from her mother. While she was in the state of needing a hit, there was no telling what she might do next.

"She's my daughter, you can't have her."

"Then start acting like it," he snarled over his shoulder. Chelsea threw her hands in the air and continued to tear apart the little tarp home.

"Thanks, you didn't have to do that," Zumi whispered.

"Why do you continue to say stupid crap to me, Kid?"

Zumi lifted a shoulder as she used the back of her cuff to wipe away the tears. It was a tough lesson to learn that not all parents are superheroes. "I'm sorry," she mumbled.

Kes nudged a milk crate over to her with his foot so she could sit down while he grabbed a five-gallon bucket from the other spare items he stored beside his tent. His ass already felt like it had a premade circle in it from sitting on one of them all night. What the fucking difference did a few more minutes make?

They sat in silence and watched as Chelsea tore apart the small home that the two females shared.

"Kes?"

"Hmmm?"

"Where do you go at night?"

He looked down at his pint-sized snooper. "Nowhere, just around."

"You're a liar," she said quietly and then shrugged. "But it's fine. I'll figure it out."

What the fuck was up with everyone being all up in his business today? "The better question is, why do you care?"

She laid her cheek on her knees, and her face turned away from him. "Anything has to be better than this?"

Kes swallowed hard. He wanted to give her a hug and tell her it would all be alright, but instead, he turned his eyes to Chelsea as she threw something shiny out of the home with a loud crash.

"Trust me, Kid. The outside world only looks better, but looks are deceiving. There is just as much sadness and abuse in the pretty houses and impressive buildings." Zumi turned her head to look at him. "They've simply mastered how to hide it better behind their shiny doors and fake smiles." He turned his head to stare into Zumi's eyes. "That makes them deadlier. Never forget that. Wanna get out of here?"

She nodded, but there was no exuberance, and he hated to see her so defeated.

"It's going to be okay, Kid." Kes laid his hand on her shoulder as he directed her away from her still screaming mother. "I promise you that."

# CHAPTER 13

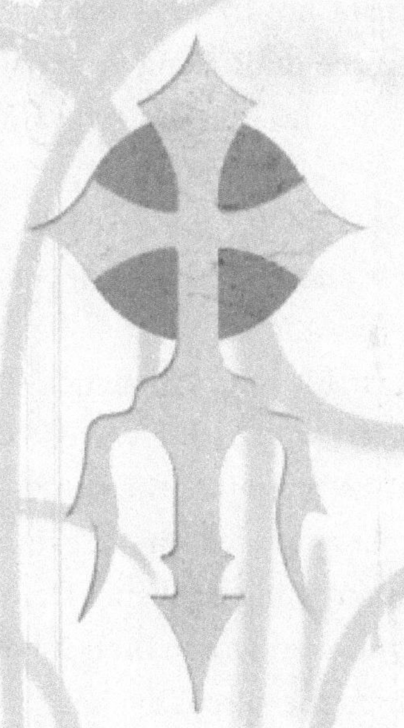

Ashley made the journey to the front door of Salvation Place she detested the fact that she was holding onto a cane. She glared down at the piece of wood as if it had offended her. At least she didn't really need it this morning. There was only a mild lingering weakness left in the wake of whatever had happened yesterday.

One thing was certain, she needed to stop drinking wine. She'd had this intense dream about Kes and didn't even remember finishing the bottle or making it to her bedroom to sleep.

Gripping the large brass handle of the church, she pulled open the heavy door to the vestibule and was greeted by the smell of the Saturday special, bacon. Her stomach growled at the greasy scent.

"Get out right now." Ashley jerked in the direction of Dennis's booming voice. There was the sound of thundering feet coming toward the inner door. She tried to jump out of the way to avoid getting hit, but her feet chose that moment not to work quickly enough. She only got a step off to the side when the door flung open, hitting her side hard. The force sent her tumbling to the floor as two men jumped over her legs and ran out the front.

"And don't come back. Oh, shit, Ashely, I'm so sorry." Dennis dropped down beside her and laid a baseball bat on the floor as he yelled for someone to come help.

"I'm fine, really. It just hit me off balance. I was unsteady with the cane, and this darn twisted ankle." She waved off the support, her body breaking out in a sweat as one after the other, people came out of the inner living area to see her sprawled on the ground like a circus act.

"Can you stand, or is anything broken?" Dennis's worried expression said it all. She definitely looked worse than it had felt. In actuality, she'd felt very little other than the jarringly hard floor slamming her jaw closed on impact. "Shit, your lip is bleeding."

She licked at her lip, and the coppery taste filled her mouth. *Just great. Now it was going to look like she'd gone a round with Mike Tyson.* She needed to get off the floor. With every person that filled the room, the walls closed in around her.

"Can you help me stand?"

"Of course, but should you move yet?"

"I'm fine, really. Just a bad ankle, and now a swollen lip."

Dennis's unbelieving stare said he didn't believe her, but he wrapped her arm around his neck and slowly stood, helping her to her feet. Once vertical and steady, he bent and grabbed the cane.

"I don't understand. When did you twist your ankle?" Dennis held out the small wooden helper.

"I guess I did it at the car wash and didn't notice until after you left. I grabbed this from the box in your office. I hope that's okay?"

"Anything you ever need from here is yours." Dennis gave her a small smile and then went to help her again, but she shook her head no.

"What was that about with the two men?" She nodded toward the now closed door.

"I caught them stealing from some of the members that were asleep. I don't mind anyone staying under this roof, but never steal from or hurt one another. That has always been our motto. Respect, is it really that difficult to ask of people?" Dennis huffed and shook his head, his face a glower of disgust.

Ashley looked around at the somber faces. "I'm good, I promise. You can all go back inside now." It didn't matter what she said. The group followed her like she was going to fall over at any moment, and she hated that more than the cane.

She was the one who helped people, not the other way around.

Head held high, she made her way into the room where she offered physical therapy and shrugged out of her jacket. A soft rapping sound had her turning to see Momma G. This was a rare occurrence. She preferred to stay away from the shelters, opting to stay on the streets—said she didn't need any coddling. Ashley understood the older woman better today than she ever had before.

"Hi there, Momma G. Are you okay?"

The older woman held onto the door frame, her feet taking small shuffling steps. "You help my back?"

"I will certainly try. Come on in and lay down." Momma G looked back in the direction she'd arrived from. Ashley knew what she was worried about and said, "It's okay. Dennis will make sure your stuff is safe and no one touches it. Come on in, let me help your back."

It was easy to see her reluctance as she chewed on her bottom lip, but she did come in. It was another mini battle getting her to remove her coat and sweater. "Can you tell me where it hurts?"

"All where." She moved her thumb in a slow circle to indicate her entire back.

"I'm going to touch you now, Momma G," she warned. She'd made the mistake of just starting an assessment one time without warning the patient, and in his mind, he thought he was being attacked. It took both Dennis and Charlie to calm him down. Now she always waited for the confirmation nod.

As soon as Momma G gave her permission, she gently felt around her neck and shoulders and down her spine. The car accident the woman had suffered had done a lot of damage, and she'd barely received any medical care once released from the hospital. She had a distinct twist in her spine and her shoulders were permanently hunched, which was exacerbated with her lifestyle and only added more strain on her spine. She'd never be able to fix this much damage, but she could alleviate some of the pain.

Momma G lay down face-first on the treatment table, and it felt good to work. To be useful, to help someone again. Scheduling the two weeks off to process was supposed to be a good thing, but it gave her too much time to think and let her mind travel down dark roads.

Twenty minutes in, her left hand began to cramp. It wasn't much. It felt like she'd been away from work for too long, and her hands were rebelling. Shaking it off, she continued on, determined not to give up, but another twenty minutes in and she couldn't open her hand. The pain was immense as the tendons and muscles rebelled against her.

Ashley sat back on her small rolling stool and gripped her fingers with her other hand to force the hand open. It wasn't smart, but the charley horse-like pain was radiating up her arm.

Momma G lifted her head, her soft eyes staring at her. "You okay?"

Ashley was so sick of that question. No, she wasn't okay, but she had to be okay. She had no other choice.

"I will be, bad hand cramp. How do you feel?" She averted the conversation.

"Better. Head no stabbing and back better." Momma G slowly sat up and moved her shoulders around.

"Take your time. I need to go to the bathroom." Standing, Ashley marched out of the room and down the hall as fast as she could without drawing attention. She darted into the bathroom, and as soon as the door closed, she flipped the lock and sunk to the floor. Tears she'd been trying to hold back burst forth, and she gasped as the panic gripped her throat, making it hard to draw breath.

Ashley wrapped her arms around her knees and buried her head as the pent-up emotions finally knocked down the wall she'd erected. Her phone picked that moment to vibrate, and she took a steadying breath so she wouldn't sound like she was in the middle of her obvious break-down as she answered the no-caller-ID call.

"Ashley Hartley here," she managed to get out.

"Hi there Ashley, this is the Mount Rose Clinic calling. I'm glad I reached you. We have had a last-minute cancellation for tomorrow at 9:00 a.m., and we are hoping you can take the spot. We'd like to get you started on your new treatment plan as soon as possible." Ashley swallowed hard and closed her eyes as she listened to the woman explain what the procedure would entail. Spending up to eight hours with an intravenous drip in her arm and hoping she didn't have a bad reaction didn't sound like a fun day.

What felt like someone else answered the questions, and when she hung up the phone, it dinged with her confirmation and pre-procedure directions.

She had no idea how much time had passed until a knock jerked her back to full awareness.

"Ashley, are you in there?" Dennis's voice was hushed and sounded worried.

"Just a sec." Pulling herself to her feet, Ashley stared into her reflection. Her eyes had dark circles and the face staring back didn't seem like it was her at all. She scrubbed at her hands with soap and hot water, the steam rising into the cool air-conditioned room.

She placed her well-crafted mask 'I'm fine' in place and opened the door. Well, at least it seemed like a well-crafted mask until Dennis's eyes found her own.

"You and I need to have a conversation in my office. Now, please."

"I'm fine, really."

"Now." Dennis didn't wait for her, and she knew the jig was up. He held open his office door, and as soon as she crossed over the threshold and it clicked behind her, the mask tumbled. She bit her lip hard as Dennis walked around to face her and placed his hands on her shoulders.

"I've been married to a strong, stubborn woman long enough to know when I'm being lied to because she doesn't want to tell me what's wrong. So what is really going on, and no more 'I'm fine.'"

Dennis had never felt more like an older brother than in that moment. She opened her mouth to speak, but only a tear-filled sob escaped.

"Come here, let it out." He pulled her into a hug, and she let herself go, let someone else take the brunt for a few minutes.

She hated that Dennis saw through her and had to comfort her and she hated it even more that she wished Dennis was someone else, someone she swore she'd never think about again. And just like the twisted and crawling roses her mother loved, Kes was creeping back into her system, sticking to her mind and heart—but all the while the sharp thorns were just waiting to make her bleed.

*Damn you, Kes Reynolds. Damn you.*

# CHAPTER 14

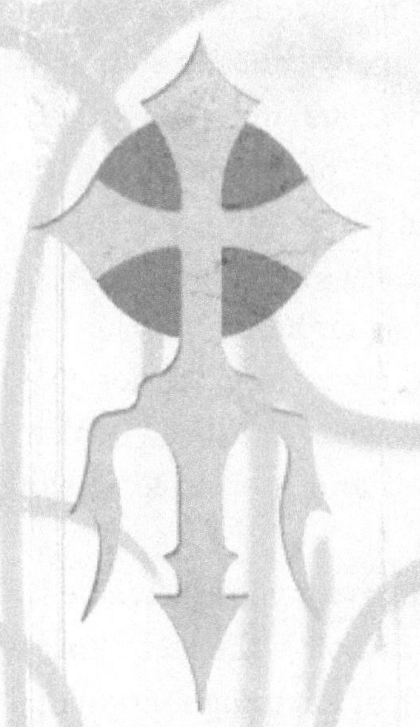

Kes arrived at Ashley's apartment just as the sun was setting and casting long shadows like fingers up and down the alley. He slipped inside the kitchen window as he had the night before to get a better look at her modest space. He needed to be quick to get back out before she got home.

Was he a stalker? It felt like he'd always been her stalker, but only because she stalked him first.

Her scent would linger in his nose or on his clothes if he got close to her. That shy smile coupled with her stunning lagoon-blue eyes made his heart hammer even when she wasn't in the room. That sexy body she hated to show off had him hard with the slightest thought about touching her, and that was all before she opened her mouth. Her sharp mind and sense of humor always had him on his toes and reliving every interaction over and over again. She'd always been far smarter than he was.

It was disturbing to be so consumed with thoughts of another person like that. He'd tried so many times in so many different ways to put his temptress out of his mind, and nothing worked.

Kes picked up a fluffy pink sweater off the back of a chair in her sitting area and brought it to his nose. He closed his eyes and took a deep breath. She had always been his, and he'd made sure no other guy in school would dare go near her.

Now he had to find a way to make her give him another chance. He needed to make right what had been stolen from him. Folding the sweater, he laid it down and proceeded to slink around the apartment like a lonely ghost.

For the most part, everything screamed 'single woman.' All she needed was the cat to complete the feel. What was strange was how the space was lacking much of anything sentimental. He always knew her to be a family person. Other than a few pictures scattered around, the walls were blank and said very little about the woman he knew.

The small spare room was the only place that really felt like her. The walls were bright and cheery with a mural painted on the window side of the room. He wandered over to the stacks of paintings and sketches that were leaning against the wall and flipped through them, taking a moment to appreciate each one. Art was an expression of the soul, and staring at the various canvases was like getting a peek into hers. He paused as he came across one that was all flowers. Little roses mixed with daisies were the only flowers he could name, but the canvas was full and bright and made the corner of his mouth turn up.

Kes leaned all the art against the wall just the way he'd found it and set his sights on the closet.

He pulled on the long string hanging from the lone bulb in the spare bedroom closet and stared at the stacks of orderly boxes, each one labeled with a year. Following the dates, he found the year he was after and pulled it away from the rest. The top was simply folded together, and he opened it as eagerly as a child opening a birthday gift.

Laying right on top was the holy grail, their yearbook. Reaching in, he slowly lifted out the heavy book with its navy cover and gold writing, the logo of their private school embossed on the front. Cracking the cover open, he heard the spine groan in protest. There she was, front and center, the captain of the soccer team.

His finger traced her smiling face, her foot on the championship ball that had won them the state championship for the first time in school history. That night had been unseasonably cool. The wind had been up, the band loud, and the excitement in the stands electric. It has been as loud as any of his football games—it might even have been louder. He'd stood in the stands cheering like any other hungry fan, but what he'd done after the game, that he regretted.

He flipped the pages until he found the one of her class. Fuck she was stunning. She still was. It was like she'd barely aged while he felt like he'd been dragged through a meat grinder backward. He flipped again until he found some random photos that were meant to be humorous, but his face fell as he caught sight of Ashley's in the background. She stood away from the others, her face sad as she held her books to her chest.

He remembered that look all too well—that look was his fault. At one point, all he wanted was to see her cry, to taste her tears. The school alienated her because he'd made it his mission to fuck with her every chance he got.

Kes closed his eyes and forced himself to remember what he'd done. He was such a fucking prick, but he couldn't stand to see her happy when he was so miserable. He had it all, and yet, he was hard-pressed to remember one happy family memory. She was always smiling and talking about her parents, and without realizing it, she'd continued to pour salt in the open wound.

Snapping the yearbook closed, he held it to his chest, his heart a drum against the thick cover. He peeked inside the box again and smiled as he pulled out her soccer uniform. The soft, silky feel of her jersey sent a shiver racing down his spine.

He dug through the box until he found what he'd been looking for from the start. He held up the flower-shaped origami he'd spent days figuring out how to make and smiled wide. She kept it. She kept it even after all the crap he did, after all the pain he'd caused.

His heart pounded hard in his chest. There was hope. To appreciate this tiny glimmer of light, he had to spend years wading blindly through the dark.

Kes froze at the sound of the apartment door closing.

*Shit.*

Jumping up, he pulled the string on the light and stuffed the origami flower in his pocket. As quietly as he was able, he put the items back in the box and closed the lid.

Ashley turned on the radio and hummed along to the song that was playing as she moved around the kitchen, the sound of keys on a counter and an oven being turned on loud in the small apartment. Kes put the box back where he'd found it and closed the bi-fold doors so nothing was out of place. Looking around the shoebox-sized room, void of any furniture, he tried to find a place to hide—there just wasn't any. The only thing he could hide under was her art easel, and that wasn't going to do much good.

"God, I need to get changed," she mumbled.

No other option available, he squeezed his substantial frame behind the door as she walked past. His pulse pounded in his ears as she stopped walking and came back. As if sensing something was off, she turned on the light. He didn't dare breathe as the seconds ticked away.

He slumped as the light was turned off and she made her way down the short hall to her bedroom.

Kes peeked around the door, and he was about to make his mad dash to the window when he heard her returning. Like a thief in the night, he resumed his position and groaned as he heard the water in the shower turn on.

*Oh fuck, she was getting naked.*

The shower door rattled and clicked, and he once more poked his head around his hiding place. He stepped into the hallway, and any determination he had to leave slipped away as he watched her shadow move behind the foggy glass.

He licked his lips as the scent of strawberry filled the air, her sweet voice picking a tune he didn't recognize, but he'd listen to her sing the fucking phonebook if she wanted. He was frozen like a marble statue that had sprung up out of her floor. He couldn't make his feet work. His eyes were glued to her delicate shape, his dick throbbing in time to her hand traveling up and down her legs.

His throat was so dry he couldn't swallow as he envisioned licking that water off her body. The sound of the shower shut off, and his brain continued to float in the blissful fog of his fantasies. The glass door rattled as it opened enough for her arm to reach out and grab a towel.

*Move, you fucking idiot.*

Darting away from the door, he snuck off in the opposite direction of where he should be going and opted to hide in the large closet of the main bedroom. He peeked through the slats as she came in with a towel on her head and another one barely covering her body. Her body wash wafted in at him, and he had to adjust his cock as the sweet berry aroma filled his nose.

This was so wrong, and yet he wasn't going to stop watching. Thankfully, she stepped out of view to finish getting changed because he was enough of a fucking douche to watch her take that towel off. He wasn't entirely sure he would've remained in the closet as images of spreading her open and tasting her as she moaned and writhed in pleasure played like a fucking porno in his mind.

Kes's back slid down the wall to hide in the corner of the closet as the light of her bedroom was switched off. That he was no longer able to see didn't matter. The image of her in that fluffy purple towel was permanently seared in his brain.

If there was any lingering doubt about how much he wanted her, it was officially washed away like footprints on the beach when the tide came in.

He wasn't letting her get away again.

# CHAPTER 15

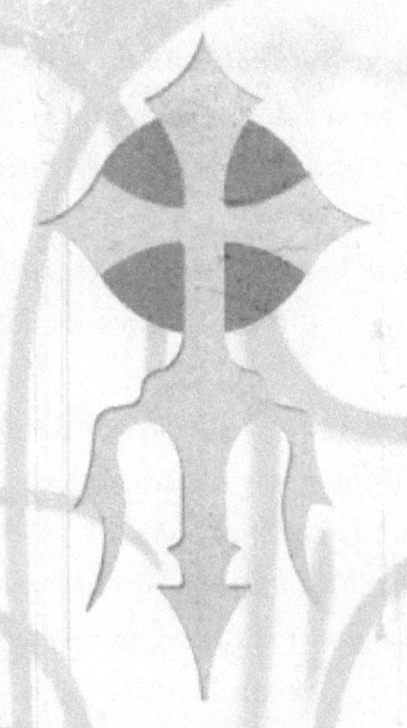

"*F*uck, fuck, fuck!" Ringo smacked the gauges as the little arms spun uncontrollably on the helicopters readouts. "I don't know what's going on."

"This bird has always been a glitchy girl." Kes rubbed the gauges with his hands like he was stroking a lover. "You just need to treat her with a little love."

"Well, your fucking touch ain't doing it. We don't even know our altitude. We need to turn back."

Kes shot Ringo a glare in the co-pilot's seat. "I'm not turning back. If we don't make it to the exfil site, then they are not getting out of there." Kes turned *his eyes back to the night sky with just enough moonlight to see the approaching mountains. He could barely make them out in the dusky skyline.*

*"Kes, this is fucking dangerous."*

*"Living is dangerous. Being here at all is fucking dangerous. I'm not leaving them." His hand tightened on the cyclic, determination flowing through his body to complete the mission.*

*"Hey, love birds. Do you feel that?" Jimmy came on over the headset. Kes turned to look over his shoulder at him. Jimmy looked as relaxed as ever with his foot resting on the frame of the open-door, M4 resting in his lap.*

*"You gonna bust my balls too?"*

*Jimmy took the toothpick he'd been sucking on out of his mouth and tossed it out the open door. "I don't give a fuck what we do. This is your whirlybird. I'm just along for the ride."*

*"See, now that is a good answer," Kes shot at Ringo. He couldn't see his eyes through the dark visor, but he knew his co-pilot well enough to know that he was getting the death stare. "Relax, man. She is going to get us there."*

*Ringo shook his head back and forth. "Something is wrong, Kes. That vibration is not normal, and now this. I'm calling us in—we need to turn around."*

*"Don't you fucking dare. It's my call, and I say we can make it and get back before the bird falls apart," he argued even as the cyclic began to shake in his hand. He turned his stare on the piece of equipment that was acting like a high-powered dildo jumping around in his hands and licked his lips.*

*"Kes, you know I will follow you into the bowels of hell, but I have a gut feeling. I know every groan this old girl makes, and this is not her 'yes, keep fucking me' sound." Ringo pointed to the gauges again.*

*"If you call us in and we turn around, you know they won't let us back out with a new bird. They will consider the mission a failure and leave the team there. Can you live with that? Cause I can't."*

*Ringo looked out the window to the dark sand below. "Mother fucking guilt card. Fine, keep going."*

*Kes held out his fist for his friend to bump just as Bitchin Betty lit up, the warning siren loud in their ears.*

*"What the fuck?" Ringo asked, plastering his face to the window. "You see anything back there?"*

*"I see jack shit. It's like the black pit of hell," Jimmy answered.*

*The alarm ceased, and Kes took a shuddering breath as his thundering heart galloped in his chest.*

*"Bad omen, man, I'm telling you."*

*Betty screeched again, and this time, Jimmy yelled to hang on as a thunderous crash hit the tail rotor. The bird jerked violently before starting to spin out of control in a vortex spiral. Ringo and Jimmy's yells were loud in his ears.*

Kes jerked and gasped as he sat up straight, his hands clenching the armrests of the chair he was propped up in—his eyes darted around the strange room as he tried to get his bearings. He rubbed at his eyes and wiped away the sweat as remnants of the dream danced before his eyes.

He slumped back into the chair he was occupying. He hadn't meant to fall asleep as he watched Ashley sleep, but he'd been so comfortable being near her.

She moaned in her sleep, her feet kicking until she'd freed herself from the confines of the thick-looking comforter.

His mouth dropped open as his eyes landed on her now exposed legs. The small nightlight in the far corner of the room gave him just enough light to see that she was completely naked. Ashley's sweet pussy was on display for his viewing pleasure with her legs splayed open.

"Holy shit," he whispered. From one breath to the next his cock stood straight, the jeans he was wearing feeling uncomfortably tight. He licked his lips as she moaned again, and this time, the simple tank top she was wearing pulled up as the comforter fell to the floor like a waterfall.

*Holy fuck.*

In all his time fantasizing about what she'd look like under her oversized sweaters and tight little jeans, he'd never come close to the real thing. Kes slid to the edge of the seat, not daring to get any closer but unable to look away.

Ashley moaned in her sleep, and he groaned in response as his cock swelled further in size. His body flushed hot, a sheen of sweat breaking out on his forehead as she drew her left leg up forming a number four shape. The movement revealed even more of her delicious-looking pussy. Kes's mouth was watering as he pictured crawling up the bed and settling between her legs to taste that beautiful mound.

His breathing was heavy, his hands gripping the chair in a death grip to not follow through on his desire. It was suddenly very clear how long it had been since he'd fucked anyone, how long it had been since he'd had the desire to do so.

Bursting from the seat, he darted out of her room and worked open the zipper of his jeans as his long stride ate up the ground to the bathroom. He stepped inside the open door, not giving a fuck that he still had his boots on. He got his aching cock freed from its material prison and let out a strangled sigh.

Kes laid his head on his arm against the cool tile, his eyes fluttering closed as he pictured Ashley in the next room. His hand feverishly stroked at his hard length as he envisioned waking her up with his tongue buried deep inside her pussy. He wanted to see the look of shock before she caved to the pleasure. His hand stroked himself faster, not bothering with trying to prolong the moment. He groaned, a shiver racing down his spine as the sound of her little moan filled his mind. He couldn't help but remember the last time he'd heard that sweet sound, before everything had gone to shit.

*"I'm going to kiss you now." Kes pushed Ashley up against the wall under the bleachers and ravaged her mouth like she was his last meal. She didn't open for him, held perfectly still like he might actually eat her*

alive. Flicking his tongue out, he traced her lips until she sighed and granted him access.

She tasted so fucking good—he was going to have a fucking boner the rest of the day after this, and he didn't care anymore. He let go of one of her trapped hands and ran his fingers into her silky hair until he could get a good grip.

Ashley moaned as he tugged back on her hair, and his tongue explored deeper into her mouth, consuming it. Her free hand found his waist, and he wished he didn't have the stupid school shirt on. He wanted to feel her skin against his. He wished he could take her to his home and pop that sweet cherry for himself.

Breaking the kiss, they were both panting hard as they caught their breath.

"Why are you doing this to me?" Her voice shook slightly, all bravado gone like the wind. "You don't even like me."

"That's where you're mistaken." Kes dropped his head to her neck and nuzzled the racing pulse under her heated skin. "I want you to go to prom with me."

"Have you lost your mind?"

Kes loved how her voice wavered as his lips traveled up the length of her neck to the delicate jawline. "Does it feel like I've lost my mind?" He kissed the skin that had been tantalizing his dreams for years. She was so soft and tasted even better than in his fantasy. The sharp intake of breath as her body finally weakened against his hold told him exactly how much she was enjoying this.

"This is the Twilight Zone. I just need to wake up," she murmured.

He smirked as he stared at her closed eyes with their long lashes that hooded her bright blue eyes whenever she smiled.

"Say you'll go with me." He placed a soft kiss on the corner of her swollen lips. "Do it. You know you want to say it." He kissed the other side of her well-abused mouth. Ashley's body was trembling like she was freezing in their ninety-degree heatwave.

"I can't. You've played me too many times, Kes." Her eyes opened, and it was his breath hitching as he stared into them. "I don't trust you."

*He smirked and laid a tiny kiss on the end of her nose. "Alright, challenge accepted. You agree to go with me the moment I've gained your trust."*

*One delicate eyebrow rose as she sucked in her bottom lip, and he was tempted to ravage that mouth again.*

*"Alright, it's a deal, but it's never going to happen."*

The memory of her taste on his tongue was as strong as it had been years ago—but now, he didn't want to take her to prom, and he didn't want to just make her moan. No, he wanted to take what should've always been his. Make her dig her nails into his shoulders as he fucked her until she screamed and came all over his cock.

"Oh fuck," he grunted as the first spurt of come flew from the tip of his cock, but his hand didn't slow. His knees shook as the next rush hit with enough force to sit him on his ass. Sheer determination alone kept him on his feet as the jets of come landed on the shower wall, his mind picturing bathing her insides.

As the last drops dripped from his cock, he had to force himself to let go as every instinct still screamed to do it again. It didn't matter that he'd need time to recoup or that it would hurt to try and force another climax so soon. None of that mattered.

He swallowed, his throat hurting as he tried to wet the dried-out area. Kes stuffed his still semihard cock back into his jeans and stumbled back from the wall. It was hard to see in the dark, but the grey tile showed a distinct smattering of white. The corner of his mouth curled up in a wicked smirk, and he was tempted to leave it, let her wonder where the truckload of come came from, and he pictured the confused expression on her face. He wanted to laugh, but opted to turn on the shower to a gentle spray. He washed off the wall and had to grip the doorframe as he shook out the rest of the rubber in his legs.

He looked toward the master bedroom. If that was the result of just looking at her, what would it be like to be buried balls deep inside her? His body shuddered with the question.

*Not tonight.*

He slowly made his way toward his version of a doggy door and let himself out. Not tonight, but it would happen.

# CHAPTER 16

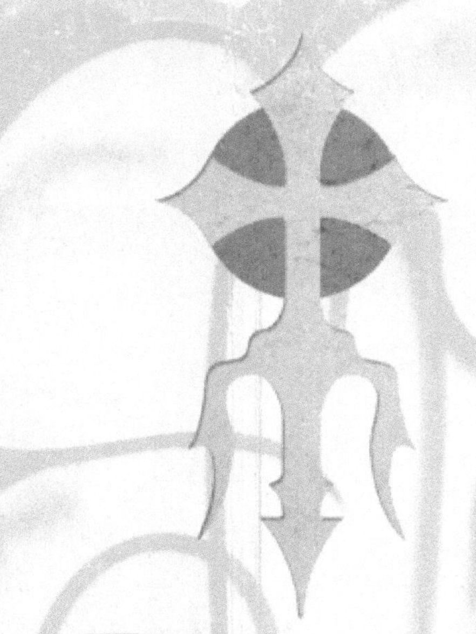

Ashley felt like she'd been in a battle last night. She woke up, and all the blankets were on the floor, and she was still restless. At one point in the night, she awoken with a start, heart pounding and sat up straight, thinking someone was in her room, but the bedroom was empty.

This was Kes's fault. Since the moment she'd bumped into him, she'd been feeling out of sorts, or more specifically, like the girl she had been and not the woman she was now.

Stupid men. Why did she have to be attracted to the dickheads? The first guy she'd dated in college was a hardcore manwhore, a cheater. The next one ended up in jail for stealing cars, and had tried to say she did it. The third one always found a way to make her pay for everything and then had tried to date her friend while they were still together. But the piece de la resistance was the jerk that had eventually caused her to get a restraining order against him for hitting her.

And here she was, once again infatuated with Kes Reynolds, the first boy to treat her like crap and break her heart. She gave her head a shake as she wandered into the bathroom and flicked on the light.

She made her way over to the toilet and had to do a double-take at the shower. "What the hell?" She stared at the distinct brown ring of dirt and water that surrounded the drain. "Shit, this thing better not be backing up again," she groaned as she flicked on the water to wash the dirt down and then waited to see if it was going to bubble back up.

Hopefully, it was just a one-off and it didn't need to be fixed. The last thing she needed was something else to have to fix. Ashley set about getting ready for her appointment. Just the thought of the appointment was making her want to go back to bed and hide under the covers like a child and yell that she was never coming out. She should call her mother. At least her mother would come and sit with her.

"No, don't do it. You know where that will lead," she mumbled.

Ashley decided that if she was going to have to sit in a medical clinic for six to eight hours, she was going to be comfortable. She pulled a loose-fitting sweater over her head, and it settled over her pale pink yoga pants. Just in case it was the type of building that loved to crank up the air conditioning, she rummaged around in her front hall closet and found a scarf and shawl that her mother had randomly knitted for her even though she lived in a hot state.

Stuffing the items into her gym bag, she grabbed her purse, phone, and the cane she hated to head across town. Thirty minutes later, she stepped out of her Uber only to stare up at the bright red letters that proudly stated Mount Rose Clinic. She licked her lips, her mouth suddenly dry, and peeked over her shoulder to see the Uber pulling away.

"I guess running is no longer an option." Rolling out her shoulders, she made her way up the long access ramp to the front doors and stepped into her new reality. This place was going to be her temporary prison every six months for the rest of her life, however long that was.

Shaking off the dread that had settled in the pit of her stomach, she put on her 'I'm great' smile for the woman at the help desk. "Hi, I'm looking for Dr. Pierce's clinic."

"Elevator is over there," the overly bubbly woman said as she pointed. "You want the second floor, and then you turn right off of the elevator. You can't miss it."

"Thank you."

The elevator doors dinged and slid open as she reached the second floor. Taking a deep breath to steady her nerves, she stepped out into the hallway and followed the signs on the wall. The woman downstairs had been correct. You couldn't miss the clinic. The walls were a deep rose, and there were brightly colored flower murals painted all over the place. Why did that seem to make it worse? It was as if the walls were designed to lie to you, to lull you into this false sense that all was okay, when in reality, nothing was okay. She was not okay, and no stupid images of gardens with butterflies were going to help.

You would need to be blind to miss the patient sign-in area. The circular formation of desks was in the middle of the room and had a giant, artistic sun hanging above it, the lights inside of it glowing.

"It's odd, right?"

Ashley turned her head to find the source of the voice. A woman around the same age was sitting in the waiting area and gave her a small grin.

"Yeah, it kind of is. My name's Ashley." She leaned over and held out her hand. She immediately regretted it as the woman struggled to lift her arm. "I'm sorry, I… ah…." She was normally so good with patients, but right now, she was at a loss for words.

"Nope, don't worry about it. I'm Daisy, and yes, the irony is not lost on me." Daisy's eyes flicked to the wall behind her, and Ashley smiled at the realistic country garden filled with the white-petaled flowers. Daisy's cool hand clasped her own. "Today is just a bad day. Normally, I would jump up and offer to show you around. You get used to the ups and downs."

Ashley bit her lip as they released the handshake. "What are you reading?" she asked, hoping to divert the conversation.

Daisy tilted the book to show off its cover. "*The Brat and the Body-guard*, by Tia Fanning. I just started. Loving it so far—you need a little sexy distraction in this place," she giggled. "How about you? Did you bring something to occupy the endless day?"

"Yeah, it's just on my phone. That way, I can download as many as needed."

Daisy smiled. "I can't argue that is awesome, but there's nothing like the feel of holding a book in your hands." Daisy nodded toward the receptionist. "You better go get signed in. Stalling only makes it worse."

"That obvious?" Ashley squeezed the strap on her gym bag hard, and the wooden top of the cane bit into her palm harder still as she stared at the slowly-rising sun.

"You can always tell the newbies. We all come in looking like wide-eyed deer about to be hit by a car. Don't worry. You'll be fine. It's really not as bad as you think it will be." Daisy fumbled around in her purse and held out a business card. Taking the card, Ashley stared at the little flower emblem with Daisy's name splashed across the front. "I run a support group if you're ever interested. It's nothing formal, just a few of us that sometimes just need someone to talk to that understands what you're going through."

Ashley blinked back the tears stinging the backs of her eyes. "Thank you, Daisy. I better get going. Have a good day."

"You too, Ashley. It was nice meeting you."

Swallowing down the lump of emotion in her throat, she made her way toward the desk and tried to stay focused on the fact she was here to get help, not to be taken out to slaughter like her brain kept screaming.

*I'll be okay. It's all going to be okay.*

# CHAPTER 17

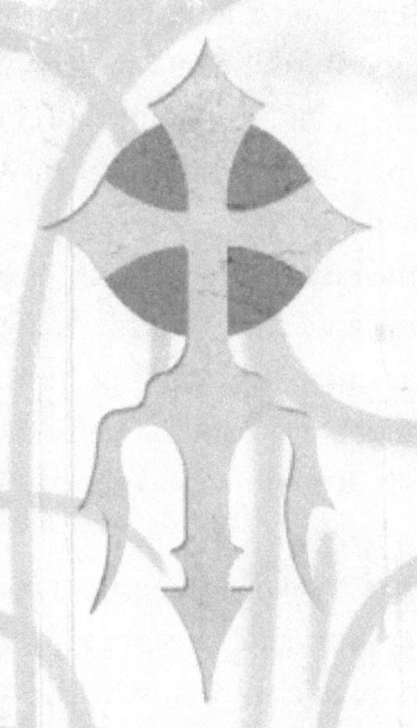

Contrary to popular belief, the best time to stalk prey was during the day. They thought they were safe, behaving like normal members of society and not the scum that chose to destroy young women's lives.

Kes sat in Baby Doll, binoculars in hand as he watched the man he'd nicknamed Slim Jim speak to some of the shadiest looking guys he'd ever seen. That said a lot because he'd seen a lot of shady people over his time on the streets. Spike's phone had been a treasure trove of dirtbags, and if he hadn't already killed him, he would've shaken his hand for all the information.

Instead, he'd taken the liberty of sending out a message on the late Spike's behalf letting them all know he was fine and just lying low. He didn't want any of Spike's associates to go underground. Nope, he wanted them going about their business as usual.

A plain black duffel bag was handed off to the shady men, and they marched off, leaving Slim Jim to look around and make sure his sorry ass didn't look suspicious. Too bad for him—he was already being watched. Fixing his suit jacket, Slim Jim marched for the blacked-out Cadillac Escalade and sped off toward the freeway ramp.

Kes tossed the binoculars on the passenger seat and stared at the red dot tracker on the monitor built into his dash. Firing the Hummer up, he pulled out into the sparse amount of traffic and followed his prey from a safe distance. He'd been quite successful in hunting his targets without the use of the fancy tech, but he couldn't deny that in times like this, his life was made easier by it. It took far less time to hunt, kill, and move on to the next target.

Slim Jim pulled off the freeway and onto a road that led out past the suburbs and into the countryside. Eventually, the dot on the monitor turned once more to come to a stop on what Kes could only assume was a farm.

He traveled to the next road over, which thankfully was a dead end with only one house on it. He made his way to the very end and parked in front of the *Dead End* sign. Hopping out, he grabbed his gun, knives, and a few other toys, just in case, and set off at a brisk jog through the dense, overgrown brush. The sun beat down on his back and head despite the fact that his face was covered with his hood up. He hated this time of day, it was always too hot and he could still feel the bright rays beating down on him in the thick heat through the material. Sweat trickled down his spine and into his fatigues. He jumped over a small log and pushed on through the scraggly undergrowth, the slender branches acting as miniature whips along his body.

· · ·

"*Keep moving,*" *Trev yelled.* "*We can't stop soldier so pick your feet up.*"

*He glared at Trev as he stood yelling at everyone to keep running like fucking ignore the sound of the bullets hitting rocks and sending fragments flying was normal. Dean was helping him as they ran and every stride was excruciating. Another torrent of bullets landed all around them, and Dean gripped him a little harder as he pushed the pace faster. Dodging the metal and dirt rain was like trying to dodge raindrops.*

Coming to a sudden stop, he shook his head and bit his lip hard to keep the memory from surfacing.

"You are the keeper of your memories. They do not keep you," he said softly as he took slow deep breaths.

The sound of yelling reached his ears, and his head snapped up toward the sound. He was close to his target. Breathing steadily and mind squared away, he ran on, weaving around the small saplings like a slalom skier. There was a trail camera a little further up that faced the farmhouse. Ducking down low behind some thick bushes, he watched the man, Slim Jim, pull a young woman from the house. The yelling boomed louder as she screamed for forgiveness. Kes's hand balled into a fist as he watched her be yanked around by her hair, tears streaming down her dirty face, and saw her sad excuse for clothing hanging off her body in tatters.

"Get on your knees," Slim Jim ordered, pushing the girl down with a rough shove. She tumbled to the dirt floor, and before Kes could even blink, the gun the man was holding went off, and the crying girl went silent. "Bury her with the others and pick one more to get rid of. We need to make room for the new shipment."

Two men who Kes had barely noticed with his focus locked on the girl stepped up and dragged her rag doll form away. Kes looked down at the large recluse spider crawling up his arm and got an idea.

Flicking the furry hitchhiker off his arm to live another day, he dashed off through the brush until he was in line with the Escalade but out of sight of the trail camera he'd spotted. He hadn't seen any more attached to the trees, but there could be more he hadn't seen, so he kept his hood up and head down as he sprinted toward his destination.

Opening the back hatch just enough, he slipped inside and pulled the door tight, locking it in place. He didn't have to wait long for Slim Jim to return, and he lay as flat as he could in the vacant hatch area as the man started the engine. Kes had to brace himself to avoid rolling around as the man backed up and took off like he was in a Formula One.

The sound of a phone ringing came over the speakers, and Slim Jim answered with a gruff, "What?"

A mechanical voice that was obviously being distorted with an app of some sort chuckled through the vehicle. "Is that any way to talk to your best customer?"

"Oh fuck, I thought you were someone else." Kes rolled his eyes as the man spent the next minute kissing whoever was on the phone's ass. The guy probably felt the thorough rim job from wherever the fuck he was.

"Are you in need of more wine?" Slim Jim asked.

"Indeed, what vintages do you have available?"

"Everything from dark to light, and even some robust, exotic flavors for you to try."

Kes ground his teeth. The urge to jump out now and slit the man's throat flowed through his veins like a fast-moving forest fire. He pictured Slim Jim's bright red blood spattering the steering wheel and windshield, his eyes wide in shock as he groped to stop the bleeding in his neck—the fear dancing in Slim Jim's eyes as they stared at him in the rearview mirror as he fucking smiled back.

"Do you have anything that is not too aged?"

"Everything from nine years to fifteen years is ready and waiting to be shipped out. Just let me know how many cases you require for your store."

"I will take a case of ten years of white wine, twelve years of dark red, and fifteen years of a more exotic blend to try. I would like to place a special custom order as well, if I could."

"Of course, what would you like?"

"I'd like to order a wine that no one else has tried. One aged to eighteen years to perfection. This case needs to be special for a very special and high-paying customer."

"Yes, of course, we can certainly accommodate that order. I will have the shipper put it together right away and will send you an invoice as well as a delivery date."

"Until next time." The man placing the order hung up, and it was a good thing, or Kes was going to follow through on his fantasy before he got what he really needed: information.

He counted down the minutes in his head, noted the direction the vehicle turned and any other distinct noises as they traveled. It took exactly thirty-three minutes and forty-one seconds before they pulled through a set of gates that whirred as they opened. Laid out like a fucking turtle stranded on it's back, he was able to see the gates close as they pulled through. Tall, black, and fancy. It was wrong that a piece of shit like this got to live in a mansion and the kids he was selling had nothing and no future. All forms of authority, like the cops, had their hands tied. He'd seen what that was like firsthand overseas. To know what was right, but the political tape was always in the way. The Righteous gave him the freedom to do what they couldn't and that was permanently take the targets out. The fact he got to do it anyway he liked, was a bonus.

The shadow of a door opening up and swallowing up the car announced they had arrived at their next destination. The Escalade shut off, and the vehicle rocked as the door was slammed shut.

"Baby Doll," he whispered into his watch now that he was alone in the car. "Track my location, and go park at the coordinates I just sent." Kes stared at the small map on his wrist. They were located in a gated community. Okay, the first task was complete. Now for task two, capture the prey.

Kes poked his head up like a groundhog and stared through the glass around the spacious garage. It was still too light outside as of now for what he had planned. Settling back down into the surprisingly comfortable trunk space, he waited like the good little predator he was.

He was formulating a plan to kidnap Slim Jim from his bed when the door leading from the garage into the house opened and the man of the hour returned.

"I need to buy a fucking lottery ticket," Kes smirked as he laid flat once more.

Slim Jim slipped into the driver's seat and sniffed. "Man, I need to get this car cleaned. It fucking reeks."

Kes sniffed himself and shrugged. He'd smelt worse.

He felt like he was a fly on a dog's ass hitching a ride. Slim Jim pulled out of his garage and sped up the street despite the late hour.

This time when he poked his head up, he watched the man in the small mirror carefully. Slim Jim was distractedly flicking through radio stations, and he wanted to yell, 'just pick one already.' On the bright side, Slim Jim wasn't registering the danger that lurked so close by. Kes slid over the seat and proceeded to lay on the floor behind Slim Jim. He took a quick look at his watch and tapped the face, hiding it under the front seat so as not to be noticed.

Kes took the chance and looked out the side window, and a grin spread across his face. He really needed to go and buy a Powerball ticket. The surrounding buildings and the scent of cookies in the air screamed that they were in the heart of the industrial section. He'd know that mouth-watering scent anywhere. The cookie factory made a mean oatmeal chocolate chip cookie and were always handing out the broken cookies in boxes for free if you came around midnight. Kes had already spent a lot of time down here and he knew most of the buildings were abandoned and the cameras were few and far between. Lady Luck sure was shining down on him tonight. Slim Jim there must have pissed her beautiful ass off.

Inch by silent inch, Kes pulled the hidden blade from his boot and got himself into position to make his strike. The Escalade slowed and turned into a warehouse empty except for a lone girl standing in the shadows.

Kes had seen her before—she worked the corner across from some of the prostitutes he'd had to help in the past. She wore a standard skimpy outfit for her trade, the short skirt not leaving anything to the imagination. Her face was done up with so much makeup that you would think she was in her twenties, but he knew she was barely sixteen. Oh, this was so not happening.

Rising up just enough, he pulled his gun instead, returning his knife to its sheath. He kept it concealed where the girl couldn't see, pressing the cold tip into the neck of the man he was hiding behind. His cock twitched as the man sucked in a shuddering breath.

"Unless you'd like your brains to decorate that expensive dash, you're going to tell the girl you've changed your mind," he growled out, his voice promising the man's demise if he didn't cooperate. "If you'd like to test me, then by all means, warn her. I will kill you both, and I will gut you like a pig before I do."

Slim Jim nodded, his hands tightening audibly on the steering wheel, squeaking on the leather. Slim Jim opened the drivers-side window, and as he did, Kes pushed the gun firmer into his neck.

"Not tonight. I have other business to attend to."

"But, you called me."

"Listen, bitch. Not tonight. Now get out of here."

"Fuck, alright. I'm going," the girl said. Kes could just make out the word 'prick' as she walked away, and he smirked.

The window hummed as it rose into position once more. "Good boy. Now turn off the vehicle and put the keys on the dash."

Kes was happy as Slim Jim's hand shook, placing the rattling keys on the shiny black surface.

"What do you want?"

"I want to play a game," he murmured in Slim Jim's ear and then laughed as the man shuddered. He was going to shudder a whole lot more before he was through.

Kes yawned as he made his way to his tent. It was blessedly quiet, with only a few souls still awake. It had been a few nights since he'd slept in his spot, but he was going to need rest for what tomorrow was going to bring.

His stride faltered as he made out a shape in the dark shadows outside his tent. His hand slipped inside his coat, his fingers wrapping around the handle of his knife, but as soon as it moved and looked up at him, he knew it was Zumi. He let out a sigh and released the handle. The girl was sitting like a little sentinel keeping watch. Her dark eyes searched his face before she jumped up and ran to him. He let out a sharp breath as the girl practically rammed him in the gut with her head. Zumi's arms wrapped around his body and held his waist tight like she was part-python.

"I thought you were dead and never coming back," Zumi said, her voice soft.

Kes wasn't sure what to do, so he patted the girl's shoulders like she was a dog he wished would sit.

"Why the hell would you think I was dead?" he asked.

Zumi's face turned up to his, a shimmering of tears in her eyes. "Cause you never stay away so long. You always check on everyone, and..." and she gasped in a breath as she released his body and stepped back.

"And?" he prompted.

"Just...trouble seems to find you," she said.

Kes raised an eyebrow at the proclamation. He wasn't sure what trouble she was referring to but was way too tired and hungry to be bothered questioning it. "As you can see, I'm not dead. I'm going to go to bed now, unless you're planning on questioning me some more, Mommy?"

Zumi rolled her eyes at him with the standard sauce that accompanied her sweet approaching-teenaged snark. "Jerk." Kes stepped around Zumi and then paused as she spoke again. "I made you beans—they're still warm."

His hand gripped the tent flap and pulled it aside like he didn't care, but he couldn't stop the rumble with the word beans. "What kind?"

"Brown with bacon." Zumi grinned as she bent over and pulled the can out of the small makeshift warmer, consisting of a tiny fire and strips of metal he'd shaped to make the pointed top. Placing a spoon in the can, she held it out to him.

"Thanks, Kid." He expected her to head home or sit down, but she simply stared at the ground.

"Where is your mother, Zumi?"

"Off with another guy, doing whatever it is she does. I mean, I know what she does, but I don't want to say it out loud."

Kes rubbed his eyes, wondering when he'd gone soft. "Come on, Kid. You can have my tent. I'll eat and then sleep outside to keep watch."

"That's not why I came over here. I don't need you to protect me all the time." She crossed her arms over her chest as she lifted her stubborn face to his.

"And yet, I would feel better all the same if you'd simply shut up and get in the tent." He pulled open the flap for the second time, making a dramatic movement with his arm like he was inviting her into a palace, not a tent on its last legs.

Her small shoulders folded in on her as she walked on past him. "Thanks, Kes."

He heard the subtle squeak of his cot moving under her weight, and he let the flap drop back into place. What was one more night sitting in a lawn chair? He'd spent months laying on dirt or hard floors, not to mention curled up in stacks of large boulders with his unit like it was the fucking Ritz.

Flopping down into the mesh chair, Kes placed the first spoonful of beans in his mouth and groaned a little. He ate them like a starving animal, shoving them into his face faster than he should, and then sighed as the ache in his belly subsided.

Kes pulled his coat firmer around his body and buried his head into the hood and high collar of the coat. He'd missed seeing Ashley tonight, and he kept wondering what she was doing and if she'd made it home safely from the church. He'd overheard Dennis talking on the phone about Salvation Place being shut down in a few weeks. He was looking for donations from someone, but it didn't sound like the conversation had gone well.

He couldn't let that happen. It was the one place he knew he could go to find Ashley without looking like a stalker. He'd make a couple of calls in the next day or two, but right now, all he wanted to think about was Slim Jim crying himself to sleep in a cage. The thought of the man naked and cold with only a small bucket to piss in as he sobbed pitifully was sinfully fun. He had made sure that the cage he built was too small for anyone over four feet to stand in or lie down in properly. By the time he saw the man again, he would be in excruciating pain, and yet it still wasn't enough for all he'd done. He needed to make his death fitting for the crime.

All the people that they'd helped to steal and traffic were put in similar cages or chained to beds and walls to be used. He wanted to make sure that those he hunted realized what the girls and boys they treated like disposable garbage felt in their grasp. It was his own sweet little piece of justice before he took their life.

His eyes were heavy by the time his meal was consumed. He took a deep breath and let his eyes flutter closed. There were way so many possibilities to kill Slim Jim. He could fillet him like a fish, spend the time to gut and skin him, but he'd done that already. He could burn him alive, but he never knew when he'd be triggered by the sight of a flame. Besides, the smell was repulsive and it stuck to you for weeks. No, he needed something new. As his body slipped into sleep his mind played over all the possibilities of how to kill Slim Jim. Like a grand ballet, each one danced across his mind.

# CHAPTER 18

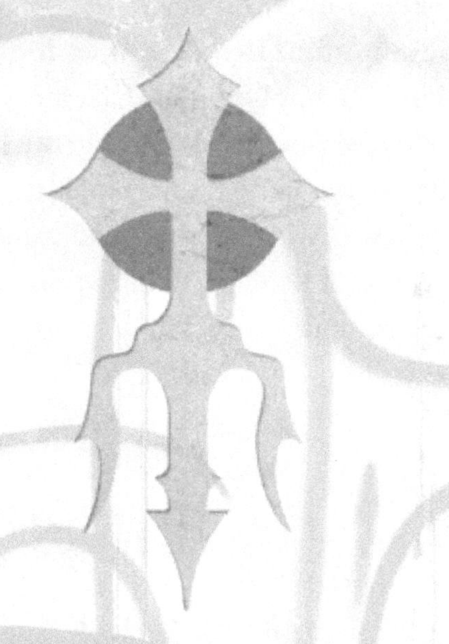

As soon as the sun started to crest the horizon, Kes was on the move. His first stop was to check in on Ashley. He'd woken up a couple times with her face in his mind, driving his protective streak over the edge. He scampered up the fire escape and decided that if he ever needed a new career, he was hitting up *The Titan Games*. The Rock was one human he wouldn't mind meeting, but the idea of his face plastered all over the world turned his stomach faster than a rotten cheese sandwich.

The apartment was quiet when he arrived. The coffee wasn't on and the kitchen and hallway were still dark. A sinking feeling in his gut gripped him, and against his better judgement, he shimmied the window open and wiggled his way inside.

Dropping to the floor, he waited a heartbeat to listen for the sound of feet or the shower—or screaming, the back of his mind whispered in a panic. Kes was swift as he moved on to find Ashley. Another thought occurred to him, that she might've stayed at another house last night. More specifically, another man's house. He ground his teeth together—he would be hard pressed not to kill the man that touched her now.

The bathroom was dark, the sink dry. The spare bedroom was likewise dark and still sparse. Kes stood outside her bedroom door and heard the soft sound of rustling. Daring to take a look, he peeked around the edge of the door frame. The drapes and blinds were pulled tight and it took a few minutes for his eyes to adjust enough to see her face in the dim light. Ashley was curled up on her side, the blankets pulled tightly around her body, her face pale. The blankets rustled again and he realized she'd shivered, and immediately he wanted to rush across the room and wrap her up in his arms.

He had to look away, and he forced himself to stop staring and stand outside her door. She was obviously not feeling well, and he rubbed at his eyes as he convinced himself to let her rest. The last thing she needed was him, and besides, he had other things he needed to do tonight and there were a few supplies he'd yet to pick up.

As he rounded the island in the kitchen to head for the window, he paused to stare at the bottle of pills on the counter. He picked them up and stared at the name he'd never heard before.

"What do you need these for?"

Biting his lip, he couldn't hold back the urge and opened her purse. He craved to know everything about her. What made her laugh or smile, what made her sad or scared. There was a new prescription in her purse, the little white bag not telling him much more than another medication name he didn't know. Was she in pain? Was she sick, maybe depressed? He hated the idea that she had something wrong and he didn't know what. Putting the white bag back, his fingers brushed something else, and he pulled out a business card and stared at the name. 'Daisy's Support Group' and a number were in a pretty gold and yellow across the card. He flipped it over in his hand, but it didn't say any more.

Kes stared off towards the hallway and the bedroom with the sleeping woman down the hall. "What's wrong, my Doll? Why do you need a support group?"

Every worst-case scenario raced through his mind like a runaway train, each possibility worse than the one before. His head jerked as the sound of shuffling reached his ears, he stuffed the items back in Ashley's purse and squeezed out the window just as her shadow was cast across the open doorway.

Kes jumped for the opening in the fire escape and, using his hands and feet on the metal bars, slid down to the next level. He pressed himself against the wall, his heart beating fast as he stared up at where he'd just snuck out of. The window didn't open, but the light didn't turn on either. He was tempted to make his way back up, but gave his head a physical shake to stop himself from acting too crazy.

She was alive and alone and he could figure out the rest later. Kes used the same quick movement to make his way to the bottom and the alley below, dropping to the top of the dumpster. Next stop was the hardware store and the garden center.

"You know, you could just buy her flowers."

Kes swore as he spun around. "Jesus-F-Mother-Fuck-Fucking-Christ." He clutched at his chest as he stared into Zumi's eyes. The kid burst out laughing and was doubled over clutching her stomach by the time she was through.

"Are you finished," he drawled, annoyance setting in.

"Yes." The rosy cheeks and shining eyes mixed with the constant biting of her lip told a different story.

"What the hell are you doing following me?"

She lifted her little shoulders and let them drop and then leaned against the dumpster. "I told you I'd figure out what you're up to." She glanced up at the fire escape. "But I'm guessing by the way you just dove out of there like your ass was on fire that she doesn't know you are sneaking in all the time, so I'm giving you an alternative. Flowers—women love them, and I know a great garden where we can steal some."

"Okay first, stop following me. Second, flowers are not going to win her over, trust me, and third, we are not stealing from someone."

Zumi sighed, the sound vibrating her lips like a horse's whinny. "So you think that sneaking into her apartment is the way to win her over? I have news for you, it screams scary-ass stalker."

Kes opened his mouth and closed it again. "Whatever, I'm not arguing with a nine-year-old about this. Now I mean it, stop following me."

He marched along the alley, his long strides eating up the ground. He hated that the kid was right. He had no more ice under him to skate on where Ashley was concerned. If she caught him going through her things or sitting at the end of the bed, she'd probably have him thrown in jail.

A small pebble scurried past his feet and he looked over his shoulder to see his pint-sized tail. "Zumi, for fuck's sake, please go home. I have things I need to do that you can't be a part of."

"Why not? I'm so bored at the camp. There is no one for me to talk to other than Momma G and she hasn't been around either, and I hate it when mom is all...." She paused to wave her hands around as she tried to think of a word. "Inebriated." Zumi smiled wide. "I learned that word from a crossword."

"Great, I'm happy for you, I really am, but you still can't follow me."

"Kes, please...."

Kes stopped and whirled around to glare down at the girl. "Zumi, there are things that I do, adult things, that you cannot be a part of, now go home. I'm not joking, go." He pointed down a side alley toward the busy main street.

Her lower lip trembled like she might cry, but the rest of her face was a ball of fury. "Fine! I didn't want to hang out with your stupid ass anyway." She ran down the alley and disappeared around the corner.

Kes pinched the bridge of his nose. Great, now he felt bad. Shaking off the crazy morning it was shaping up to be, he continued on to his destination, which would hopefully put a big old smile on his face.

# Chapter 19

Kes was like a sewer rat. He knew every tunnel and long-lost secret entrance. He could even list nearly every abandoned building in the state. Was that a broad declaration? Maybe, but he'd spent time making his way from one end of Cali to the other, and he wasn't visiting for the tourist sights.

He currently was sitting on an empty crate with his feet crossed, giving his new friend some space to ruminate about the situation he was in before taking the next step in tonight's soiree. If it wasn't for the high-pitched screaming that would start and stop like a broken record, he easily could've meditated in the otherwise-quiet and spacious warehouse.

"Please, I promise I'll change," the man blubbered. "Just take me to a hospital." Tears and drool ran down the front of Slim Jim's face as he continued to beg.

The hospital was the last place he intended on taking the useless piece of human garbage. Kes glanced up at his hanging friend. The skin along Slim Jim's naked, overindulged body was slowly burning away. He was hypnotized by the sight and lulled into calm by the sounds of his shrieking. He'd seen this done to one of their own overseas, but this was only his second attempt, and he had to admit, it was amusing and deliciously morbid.

The young soldier, Stew, had been nineteen, just a kid, still wet behind the ears with grand ideas of saving the world—a world that didn't want to be saved, but he hadn't figured that out yet. In reality, Stew hadn't been any younger than when he'd ended up in the Sandbox, but he was so much more naïve than Kes could ever remember being. Stew was out doing patrols when he disappeared. They had no idea how he was taken away from his unit without anyone noticing. A group of them had volunteered to do a search of all the local abandoned villages. Kes was sure some of those that found him just like Slim Jim was now and wished they never had to see such a thing.

He'd been stripped naked and hung outside by his wrists from a makeshift flagpole. They'd used a cocktail of old battery acid and hydrochloric acid dripped all over his body at a deliberately measured pace to maximize pain. There was no helping Stew when they'd arrived. He was barely alive and in excruciating pain, begging for someone to end his life. All of his skin had been slowly burned off his body. The abductors left him alive, his muscle tissue exposed to the elements. Near death, but not quite there yet. Birds had started to swoop in and take their fill of Stew's ruined flesh. It was one of the most disturbing things he'd ever seen, and the image of Stew's face, or what was left of it, anyway, was forever burned into his mind. Stew's sergeant had been shaken, his eyes wide as he stared with a horrified expression at his young soldier. Being the only other sergeant with the group, Kes had taken it upon himself to put the kid out of his misery.

Clawing his way out of the memory, Kes squeezed his shaking hand and then shook out the tremble like he was shaking off water.

*Fucking memories.*

A sharp, piercing scream reached his ears, and he glanced up to see that Mr. Slim Jim was thrashing around in the bindings, his skin, mottled with different stages of damage from reddened to blistered, beginning to bubble and slough off. A few drops of the liquidized skin lay in speckled droplets on the concrete floor. Deadly vapors rose into the air every time his little invention released another drop on Slim Jim below. The stench of the corroding flesh would've churned his stomach if he hadn't smelt the scent of burnt flesh for months. Now, that scent was a part of him as much as any of the scars he wore.

He'd made sure to sit far back from the show, a mask on his face. He figured he must look like a character out of the movie *Dune* with his hood pulled up in place like an apocalypse had descended upon them.

"Please, make it stop, please just kill me already. P-please."

Kes cracked his neck, his eyes finding the desperate eyes of Slim Jim. He knew his real name, but it didn't really matter at this point who he was. After tonight, he would be no one.

"Why should I grant you a fast, painless death?" He folded his hands in his lap, his eyes finding the pleading eyes of Slim Jim. "Tell me one good reason, and I will put a bullet through your head right now." Kes held up the gun lying beside him on the large crate.

"Because I'm…."

"Don't say sorry. We both know you're not sorry for kidnapping, raping, selling, and murdering young women and children. If you are sorry for anything, it's that I found you. I am giving you an opportunity to give me one solid reason to free you from this agony. Don't screw it up by saying sorry."

Slim Jim licked his cracked lips, a corner of which had already been hit by the deadly acid, leaving a dime-sized hole and exposing his jawbone. "I can fix what I did."

Kes laughed the sound coming out very much like Darth Vader from behind the mask. "Okay, you have my attention, continue."

"I can stop all shipments, I can cancel all contracts, and I can set the girls here in the city free. I will do all this before you kill me. Just please, give me a quick death." The blubbering and screaming echoed off the walls as another drop fell from the slowly rotating container above Slim Jim's head. It was actually quite brilliant. He'd placed the slowly dripping contraption on a small track, so the acid hit in a different location every time a new drop was released.

Kes patiently waited until the screaming subsided and only ragged breathing remained to accompany the steady whimpers.

"So here's the issue with that offer. If you do all that, then I don't get the opportunity to get my hands on all those you're working with. And trust me when I tell you, I'm looking forward to it." Kes lifted a shoulder in a half-hearted shrug. "Besides, I already have all your contacts and appointment dates, thanks to this baby." He held up Slim Jim's phone before tucking it into his pocket.

Slim Jim's lower lip trembled, his head sagging in response.

"How do you do it? I'm genuinely curious." Kes sat up straight and rolled out his shoulders. It had been a few hours since he settled himself on the box, and his body was announcing that he'd been still for way too long.

"Do what?" Slim Jim glanced up at him, his cheeks and eyes glossy with tears.

"How do you traffic and murder young children like they are cattle and then go home and fuck your wife and kiss your children goodnight?"

Slim Jim looked away from his steady glare but failed to answer the question.

"Don't have an answer, or don't want to tell me?"

Again, there was only silence.

"It doesn't matter—I was only curious. You should be thankful that I'm the one that decided to end your miserable life and not one of my associates."

A flash of anger mixed in with the fear in Slim Jim's eyes. "Thank you? Are you crazy?"

"If I were a different kind of man, a different kind of animal, I'd make you watch me do to your children what you allowed done to so many others before I killed you."

The chains rattled as Slim Jim jerked hard, his eyes flaring with hatred, an emotion that Kes was used to seeing on the faces of those he killed, and on some that he didn't. "Don't you touch my kids!"

Kes smiled, although Slim Jim couldn't see the reaction. "I said, 'If I were a different kind of animal.' I'm not like you—I don't kill innocents. Not even to fuck with scum like you."

Kes groaned as he pushed himself up from the awkward lotus position he'd been holding and stretched his body out into a warrior pose. Hands to heart center, he slowly turned to stretch out his other side before lowering his hands to the crate. Taking a slow breath, he flexed his hands and pushed up with his feet until he was in a flying pose.

"What is wrong with you, man? Are you doing fucking yoga? Why can't you just take me to prison or kill me like a normal person," Slim Jim yelled before screaming wildly as his angry thrashing jostled a larger dose of the deadly liquid down on his shoulder.

The sharp echoing thud of something smacking against the concrete had him jumping up straight and spinning around. His eyes focused on the mangled mess of boxes and other discarded items. There wasn't much left that could be considered useful, but what had been left behind was piled in a row from one end of the building to the other. The building was condemned, part of the roof having fallen in, and the long streams of plastic curtains waved back and forth, making it harder to see who the fuck was in the building with him.

The man hanging from the chains disappeared from his mind. He was zeroed in on what had caused the bang. The slim sliver of moonlight shining through the hole in the roof was just enough to show a shadow moving. Before his eyes fully focused on the moving figure, he took two long strides and leaped off the large crate, breaking into a full sprint toward the intruder. Kes snatched his blade from the strap he kept under his coat, easily pulling the sharp knife free of its sheath.

The intruder took off behind the boxes, the size of the shape confirming it was indeed a human and not an animal. He couldn't get a good view with the random pieces of plastic hanging between him and the fleeing shadow. The intruder kept disappearing completely behind the taller stacks of debris, leaving him to rely on his hearing to follow the rhythmical thumping of feet to track his pray. It didn't matter, though. He was gaining ground, and Kes knew where they were heading before they could even angle in that direction. All doors but one were chained from inside the building with links as thick as his forearms. He knew because he was the one that had placed them there. This was a building he'd used before, and he enjoyed the game of watching those he trapped trying to get out like mice in a maze.

The intruder must have snuck in while Slim Jim was screaming. That had to be the reason he didn't hear the noisy door.

With a final burst of speed, he grabbed the back of the intruder's puffy black coat that blended in with the dark, unlit corners of the building before they could make their great escape. Kes lifted them easily into the air, a sound of rage ripping from his throat as he slammed the small body against the wall. He put the knife to their throat, but his hand stilled as small hands gripped his forearm. His eyes flicked to the chipped black nail polish and then to the size of the intruder and the jacket. Up close, he knew that jacket—he had just fucking purchased it.

Grabbing the hood, he ripped it back from the hidden face and groaned. "Zumi, for fuck's sake. I almost slit your throat."

Kes pulled down on the mask he'd been wearing so she could see his face properly in the dim shadows of the unlit area. Zumi's bottom lip trembled and her eyes held unshed tears, but she didn't cry or scream for help.

"Are you going to kill me?" Her small chin nodded toward the area where he had his guest hanging. "Like him?" A tiny whimper did escape her lips then, and he sighed.

"Really, Kid? Do you think I randomly kill people for fun? Well, most times it's fun, but it's never random." He gave her his best 'don't be stupid' face when Nezumi continued to stare like a frightened mouse. "No, I'm not going to kill you."

"Even if I ran out of here and told the cops you were killing some dude?"

His lip curled up. "No, not even then. I would prefer it if you didn't—it complicates things. But regardless, no, I'd never hurt you." Stepping away from the wall, he gently lowered her to the ground and let go of the jacket.

Zumi took a few little sideways steps toward the exit, fear still dancing in her dark eyes. "I'm serious. If you want to run, then go. I will not come back to the camp and will move so you feel safe."

"That wouldn't make me feel safe," she mumbled, and he didn't know what to say to the terrified but sweet admission.

"Why are you here, anyway? I swear you're like a fucking tick on my ass today."

Zumi stuffed her hands in the coat and looked at the door and then back up at him. "You swear I could just leave?"

He slipped the knife into its hidden sheath and crossed his arms over his chest while taking another step away from her. "Go for it. I didn't invite you to this party—you crashed it all on your own. But, I can tell you I've never hurt an innocent willingly, and I'm not going to start with you."

Sighing, she mimicked his pose. "So, you've killed innocent people unwillingly?"

He looked away from her keen eyes and shrugged. "I had to do my share of shit while I was overseas. Now, I've answered your question. You answer mine. Why the hell are you here?"

Zumi ran her foot along a crack in the concrete, the action so child-like. "I wanted to know what you do. You wouldn't tell me. I told you I'd find out, so I did."

Kes shook his head back and forth in disbelief. "And what was I supposed to say I do, Zumi? 'Oh, you know, nothing much, other than murdering people?'" His voice dripped with sarcasm, and Zumi rolled her eyes at him.

"I can handle it." She looked away from him, her eyes on her boots once more.

"Oh really? So you're telling me that it's perfectly acceptable to tell a nine-year-old that you murder people for a living? I guess that explains what's wrong with the school system these days. They're too soft."

"Ten."

"What?"

Zumi sighed again and crossed her arms as she leaned back against the wall. "I was nine, but today is my birthday. I thought you'd remember. You always remember. We normally spend the day hanging out, and I kinda thought you were making a surprise or something for me. Stupid, I know. I'm sorry." She hadn't looked up from staring at her worn eight-hole shitkickers. Her voice was so dejected, making her seem smaller than she was.

Kes closed his eyes and pinched the bridge of his nose as the guilt washed over him. "Shit, Kid, I'm sorry. The opportunity to take down this guy came up, and I got preoccupied. I barely know what day of the week it is these days, but I should've remembered your birthday."

Their whole incredibly awkward/crappy conversation, with the sound of a man's screams serenading them in the background, was just seeming all sorts of wrong.

Zumi turned her head toward the noise and then looked up at him. "What did he do, anyway?"

"He's a trafficker," Kes said, not elaborating.

"Drugs, weapons, or people?" Zumi asked, and at that moment, he realized just how fast the kid had needed to grow up. Kes blinked as if seeing her for the first time. She was so much more grown-up than he'd ever noticed. At ten, she should be thinking about doing her hair or shopping or playing sports, going to movies, maybe thinking about school dances or finding fucking ways to save the world from hunger. Instead, she had to worry about meals, keeping a roof over her head, and predators like Slim Jim, all the while having to mother her own mother. She definitely should not even be contemplating what type of trafficker Slim Jim was. His eyes roamed over her face, and the eyes that stared back at him were not those of a kid but those of a marred soul that had seen way too much already. Her life had barely begun.

"Are you going to answer? Why are you staring at me like that?" she asked with her full-snark preteen attitude in place.

He smirked and crossed his arms over his chest. "Human. Kids mostly, some adults, and gender didn't matter."

She nodded and pushed off the wall. "You torture people before you kill them. Why? Why not just kill them?"

It was a good question, one he'd asked himself and didn't like the answer to. "Why not? They don't deserve their last moments to be fast or peaceful. They deserve hell raining down on them, and that's what I bring. I'm the hellfire that rains all over their fucking parade."

"Um, you need to lay off the old action movies. You're starting to sound like one."

Kes looked around the warehouse and then back to Zumi. "Did you just fucking sass me over my amazing explanation?"

"It wasn't that good. It was a little cheesy." She gave him a shrug and then smirked. "Well, if you're not going to kill me, then I guess you should go finish what you were doing. I'll wait here."

"No, that is not happening. It could be hours or, maybe if I'm really lucky, a day before he dies."

"Kes?"

"Yes?"

"Just kill the guy already, then we can go get my birthday ice cream. Even though it's free, I'm willing to take that as blackmail payment to keep quiet. Best part is that they're open all night for the annoying tourists." She beamed up at him, and he couldn't find the words to stop the swirl of confusion that was happening right now. He felt like looking around for a camera because his ass had to be getting punked.

"You want ice cream? After seeing that?" He thumbed over his shoulder to the wails that were growing loud once more.

"Yeah, why not? Do you need to bury him or something? 'Cause I could help to hurry things along." Zumi took a couple of strides in the direction of Slim Jim, and Kes reached out, grabbing the back of her jacket, freezing her in place.

"What the fuck do you think you're doing?"

"I was gonna go help." She smiled up at him, and he shook his head no.

He gave Zumi a hard glare. "You're not helping anything. Now, go wait outside." Kes pointed to the door and waited until Zumi finished her attempt at defiance.

As soon as the door clicked back into place, he growled under his breath. "What in the actual fuck?" A long list of swear words was grumbled every stride as he stomped back the way he'd come. His mind wouldn't stop running in circles that made no sense. How the hell did he get himself into such a mess, and more importantly, how the fuck was he going to get back out of it?

Grabbing the gun off the crate where he'd left it, he turned to Slim

Jim, who'd had an unfortunate moment when the acid dripped down into his eye while he was gone. The weeping socket was right out of a horror movie as the gooey remnants of his eye slid down his disfigured face. It explained the hysterical screaming. Shit, it was just getting to the good stuff.

"Well, it looks like today is your lucky day." Before Slim Jim could ask the question, he raised the gun and shot him in the head. Slim Jim's head rocked back with the impact as the bullet found its mark. Slim Jim sagged forward, his body going limp as death claimed him.

Kes took a moment to assess the amount of liquid that was left in the special plastic container and figured that by the time it had finished dripping, the man would be reduced to a puddle of unrecognizable flesh on the floor. He'd hose him down the drain later.

Stuffing the gun in the back of his jeans, he stomped toward the door. There had to be a full fucking moon out. That was the only explanation for this shit. Worst self-assigned guardian on the planet, that was him.

# CHAPTER 20

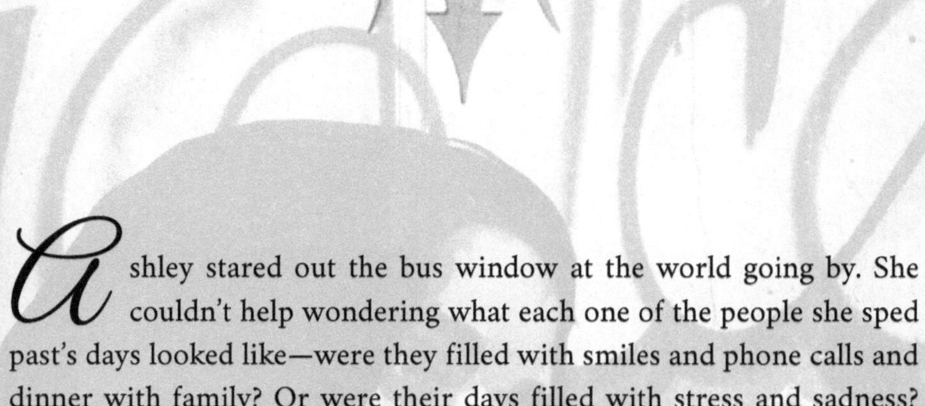

Ashley stared out the bus window at the world going by. She couldn't help wondering what each one of the people she sped past's days looked like—were they filled with smiles and phone calls and dinner with family? Or were their days filled with stress and sadness? With bills to pay, and illnesses to treat.

She closed her eyes and wiped away the tear that was slipping down her cheek.

. . .

"*So, what does this mean, Ashley?" her boss asked. Camilla sat behind the white desk that practically glowed in the fluorescent lighting.*

*"For now, only that I will ask to modify my schedule to take a few less patients in a week. There are some appointments I'll need to attend, but I can give you those dates months in advance." Ashley kept her voice calm and reassuring even though she felt anything but as she stared into Camilla's eyes.*

*"I'm really sorry for what you're going through, but we are already short-staffed, with backed up waiting lists as long as my arm. What you're proposing is only going to make things worse."*

*"Can you hire a part-time person, someone that can take the extra load?"*

*"I'd love to do that. I've been asking to hire another physiotherapist for over a year, and the owners keep refusing. I don't know if I can make this work for very long, and I hate saying that to you because you've been a fabulous employee, and I don't want to let you go."*

*"You're firing me?" Fear ripped through her body, a hot flash of panic blooming, making her hands shake. "How would I pay for my medical bills without the insurance?" she asked, her voice shaking slightly.*

*"No, not yet. But Ashley, you have to know that I can't have you not working for days and weeks on end when your symptoms worsen."*

*Ashley bit her lip, her mind racing and calculating numbers in her head. "What if I donate twelve hours a week from my salary toward hiring someone part-time."*

*Camilla leaned back in her matching white chair, the springs squeaking noisily. "It doesn't work like that." Her boss sighed as she turned her head to look out the window. Her reddish bob and crisp yellow suit seemed like too much color in a room that was void of anything other than white. "Let me see what I can do. For now, we will cut your workload back by one patient a day."*

*Camilla turned to look at her once more, and Ashley knew by the look in her eyes that it was out of her hands. This was the best she could offer until a higher power decided to kick Ashley to the curb like a bag of garbage. What happened to loyalty? She'd worked there since she'd graduated and she put in extra hours for free because she hated to see people suffer in pain.*

*How ironic that she was the one now suffering, and they were ready to turn and look away.*

*"I guess that will have to do." Ashley glanced down at the cane lying across her lap and wanted to stand and heave it across the room. Smash the window and anything else she could hit in her path.*

*"I really am sorry, Ashley. I'll do the best I can to keep you on for as long as I can. I promise you that."*

The bus slowed and the door dinged, but the sound didn't register. "Sweetie, are you not getting off here?" The driver's voice came over the speaker, and Ashley's head jerked up. She looked out the window, and her brain kicked back into gear.

"Sorry," she called out.

Standing, she made her way down to the side exit and out onto the sidewalk. She stared up at the large church and sighed. As bone-tired and mentally exhausted as she was, she wasn't missing the little bit of time she had left to volunteer here. This place felt like another home, and was sometimes more comforting than her lonely little apartment.

She made her way inside. The sounds of those that made this place their home had her spirits lifting. There seemed to be a party going on, and she smiled wide as she stepped into the large eating area and watched the people laugh and cheer. Dennis spotted her and waved before practically running toward her, his face glowing with excitement.

"What's going on?"

"A miracle," Dennis exclaimed, and those closest held up a piece of cake and yelled 'amen.'

Ashley smiled wide as Dennis wrapped his arm around her shoulders and guided her to the office. "I got a call from the building owner today."

"I take it he changed his mind and isn't going to kick us out or sell?"

A surge of energy flowed through her body, the joy in the place infectious.

"No, even better." Dennis's eyebrows lifted, the smile so wide on his face she thought it might split it in two.

"Well, don't keep me in suspense. What happened," she asked as they reached Dennis's office. She hung up her jacket and purse and turned to stare at the man, who was now sitting at his desk. "Dennis, are you okay?"

"Yes, oh my god, yes. Sorry, I'm still in shock. Come sit down. You are going to need to sit down when you hear this."

She wandered over and did as he asked, her butt finding the simple wooden seat. "So, the place sold, but," Dennis held up a finger, "the new owner not only wants to keep this place what it is, he is going to fix up all the problems with the building and has already purchased the old apartment complex next door. He's planning on tying the two together so this place can triple in size, but the extra funding that's being provided will allow us to do so much more. We can have proper training for those that are trying to get back on their feet. Counseling sessions for those suffering from addiction and mental health. Ashley, this man is a godsend."

She couldn't keep her mouth from falling open. It all sounded way too good to be true. It was a massive undertaking that would cost a fortune. "Who is this person?"

Dennis shrugged. "I don't really know."

"What do you mean you don't know?" The skeptical part of her brain was waving a red flag.

"The man's lawyer came by, said that he wanted to stay anonymous, but showed me the potential plans for the expansion and—," Dennis stopped and laid his hands on the desk. "This is what we wanted, what we've prayed for, so wipe that look off your face. Everything is going to be alright. Someone up there is smiling down on us today." Dennis pointed to the ceiling, but she knew what he meant.

She wanted to argue, wanted to mention all the complex issues with the situation, but she couldn't do it. Dennis stood from the desk and came around to her. The smile and look of hope on his face was something she couldn't shatter, at least not now. Besides, she needed something to celebrate.

"Come on, let's go get you something to eat. I ordered a truckload of pizza." Dennis smiled and held out his hand for her to take.

A sliver of hope wound its way through her chest and wrapped around her heart. If this miracle could happen, maybe there was hope for one of her own.

# CHAPTER 21

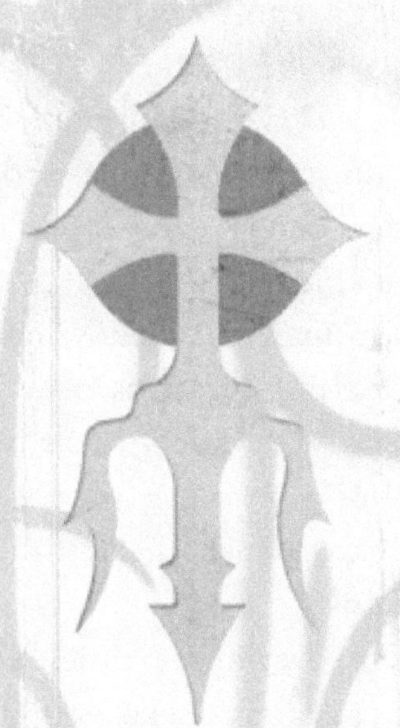

$K$es stood outside his place, lost in thought, before resuming pacing the short distance from one side of his tent to the other. His feet kicked the small pebbles on the crumbling concrete as he went, sending them skittering away.

A flash of blue tarp moving caught his attention, and his gaze landed on Zumi as she stepped out of her hiding spot. She stretched and yawned, looking like a little gremlin, which made him smirk.

He lifted his hand and waved her over. She rubbed her eyes and shuffled sleepily in his direction. As long as Kes had known her, he'd never known her to be a morning person, and it didn't look like that was changing anytime soon.

"Mornin'," she said and shook her head as another yawn gripped her.

"So I've been awake all night thinking." He stopped talking and continued to pace.

"Okay?" She lifted her eyebrows at him as he walked past and then back again.

"Shit, this is a dumb idea." Halting his crazy little march, he fixed her with a hard stare. "How do you feel after yesterday and, you know…?"

She lifted her shoulders and let them drop. "I don't feel any different. Dude was a bad guy. You killed him."

"Shhh." Kes looked around, but luckily, no one else seemed to be awake or in earshot. Crossing his arms over his chest, he tapped his bottom lip with one hand. "You know there is something wrong with that thought process, right?"

Zumi contorted her face like she'd eaten something sour. "Um, isn't that the same way you think?"

"That's my point. I'm over three times your age, and I've lived through hell. You're ten. For fuck's sake, you shouldn't be thinking like that," he grumbled.

"Kes," she said, laying her hand on his arm like she was trying to reason with a child. "I'm currently living in a tent under a bridge and have had the cops cart me away to foster care more times than I can count. I always end up getting stuck with a family that sucks, so I just end up running right back here. I've had two heart surgeries and lived in a hospital for months close to death. My mother is a prostitute that comes home high or drunk every night, smelling like cologne and sex. I have to sneak into school because I can't get my mother to register me anywhere, but my plans don't have me living on the streets forever, so I do what I have to. My life is not exactly normal."

Her hand dropped to her side, and she looked up at him with an emotion that he couldn't put his finger on. "I've seen people beaten, shot, overdosed, jump off this very bridge to commit suicide, and show up floating in the water." Her eyes flicked away, the sun's morning rays just high enough to bath her face in golden light. "You're the closest thing I have to a real family, so if you say that what you did had to be done," she lifted her hands out to the side in a shrug and then let them drop. "Then it is what it is."

Kes processed what she'd said, the words seeming like they should never be said in the same sentence, let alone out of the mouth of someone so young.

"Alright then," Kes sighed, still not sure this was a good idea, but he'd certainly had worse ideas than this.

"What does that mean?"

"It means that I'm going to get you into school, don't worry about the how. It also means that you're going to come with me today. I want to show you why The Righteous gets us to do what we do, and if you have the stomach for it, then I'll train you to defend yourself, and one day, if you choose, you can help people the way I do, or find your own way.

Her mouth dropped open and her eyes went wide like a funny little GIF. "Are you fucking serious?" Zumi squealed and lunged at him, gripping him in a hard hug. "You mean there are more of you? It's like a whole secret club?"

As she leaned back, smiling up at him with way too much excitement in her eyes, a more logical part of his brain screamed that he was a fucking idiot. "Yes, to all of it, but this stays between us. You don't tell a soul. Do you understand?"

Zumi stepped back and picked at her black nail polish. "Pfft, easy. I'm a vault. Besides, I already know so many secrets, I could blackmail half the politicians and corporate CEOs in this state."

His lip curled up. "Oh really? Do tell." Kes placed his hand on her shoulder, ushering her to where his Baby Doll was stored.

umi was worse than a kid in a toy store when he introduced her to his Baby Doll. She'd always been fascinated with technology and had tried to sneak off with his phone on more than one occasion. She was still smiling as she asked the Hummer one question after another, soaking up the knowledge like a miniature sponge. Everything from facts about other countries to how her software worked.

"Okay, enough with the questions. I need to talk to you, Zumi. Baby Doll, end conversation with Miss Zumi."

"Conversation terminated."

"Awww." Zumi bounced on the seat, her dark eyes shining as she looked at him. "What's up?"

"You need to stay in the vehicle when we get to the house, which is just up the road." Kes tapped the control panel and the screen shifted, showing their location. Hitting another button gave him a satellite image of the property that allowed him a zoom function.

"You are like a fucking super spy. I knew it," Zumi said. She scooted to the front of her seat as far as she could go, her eyes staring at the image on the windshield. "It looks like there are four vehicles, one really fancy one, and at least three people outside," she pointed.

"There will be more men inside."

"So why are we here, anyway?" It was the first time that Zumi had asked what exactly he was roping her into.

"I'm here to kill them and show you why I do what I do."

The cheery smile slowly slipped from her face. "You mean like you did with the guy at the warehouse?"

He gave her his best blank stare. "Would that be a problem?" He had no intention of torturing these men. It was a quick slaughter today. He wanted to get the victims being held inside to a safe location before the operation realized that something bad had happened to Slim Jim and they moved the kids into hiding.

"No, not really. That's just a lot of torture on an empty stomach."

Unable to stop the surprised amusement that welled up inside him even if he wanted to, Kes burst out laughing. "You may make a great sidekick yet," he said, earning a grin.

"One day, you will be my sidekick." She crossed her arms over her chest and slid back in her seat. Kes had no doubt that she was telling the truth about that.

"Okay, well, until that glorious day, this is what's going to happen. First rule and most important rule—you listen to whatever the fuck I say and do what I ask to the goddam letter. If you don't, you can get me, yourself, or innocent people killed. Do you understand?" Kes barked out like he was still a sergeant.

Zumi's eyes were large as she looked up at him. "Yeah, I understand."

"Good, so when we pull up, you're going to stay inside Baby Doll and not fucking move or touch anything until I say it is safe to do so. Are we clear?"

"Yes, we're clear," she said, with no hint of humor or teasing in her voice.

"Good, 'cause we're here." Kes pulled off onto the same backcountry road he'd traveled two days earlier, but this time he pulled into the driveway and not the dead end. "Baby Doll, open back weapons hatch." He stopped near the end of the driveway out of view of the house. He hopped out to open the back door and grab what he wanted—two handguns. He checked the chambers and slipped them into their holsters before stuffing extra clips into his pockets. The throwing knives were already in their sheaths, and he tossed the strap over his head so the knives lay flat against his chest. Finally, he pulled out his M4, which was already locked and loaded. He slipped the strap of his gun over his head, swinging it around so the rifle sat against his back. He doubted he'd need it, but it was better to be over-prepared.

"Okay, I'm going to sneak around the house and come in through the back door. Don't worry about the men trying to escape. If they come toward Baby Doll, she will keep you safe. She has a state-of-the-art intelligence system that will get you to safety if you were in any danger. Baby Doll has a tougher exoskeleton than a tank and this glass..." He stopped to tap the windshield. "Can handle an RPG. She is a lean mean Batmobile like machine.

"Batmobile? Really?" She crossed her arms and lifted an eyebrow at him.

"Just go with it."

Zumi looked a little unsure about what she'd signed up for as she stared at the weapons draped on his body. "I need to know now if you want out of this."

"No, I'm all in." She lifted her chin, and he nodded.

"Alright, fly time. Baby Doll, move to the coordinates I set and go full lockdown." He closed the door and ran into the trees that surrounded the property. His guns all had silencers on them, and as he ran, he shot out the trail camera that he'd picked out before, along with the new one he hadn't seen the first time he'd been here. The loud rock music began to blare from the front yard and was quickly followed by the sound of pinging as bullets found the target.

He could hear the men yelling back near Baby Doll for whoever was inside to get out. The blackout windows wouldn't allow them to see inside, heightening their anxiety over the strange vehicles sudden appearance.

That was what he was hoping for—he wanted to draw as much attention as possible to the front of the house. Small branches snagged on his jeans and whipped him in the face, making him want to swear as he ran. Kes smirked, though, as the shooting started in the front yard, the distinct sound of pinging reaching his ears as the bullets harmlessly bounced off the hard exoskeleton of the high-tech military-grade vehicle.

Using the sound as cover, he burst through the trees and ran for the back door, kicking it open with a loud bang. Guns raised, he was like a man possessed. He'd already memorized the simple old farmhouse's layout. It had two levels—five small rooms on the main level and six even smaller ones on the second floor. Kes dove into the room on his right and didn't hesitate to shoot the two guys staring out the front window. They collapsed to the ground, but not before one of the guy's blood splattered the front window.

*Well, that's unfortunate.*

Now he just had to hope the guys outside didn't see it until he was ready. Spinning back the way he'd come, he ran across the hallway that led to the front door, which was hanging wide open. He ran into the kitchen and stared at the back of the shiny cue ball head of a guy eating what looked to be spaghetti. He seemed totally unfazed by whatever was going on in the front yard.

"It's a shame you won't get to finish that. It smells good," Kes said and shot the man execution-style before he could even flinch. His head fell forward, the new hole in his forehead bleeding onto the plate and mixing with the bright red sauce.

The door to the tiny shitter was closed. A man's voice was calling out, wanting to know what the fuck was going on. He was about to find out. Kes's foot found the center of the door, the wooden door breaking off its hinges as it crashed in on the man. This one was going to be entertaining for the cops to find. He could see the headline now, "Such a Shitty Way to Die."

Smirking, he opened fire, the wood splintering and flying in all directions as the man jerked under the weight of the door from the bullets finding their mark. Blood dripped onto the floor, the speckled red like vivid art against the faded white linoleum floor.

He turned around just as a man came running down the stairs. His guns clicked empty, and he cursed under his breath as he grabbed the knife tucked inside his jacket. Thankfully, the guy didn't have a weapon, and despite his large size, he didn't have proper combat training.

"I'm gonna crush your fuckin' skull," the man growled out, his voice thick with some form of a European accent.

Kes grinned at the man, the humor not reaching his eyes as he waved the man forward with the hand that didn't hold a hidden knife. Kes kept the knife behind him until the man was a stride away. Like a cobra strike, he struck with his free hand and caught the man in the throat, the movement only driving the large man back a step—but the hit did its job of effectively blocking off the man's windpipe. Eyes wide, the guy grabbed at his throat, and Kes swung his large blade, cutting off a finger and slicing a gaping line like a smiley face in the man's throat. Changing his grip on the knife, he struck again, slamming the long blade up through his jaw and into his brain. Kes's muscles flexed as the man went slack. He watched the knife pull free from the gaping mouth and gave him a push in the chest. He had the sudden urge to yell 'timber' as the guy fell like a loud tree crashing in the woods.

Jogging around the guy, forgetting him already, he hurried up the stairs just as the guys outside stopped firing.

Reaching the top landing, he looked out to see them still distracted and approaching the undamaged vehicle. He put the knife away and reloaded before dashing to the first door at the top of the stairs. He flung it open, and the man inside, wearing nothing more than a white tank and black socks, jumped off the bed and the girl he'd been fucking. The girl let out a small scream as the man fell back onto the bed with a bullet in his head, narrowly missing the girl.

"Stay in here until I say it's all clear," he whispered.

She furiously nodded her head, but he needed to move faster just in case she got any bright ideas.

The next two rooms were empty, but the last one had a group of girls huddled in the corner and a man with a gun guarding them. The guard was quick with the gun but a terrible shot, as the bullets thudded harmlessly in the wall beside Kes. The sounds from the shots were a problem. He didn't want the men outside to storm in. The more people inside, the harder it was to defend himself.

"Baby Doll, alarm on," he spat out as he shook his head in disgust at the man with the shitty aim. He fired as a loud blaring started outside. It was loud enough to wake the dead. Kes's aim, unlike the guard's, was true. The two bullets sailed through his eye sockets and blew the back of the former gunman's head off.

The cluster of girls squealed and scurried over the bed as blood and the dead body fell toward them. His eyes roamed over the small group, all not much older than Zumi, and repeated the same thing he'd ordered the other girl to do before sprinting back the way he'd come. Peeking out the window as he jogged down the stairs, he could only see two of the three men that had been on the front lawn. He was not a fan of hide-and-seek, but he hated using the vision tech. It seemed like cheating to him.

By his count, he still had six shots left with each gun. He bolted through the open front door onto the covered porch and opened fire on the guy pulling on the passenger door handle while yelling for it to be opened. The man crumpled to the ground, his hand still gripping the handle.

Thumping vibrated up his legs from the floorboards as a man he couldn't see began running around the wrap-around porch straight for him. Making a last-second judgment call, he flipped the gun in his hold and jumped in the air as he slammed the butt on the man's nose. Blood splattered across the man's face with the powerful impact as a massive cut opened up across his nose and cheek.

Spinning out of the way of the guy's momentum, Kes drove him to the ground face-first as he yelled. Kes's boot was pressed firmly into the middle of his back, and a bullet quickly found a new home in the back of his head.

Jumping down the rotting stairs, he let out an evil little laugh as the last guy shook, trying to reload his automatic weapon.

"This would be a good time to run," Kes said, the corner of his mouth lifting as malice burned in his chest. Dropping the gun, the man ran for the trees. Yanking two throwing knives free, he let them sail and caught the guy in the back. His spine arched as his feet stopped working, and he fell forward to land flat on his face in a prickly bush. Kes snorted and then sobered as the sound of a yell and the bang from a bullet coming for him rang out. He jerked to the side as the bullet barely missed him, hitting Baby Doll instead. Kes grabbed the guns in his leg holsters, his mind once more reviewing the layout of the farmhouse. The fucker had to have been holed up in the basement or a secret magic trunk because he'd cleared what were supposed to be the only two active floors. The basement was unfinished, a dirt floor with a low ceiling. Who did this guy piss off to end up in the basement?

The man was as wide as the fucking door frame. He had to duck to get through, but he didn't raise his gun like Kes expected. Instead, he tossed it to the side.

"Come on, fight me like a man," Beefcake said.

He put the guns in his leg holsters and nodded, waving the guy forward and taking a fighting stance. When Beefcake reached the bottom step, Kes grabbed his guns and opened fire until his clips ran dry. The guy stared down at the holes in his chest and then up into his eyes before he comically fell forward like a cartoon character.

"I'm not that fucking stupid, but thanks for coming out," Kes said, putting his guns away into their holsters. Kes turned and walked to the passenger side of the Hummer. The guy he'd shot still had his hand wrapped around the handle from falling to his knees facing the door like he was praying. The fucker better not have gotten blood on his ride. Getting a grip on the piece of trash, he pulled him off the door, throwing him onto the driveway. "Baby Doll, code word Ashley."

"Codeword received, lockdown disengaged." The doors clicked as they unlocked, and he opened the door to see Zumi sitting like a statue, eyes wide and as white as a ghost. "So Kid, you still think you want to be a part of this?"

"Fuck yeah, I do," she mumbled and then slowly turned in her seat to face him.

Kes shook his head, not able to comprehend this kid. "You kinda worry me, Zumi."

"You were all like the pow, pow, and then knife and more pow." She used her hands to demonstrate as she hopped out of the truck and stared at the man he'd just tossed aside.

"Okay, enough of that. Let's get something straight. This may seem like fun and games, but these men are dead, so don't be crass. For better or worse, they are never going home. Keep in mind that they may be assholes, but they still have people that love them, and every time you take a life, a little more of your soul darkens. Don't ever take that lightly, Kid. It should never become nonchalant to take a life. Do you understand?"

Zumi crossed her arms, looked around, and then slightly nodded her head. "Yeah, I'm sorry. Still, you seem to enjoy it."

He stared into her overly-keen eyes and sighed. "Kid, my soul died a long time ago. What's left of it finds comfort in helping others in the only way I know how, but you don't want to be broken like me." He rolled out his shoulders and cracked his neck, the noise loud in the silence.

"Okay, come on. Let's go and finish the job." He'd closed Baby Doll's door and taken a step toward the front door when Zumi pulled on his jacket.

"Kes, if something ever happened to me, like if men like this had me." She looked up at the weathered whitewashed walls and the peeling paint on the shutters. "Would you come save me?"

He pulled Zumi into his side, his arm wrapping around her small shoulders. "I'll always come for you, Kid. Always."

# CHAPTER 22

Kes made sure Zumi had a full belly and was asleep in his tent before he took off for Ashley's. He hadn't been near her for a couple of days, and it felt like a lifetime since he'd been able to smell her body wash or watch her as she did her nightly routine so he could pretend even for a moment that he was worthy.

His phone vibrated, and he pulled it out and took a look at the message from the unknown sender.

'Packages are safe' was all it said, but he knew it was Wolf.

Kes stuffed the phone into the back pocket of his jeans and kept walking. If there had only been one kid in the place then he would've had enough resources set up here in Cali to take them, but because of the number of kids he had to find care for them. Their families, if they had any, would be reached out to, and if not, then safe and stable homes would be found. One thing was certain, he didn't trust the fucking government to do its job right. Jaded after what happened in the Sandbox…maybe, but anyone would be. Other than Trev and Arek, the only people he trusted were Morry, Dean, and Wolf. Wolf had set up a network across the states to extract children from dangerous situations. The group would look out for them until a stable home was located or they were smuggled back into the countries they came from. Many of the children didn't chose to come to the US and their loved ones had no idea where they were. Parents woke every day to find their children gone, and the local police didn't have the resources to hunt them across the world.

Zumi had slept all the way back to their camp after they made arrangements for the girls and got them to the meetup location. As the girls walked up the stairs of the bus Zumi had given them a wide reassuring smile and waved—it was the happiest he'd seen her in a long time. She said she felt good helping and was excited to start training. Kes still didn't know if the whole thing was a good idea, but the kid was different —she was like talking to a pint-sized fifty-year old. She was an old soul and half the time he didn't know who was looking out for who. Most of the time she was a hell of a lot smarter and more mature than he was. She'd been a huge help, especially in talking to those that looked at him with the same fear as they had their captors. Zumi'd shocked him further when she started speaking Spanish to a pair of girls that didn't speak English. He had no idea where she learned it. *Freaking smarty pants.*

He was turning the corner to Ashley's apartment's back alley when his phone rang, vibrating inside his jeans. Pulling it out again, he sighed as he read the caller ID.

"Hey, Trev."

"I didn't expect you to answer. I was planning on leaving a message."

"I can hang up and you can call back if you want?" He teased and smirked as Trev snorted on the other end of the line. It was fun teasing Trev. He'd always been good to him, and as much as he tried to resist it, he liked the man as much as he respected him.

"No, this is better. Now you can't say you didn't get the message."

"Oh, this isn't sounding good."

"Relax, soldier. I want to invite you to my wedding." Kes pulled the phone away from his ear and looked at it like he couldn't have heard right. "Yes, I'm serious."

"It's seriously creepy when you do that, Trev."

A deep chuckle sounded on the other end of the line. "I just know you. And yes, I want you to be there. It would mean a great deal to me to have you stand in as a groomsman."

He didn't know what to say. "Trev, I don't know. I mean, that's a big deal."

"It is, and I want you there. Please don't deny me this small ask."

Kes licked his lips. "Is this an order?" he asked, smirking.

"If it must become one, I'm not above resorting to such tactics."

Kes looked up to the dark night and the glittering stars. "Yes, I accept, but don't expect me not to make a scene, and I don't do speeches."

Trev laughed. "I wouldn't expect anything less. Have a good evening stalking whoever is in your sights." The line went dead, and Kes looked around the dark alley like he was going to find Trev hiding behind a dumpster.

"Shit, what did I just agree to?" he mumbled as he looked up at Ashley's apartment building and to her floor.

This was playing a dangerous game. He didn't have a strong will where Ashley was concerned, and even though he should leave her the fuck alone, he couldn't do it. The dumpster was still in the same spot, and with a burst of speed, he was able to jump up and land on the lid with a soft thump. The old metal creaked underfoot as he stood, and he wondered if he was going to end up inside the fucking thing one of these nights when the lid folded in on itself.

Scaling the fire escape fast enough to make Spiderman jealous, he peeked through the window into the dark apartment. As he checked the time his watch glowed, reading ten o'clock. He was surprised she was asleep already, but then again, maybe she wasn't home.

Grabbing the window, he gave it the good old twist and shimmied the thing loose from the bottom. Like the other nights he'd done this, he slipped in like a shadow and squatted on the kitchen floor as he listened. Not hearing anything, he stood and made his way along the hallway toward her bedroom.

The small night light provided just enough of a glow that he caught a shadow heading out of her room. He dove into the spare room but didn't have enough time to hide behind the door before the sound of Ashley's feet on the un-carpeted hallway made it clear she was too close for him to try. He laid his back against the wall on the same side of the room and moved as far away as possible. His heart was pounding hard as he heard her pass the door and pause.

"Hello?" Her sweet voice called out as if sensing him. His blood warmed with the thought—he wanted her to feel him, alright. He had to give his head a physical shake as the image of spreading her wide as he pounded home ran wild through his mind.

He swallowed hard as every part of his body flexed and drew up hard with just that one word. It was a good thing she'd never realized the power she had over him.

As the sound of her feet continued on, he jumped into action and darted out of her spare bedroom. The sound of her moving around the kitchen and running water had him stupidly heading in her direction rather than the hiding spot in her closet.

*What the fuck are you doing, you idiot?*

Although the question swirled around in his brain, he couldn't help himself as he peeked around the corner and watched her get a glass of water. Fuck, she was sexy. She was wearing a tank top and these tiny little shorts that barely covered her delicious ass. He licked his lips as he watched the material move as she did, teasing him and inviting him to touch. The heat was like a flash throughout his body, and the regular freezing cold showers of the Sandbox suddenly sounded appealing.

*Oh, shit.*

He watched with dread as Ashley's eyes landed on the window that he'd left slightly open to make a quick exit, and her whole body stilled, glass halfway to her mouth.

*It's nothing. Just go back to bed, Ashley.*

He tried to will her with his thoughts, but unfortunately, he still hadn't been granted that superpower. Like a horror movie, he watched Ashley reach out and pull on the bottom of the window with her finger-tips. The top stayed hinged allowed for a perfect doggie-style entrance.

Her hand was shaking as she sat the glass of water down and grabbed her small purse off of the island. She dumped the contents, a small whimper escaping her mouth as she moved the stuff around like a bunch of mahjong tiles.

*Shit.*

Kes stopped his staring and leaned up against the hallway wall, trying to decide the best way to handle the situation.

"Who's there?" she called out. "I know someone is in here, and I'm calling the cops right now, so you better fucking run while you have the chance," she said a little louder, but her voice shook.

Kes didn't want to be found, but he hated that he was scaring her more. He'd scared her enough already to last a lifetime—he'd take whatever punishment she doled out. As he stepped around the corner into the door frame, Ashley let out a small scream.

Her eyes were wide, her complexion that of a ghost as her body trembled. It was easy to see the terror in her eyes, and he hated to see that. He wanted her heat and her passion as he took her anger and swallowed it down, but he no longer wanted her fear. The part of him that craved that died a long time ago.

She wasn't holding her phone as he expected but instead had a hold of a large knife from the wooden block of knives on the counter. Her hand wavered back and forth as she held it in front of her body.

"Hi, Ashley," he said, trying hard not to sound like the crazy stalker guy he must seem like.

"Kes? What are you doing in my home?"

He dared to take a step into the kitchen and pushed back his hood so she could clearly see his face. He could hear her intake of breath, and it wasn't fear that made her body shiver. He slowly moved toward her like he was approaching a wild animal.

"I wanted to see you," he said, taking another small step.

"So, you break into my home?" Her eyebrows shot up, and it was the most adorable look. Fuck, he wanted her. He could smell her sweet strawberry scent, and his head felt light.

He glanced at the knife still tightly grasped in her hand and took another small step. Ashley matched his movement and backed up until she was pressed against the counter.

"Do you want to stab me?" He looked at the knife again, and she followed his stare. "I wouldn't blame you if you did." He stepped close enough that the sharp tip of the blade was pressing into his gut. "I certainly deserve it," he said, his voice coming out strangled with need from being that close to her. He would fucking impale himself on the knife if she asked him to.

"I...I...I should." She lifted her chin at him, her blue eyes glittering in the moonlight that was filtering into the kitchen.

"I wouldn't blame you." He reached out and trailed the back of his knuckles down the side of her face. Her hand shook more, and he gently grabbed her wrist and pulled her hand away from his body so he could step in closer. "I don't think that's what you want to do to me."

"Oh yeah?" she said, her jaw locked as she glared at him, but her shaky voice gave her away.

"Yeah." Kes stepped in close enough that their chests were almost touching, and he could feel the soft vibration coming off her body. "Drop the knife, Ashley."

Her eyes flicked to the knife that was now being held harmlessly over the counter. She blinked like she wasn't sure when that had happened, but he could feel her fingers relax as she released the blade with a clatter. "Oh, fuck, you should've kept the knife." Her eyes went wide a moment before he cupped her face and crashed their lips together.

Ashley was stiff under his touch, but he wanted her to melt. He nibbled at her bottom lip and groaned as she opened her mouth for him. How had he stayed away from her for so long? He was frantic to be closer, to feel more, to slide into her heat and claim her. He knew she'd let her final guard down when she moaned and mimicked his position, her fingers pressed into his neck right over his pounding pulse.

Kes released her face and traced the outline of her body. He loved the small whimpers she made with every touch. Reaching for her waist, he traveled lower until he could grip the perky ass that he fucking loved. Her body pressed harder into his own, and his kissing amped up as frantic need coursed through his body. Lifting her so she could sit on the counter, his fingers slipped up the legs of the temptingly flimsy boxer shorts she was wearing. Her skin was so soft that there was nothing he could think to compare it to, but he greedily caressed her skin as he stepped between her legs. He pulled her so that she was on the edge of the counter. The heat of her pussy seared through the layers of clothes he was wearing. Ashley shivered and let out a little moan as he pressed himself into her harder. He fucking wanted these clothes out of the way. The temptation to unzip himself and shove the material aside was a choir in his head.

He had to stop kissing her or he was going to climb on top of her and fuck her on her counter. But he couldn't do it. He couldn't make himself let go of her ass or stop the voracious kiss that was consuming him. The only thing that had ever come close to what he was feeling was his first glass of water after spending a month on the run in hell.

Luckily, Ashley pulled back with a small gasp and touched their foreheads together, both of them breathing like they'd just run a marathon. Kes ran his fingertips up her arms and smirked as goosebumps rose from the simple touch.

"You've always made me stupid, Kes, and I hate you for it," Ashley mumbled.

He couldn't help but chuckle and then stood straight as he smiled wide at her. "That is the best compliment you could ever give me." He placed his hands on the counter and leaned in, tempted to kiss her again as she licked her swollen lips. "Do you really hate me, Ashley?"

Ashley could never keep what she was thinking off her face, and that hadn't changed. Her eyes, which seemed to glow in the dim light, looked away from his as she sucked on her bottom lip. Using the tip of his finger on her chin, he made her look at him once more, the eyelashes that always reminded him of butterfly wings slowly opening and closing as she tried her best not to look away.

"I should hate you." Closing her eyes, she sighed, and he could feel her composing herself, trying to stuff her emotions away. "You've hurt me so much. I waited for you like an idiot in my prom dress until the hall emptied out and I was the last one left. I was the laughingstock once again, a final emotional teardown by the great Kes Reynolds. I was so furious that I went to your house to give you a piece of my mind and your father said you were out on a date. You played me for a fool, Kes. Over and over, you tortured the shit out of me and enjoyed my pain, and then, just when I thought you might've changed, you—," she stopped talking, and this time, when she tried to look away, he let her.

"I know what it seems like, but it wasn't like that," he said, his voice soft. "And I wasn't out on a date."

She gave his chest a shove, and he was tempted to stay, but that was the old him rearing his ugly head. Kes stepped back enough for her to hop to the ground, and she immediately slipped past him until they had the island in between them.

"It's been ten years. Where the hell have you been all this time? I hope you don't think I've just sat around waiting for you to wander back into my life. I've dated, I have friends, I finished school. I have a job I love," Ashley listed off as anger simmered in her eyes. "I don't need you trashing my life again, Kes, tearing me down until I don't recognize myself anymore. That's what you did to me. I could barely look at myself in the mirror and not feel ashamed, and I won't let you do it again."

Guilt spread throughout his body. She didn't know why he'd done what he had, but it didn't matter. She was right. He'd tortured the shit out of her long before prom night—and a part of him enjoyed her fear, enjoyed her tears, enjoyed finding ways to be around her. He was so fucked, and the irritated expression she was giving him only made him want her more. Kes placed his hands on the island to keep them from doing something stupid.

"Ten years, eleven months, two weeks, and three days."

"What was that?"

"That is how long it has been since the night you think I fucked you over. I've never stopped counting, and I've never stopped thinking about you."

Ashely didn't move. She barely blinked as she stared at him. He let the uncomfortable silence continue until she cleared her throat and looked away from his stare. He was telling the truth. No matter what they had experienced individually in life or with other people, she'd been his one constant. The one that got away, the one that he was forced to leave behind, but his heart had never let go of. He'd begged to whoever the fuck was up there, more than once, to go back in time, but he wasn't that fucking lucky.

She crossed her arms over her chest, and he smirked as she pinched the bridge of her nose just like he did when he was stressed. He couldn't remember who started it first, but the fact they both still did the action made the possessive part of his personality stand up and cheer.

"How the hell did you find me? It's not like I have a listed address," Ashley finally asked.

"Would it creep you out more or less to know that I followed you?" He leaned a little more across the counter and smirked, loving how her cheeks pinked and her pupils dilated. Some would call him fucked up for watching her so closely, but she was turned on by what he said, which made her just as fucked up. They'd always been perfect for one another. He had excellent people-watching skills, and when it came to this woman, he watched everything. He'd gotten so good at knowing her that with a quick look toward her in the hallway, he'd know what she was thinking and where she'd be heading.

"That definitely creeps me out," she lied, and he let out a small bark of laughter but didn't call her out on it.

Ashley smacked herself in the forehead and groaned. "You've been here before, haven't you? That was why my stupid shower looked dirty and why I kept feeling like I wasn't alone. I thought I was losing my freaking mind, Kes. How long have you been sneaking in here, you stalker?"

"Guilty as charged." Kes took a step around the island, and his cock surged painfully hard as she licked her lips but took a step away. For each step he took, she mirrored it until they looked like they were in a slow-motion chase.

"Keep it up, Ashley. You know it will only make me want you more."

He could almost taste her arousal from where he stood. His mouth watered, and he desperately wanted to bury his face between her thighs and make her scream as she came. The better man in him was freaking out and ordering him to leave the house, to leave her alone and never come back, but he'd never been much for listening to that asshole. She was his kryptonite.

She held up her hand, and he stopped moving only when it came into contact with his chest. "I'm not talking to you anymore about anything else until you go shower. You stink worse than my garbage on a bad day. I'd show you where the bathroom is, but I guess that's redundant." She shook her head like she was trying to clear it of the idea of letting him stay longer. "Just put the pile of clothes you want to be washed out in the hallway, and I'll throw it in the laundry while you're showering."

"Are the cops going to be waiting for me when I get out?"

She narrowed her eyes, those beautiful blues becoming mere slits. "I haven't decided yet," she said, but her tone said the complete opposite—she had no intention of turning him in.

"Alright, then. I guess I'll have to take my chances. Whatever happens next is in your hands." Kes smiled as he turned and marched out of Ashley's kitchen like he owned the place. He at least wanted to give her the illusion that she could kick him out and tell him to never come back. Deep down, they both knew she wouldn't do either of those things, and he would put up a fight even if she tried. He was certain of that. Just as certain as he was that he'd lay down his fucking life for her, and just as certain that he would get down on his fucking knees and beg at her feet like a dog to have another shot at a relationship.

He glanced over his shoulder as he stepped into the bathroom and flicked on the light. Ashley stood in the doorway of the kitchen, and even though he couldn't make out her expression in the shadows, he could feel the weight of her gaze, like a hand caressing his body.

From the first moment he'd met her, it had been like this between them, and it only got stronger the harder he fought it. So, he wasn't going to fight it anymore—she was going to be his, and for good this time.

# CHAPTER 23

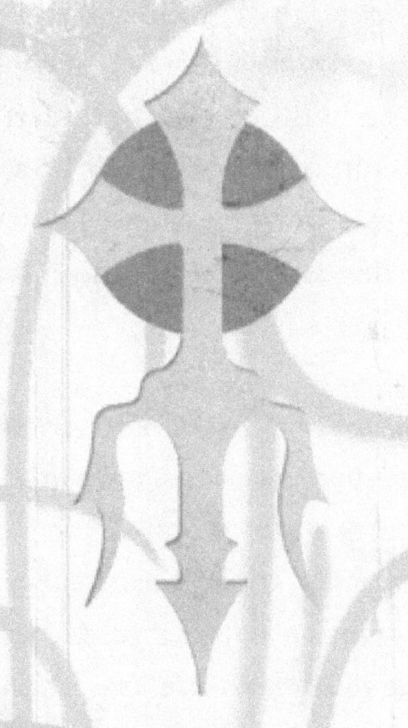

Ashley did laps around her island like she was in the world's smallest track race. She paused at the door and listened, but the shower was still running, the same as her washing machine, which she was going to have to sanitize when the load was done.

She'd promised herself if she ever saw Kes again, she'd never let him back into her life, back into her heart. For shit's sake, she had a whole speech planned, had recited it in the mirror for months after he never showed up to prom. She'd stood like a loner inside the hall, waiting for him like an idiot. It gave everyone one more good laugh before she never saw the asshole seniors again.

Ashley rubbed her eyes before resuming her lapping of the small kitchen. But, here she was, with him breaking and entering, and instead of calling the cops, she offered him a shower. He made her stupid. It was as if her brain misfired, and all logic danced a jig on its way out the door.

Ashley slumped into one of the island stools as she tried to stop her raging hormones long enough to think straight. She needed to think about what an asshole he was and not how he could still make her panties melt off her damn body, or how her heart pounded so hard it felt like it was going to leap out of her chest. Or how her stupid imagination pictured this amazing relationship where he actually cared about her. Placing her head in her hands, she let her mind travel back in time.

*shley raced toward her target. The girl she was zeroed in on was not paying attention the way she should. Ashley stripped the ball off the opposing striker with a quick move that she'd practiced for months. Taking advantage of the open space, she streaked across the green grass, keeping the ball well in front of her. The game was tied on a bogus penalty kick, and she wasn't going to see her team dragged into overtime or the championship determined by a penalty kick shootout because the ref had it out for her. She wasn't much for conspiracy theories, but all season that ref was causing her issues, and she'd groaned when she saw the lineup card and the ref's name.*

*The crowd roared as the school colors waved wildly from the sidelines. Her teammates' shouts to keep going and the thunder of feet behind her, faded into the background with every stride she took. The only sound in her ears was her own breathing as she honed in on her destination. It was just her and the goalie, and she knew exactly what she wanted to do. She faked a kick of the ball to her strong side, and the goalie fell for it, diving to the left. Her hands outstretched as she reached for a ball that would never arrive. With a move she'd only ever tried in practice, she kicked with her nondominant side and held her breath as the ball headed for the top right corner. The ball seemed to be spinning in slow* motion, the black and white pattern rotating as it hit the corner of the goal post and bounced into the net.

Screaming, she jumped around as her teammates surrounded her and jumped up and down. She'd never felt such joy, such satisfaction in her entire life. Her parents were in the stands, and she raised her hand and waved where she knew they were sitting, but it was the raven hair and amber eyes of Kes Reynolds, watching from the bottom bench of the bleachers, that had her heart pounding. He slowly clapped his hands together, a smirk she'd seen in her dreams on his face.

Turning away from the guy that had become her constant torment in a hundred different ways, she continued the celebration with her team.

"*H*artley, come in here," Coach called out as they moved passed his office on their way changing room to wash off the dirt and sweat of the game.

"I'll meet you at the party," she said to the other girls and peeled off to go see Coach. He closed the door and she took a seat, unable to stop the smile that was plastered on her face.

"That was a hell of a move you made out there."

"Thanks, Coach."

He picked up his pen off the desk and tapped his chin. "Have you considered your options for playing at the college level?"

"Not really." Ashley lifted her shoulders and let them drop. "I love the game, but I don't see myself playing outside of here."

"I'd like you to consider it, Ashley. You have the talent to do really well at College and there are scholarships that will pay for your school, which I know you're interested in."

*By the time she and Coach were done talking, the rest of the girls were getting dressed or already heading to the afterparty. She let the hot water of the shower soak into her shoulders as her whole body ached. She rolled out the shoulder that had taken a particularly nasty hit.*

*A soft thump echoed from the locker room area. She sucked in a gasp and pulled her head out of the water, her eyes searching the empty locker room for a cause. She needed to lay off the horror flicks because serial killer images were dancing behind her eyes. She stepped back under the spray but was unable to relax. Slapping off the tap, she grabbed her towel, wrapped it around her body, and shivered as she padded down the row of lockers toward hers.*

*Ashley stared at the bench and then at her locker. Where the hell were her clothes? She could've sworn she'd left them on the bench. She yanked open the metal locker, and it was void of everything. Her jacket and shoes, along with her purse, were all missing.*

*"What the hell?" She stepped back from the locker, her heart picking up pace.*

*"Missing something, Doll?"*

*Ashley let out a little scream as she jumped around to see Kes and a couple of the cheerleaders leaning casually up against a nearby locker. It was like they were fucking magic and able to appear out of thin air. The girls giggled their annoying, 'I think I'm better than you because my daddy has money' laughs as they held her clothes to their chests.*

*"What the hell, Kes? Can't you let me have one good night? Give me back my clothes." She tried for anger, but she was nervous for whatever it was they had planned. She'd known Kes and his creepy Stepford Wives long enough to know they wouldn't be content simply taking her clothes.*

*"You really should learn to lock your locker, Doll." He smirked, and she shivered for a whole different reason.*

*"And you really shouldn't be in a girl's locker room. I'm sure Coach would be pissed."*

*Kes pushed away from the locker, and she stumbled back as he stalked toward her. His eyes were always intense, but the way they roamed over her legs and up to her eyes made him look more predatory than normal.*

*"Would he, though? I mean, Coach loves me, and I know you made a cute little play out there, but let's face it, you're not going to make his career. You'll never be anything more than a high school memory for him." Ashley sucked in a sharp breath as her back came into contact with the cool metal of the lockers. She gripped the front of the towel closed like it would somehow protect her. "While I'm one of the most sought-after quarterbacks to graduate this year. Who do you think he will believe?" Leaning against the locker with one forearm, he let his eyes flick down to her tightly-fisted towel. "I like this look."*

*"Pervert."*

*"Maybe."*

*"What do you want, Kes?"*

*Kes leaned in close to her ear, the heat of his body pressing into hers, and she bit the inside of her lip hard so as not to moan with his closeness. He was a horrible person, and she was worse for wanting him. Her body always felt like it was on fire when he was near, like a lit wick being doused with accelerant—her gut clenched, and her blood seared in her veins.*

*"What I always want," he said, the dimple in his cheek showing as the corner of his lip lifted. She swallowed hard as the girls ran for the door. All she could think was, 'No, don't leave me with him.'*

*Grabbing her by the arm, he held open her locker door with his other hand and her eyes went wide. "What are you doing?" She pulled hard on her arm, but he held her easily as he gave her a hard push into the stupidly wide locker, which she had thought was cool until that moment. Unable to grip the edge of the locker or fight back without letting go of the towel, she resorted to screaming like a banshee.*

*"Help, Coach!" she yelled, and it only made Kes laugh.*

*Panic clawed at her throat as he gave the door a hard shove and it slammed* in her face. "No, no, no. Kes, please don't do this. I'm claustrophobic." Even as she begged, the sound of a lock clicking was loud in her ears.

"See you later, Baby Doll."

Ashley could see his feet through the slats walking away, and then the room was plunged into darkness. Her fist hit the locker as she yelled hysterically. "Kes, come back. Please come back. Don't leave me in here."

The room was illuminated and then plunged once more into darkness as the door opened and closed, sealing her fate.

"Oh my god, oh my god, don't panic. Just breathe." Ashley clamped her eyes shut even though it didn't matter if they were open or closed. It was pitch black regardless, but that way, it felt like the darkness was controlled. Her heart was hammering like a drum in her chest and a sharp pain started, making her feel like she was having a heart attack. She gasped as she tried to draw a deep breath, but it was like she couldn't suck in any air. Tears streamed shamefully down her cheeks as the panic she was trying to hold back gripped her throat a little tighter.

"Breathe in, breathe out," she whispered softly, but the words were reduced to incoherent blubbering as she lashed out at the door with her hands and feet until she could barely stand because her muscles felt so weak. Her right hand seized up, a radiating pain shooting up her arm as the fingers ceased to work properly. She clenched the towel, trying to keep it in place.

Her back slid down as far as she was able to in the small space as she dropped her head forward, the terror making her lightheaded.

"I can't pass out, don't pass out." Her muscles were full-on spasming, and she cried out as the debilitating agony coursed through her body like a steady throbbing.

By the time Kes returned, her feet were numb. Her entire body was shivering from the cold and fear. She was able to register the light coming on but couldn't bring herself to be hopeful. Arm shaking, she gripped the damp towel around her body, unsure if her limbs would move if asked.

"Shit, Ashley. I didn't mean to leave you in there so long," Kes said, the lock rattling.

*Her eyes flicked up as the door was opened. Kes stood in her way, the look of worry barely registering as her body was gripped with the overwhelming urge to run. Leaping from the cramped space, she slammed into Kes, forcing him to step back and land on his ass on the bench.*

*She turned and bolted for the door, not caring that she was only in a towel and her feet were bare.*

*"Ashley, come back," Kes yelled, but she kept running. Tripping over her cramping legs, she hit the ground with force, knocking the air out of her lungs, but even that didn't stop her. She stumbled to her feet and ran like a bear was on her ass. She could hear Kes chasing her, and it might as well have been a bear. She slammed her body into the door leading outside and took off into the night for the only safe place she knew, and that was home. Rocks bit into her feet and the towel whipped open, giving everyone she passed a show, but none of it mattered. She was done, she couldn't take it anymore.*

*Kes Reynolds had won.*

"Are you okay?" Ashley jerked with the sound of Kes's voice. She quickly wiped at the tears running down her face as she nodded, plastering a fake smile on her face.

"Yeah, I'm fine." She stood from the stool and busied herself with making a comfort drink. Grabbing the can of hot chocolate, she pulled down one cup and froze as hands rested on her hips.

"You're not fine. What's wrong?"

"I'll be fine, just a bad memory. Did you want some hot chocolate?" She didn't believe herself and knew Kes wouldn't either. She tried to resist as he used her hips to slowly turn her to face him.

In her haste to look away, she hadn't noticed he was only wearing a towel around his waist. She should've known that would happen. It wasn't like she'd offered him any of her way-too-tiny clothes to put on. Water droplets were still clinging to his body, and she couldn't help but watch a particularly naughty droplet as it slid down his rock-hard abs to disappear behind the towel. She'd never wanted to be a towel so bad in her life. Tattoos traveled down the left side of his body, and his chest had a freakish-looking reaper as the centerpiece, but even that didn't deter her focus. Nope, instead, all she could think about was tracing every black line with her tongue. She pinched her leg hard, her nails digging in desperately, trying to kick her brain back into gear. He took another step toward her, and she heard her own intake of breath as his shoulders flexed. The single light that was on over her stove only dimly lit up the room, casting deep shadows along his body, but there was no denying that he was no longer the boy from her high school fantasies. Kes as a man was so much more than she could've imagined.

As her eyes traveled up his strong legs, the towel cutting off her view, she licked her lips, her mouth going completely dry. He took another small step like he was gauging if she would run, but he need not have worried there—her feet were glued in place. She didn't think her legs would work even if she wanted to bolt.

"Oh my god, what happened," she asked as he stepped further into the light. Her hand instinctively reached for Kes's right arm and the side of his body, where a large area of skin was mottled with scarring that didn't quite match the rest of his smooth perfection. She ran her fingers softly over an area that didn't look like the rest of his skin, and yet it somehow made him more perfect, more human, more everything. Ashley's eyes flicked up into his intense amber stare.

"You answer my questions. I'll answer yours."

She didn't think she could hate herself any more, but as he reached out, his hand gently caressing the base of her neck before his fingers ran through her hair, she could feel her tough resolve slipping away. Ashley covered her mouth and looked away from him. She was going to have a full breakdown, and he'd enjoy that way too much.

Clearing her throat, she forced herself to look him in the eyes. "I was remembering the night of the championship game."

There was no need to elaborate. They both knew which night she meant. His face was as serious as she'd ever seen as he picked up her hand and laid it over his heart.

"You will never know how much I'm simultaneously ashamed of that night and what I did to you while also happy that I did it." She glared at him and tried to pull her hand away from his chest, but he held it firm. "I'm happy because it was the first night I realized that what I was doing had gone too far—that what I had been doing surpassed teasing or…" He swallowed hard and took a deep breath. "Or, doing it just to see if I could get a rise out of you, or make you as miserable as I felt. I know this is going to sound dumb, but at the time, your resilience made me angry, because I was weak and I had none where my father was concerned. I know how this sounds, and I wish I could try and explain it better than this, but on some level I'd found a way to believe you were okay with it. Like you understood that under it all I actually liked you."

She shook her head in disbelief and yet ironically, she believed him. "The night of the championships there was this look in your eye and it all clicked that what I'd been doing had been hurting you, like actually hurting. I crossed a major line that night, and I had to look myself in the mirror and deal with the knowledge of my actions. The image of you running from me, the look of sheer terror in your eyes, was seared into my mind." She could feel the tears stinging the backs of her eyes again and was shocked when Kes reached out and wiped away a stray tear that was slipping down her cheek. "I'm sorry for that night, but I'm also sorry for so much more that I can't take back. I was an asshole because I thought I needed to be. I liked you, and I thought I could never have you."

"You make no sense, Kes."

Kes leaned down and placed a soft kiss on her forehead. "There is so much to explain, but for now, just know that I'm sorry more than I can put into words that I ever hurt you."

"Why did you leave me alone at prom? Will you tell me that? Why did you convince me that you'd changed only to crush me all over again? I can't even tell you what that did to me." She tapped her head and rubbed at the old pain in her chest. "I was broken, Kes. You broke me again, and I kept asking myself, 'why me,' what the hell was wrong with me? What did I do to you that you hated me that much?" She hated to cry in front of him, to give him her tears, but the waterworks were in full effect the moment he pulled her into his arms and held her. She was so weak—she wanted him, even after all he'd done, and she couldn't deny that she'd fallen in love with him years ago and the emotion had been tampered but never burned out. It was just dimmed for a while, but it was blazing strong tonight.

"I'm so sorry," he mumbled into the top of her head over and over until the tears slowed. Ashley clung to his hard body like he might disappear again if she let go. "The night of prom, I got dressed to pick you up, but when I got to the living room, my father was uncharacteristically home from the office. He came over to me. At first, I thought he was going to congratulate me or tell me to have a good time. I was stupid to get my hopes up like that, the man never said a word to me that wasn't intended to cut me emotionally, so why I even thought it was a possibility, I don't know. Instead, he said, 'I got a call from one of your friends. They are concerned that you're heading down an embarrassing path.'" Kes paused, and she listened to his heartbeat under her ear as she waited for him to continue. "He didn't have to tell me who called—Vanessa, the cheerleader I'd broken up with, was livid when I told her that I planned on taking you to prom. It was something she had done just to ruin my night. God, I hated that life. Always keeping up appearances, always hanging out with the right people, wearing the perfect clothes, and sucking up to all the people my father considered worthy. Everyone was always so manipulative and deceiving, it was a terrible way to live. To never be yourself, feel like you can be yourself, it does something to you." He took a deep breath and rubbed a circle into her back, his hand so warm on her skin. "It doesn't excuse what I did to you, but…."

Kes pulled back, and she looked up into his earnest expression. It was the first time she'd heard him say how much he hated his life. She'd always assumed it had been sunshine and rainbows being a Reynolds' man—the world dished out on a silver platter for the taking. He ran his thumb over her bottom lip, and she was tempted to suck it into her mouth, but she needed to know what had happened that night.

"I told him I was going to prom, and he couldn't stop me. I marched to the kitchen and grabbed the keys off the counter, and my father grabbed me by the jacket and hauled me back." He rubbed a hand over his face, a deep sigh leaving his body. "We argued, and it got heated. I told him I was done pretending to be someone I wasn't, and he was having none of it. When I went to leave again, he grabbed my arm. I lost my temper. I punched him so hard, Ashley. There was blood everywhere —I broke his nose and cracked his jaw. In a rage, I went for him again. There was so much pent up emotion, and by that time, my mother had called for the security. It took three of them to pull me off him. I think I would've killed him if they hadn't been there. I barely remember my fists hitting him over and over."

"Oh my god, Kes."

He stepped back and sat down on one of the island stools—his eyes fixed on his hands fisted in his lap. "I know, it was an over-the-top reaction, but I'd been so angry and bitter and resentful and—I hated my life so much and for such a long time. He didn't call the cops. Instead, he called a friend that pulled some strings and had me carted off to a military camp for troubled youth."

"I wondered what happened. I mean you simply disappeared, but Kes I have to say I figured you were off laughing it up while on the European trip you said we'd go on."

"No, oh god no. Man I was such a dick you thought I ran away from prom to go on a vacation to rub your nose in it? I mean you know you were a fucktard when?"

She squeezed his hand and offered a small smile. She wouldn't lie to him, it was exactly what she thought and he needed to know.

Kes pinched the bridge of his nose. "I'll finish telling you what really happened. My father told me I should be thankful that he wasn't having me arrested and charged as an adult since I was eighteen. When my time was up, I decided to enlist. I didn't want to go home. I couldn't go home. I was too embarrassed to face you, and even if I had, what kind of life could we have? I needed to grow up and break the chains my father had on me. The Navy gave me that, it allowed me to be my own man and make money my father didn't control." His eyes lifted to hers, and the pain he kept hidden under his cocky exterior was laid bare.

In that moment, she knew she was done. She was going to do something stupid, her heart pushing her to close the short distance and cup his face. "I wanted to prove myself as a man before coming home to you, prove I was worth your time, but as days turned into years I felt like I couldn't face you. That you would've moved on and you were better off —I was a broken man when I first got back. Ashley, I never wanted to hurt you again, and there is nothing wrong with you. There never was." His hand slid around her waist as she laid a soft kiss on his lips. "You're beautiful. You've always been my angel, and I'm sorry I plucked out your feathers."

"I'm no angel." The heat roared through her body with his words, her face hot with the blush she knew would be there.

"You've always been my angel, my hope amongst the dark. When I didn't think I could go on, it was your face I thought about." Kes pushed her hair back from her face and stood, connecting their lips and sending a shockwave through her body. She gasped as he deepened the kiss like he was going to devour her. "Tell me you want me," he mumbled against her lips.

"Are you going to walk away this time?"

Kes smiled against her lips. "Never again."

She nodded, and even as her mind was trying to back away from the steep cliff, her heart pushed her over the edge. "I want you."

She squealed as he pulled her up so she could lock her legs around his waist. "You really should've kept the knife, Ashley. There's no going back for me now."

God, help her. That statement only made her want him more.

# CHAPTER 24

es was ravenous as he marched down the hall with Ashley clinging to him. Her body felt perfect pressed up against his, like this was where she was always meant to be. As soon as he rounded the corner to her bedroom, he pushed her back up against the wall.

"Oh fuck," he said, his voice close to a growl as he broke the kiss and latched on to the soft skin of her neck. He swirled his tongue around on the delicate area as her decadent berry scent filled his nose and traveled through his body like a drug.

His cock had found an escape from the fluffy purple towel, and he could feel her flimsy boxers, the only barrier between him and what he craved.

"Oh god," she moaned, her hands gripping his hair and pulling him harder into her neck as he rubbed himself against the crotch of her little shorts. She was going to have a massive hickey when he was through, and she welcomed it. She was his. She'd always been his, as he'd always been hers.

"I've wanted to do this since the first moment I laid eyes on you," he whispered into her ear, loving her little inhale of breath and how she ground her mound into him harder. Sliding his hand up the underside of her leg, he felt the material easily move aside for him to find what he was after.

"Oh shit, Kes," she groaned as his finger slid into the slick walls of her pussy.

Ashley's eyes were half-closed, her mouth parted, and he wanted her to groan. No, he wanted her to yell and swear into his mouth so he could capture every single sound. He kissed her again as his finger slid easily back and forth, teasing her swollen lips. As he made a little circular motion on her clit, she whimpered into his mouth as she tried to grind harder on his finger. Her grip on his sides tightened along with the hold she had on his hair. Kes reared back and sucked in a deep breath.

"Please don't stop," she begged and wiggled around on his finger.

"Oh, I'm not stopping. Take your tank off," he managed to get out as he battled back his own raging need. If he never did anything else right, he was going to get this moment between them right. He was going to make sure she was writhing in pleasure before he even got a taste.

Ashley fumbled with the bottom of her cute pink tank top and ended up elbowing him in the chin in her haste to yank it over her head. It was a good hit and was going to leave a mark, but all he could do was laugh. She peered at him through the small opening between her tangled tank top and arms, making him laugh harder.

"Oh shit, I'm so sorry," she pleaded.

Reaching up with his free arm, he helped her struggling arms out of the material and loved how her hair fell around her face in a wild mess. That's how her hair should look all the time—like he'd just fucked her all night.

"Don't be sorry, Doll. I've earned worse than that from you. Would you like to give the other side a shot?" Kes smirked as he offered his jaw up to more abuse. She could abuse him all day, any day, and he'd gladly take every bit of it and beg for more. "Or would you rather me do this?" He wiggled the finger still deep inside her and savored the instant moan. The normally sweet expression she always wore slipped and showed that his sweet beauty was a vixen under it all.

With a dip of his head, he took one of her sexy little nipples into his mouth and teased the hardened nub. Ashley's hands found his hair again, and he grinned against the delicate mound as she pulled his head harder into her chest with a breathy gasp. As his tongue twirled around the sensitive flesh, he withdrew his finger and teased her by dipping just the tip of his finger into her heated core. She was so tight and wet, and the little moans as she writhed around were amping his need higher than he ever thought possible.

"Oh fuck," Kes groaned as he switched nipples. His cock ached to be where his finger was slowly pushing deeper. He could almost feel it on his cock as her walls clenched around his advancing digit.

"Kes, oh my god, I'm so close." The words strangled in a moan were words he'd dreamt of hearing. He smirked as Ashley whimpered when he added a second finger. "Oh fuck!" She bucked in his hold, the action making him pant almost as hard with his carnal desire to be inside her.

"Right there?" He curled his finger just enough to apply pressure to where he knew her G spot should be.

"Oh, oh, oh," she said, her eyes fluttering closed.

His eyes were drawn to the darkening hickey on her neck like a vampire drawn to blood. He smiled as his lips latched back on to the same spot. Closing his eyes, he allowed his body to soak up her reaction.

He wanted to know what she liked, what she craved, and he planned on making sure that she always got what she needed from him from now on.

His breathing quickened along with Ashley's, his heart pounding hard in his chest as she whimpered and clenched her legs hard around him. With a sudden wild scream, she arched her back, her walls clamping around his fingers like a vice as she came.

"I'm…oh…Kes," Ashley yelled and slid her arms around his neck, squeezing him harder as his fingers continued to toy with her, drawing out her orgasm as long as possible. A shiver raced down his spine at the passion-laced way his name rolled off her tongue. It was sweet, sweet music to his ears.

There was never a doubt in his mind that he loved and adored her, but from this moment on, he was going to make sure she knew how much she meant to him.

As the quaking subsided, he slowly slipped his fingers out of her dripping pussy and made sure she was looking at him as he brought the digits to his lips. Ashley's cheeks reddened to a dark shade as he sucked the fingers into his mouth with a groan.

"You taste like heaven."

"Oh stop," she whispered, looking away from his eyes.

"Never, I'll never stop telling you how perfect you are." Ashley's eyes flicked back to his, and the shy look in her eyes was like gasoline pouring on the fiery passion in his gut. "Fuck, I want you so bad."

Ashley bit her lip the way only girls can do that makes them look sexy as hell with the simple act. "I want you, too," she said softly as her fingers played with his hair.

"I need to clean you up first."

Her eyebrow lifted in obvious confusion, but when she opened her mouth to ask the question he knew was coming, he simply laid a finger on her lips and let her feet slowly drop to the floor. Hooking his fingers in the adorable cotton boxers with little bunnies all over them, Kes lowered himself to a squatting position and slid the material down her legs.

Tossing them aside, he skimmed his hands up her legs and loved how goosebumps trailed in their wake. He took a moment to simply appreciate the view of her body. His eyes trailed the lean legs he yearned to have wrapped around him again and then up higher to admire the slick folds that had his tongue tingling for a taste. He looked up at her, and his breath caught as he stared into her shadowed face. She'd always been beautiful, but now she was so much more than that. He couldn't describe it, but she exceeded every memory he'd kept locked away of her in his mind. It was like he'd been watching a black and white movie, and now he was getting to see her in color for the first time.

Kes turned his attention to the prize that was before him. "Spread them for me." He tapped her legs and couldn't have been more pleased when her shaking legs stepped farther apart. He focused his attention on the inside of her thigh, savoring the sweet flavor of her juices as he licked the thin line dripping down her leg. A gentle moan reached his ears as he switched legs, making sure to give them equal attention. As he made his way closer to her core, her body trembled in his hold. He couldn't resist—he needed a better taste. His tongue slipped between her delicate folds.

His tongue dove deeper, the gasps and squirming of her hips driving him wild as she rubbed herself on his face. He gripped her legs harder, which gave him a better angle to take the sensitive nub of her clit in his mouth. He sucked hard, drawing it away from her body as it began to harden with excitement once more.

"Fucking hell, Kes. I can't stand much longer," Ashley gasped.

Kes glanced up and growled into her pussy as he watched her enjoy what he was doing. Her face was a perfect picture of pleasure—flushed with that lush bottom lip drawn into her mouth—her eyes were half closed as her hands roamed over and gripped at her breasts. He waited a little longer even though his cock was aching, throbbing between his legs for release. He refused to touch himself yet—the only pleasure he'd receive was between her legs tonight. If she suddenly turned him away, then he'd leave hard.

"Oh, god," she whimpered, and he knew she was close again. Reluctantly he let go, and the pout that greeted him as he stood to his full height made him laugh.

"Were you wanting me to finish something, Doll?"

"You know I do."

Bracing a hand on the wall, he leaned forward and whispered in her ear. "Then say it. Tell me what you want, and it will be yours." She could've asked for the mother fucking moon, and he would've found a way to yank that thing out of the sky for her.

"Fuck me," Ashley said so quietly that he barely heard the words.

"Louder."

She sucked in a deep breath as she shook out the blonde hair around her face—she reminded him of a high-spirited horse shaking out its mane before it sprinted off. To make sure she didn't decide to do just that, he gripped her hips and pressed the length of his cock against her stomach.

"Say it louder. Say it like you mean it," Kes commanded as he teased himself back and forth across her stomach.

Ashley bit down on her bottom lip as her eyes locked with his. "Fuck me, Kes. Make me forget my own name."

"Gladly." He crashed his lips against hers and stole the little noises she made that drove him crazy. He gripped her hips and easily pulled her up to his body so she could lock her legs around his waist once more. He turned and made his way to the bed, holding her tight as he knelt down and laid her out on the bed. As he broke the kiss and pushed himself up, she released the death grip she had on him. He raised up just enough that he could grab the towel that was in his way and yanked it off, throwing it off the side of the bed.

"Are you sure about this?" he asked.

Ashley nodded, a sexy little smirk gracing her lips. "I may be crazy for letting you anywhere near me, but I can't lie and say I don't want this. I've wanted this, and I've wanted you, for a very long time. Life is too short not to grab happiness when you can."

"If you're crazy, there's no hope for me because I've wanted it longer." Kes slid his hands down her calves and gripped her ankles as he lifted them up. She let out a squeal as he pulled her closer and spread her legs in a wide V. "Now that is a sight I could stare at all day, every day." His voice was ragged as he stared at the spread pussy that was calling to him like a siren's song.

He sucked in a sharp breath as his hand gripped his dick and rubbed the weeping head between her pussy lips until he was soaking wet. As the tip pressed into the tight grip, his muscles shook with the effort it took not to just slam himself home.

"Oh, fuck," he said through clenched teeth as inch by inch he sank deeper until he was fully embedded inside of her. Sweat trickled down his back, matching the line that slid between the valley of Ashley's heaving breasts.

Her arms reached out to the side and gripped the thick comforter in tight fists. "Don't be gentle," she panted out.

"What?"

The look she gave him was that of a primal animal. She arched her back and groaned before answering, "I said don't be gentle. Fuck me hard, Kes. Make me scream."

She didn't have to ask him a third time. Sliding back, he didn't hold back as he slammed home, rocking her body with the force.

"Oh fuck, yes. That's it."

"God dammit, you feel too good." He clenched his eyes shut as he tried to stave off the orgasm that was rapidly building. He let the starved and wild part of himself loose, his hips thrusting as hard and fast as he could. The bed's headboard banged noisily against the wall in time to the sound of slapping skin as they came together. Kes let go of Ashley's ankles so he could grab the wrought iron bed frame for more leverage.

"Fuck, yes," Ashley screamed as the walls around his cock clamped down hard. "Kes," she yelled his name and grabbed his shoulders, her nails digging in, and it was the sweetest pain he could ask for as she arched up into him, her pleasure taking over her body.

Letting go of the last bit of control he had, he lost himself in the feel of her and the sound of her voice calling out his name. With a final thrust, he rammed forward into her, and every muscle flexed as he cried out the powerful orgasm that rocked him to his very core. If it was possible to feel torn apart and put back together again at the same time, then that was what he felt as the final stream of come left his body.

Gasping, he fell forward onto his forearms, careful not to lay his weight on Ashley. His heart hammered hard like a jackhammer in his chest as they lay there in the quiet aftermath.

Rising up enough that he could see Ashley's face, he froze as he watched the tear travel down her cheek.

"What's wrong? Did I hurt you?"

She shook her head back and forth before a small smile pulled up the corners of her lips. Her hands shook as she reached up and ran her fingers through his hair and down the sides of his neck. Finally, she trailed her fingers along his shoulders.

"Did this really happen? Am I awake, or is this another one of my dreams?"

Kes smirked and softly touched her swollen lips with his own. "If this is a dream we're having together, Doll, I never want to wake up."

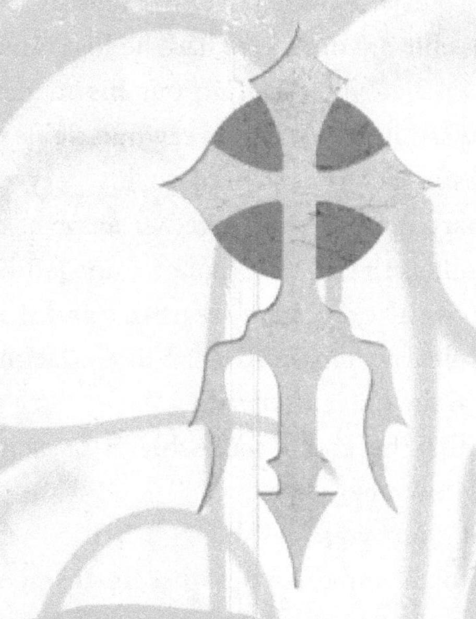

shley kept wanting to pinch herself to make sure it really was all real. Kes Reynolds was in her bed, laying in her arms with her head over his heart. She lifted her head slightly and stared at his peaceful expression. Those thick, dark eyelashes that stood out against his softly tanned skin would make any woman jealous.

Taking advantage of the few moments of quiet, she took in the man that had become the one, overwhelmingly constant thought she had for so many years. The tattoos were beyond sexy, and yet, as she stared at them closer, there was a lot of pain expressed in the artwork. Tears, graves, skulls, and the shadowed face of a soldier laid out on the ground were only a few of the images making up the intricate mosaic, but it was the flames and the ghosting of a hand among the flames that made her shiver. Her eyes flicked to the area on his side and the arm that had been graphed. She wondered if that was how he was injured.

"I can feel you watching me, Doll." Kes's low voice made her jump, but his hand simply pulled her a little closer to his body.

"How long have you been awake?"

"I don't sleep much. I've been awake most of the night."

Those amazing amber eyes fluttered open and heat stirred in her gut with a single glance from them. He put his opposite arm behind his head, and the movement showed off his biceps. She couldn't stop herself from staring.

"I really like you staring at me like that."

"You're a prat with a one-track mind."

The smile that spread across his face was devious and so like the teenage version of Kes, back when she'd thought he was so carefree.

"I'm not sure what that is, but if it means I'm a rockstar in bed, then you can call me prat all you want."

She pushed herself up and rolled her eyes. "Oh, lord. It means you're a brat, jerk, pain in my butt," she teased and went to stand.

Kes reached out and wrapped his arms around her waist, pulling her back until he could roll on top of her. Easily pinning her to the bed, he rained soft kisses along her neck that made her giggle but also stirred the desire in her gut. It was like a light switch being turned on.

"I missed that sound," he said as he pulled away from her neck and played with the ends of her hair.

"Me laughing?"

"Yeah." Kes's face was somber as he kissed her cheek, but there was something so sweet about the act that it had her breath hitching with emotion.

"Can I ask you something?" Ashley watched the goosebumps follow her fingers as she trailed them up and down Kes's arms. There was something so satisfying about having that effect on him.

"Of course, Doll. You can ask me anything."

"Who was the girl you were with at Salvation Place? I mean, is she your daughter?"

Kes's eyebrows shot up with the question.

"I mean, it's fine if she is unless you're still with her mother, or—oh, god, are you married? Am I committing adultery?"

Kes laughed, his body vibrating as he laid his head on her chest and continued to rumble as if he'd lost his mind. "Stop the runaway train," he finally said, lifting his head and wiping the tears of laughter off on the back of his arm. "I haven't laughed like that in a long time."

"At least I'm good at one thing," she muttered, wanting to smack him. But she loved the smile on his face more.

"You're great at many things," he teased as he pressed his hips forward, making her gasp with the feel of him rubbing between her legs.

"Answer the question, Mister."

"No, Zumi is not my daughter. I met her when I got back to the country. She was only around six at the time. Her mother is not mentally, emotionally, or physically able to provide a stable situation, so I keep an eye out for her. She's a good kid. And no, I don't have a girlfriend, a wife, or any real exes, for that matter. Most people are not interested in a homeless guy."

"We'll get to that topic at some point, but will you tell me how you got injured first?"

Shadows of sadness and something else, maybe pain, crossed his eyes.

"Do they bother you?"

"The scars? No, never." Ashley placed her hand on his once badly injured side, and his eyes closed, hiding away his emotions from her. "It must have been a lot of surgeries."

"Too many surgeries, so many hours in a bed staring at the ceiling with only my thoughts to keep him company. It was a dark time and I had serious issues kicking the pain meds afterward. I had a friend help me, but that was many more months of a different kind of pain."

Kes rolled himself off her and pushed himself up into a sitting position. She tentatively followed suit and wrapped the sheet around her as she sat cross-legged beside him. He was quiet for so long she wasn't sure he was going to open up at all.

Clearing his throat, he said, "As I mentioned, I joined the Navy when my father finally gave the okay to free me. If he'd known that I wouldn't come running back, he probably would've kept me locked up as long as he was able to pull the strings." Kes rubbed his eyes and drew his one leg up. He wrapped his arm over his knee. "I loved the idea of flying, so when I was looking at all my options, I decided that a helo operator was what I wanted to be."

"Helo?"

"Sorry, I mean helicopter."

Ashley held up her hand. "Wait a minute, are you telling me you know how to fly a helicopter?"

"Yeah, I do. Does that turn you on?" Kes gave her his standard panty-dropping smile, the dimple in his left cheek making its rare appearance.

She gave him a shove, not that it moved him an inch. "Be serious."

"I am serious. I'll find a helicopter and fuck you in the back if you want me to. Hell, I'll take the bird up and have you ride my joystick in the air."

"Oh, for the love of god."

The deep rumbling laugh sent heat racing down her spine. "You're so fucking adorable when you're annoyed. I've always loved that about you." Ashley bit her lip, her eyes darting to the sheets with the compliment. "Yes, to answer your question. I'm a pilot, or I was one, anyway."

"What happened?"

Kes lifted his shoulder and let it drop. "We were on a top secret mission, and it went wrong. The helicopter I was flying was hit, and we went down. I got burned." He looked down at his side and then back up at her. "The others didn't make it out at all."

Ashley reached out her hand and laid it on his arm. "Kes, I'm sorry. I can't imagine."

"It is what it is. We all die at some point." Ashley looked away from his face, the last statement hitting a little too close to home. "Anyway, I still put my skills to use, but in the private sector. Enough about me, what about you?"

"Me? What do you want to know?" she asked as a nervous sweat broke out on her hands and she discreetly wiped them on the blanket.

"What do you do for work? I don't see a ring on your finger or a man pounding down the door to try and kill me, so I assume you're not with anyone. Do you still hang out with that weirdo girl from high school?"

Ashley laughed, happy that he picked easy topics. "Trish is not a weirdo, well no more of a weirdo than I am, at least, and yes, we still hang out, but she's an award-winning photographer now and is barely in the country anymore. As for work, I'm a physiotherapist for people who have been in severe accidents or had a stroke, or really anything that requires them to learn how to live in pain."

"I thought you wanted to be a doctor or a veterinarian—how did you end up in physio?"

Ashley's face flushed bright red, and she cleared her throat before speaking. "Senior year was tough for me. You were always going to be gone, but it was just...." She sighed and looked away, not wanting to bring up his prom again. They'd already been through that. "I decided to drop out. It took me two years to get my high school equivalency." She gave a shrug and braved looking him in the eyes. "When I made it into college, it only made sense to take something that required fewer years and less money to complete since I lost all my scholarship money."

"Why the heck would you drop out? You had the best average in the entire school. The teachers tried to find issues with your work and couldn't. You used to have perfect test scores and even got the bonus questions right."

Ashley sucked in her bottom lip and couldn't look him in the eyes. It was embarrassing.

"Wait a minute, is this because of me? Please don't tell me you dropped out because of the whole prom thing?"

"Not entirely, but that didn't help." She drew her knees up and hugged them to her chest. "My mom had breast cancer, and we found out after you disappeared. Between worrying about her and feeling like I somehow drove you away—I just couldn't focus. My grades slipped, and I just needed some time. Dropping out gave me time to help my mom while she was recovering. She's fine now, but the surgery and the chemo were intense."

"Ashley, I'm...fuck, I'm so sorry. I would've been there if I could, I swear I...." Kes balled his fists, the anger palpable as he stared at the wall.

"It's okay. I get that you physically couldn't be there." She smiled and patted his arm. "As for dating. You, sir, put me on a path of crash and burn in that department."

She laughed even though Kes's serious face turned dark.

Nervously, she kept talking. "It's been a string of bad decisions, really. The last guy I dated, I ended up having to file a restraining order on, so my taste hasn't improved."

Kes's eyes narrowed into slits, the muscles in his body flexing, and for a moment, she thought he was going to pounce on her. That look was so intense. "What did he do to warrant a restraining order?"

Ashley swallowed hard as Kes continued to stare at her like he was peering into her soul. "Can we just change the topic?"

"Not until you tell me what this guy did and his name."

"Why? What are you going to do? It's all in the past, long forgotten." She tugged at the blanket, smoothing out the wrinkles. She couldn't put her finger on why, but she'd put money down that if she told him Kevin's name, Kevin would end up with two broken legs.

"The organization I work for now is a group that puts guys like that on a list, so if they hurt anyone else, we are ahead of the game and can bring them in faster."

"Like bounty hunters?"

Kes rubbed his jaw, the corner of his mouth curling up. "Yes, very similar to bounty hunters."

She couldn't quite decipher the look he was giving her, and she wasn't sure she believed him, but she found herself saying his name anyway. "He got drunk and hit me, but it was only once. I kicked him out. The restraining order came into play because he didn't like being told to get lost."

Kes's jaw muscles twitched, a dark hatred burning in his eyes. She swallowed hard as she spoke next. "His name is Kevin Matthews, but Kes, seriously, it happened over a year ago. I doubt that he's ever going to be a problem again."

"You're right. I doubt very highly he is," Kes said, but the way he said it had her blinking and her mind running to see if she could find a double meaning in his facial expression. He sat there quietly and simply stared back, but the hair stood up on the back of her neck like the energy in the room had shifted.

Giving up, she swung her legs over the bed. "I'm going to go get a glass of water. Do you want anything?"

"Water would be great."

Nodding, Ashley stood and took two steps when her next stride simply didn't happen. The force of the missed stride sent her flying forwards, and she caught her shoulder on the bed and then landed hard on the floor in a heap. She cried out as she landed on the wrist that had already taken a beating with her last embarrassing fall. Mortification raced through her body as Kes suddenly appeared by her side.

"What happened? Are you okay?" His voice was so soft, so concerned, and that was her breaking point. All the emotion she'd managed to push down or ignore over the last month stormed to the surface in a turbulent rush that she couldn't control.

The shower of tears was immediate, and she smacked at Kes's hand as anger mixed in with the other brewing emotions.

"Don't. Don't touch me." She batted away his hand again as he tried to touch her. Even though she could barely see through the tears that were making everything blurry, she looked up at Kes. "I bet you're loving this," she spat out in between the sobs. "My greatest humiliation, and you get to witness it. Have your laugh, Kes Reynolds. Come on, do it," she yelled, shying away from his touch as his hand tried to move the hair out of her face. "Just go away, Kes. For fuck's sake, just leave me alone." Testing out her legs, she pulled them close to her body and hugged them tightly as the crying intensified along with the pain of rejection that pressed in on her chest.

She expected him to stand and storm out as she yelled again for him to leave, but instead, he cupped her chin and forced her to look at him. "Tell me what's wrong, Ashley."

"Nothing's wrong. I just want you to go."

"You're lying, and you're lashing out. I'm not that same boy that hurt you, and I don't like seeing you cry. Now tell me what's wrong. It was like your legs didn't work properly, why?"

"Why won't you just go away? This is hard enough without having to look at you and know you're going to run when you find out the truth about your so-called perfect little doll," she said sarcastically.

"You are perfect, and I'm not running anywhere. Ashley, I need you to really hear me. You're the only person that I ever loved. I have from the first moment I laid eyes on you." She blinked through the tears, but the fear that had turned into a living creature in her chest only tightened its hold as Kes spoke. Not because she was scared of him, but because she was terrified of the fact that she'd always felt the same way about him. "Yes, you heard me right, I have loved you for over fifteen years, and not for one day that has gone by have I stopped. You've always been my everything, my home base, my heart, and my soul. I know I was a fucking prick before, and I had the worst way possible of showing you how I felt. Call it immaturity, call it asshole syndrome, call it scared. I don't care how you categorize it, but I swear to you that whatever it is that's wrong, I'm not going anywhere."

"I don't know how to believe you."

"I can only prove I've changed with time. Words are cheap."

She looked away from the earnest stare that was making her want to cave. She wanted to hand this problem over to somebody else and scream from the top of her lungs for someone to help her through it, but how could she trust Kes after everything? Even if he did seem different.

He moved until she was forced to look at him or play a stupid game of continuously turning away. "Ashley, now that I finally have you, I would scour the fucking earth to find you. I'd crawl through hellfire, even a rain of bullets, and stare down an army to get to you. You're my one, and I'm never letting you go. Unless you really want me to go, but if you say it, you need to mean it 'cause I'll know if you're lying to me."

The tears transformed into body-wracking sobs that made it hard to catch her breath as they escalated into panicked hysterics. The walls around her heart fractured, giant chunks of the perfectly-crafted armor falling away, leaving her exposed. She was feeling something deep for the first time in what seemed like a lifetime.

Kes picked her up in his arms, and she wrapped her arms around his neck as she buried her head in the crook of his neck. She never wanted anyone to see her like this, but she especially never wanted Kes to see her this weak or vulnerable. She was only going to get worse. Somehow, she'd managed to convince herself that, like Salvation Place, she too would get a miracle, but there wasn't one coming for her. There was no magic wand to stop the progression completely, and it was inevitable that she would become a burden on someone. As much as she hated the idea of Kes knowing, she equally hated the idea of dealing with this alone. She couldn't let him in if he couldn't deal, and if he was going to run, she'd better know now because, god help her, she couldn't take him ripping her heart out again.

As the uncontrollable crying eased, she realized he was sitting on the bed holding her and rocking her back and forth as he whispered, "I love you," into her hair. Leaning back enough so she could see his eyes, she could tell the emotion was real. Their connection had always been there. She'd always just pushed it aside and considered it a sick fascination because of all the other shit and hurt between them. He was still who she dreamed about, the ache in her heart, and the passion only he could ignite with just a look had never left, but their love may not be enough. He may not be prepared or willing to stick it out when the shit got real bad. And whether it was a year from now or fifty, she was going to get bad.

"If I tell you this, you need to be sure that you're not running. I can't…." She looked away from his eyes to compose herself as her bottom lip shook. "I shouldn't have slept with you. It was a mistake to do something like that with someone, but especially with you, without being upfront." Her body trembled as she tried to fight off the tears trying to take over again. "I can't deal with this right now."

"First of all, you didn't pursue anything with me that I didn't want, and Doll, I was in your house, like a freaking stalker. I've been here watching you sleep for weeks. If anyone pursued anyone, it was me pursuing you."

"Good point." She couldn't help but laugh a little as she wiped the tears off her cheeks with the back of her hand.

He gave her a reassuring smile. "Ashley, stop picturing the worst. I know I deserve it, but I'm not going anywhere. No matter what it is you tell me, we'll face it together. I don't have a father telling me what to do anymore, and while I was away, I grew into a man you can trust. Believe me when I tell you I'm all in if you'll have me." He kissed her forehead, and she nodded as her mind worked at forming the words. If she said them out loud, if she admitted to him what was happening, then it would become that much more real. She could no longer deny how bad it was, and that was just as terrifying as who she was telling.

"Tell me, Ashley," Kes prompted.

His eyes were filled with so much compassion that the words choked in her throat as she opened her mouth.

Composing herself, she swallowed down the shame she felt—if he ran, then he ran. Taking a deep breath, she said the words that she could never have imagined having to say until her body had turned on her worse than any bully.

"I have MS."

*H*is heart pounded fast, and his first thought was selfish. How much time did she have? Fear turned to ice water in his veins as his mind jumped to the worst possible scenario. Kes leaned back and searched Ashley's face for any sign that this was a hoax. Not that he actually thought she would make something like that up, but it seemed so unbelievable, so unfathomable.

"I don't understand. There has to be a mistake. You're only twenty-nine," Kes said, his brain racing to remember anything he'd heard about the disease.

"It's not a mistake, Kes. I get it if you want to leave. Just do it now. That's all I ask." Ashley looked away from him, and it hurt how much she didn't trust him. That was on him. He'd never given her a reason to see him as anything other than the school bully that played with her and hurt her in a game of cat and mouse.

He tipped her chin up to look at him, his thumb running over her bottom lip—her eyes were so red and so pained. She'd never ask him for help—she was too stubborn and strong for that. It was part of the reason he loved her so fiercely, but he wasn't giving her the chance to ask.

"I told you I was all in no matter what."

"I know, but that was before you knew what you would be getting into," she said so softly he could barely hear her.

"I still don't have a goddamn clue what I'll be getting into—what I know of MS is bits and pieces, but it doesn't matter. I'm here. I'm in. I'm whatever the fuck else you want to add to that sentence. You want to cry on me, go for it. If you need me to go to doctor's appointments, I'll be there. You want me to make you dinner, I will. Well, I wouldn't suggest that one too often unless you are a super fan of macaroni and cheese or beans out of a can."

Ashely laughed. It was a short, sweet sound even as the tears continued to flow, but at least some of her normal spark was showing in her eyes.

He laced their fingers together and brought her fingers to his lips to kiss every single one. "I've missed the opportunity to have so many years with you, so many memories. I'm not wasting anymore."

She slowly nodded and sighed as she obviously accepted what he said, but there was still doubt under the surface as she leaned into his chest. "What do you want to know?"

"When did you find out?"

"Not long before I bumped into you again. I'd apparently been dealing with it for a long time. I just didn't know it. I took tripping or dropping items as me being clumsy or rushing and not paying attention. The tightening sensation I have all the time now around my midsection, I reasoned, was nothing more than working too much and tight muscles." She stopped and ran her fingers along his forearm. If he could purr, he would've fucking purred in her ear—it felt so good. "It got to a point where even I couldn't make excuses anymore. I began getting tested over a year ago, but they just figured out it was MS. Kind of a process of elimination. It could've been any number of things." He held her tighter and kissed the top of her head. "Kes?"

"Yeah, Doll?"

"I'm scared," she whispered, and yet her sheer terror was as evident as if she'd screamed the words.

No two words had ever had a stronger effect on him. Ashley had always been fearless, even when facing him and the rest of the fucktards he'd once called friends. She'd stood tall and didn't let life drag her around like he'd let his father control him. If she was scared, then he was terrified, but he couldn't say that.

"I have your six now." He kissed the top of her head and buried his own fear.

A soft whimper that broke his heart left her lips as she held on to him with a death grip. He was going to find out everything he could about the fucking disease, and if there was anything he could do to stop it, come hell or high water, he was going to make it happen.

# CHAPTER 26

$\mathscr{A}$shley had the worst time concentrating at work. The conversation from that morning with Kes had been running on a loop in her mind. She shifted between giddy schoolgirl and wanting to smack herself and yell at herself for being an idiot.

It had been the same in high school. Her stomach was always a mixture of emotions that seemed to contradict one another like mixing oil and water together.

"Here you go," Ashley said, smiling at the newest member of Salvation Place. She held out the bowl of chili for the man to take.

"I get all this," he asked as he stared at the bowl with wide eyes.

"Yes, and we have enough for seconds. There are also buns and coffee down there. Help yourself." The man she offered the bowl to took the offering but just stared at it. "What's your name?"

"My friends call me Stiles."

"Well, Stiles, I don't know if you have a place to stay, but if you talk to Dennis, he can let you know if a bed is available."

Stiles ran his hand through his grey beard, making him look like an elderly grandfather figure. "I wasn't always homeless. I…I just don't know where north is anymore." He shuffled off before she could ask what he meant.

"Hi," a small voice said, and Ashley startled and grabbed the table to steady herself. The young girl she'd seen before with Kes, Zumi was standing there and smiling like she'd won the lottery.

"Zumi, right?"

Her eyes slightly narrowed as she turned her head like a baby bird inspecting her. "Kes told you my name?" She beamed. "Good, I like you."

"Thank you. Did you want something to eat? We have plenty." Zumi bit her bottom lip as she looked at the large pot. "Come on. I'll eat with you—I need a break anyway."

"It's a deal."

Ashley almost burst out laughing—Zumi sounded exactly like Kes. The inflection of how he'd say it was down pat. Ashley held out a bowl to Zumi to take and spooned one up for herself before they made their way toward a table and sat down.

"Oh, I'll go grab buns, be right back," Zumi said and dashed off like a high-speed sprite—she was back again in a blink. "I love the decorations." Zumi pointed to the lights and the large tree Dennis had brought in for Christmas. It did have a magical feel with all the lights glittering.

"So Zumi, tell me about yourself."

Zumi ripped a piece of the bun apart and dunked it in the chili before stuffing the piece in her mouth with a small moan.

"Not much to tell. I live with my mom. I'm ten, and I like fast cars."

She gave a little grin before rambling on. "I'd prefer you tell me about yourself. How did you and Kes meet? I know you two must know one another—he never pays attention to anyone. Well, anyone other than me."

Ashley flushed, her mouth hanging open as she stared at the young girl. "Well, um. Uhhh…."

"Come on, don't be shy." Zumi smiled, and Ashley couldn't help but laugh as she took in the Joker-like smile, red chili staining her cheeks.

"You're pretty forward."

Zumi raised her shoulders and let them drop. "I am what I am."

Once again, she sounded like Kes. It was easy to see that the young girl was taken with him. "Yes, Kes and I know one another. We met in high school."

"I knew it," she yelled, the sound muffled as she talked with half of the bun sticking out of her mouth. "You two just had this look. Did he stay at your place last night?"

Ashley choked on the mouthful of chili she was in the middle of swallowing. Coughing, she waved a hand at Dennis to show that she was fine as he made his way over. "Maybe we should change the topic." Ashley glanced to meet the eyes of all the people sitting around them who were obviously tuning in. She pushed around the chili before finally taking a mouthful.

"That's a total yes, but fine. What do you want to know?"

"Why don't you stay here? It has to be warmer and comfier than out there." Ashley nodded toward the exit.

Zumi shrugged. "I can't get my mom to come to a place like this, and I can't leave her on her own. She can't take care of herself," she said very matter of factly.

Ashley stared at the top of the young girl's head as she processed that sentence. She was tempted to point out that someone her age shouldn't have to be the parent, but instead, she asked a different question. "Okay, but why not come in for at least a meal a day?"

"I'm not big on handouts."

"Well, in that case, you could volunteer a few hours a week in exchange for meals. We are always needing help, and I get wanting to pull your own weight—that would accomplish both things."

Zumi's chewing slowed, and Ashley could almost see the gears in her mind turning. "What would you have me doing?"

Ashley took another bite of her own meal before wiping her mouth and continuing. "Could be helping prep meals, or serving, and there is always cleaning that needs to be done. This is a big place. There is always maintenance to keep it going."

"No toilets. I wouldn't want to clean one of those." Zumi made a retching face that had Ashley laughing.

"Okay, no bathrooms, deal. How about you come around four o'clock tomorrow, and you can do an hour of work and have dinner before you leave?"

The corner of Zumi's mouth curled up. "That's why he likes you."

"Who?" Ashley asked, although she was pretty sure they'd somehow gotten back on the topic of Kes.

"Kes. He likes you because you're smart, you're beautiful, and you're definitely kind for a Dweller." Zumi crossed her arms over her chest. "The problem is, I think you're too nice for him. You're going to hurt him. You're not allowed to hurt him or chase him off. We need him here."

"What?" This was like opposite-universe day. Kes was the one that had always done the hurting, not the other way around. "I wouldn't hurt Kes, and what's a dweller?"

"Dweller is what you are." Zumi shrugged like that was supposed to explain everything. "The thing is, Kes is a hero, and he protects us. He protects everyone, including you, but I don't think you'd like what he does, and I don't want you ruining him." Zumi leaned forward, her voice lowering as she gave the best glare Ashley had ever seen on a kid.

Ashley's mind was running full tilt. "Do you mean what he does for work? Because he already told me he's a bounty hunter."

Zumi snorted. "You could call it that. What I'm sayin' is he makes sure mean jerks never hurt people like you or me, and if you're as square as I think you are, then you're gonna hurt him when you find out." Zumi stood and grabbed her now-empty bowl. "Or maybe you'll actually be cool and prove me wrong. I'll take you up on the work and food, thanks." Zumi was gone before Ashley could form the next word.

Ashley swallowed the lump in her throat. What the hell had Zumi meant?

*A*shley waved to Charlie and Dennis as she headed out. The night air was warm, and she sighed, longing for cool wintry air when it got close to Christmas. She'd spent one Christmas with Trish in Banff, and it was still her favorite holiday. The large, glittering, castle-like hotel with the snow-capped mountains in the background, spiced hot chocolate, and every store decorated for the season had felt so festive, so perfect. The best parts were the horse-drawn sleigh ride and curling up with a glass of wine by the fire with snowflakes fluttering to the ground outside. Ashley smiled as the memories flowed through her mind. She could almost feel the chill.

"Hey, Doll."

"Jesus H—." Ashley spun around to see Kes casually leaning against the wall of the church, his hood in place and hiding his face from her. She clutched at her heart and glared at the man as her pulse pounded hard in her chest.

"It seems a little warm to be wearing a turtleneck."

Even with the hood up, Ashley could picture the arrogant smirk. "Well, it was either that or get sent to the emergency room since it looks like someone tried to choke me to death."

"That's not what it would look like if you were choked." Kes pushed the hood back off of his face as he stepped away from the wall. Zumi's conversation rushed to the front of her mind as he stepped closer. She didn't know if it was the conversation that was altering her perception of Kes, but he seemed lethal tonight. The way he moved and spoke sent a shiver up her spine, and crazily, straight to her nether regions. It was official, she'd lost her mind.

"Oh, really, and what would that look like?"

His presence was enough to make her lightheaded, so she swayed on her feet as the man gripped her hips. "It would leave a handprint around your neck," he said as he kissed her cheek. Using the tip of his finger, he pulled the collar away from her neck. His eyes were glued to the spot on her neck where a large hickey announced she'd been naughty.

She'd read too many sexy Santa books because her mind kept picturing Kes stripped entirely naked of everything except for red velvet Santa pants and a hat. She bit her lip as her body flushed unbelievably hot. It was like someone had turned the heat inside her body up to a thousand.

Kes placed his lips against the jumping pulse in her neck, and for a moment, she forgot where they were. "You're so sexy. I don't know if I can wait to get you to your apartment to get you naked, but then it would ruin my plans to fuck you up against your window so everyone can see."

Ashley's mouth fell open. "You wouldn't?"

Kes grinned wide as he lifted his head from her neck, the teasing glint in his eyes that always made her think of the bird he was named after evident. "No, I wasn't serious. But Doll, if you asked me to, I'd fuck you on this sidewalk right now. In fact, there is literally no place I wouldn't do it and nothing I wouldn't do. Except add someone else. I would rip any other guy's dick off his body if it came anywhere near you."

She lifted an eyebrow at him. "I bet you'd be fine with another girl, though?" The words were bitter in her mouth. She never wanted someone else to touch him.

He paused, giving the idea obvious consideration, and the heat that was already burning inside her body was dangerously close to shifting to an angry shade of green. "In theory, it sounds like fun, but honestly, all I want is you. So, the answer is no. I wouldn't want another girl involved. If any girl would do, I wouldn't have spent the last fifteen years pining over the one in front of me."

Butterflies took flight in her stomach as she searched his face for any sign of a lie. "You really mean that, don't you?"

Kes's hands left twin trails of searing heat as they moved around her hips around until he cupped her ass. He drew her into his body, and she could feel the hard length of him pressing into the front of her. All she wanted was to jump on that way-too-sexy body and ride him into the ground. Her hands twitched, and she had to order herself not to grab for the front of his jeans. If she started that, there was no doubt in her mind Kes would finish it. Former church or not, fucking on the stairs like a pair of rabbits with the statue of Jesus on the lawn wasn't her cup of tea.

"Yes, Ashley, I mean it. You're all I ever need."

Rising up on her tiptoes, she grabbed his face. He was still too tall for her to reach, and Kes gave her a panty-melting smirk before he dropped his head down to meet hers. The world and its problems melted away. The feel of his soft lips and firm hands made for the perfect combination to lose herself. She never wanted the moment to end. She wanted to stand right there on the steps until the sands of time took them both. It would've sounded ridiculous to anyone else, completely unbelievable and exaggerated, but for the first time since he was forced to leave, she felt whole. Like she was finally able to breathe after being reunited with the other half of her soul.

Kes broke the kiss, and they stood there panting as they continued to hold one another as if the other could disappear any second.

"Come on, I have a surprise waiting for you at your home, and if I kiss you too much longer, I'm going to do something wildly inappropriate."

"Maybe I want you to," Ashley said and smiled as Kes groaned, his eyes flaring with the same passion she was feeling.

The sound of voices reached them a moment before the large wooden door pushed open.

"Good night, Charlie," Dennis's voice called out. It gave them just enough time for Kes to release her face and slip his hand into hers as he stepped off to the side. "Oh!" Dennis's eyes went wide, his mouth falling open as his eyes flicked from Kes to her and then down at their hands.

"Dennis, this is Kes. He's…." Ashely paused, looking up at the man beside her.

"It's alright. I don't need an explanation." He smiled and waved as he practically jogged away. "Have a good night, Ashley. You deserve it," he called out as he reached the sidewalk.

Her face flushed again but for a different reason this time. "You think he knows that we were…you know?"

"Oh, he definitely knows you were all over me like a horny teenager," Kes teased and bumped her shoulder, making her laugh. "It's just as well. You are way too tempting. I need to get you home."

Twenty minutes later, they were walking into her apartment, and she stopped dead in her tracks. Christmas music filled the apartment. The smell of something like cinnamon and other holiday spices was making her mouth drool.

She turned to look up at Kes. "What's going on?"

The corner of his lip curled up. "You have to come and see. The key you gave me was quite useful." He grinned widely, his whole face lighting up.

"Hmm," she said, a little nervous to see what he'd done.

As he gave her hand a tug, she followed him the short distance to her living room, and her mouth fell to the floor. Everything was decorated. Little white lights glittered from every corner, and a Christmas tree that was so tall the star on top was touching the ceiling next to the windows with an array of red and gold decorations sparkling from every limb. Large poinsettias sat in every available space, along with green garlands. There was so much holiday sparkle that her eyes could barely take in everything.

"Oh my god, Kes." She covered her mouth as tears welled up in her eyes.

"Do you like it?"

She turned around to look up at Kes, who seemed nervous for the first time since she'd met him. "Like it? I freaking love it. This is stunning. It's perfect." She looked over her shoulder, not wanting to take her eyes off the beautiful sight. "How did you get all this done?"

"I kind of had help. I hope you don't mind?" Kes cleared his throat. "Zumi, you can come out now."

The dark-haired girl stepped out of the kitchen, and Ashley barked out a laugh as she took in Zumi. She was coated from head to toe in flour. Zumi was wearing her 'Viva Las Vegas' apron, which was way too large for her small frame. The sheepish expression was too adorable for Ashley to even contemplate being upset.

"I'm sorry. I spilled the flour and was trying to get it cleaned up before you guys got back," Zumi said, looking down at her hands as she wrung them together.

"That's okay. A little spilled flour never hurt anyone," Ashley said, smiling. "Whatever you made, it smells wonderful."

Zumi looked up at her, the corner of her mouth pulling up like she was trying not to smile. "I hope you don't mind, but we bought the crust and I used your recipe to mae an apple pie. Kes tried to help, but honestly, I thought he was going to burn your apartment down. I mean the oven clearly says bake and he tried to broil the first curst attempt."

"Hey, you promised not to squeal, besides I wasn't that bad," Kes said, his face morphing into the perfect pout, making them all laugh.

Tears pricked Ashley's eyes. "Excuse me for a minute." She shamefully fled at a spirited walk down the hall to her bedroom and closed the door. She covered her mouth as the tears fell in twin streams down her cheeks.

The door opened, and she knew it was Kes coming to check on her before he wrapped his arm around her waist. "Hey, are you okay?" he softly asked as he hugged her from behind.

She nodded, but the stupid emotion wouldn't stop squeezing her chest like a vice.

"Why is it I don't believe you?"

She let out a little burst of a laugh and turned around in his arms. "I'm sorry I'm such a cry baby, I just…."

"Did I overstep? I know that Christmas is still a couple of days away, but it didn't look like you were going to decorate, and I remembered how much you loved the lights." She stared up at him in wonder. She'd had no idea he'd paid that much attention to the things she liked or that he'd even remember this many years later. "Zumi and I can go, and if the decorations are too much, I can take them down. Those dirty, glittering little bastards of joy."

"Oh my god, stop," she giggled and shook her head. "I'm just so happy. I know you wouldn't think it, but—Kes, I feel like I woke up in the middle of a romance novel, and it feels wonderful. But not only am I waiting for the other shoe to drop where you're concerned, I also have this stupid disease hanging over everything I do. The emotions are all conflicted." She rubbed at her chest. "I'm beyond happy, and yet I'm terrified and angry at the same time."

He pulled her into his chest and hugged her tight. "There is no falling shoe coming from me, and you can be as happy or as scared or as sad as you need. You don't have to hide from me. I'm here, I promise I'm here," he mumbled into the top of her hair.

"Thank you, Kes."

"Come on, let's go get some pie. Zumi will kill me if I don't try her hard work."

The surreal moment continued as he kissed her lips and led her out of the room to their Christmas paradise.

# CHAPTER 27

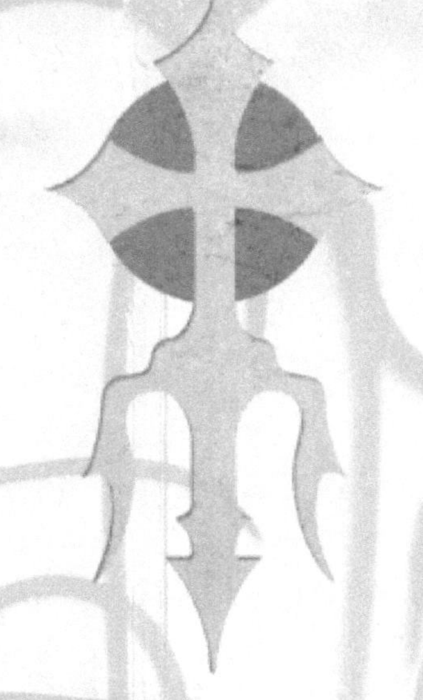

Kes stepped out of the way of the little fist that was coming for his stomach. Reaching out, he gripped Zumi's wrist in his hand and gave her a quick pull and twist, depositing her on her ass in the sand.

"Ugh!" Zumi grabbed handfuls of the little beige granules and threw them at his pants. They bounced harmlessly off the jean material and blended back in with the beach once more.

"That is definitely not going to work. At least try for the eyes," he drawled as he stepped away and grabbed the bottles of water he'd stuck into the sand. Picking them up, he tossed one to Zumi, who caught it out of the air, and then cracked open the lid of his own.

"This is impossible. You're just too much taller and stronger. It's not fair," she grumbled.

"Of all people, I didn't think I needed to explain to you that life's not fucking fair. Now, do you want to quit, give up, and walk away? If so, tell me now. I'm not wasting another minute trying to train someone that has no drive or fight in their gut to continue on at all costs."

Zumi looked down to her lap and the bottle in her hands, then up at him. "I hate being so small. I'm useless."

Kes squatted down and waited until she looked him in the eyes. "Where is this coming from?"

Like a marionette controlled by her strings, she lifted one shoulder and let it drop dramatically and then proceeded to do both as he continued to stare.

"Where is the girl that followed me around until she found out what I was up to and managed to sneak into a warehouse as quiet as a church mouse? Where is the girl that offered to help bury a man and helped me free eight young girls no older than herself from a bunch of traffickers? We gave them a new try at life. Where is the girl that finds ways to better herself despite the shit hand she's been dealt?" A single tear trickled down her cheek. "What's really going on, Zumi?"

"I didn't really help." Her voice was soft as the morning breeze. Her dark eyes found his. "At the trafficker's place, I didn't really help."

"Says who?" he asked, and she looked away at the water as it slowly came onto shore and then back out to sea. When it was clear she was going to remain silent, he continued on. "Zumi, the girls that we helped only felt safe getting into my friend's bus because of you. I think they would've tried to run if it had just been me there. I'd say you did way more than enough."

"That was nothing. I only talked to them."

"And? Helping people isn't always about smashing bad guys' faces in. You know that. So I'll ask again, what is this really about?"

"I was supposed to go for my check-up for my heart next week, but my mom is refusing to take me. She says I'm fine, and if I need to go, I can go by myself." Her eyes lifted to his, and there was way too much sadness in them for someone so young. "Do you really think the doctor is going to let me wander in without a parent? I'm a minor, but no matter how much I beg, she says no. It's her fault I even have a heart problem. If she'd just gotten a normal job and eaten healthy food, maybe I wouldn't be so weak, so tiny, so…me." Letting out a wail, she slammed her fists down into the sand over and over until she was panting hard. "I hate her. Why did she have to have me in the first place?" The tears were quick, but Zumi scrubbed them away, the anger overriding the sadness.

Kes waited until Zumi calmed down and then slowly stood and held out his hand to help her up. "Come on, Kid. You're going to keep working at this until you can kick my ass." She sighed and rolled her eyes. "I'm serious, get your ass up now," he barked out, and Zumi's eyes went wide, but she pulled herself to her feet and dusted off the sand.

"I wish I could offer you pretty words about how everything will find a way to be alright, that your mother will turn her shit around, but I can't, because honestly, I don't have a fucking clue what will happen and there will always be someone or something wanting to grab your leg and drag you under if you let them." Clutching his sweater with his hand, he yanked up the side that showed off the large area that still held scars from his narrow escape from death's fiery grasp. "You see this?"

Zumi's eyes went wide as she stared at the scarred skin that he'd never shown her.

"I've lost, Zumi. I've endured unimaginable pain, and I've definitely felt the soul-crushing weight of being useless more times than I can count." He let the sweater fall back into place. "It's not the physical body that matters. Your first lesson must be to understand that your strength to overcome has to start here," he tapped the side of his head. "And here," he moved his finger over his heart. "We all have crap. Every person walking past you on the street has had to deal with some form of crap in their life. What you're failing to see is that you've already proven you have what it takes to grab this life by the ball sack and drag the fucker around." Reaching out, he softly tapped her between the eyes. "You need to stay strong here, or what I'm showing you won't matter. Your size at first glance is a disadvantage, but it can be turned into an advantage if you let it. Do you understand?"

Her chin lifted and her water bottle crinkled as she gripped it tight. "I think I do. You're saying that you can show me how to turn my itty-bitty size into a lethal weapon of death." She smiled as she teased him. "But, I need to stop being a pouty brat if I'm going to learn anything."

Kes laughed hard and smiled wide. "I really like you, Kid." Zumi blushed and looked down, a grin finally breaking her features. "So why do they want to see you next week?"

"I don't know. I got the message and called back saying my mom was busy, so they told me to be at the hospital with my mom by ten in the morning next Tuesday." She rubbed over her heart. "I think it's something bad." Her bottom lip trembled as she stared up at him like she hoped he had the answers.

He really fucking wished he could tell her something comforting, be the hope she needed. The problem was, he had no idea what her condition was, so he couldn't offer false hope.

"New rule."

"You have a lot of rules."

He smirked as he tried not to laugh. "It is what it is. Do you want to know it or not?"

"Fine, give it to me." She shook out her hair and straightened her shoulders like a small soldier, and he realized that over their time together, he'd slowly started to see her as real family. She wasn't biologically or legally, but some of the best family he'd ever known wasn't related to him by blood, and she was no different.

"Don't worry about things you don't know. This appointment could be anything from a routine check-up to the worst-case scenario or anything in between. Until you have answers, don't panic. That goes for any situation you find yourself in. Think shit through. That is what will save your life."

"Alright, that's kind of a good rule," Zumi said with the best deadpan expression he'd ever seen.

"See, this is why I keep you around, for the entertainment." He grinned wide, and she followed suit. "So, look, this is what's going to happen. I will take you to your doctor's appointment next week. See, one problem already solved. Now get back into position. We have more work to do. If they're going to tell you you're dying, you might as well go out fighting."

"Ha, ha, so funny." Zumi crossed her arms over her chest and cocked her head in a perfect disapproving look. "What are you going to tell them when they ask who you are to me?"

"Take your pick. I can be your hot uncle, your savvy older brother, or how about your long-lost cousin Leopold that was just found wandering the Amazon Jungle?"

Zumi snickered. "Please don't say that."

"What's wrong with Cousin Leopold? Is he a jerk? I'll kick his ass if he's a jerk."

She tried hard not to laugh but failed. Her giggle was infectious as she shook her head at him. "There is something wrong with you, Kes, like really wrong."

"Kid, I've been trying to tell you that for years," he said as he dropped his water bottle to the sand. "But there must be something equally wrong with you, 'cause you keep coming back for more."

Zumi copied his actions and moved into position, her face turning up to his. "Thanks, you know, for everything."

"Don't thank Cousin Leopold yet. Knowing him the way I do, it's very likely he'll embarrass you at the doctor's."

"You wouldn't dare."

"If you get that knee kick in on me that I showed you, even once, before we're done, then I will be on my best behavior, but if not? What can I say? Yo cuz really likes to go on bout his time in the jungle and how he picked up strange warts on his ass and a green fuzz between his toes." Her mouth dropped open in horror, making him roar in laughter.

"I'm getting that kick in. Let's go."

It was dark by the time they finished, but Zumi had gotten the knee kick down. The slight limp he was now sporting was proof of that. He'd grabbed them both crab rolls and ice cream from one of the little shops along the beach and made sure she got back to the tent to sleep off her exhaustion before heading out to find Ashley at the church. She'd said she wanted to help over the holidays and make sure everyone felt cared for and had everything they needed.

He was really looking forward to having her to himself, and what could he say? He really wanted to get her naked again. The day they'd decorated Ashley's house, he'd taken Zumi back to the encampment after they all scarfed down the apple pie. It had turned more into an apple crumble, but it was surprisingly tasty. He'd been tempted to rush back and crawl into bed with her, but she'd seemed worn out when they left.

His lips curled up, and his stomach got all fluttery as he thought about getting her home and into the shower. He rounded the corner of the church just as a small scream yanked him out of his thoughts. His eyes flicked to the scene at the bus stop, and an uncontrollable rage coiled in his system like a living dragon roaring to life.

Kes marched across the lawn toward the backs of the two men that were looming over Ashley as she sat on her ass. The one guy was going through her purse and dumping the contents onto the ground.

One glance at her terrified face and he was ready for murder. He ran the final few strides, and using the momentum, he jumped and snapped his leg out in a vicious flying sidekick. His boot was squarely aimed at the man on the right's center mass. The blow caught him perfectly in the middle of his back and sent him forward with such force he crashed through the glass wall of the bus stop. Ashley screamed and covered her head as little pieces exploded and rained down on her.

The burning fire in his belly didn't ease. If anything, it only amped higher as the second man spun around to see where the attack was coming from. Kes stepped on the end of Ashley's discarded cane. The thing stood up straight so he could grab it.

"What the fuck?" the second assailant yelled in confusion.

Those would be the only words he got out, as the rounded handle of the cane found a new home in his gut, driving the air from his lungs. With a quick snap of his wrist, he brought the handle up to crack the man under the chin before he reached back and, with a sickening crunch, brought the wood around into the side of the man's jaw. The power of the impact knocked the man out and most likely broke the bone, but he didn't care. He glared even as the man's eyes rolled back in his head and he collapsed like a sack of potatoes at his feet.

Glass crunched under his feet as he stepped toward the man that had sailed through the glass. Blood decorated the little pieces as the man stumbled to his feet, cutting his knees and hands in the process.

Wide, terrified eyes found his, and a rumbling growl escaped his lips as he pictured ripping the man into two. The guy took off in a fast dash to try and escape across the street, but he wouldn't let him get away that easily. Changing his hold on the cane, he threw it with deadly accuracy, the piece of spinning wood catching the guy between strides in the backs of his legs. He sneered as the wood did its job and tripped the running man, sending him flying across the pavement face-first. An oncoming car laid on the horn and its tires screeched, narrowly missing the man as it came to a stop inches from his body.

Kes took a stride toward the man, the wave of fury still riding him, until he heard his name. "Kes, stop!" He looked back at Ashley—her eyes were surprisingly calm, but she was struggling to get to her feet. "Let him go. He's not worth it."

He glanced at the man that was now limping to his feet and shuffling off, and every instinct in his body screamed to run him down, detach his head from the rest of his body, and post it on a pike somewhere. His nostrils flared as he sucked in a deep breath trying to rein in the wild, dark urges.

"Kes, please help me up."

The soft request was like a bucket of ice water dumped on the burning inferno. He stepped over the still-unconscious man and was in the middle of helping Ashley stand when Dennis and the caretaker Charlie, along with a few other members of Salvation Place, came rushing out the door.

"Oh my god, Ashley. Are you okay?" Dennis asked, his face as white as a ghost.

"Yeah, I'll be fine," Ashley said, even as she winced trying to stand. "I seem to end up on the ground a lot lately."

Kes's jaw twitched as he gripped her side and helped steady her with his body. He watched Dennis's panicked face closely as he looked down at the knocked-out man.

"This is the same jerk that was here the other week and was trying to steal. Don't you remember? They hit you with the door when they ran out. I should've called the cops," Dennis rambled, his hand going to his forehead.

Kes's hand gripped Ashley's side a little firmer. "You mean they hurt her once already?" His voice was like steel as he glared at Dennis from under his hood. "And you didn't call the cops?" he bit out.

Ashley looked up at him and placed a hand on his chest. He flicked his eyes down to hers, and he knew she was silently asking him to drop it. He didn't want to. He wanted to demand answers from Dennis. He wanted to race across the street and find the fucker that got away, but instead, he nodded to let her know he would behave.

"I'm so sorry, Ashley. He's right. I should've called the cops. I didn't think they'd be so bold as to come back."

"It's okay, Dennis. I'll be fine," she said as sirens drew closer.

Kes looked up in the direction of the oncoming police and ground his teeth together. *Great.* "I can't be seen by them," he whispered in her ear. "I'll be over there until you're ready to go." He nodded toward the alley, and she lifted her brow at him in obvious curiosity, but then simply said, "Okay."

He slipped into the shadows and blended in with the night as the flashing lights pulled up to the bus stop, now a flurry of activity. Ashley looked over at him once as she was giving her statement, but if she said anything about him, they never looked his way. He leaned against the dirty brick and was tempted to leave. He was toxic, and he never should've pushed his way into Ashley's life again. He'd almost killed those two men and ripped out their hearts in front of her. He pinched the bridge of his nose and watched as the man that had been knocked out was loaded into the back of the cruiser and driven away.

As Ashley looked his way and held out her hand for him to go to her, he knew there was never going to be a way to walk this back. His heart was hers.

# CHAPTER 28

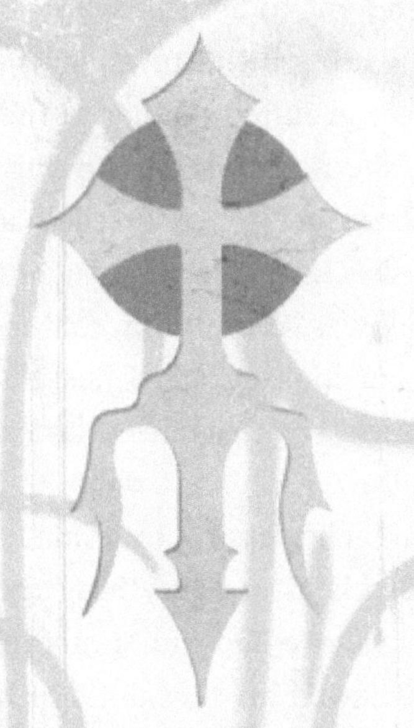

Ashley slipped her fingers into Kes's hand, and the simple contact eased the nervousness and stress that had settled in her chest. He'd kept his hood firmly in place, but she could feel the weight of his stare, and she gave him a small smile.

"Thanks for not saying anything about me," he said, finally.

"You're welcome, but why exactly is that, Kes? Why do you not want to be known or seen? You always seem to be hiding. Are you wanted by the police?"

"No, I'm not." He paused and looked around at the few rubberneckers that were still hanging around. "We should talk about this in private," he whispered.

"Fine."

He pulled his phone out of his pocket. "Baby Doll, meet me at my location." Ashley crossed her arms over her chest, her heart thudding a little faster. Had he been lying to her this whole time? Did he have somebody else on the side? Adding insult to injury, he'd given them both the same pet name. Her teeth ground together as the jealousy rose in a rush. Whoever this girl was, she was going to rip her hair out from its roots. There was only one other time in her life she had felt this violent over a man, and shock of all shocks, it was once again over the one standing before her. What the hell was it about him that made her so crazy?

A soft chuckle had her looking up to Kes. She was just able to make out the shadow of a smirk. His lips curled up further, making her want to smack them off his face.

"Is someone jealous?" The teasing tone made her hand twitch. How could he tease her like this after everything they'd been through? She looked away from him before she did something insane like jump on him like a wildling and clawed his eyes out. His hand snaked around her waist, and before she could pull away from his touch, he trapped her to him with his iron-like grip. "I love seeing you jealous," he leaned in and whispered in her ear. "It makes me hard," he baited, dropping his head and nuzzling at her neck like a cat would.

"You're a jerk, and an asshat, and a number of other things that I can't think of with you doing that," she said between gritted teeth.

"I can't deny any of that, but Baby Doll is not what you're thinking. You're the only woman for me," he said, raising his head and locking his eyes with hers.

The emotional storm that was brewing like a tropical hurricane slowed as she stared into eyes that held no teasing. With the anger turned down a notch, she had to ask, "Then who is Baby Doll?"

"You'll see. Here she comes now." Kes nodded down the street, and

Ashley looked over her shoulder as a shiny black Hummer pulled up to the curb. The blackout windows made it impossible to see who was driving. "Come on, let's get you home."

Taking her hand, he led her to the passenger side of the vehicle, and she held her breath as she waited to see who was behind the wheel as he opened the door. The remaining anger turned into confusion as she stared at the empty driver's seat.

"Um...."

Kes laughed, his deep baritone voice instantly making her body squirm and warm in all the right places. "Go on. She is safe."

Ashley stepped up into the tall vehicle, and Kes closed the door before rounding the front and jumping into the driver's side. He pulled his hood down and smiled at her.

"Baby Doll, this is Ashley."

"Hello, Ashley, it is nice to meet you," the AI responded, and he laughed as Ashley looked into the backseat and then at the dash with the same wonder that Zumi had.

"Baby Doll is the vehicle?"

"Yes, she is a high-tech AI, complimentary of my employers, that can do pretty much anything other than make my meals. I haven't figured out how to get her to do that yet."

"Wow." Ashley held up her finger as she thought. "Wait a minute. You named your vehicle after me?"

His cheeks reddened ever so subtly, but Kes was most certainly blushing. "I never thought I'd get to see the real one again. This way, you were always with me."

She opened her mouth and closed it again as no words came to her. It was the strangest and sweetest admission she'd ever heard. She peeled her eyes away from his stare, a glimpse of pink paper catching her attention. Reaching out, she picked up the small lotus flower that he'd given her as part of his prom proposal. The beautiful flower looked so much smaller now in her hand, and yet it still had her biting her lip with the powerful spark it ignited. Memories of him getting down on one knee like he was proposing in front of the entire school were as vivid in her mind as him sitting beside her now.

"Is this…?"

"Yes. I'm not proud I took it, but the first night I snuck into your place I was searching for it." She looked over at him, and he swallowed and looked away. "I thought if you still had it, then maybe there was hope that you still held onto thoughts of me as much as I'd been hanging on to thoughts of you all this time. I know it was stupid." His hands gripped the steering wheel hard, and she reached out and laid her hand on his forearm, the muscles relaxing under her touch.

"I don't think it's stupid. I hung on to it for the same reason. I felt so stupid for thinking that if I hung on to it, then one day, you'd come back. Like magic, you'd walk through my door. I didn't expect you to crawl through my window, mind you."

Leaning in, Kes cupped her cheek, and a spark of electricity raced through her system as his lips brushed against her own.

She opened her mouth to say 'let's go home' when her phone rang, the thing vibrating in her pocket. Pulling it out, she groaned as she saw Mount Rose on the screen.

"Ashley here," she said as she hit the little answer button. She sighed and nodded even though the woman on the other end of the line couldn't see her as she listened. "Yes, okay, I will be there." She hung up the phone and stared at the thing in her hands.

"What is it? What's wrong?" Kes asked.

"I need to go for a follow-up appointment the day after tomorrow." She rubbed her eyes, not wanting to deal with any of that right now, just as the Hummer began to ring. His eyes swung to the display with the name 'Trevor Anderson' on the screen.

"Are you not going to answer it?"

"No, you're more important."

Curiosity had her reaching out and hitting answer for him and then wanting to laugh at the look of disbelief on his face. "Kes, are you there?" came a smooth voice that reminded her of fine wine. Now 'this' was a great distraction.

"Yes, I'm here. I have a friend with me."

"Hi," Ashley said, and there was silence for a heartbeat too long, making the silence awkward.

"Hi, back. Maybe this is a very appropriate time for me to catch you, Kes."

"Oh really, and why is that, Trev?" Kes asked. He shook his head and rolled his eyes like he was annoyed by the conversation.

"I was calling to invite you to Christmas dinner tomorrow evening. I would love it if both you and your mystery guest could attend, along with the young girl that you've taken under your guidance." There was a soft, challenging undertone to the request, and Ashley bit her lip as Kes's mouth fell open.

"Keeping tabs on me, old friend?" Kes said 'friend' like the word was bitter on his tongue.

"No more than you do of me, 'friend.'"

"Sometimes I could really…."

Ashley cut Kes off before he began threatening Trevor. "We would love to come. What time would you like us to arrive, and is there anything we can bring?" she asked, and then had to bite her tongue to stop from laughing as Kes's exasperated expression turned in her direction. He kept waving his hands like he was trying to tell her 'no,' but she had this sudden urge to meet someone that obviously knew him before he came back into her life.

She had a lot of unanswered questions. Ones like…how does someone homeless own an expensive Hummer, and what exactly did Zumi mean by he protects those like her? She had a feeling that at this dinner she might just get the answers she was after because Kes was guarded and had already danced around a couple of her questions regarding his past.

"Well now, it's settled. I will see the three of you tomorrow around six o'clock. There is nothing for you to bring, my dear, but I appreciate the offer. Besides you're brining Kes. I'm sure he would've avoided the meal altogether, let alone offer to bring something."

Kes laid his forehead on the steering wheel as he whispered a blue streak that once more made Ashley want to smirk.

"I'm Ashley, by the way, and we'll see you tomorrow at six. Thank you so much for the invitation. We didn't have any plans, so this will be really nice."

"Excellent, I look forward to it, Ashley. Have a good evening, Kes, and don't think I don't hear you swearing." Kes lifted his head, his lips pursing like he was gearing himself up for a meltdown. "Maybe with Ashley's delightful presence, you'll finally learn that a cave is not the best place to dwell. I like her." The line went dead before Kes could say another word.

His glare found her, and instead of being scared, she laughed until her sides hurt and tears were blurring her vision. Whoever this Trev was, she already liked him. Anyone that could get under Kes's skin so thoroughly needed a freakin medal.

# CHAPTER 29

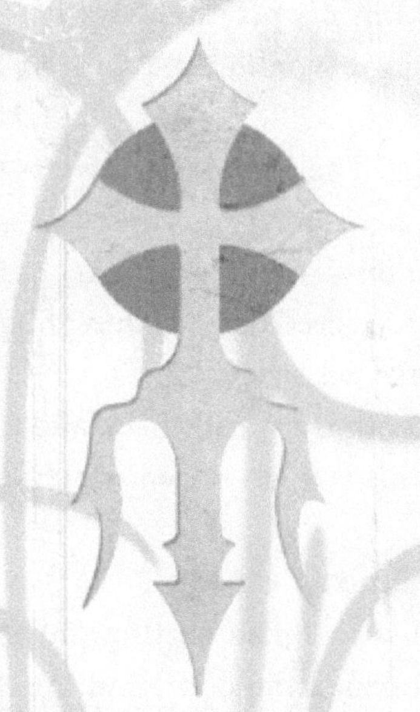

Trev stared at the large table with the ten table settings and couldn't keep the smile off his face. This was not something he'd allowed himself to dream about for a long time, but J.J. squealed as he ran past, closely followed by Simone, who was demanding that he give her phone back, and his heart warmed.

Trev's life had gone from orderly to chaotic, but it was a different kind of perfect. As J.J. went by once more, he snatched the adorable thief up who let out a loud screech like he was a miniature pterodactyl.

"Hi, Uncle Trev," he said in the cutest voice possible, his big brown eyes begging to be let free to cause more havoc.

Simone came to a panting halt and bent over as she rested her hands on the pretty red dress she was wearing. "He took my phone," she gasped.

"No, I..." J.J. started, but Trev gave him a hard stare, and J.J. sighed, giving up the lie as he held out the phone.

"Say you're sorry, J.J.," Trev prompted softly.

"It was only for fun. I wouldn't hurt it," he pouted, his bottom lip sticking out.

"That's not the point. The phone is not yours to take, and Simone has pictures of her and her father on there. If something accidentally happened, how do you think that would make her feel?"

He watched as J.J. pondered his question. "She would be sad."

"Do we want to make her sad?"

J.J. shook his head enthusiastically back and forth just as the doorbell rang. He placed J.J. on his feet but stared at him until he crossed his arms and sighed.

"Fiiiine. I'm sorry, Simone."

He left the two kids to finish sorting out their issues so he could answer the door. He opened the door, and for the first time since they served together, Kes was not wearing something that looked like it was pulled out of a dumpster.

Kes's hand was protectively wrapped around who he presumed was Ashley, and a dark-haired girl with large doe-like eyes peeked out from behind Kes. At first glance, anyone would've said they made an adorable family. That was, until you took in the scowl that was on Kes's face.

"Welcome, I'm Trev. You must be Ashley." He held out his hand for Ashley to shake, and her smile was sweet as she returned the gesture. She gave off a vibe of warmth and tranquility, and he suddenly understood why Kes was drawn to this woman. For as long as Trev had known Kes, his soul had been a turbulent sea that was always at odds with itself. This woman was like a lighthouse in a storm and the perfect fit to tame the waters.

"Yes, I am. I'm Kes's...." She paused and looked to Kes, and her mouth fell open as if the right words were lost to her.

"Ashley is my girlfriend," Kes filled in, raising Trev's eyebrows with the firm proclamation.

Ashley seemed equally shocked by the announcement but hid it and recovered quickly. "The pleasure is mine. It's nice to finally meet a friend of Kes's."

"Likewise." Kes had always been more of a loner and was definitely not the type to place a label on anyone. If he called you friend, brother, or girlfriend, it was the equivalent of saying 'this person is mine and fuck off.' This meant Ashley was important, and Trev was more intrigued than ever to learn more about the woman that managed to lasso the flighty Kes.

He turned his attention to the young girl that looked to be around Simone's age despite her petite size. "You must be Zumi."

The young girl looked up to Kes and he nodded, indicating it was safe to speak. Quite the interesting dynamic indeed.

"Yes, I am." The girl held out her hand for him, and he made sure to give her as firm a handshake as she offered.

"Well, come on in. Some are in the kitchen, others are still getting ready, but we should still be on time for dinner." Trev stepped out of the way for the three to make their way into the hallway.

"It smells amazing in here," Ashley said, then gave Kes a sharp poke with her elbow.

Kes rolled his eyes but cleared his throat. "Yes, it really does. Thank you for inviting us to dinner."

"Hmm, you're still a terrible liar, but at least you brought two enjoyable guests," Trev said, giving Zumi a wink as she snickered.

J.J. and Simone ran toward the kitchen as Sally called out that the hors d'oeuvres were served. J.J.'s feet skidded to a halt, and Simone almost collided with him as he looked Zumi up and down. She crossed her arms and stared back like she dared him to make a rude remark.

The corner of Trev's mouth turned up as J.J. smoothed the front of his shirt and fixed the Christmas suspenders he was sporting before he raised his chin and held out his hand. "Hi, I'm J.J., do you want some or-herves?" J.J. asked, and Zumi smiled.

"I think you mean hors d'oeuvres," she answered as she shook his hand.

"Meh, my word is better," he said, and then he yanked on her arm as he took off running. He was practically dragging Zumi behind him.

"I'll be a monkey's uncle," Arek said as he sauntered down the hallway. 'This should be interesting,' he thought as Arek opened his mouth again. "Well, if it isn't Bird Boy."

"Don't call me that, Arek," Kes warned, his voice low and threatening as the two stared one another up and down like two prizefighters might.

Trev cupped Ashley's elbow and very gently pulled her away from Kes's side. Confusion crossed her face as she looked up at him, but he didn't offer an explanation. She'd find out soon enough. Arek and Kes had always had a special relationship. It was much akin to a powder keg and a match.

"You're just as crusty as ever, I see." Arek rolled his eyes as he struggled to get the button done up on his sleeve. "I'd say you need to get laid, but it looks like that's not helping improve your sunny disposition either. Then again, maybe she's smart enough to hold out. I mean, I don't know anyone that would willingly want to touch your snake-bitten ass." Arek crossed his arms and gave Ashley a flirtatious wink. Trev knew he was doing it solely to get under Kes's skin, and it definitely had the effect he was gunning for.

Kes practically growled as he took a step in Arek's direction. "And you have just as big of a mouth as ever, you arrogant dick."

"At least I have one. Has yours rotted off yet from living on the streets like a rat?" Arek matched the aggressive step toward Kes.

"Has anyone sacrificed their life for you recently?" Kes bit out, taking another step closer, and Arek's nostrils flared with rage.

"I don't know. Have you crashed and left anyone to die lately? How are you sleeping at night?"

"About as well as you, I'm sure."

"Ringo screaming your name still dancing in your mind?"

Arek balled his fists, and Trev could feel the breaking pointing coming. The tension was thick in the air.

"You would bring that up, you son of a bitch," Kes roared and leaped at Arek.

The two men rolled backward into the living room like a pair of bears, their fists flying.

"Oh my god," Ashley gasped and covered her mouth as Arek cracked Kes across the face with a right hook, only to be flipped onto his back and receive the same treatment.

"Come, Ashley. I'll take you to meet the others and show you around while they sort this out." Trev gave her a gentle tug to guide her from the hallway, her expression one of wide-eyed alarm.

"But, will they be okay?"

Trev glanced at the two as they tumbled across the room and smashed into the living room table, sending everything crashing to the floor with a wild, animal yell.

"Yes, this is foreplay for them."

"Oh, okay," Ashley said as he led her into the kitchen.

"Can we go watch, Uncle Trev?" J.J. asked a little too enthusiastically as more crashing and yelling could be heard.

Trev sighed as he shook his head. No, he should've known there wasn't any point in telling Arek to behave himself. That always back-fired. Who was he kidding? They were always going to do this, no matter what.

# CHAPTER 30

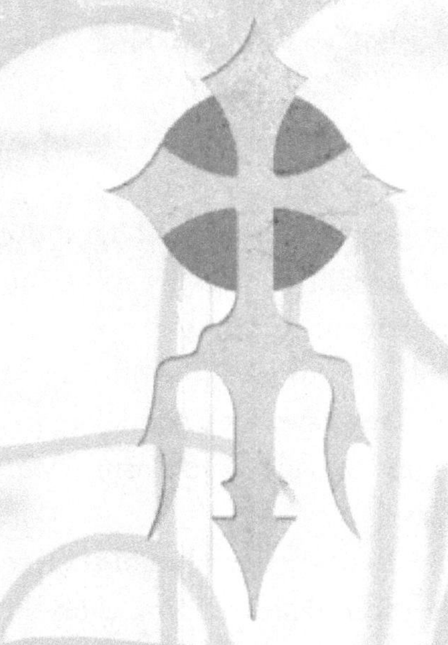

*K*es winced as he took a sip of his wine and the split in his lip screamed. Fucking Arek and his big fucking mouth.

Ashley laughed beside him, and he glanced over to see her fully engrossed in a story that Cody and Renee were telling her. He had no idea what it was about—he'd tuned out most of the conversation—but he simply couldn't remain angry with her around. Besides, it had been delightful teasing his beautiful doll all evening. Stroking her thigh had earned him a heated glance that would've melted his fucking panties off if he wore any.

The two women laughed again and began fawning all over Arek's tiny spawn. Kes couldn't believe that fucker was a dedicated father. He wasn't sure if it pissed him off more or less that Arek had gotten his shit together before he did.

"Can I?" Ashley asked, the joy in her voice infectious.

"Of course, here." Renee handed over the bundled-up little boy in the camo blanky, and Kes couldn't stop staring at Ashley's elated expression as she made that baby talk that only women seemed to know how to do naturally. Well, at least in his experience. He hadn't seen his father even once treat him like he was anything other than the chosen sperm to take over the family billions.

Kes glanced up at Arek, whose eyes were glazed as they remained glued on his son. The stupid little smile on the guy's bruised face had him wondering what it might be like to be a dad. It was a ridiculous notion—there was no way in any hell he was cut out to be a father, and yet, as Ash rocked the tiny boy, his heart seized for a beat in his chest. He blinked and looked away as the bitterness reached up and grabbed him from the dark reaches of his soul. His hand had clenched in his lap when Ash's fingers slid down his arm, and his body relaxed.

"You okay?" she mouthed silently.

He tucked a stray piece of hair from her delicate updo behind her ear and stared into the sweet blue eyes that could wash away all his pain with just a look and nodded. She looked stunning in her red dress—the shimmering material clung to every curve and had a low, sweeping neckline that was driving him wild.

A loud crash followed by laughter had everyone turning to see the life-size Jenga game scattered on the floor. Kes smiled widely as Zumi laughed with the other two children. This was something she never got to do—to simply be a child, to not worry about a meal, to dress up and feel more than fear or responsibility. Ashley had taken it upon herself to go shopping and buy Zumi an outfit for dinner. When Zumi had seen the dark green dress and black patent shoes, he thought she was going to cry. He'd never seen her so excited.

Ashley laughed at a story Cody was telling, and he couldn't stop staring at her. She was incredibly sweet and caring person who put everyone else first, and on top of that, she put up with the likes of him. He couldn't wrap his head around why she was the one that ended up with this debilitating disease. Why not himself? He'd been a fucking prick most of his life—if anyone deserved to have that happen, it was him. She didn't, she didn't deserve any of it.

As if sensing he was in the middle of another mental self-destruction episode, Ashley turned her body slightly and leaned into him so her back touched his chest. He sighed and wrapped an arm around her shoulders. He wanted nothing more than to find a corner and curl up with her.

Kes could feel Trev's eyes on him, and he looked up to lock eyes with the man that he respected more than anyone else on the planet, regardless of how much he liked to pull his chain. For all his perfection and arrogance, there was a kindness to Trev that most never saw. Kes cleared his throat and had to look away from the intense stare of the man as he gave him a small nod. It was so slight no one else would've picked up on it, but Kes could feel the emotion clogging his throat. Even though they were the same age, it always felt like Trev was so much older—he had this way about him that made everyone feel safe, and that as long as he was in charge, they'd all make it out alive.

"Well, everyone, if you don't mind moving into the sitting area for coffee and dessert, I do need to steal Arek, Cody, and Kes for a few moments, but we won't be long." Trev stood from the table, and everyone followed suit.

Kes chuckled to himself as he stood from the table and gave Ashley a kiss on the cheek. "Well, that all seemed very Godfather-like," Kes said as the door closed on the office. "Let's all go to the office to discuss matters of death and destruction."

"Well, I hope it doesn't come to that," Trev said as he leaned against his desk. "Would anyone like a drink?"

"Do you even have to ask?" Arek jumped up from the loveseat to retrieve his drink alongside Cody, but Kes waved off the offer.

"Alright, I wanted to make sure we spoke briefly as I've been hearing grumblings that the verdict could come down next week."

"How do you know that?" Kes asked.

Trev smirked as he sipped his drink. "I have my ways. It would be best for you to know as little as possible. The point is that I need to make sure we are all ready to do our parts."

"I'm ready whenever. I've already scoped out the route and hidden my supplies nearby for go time," Kes said.

"Always the go-getter," Arek said.

Before he could snipe back, Trev spoke. "Enough, Arek. You and Kes can cock fight another time, I'll even buy you spiked collars for your dicks for the occasion, but right now, we need to focus." Kes was shocked when Arek listened, even though it looked like he had to bite his tongue off to do it.

"I'm ready as well," Arek said, crossing his arms.

"Are you sure that I can't do anything to help?" Cody asked.

"No, you will be in the courtroom with me, and it will seem suspicious if you are not there when you've been by my side the entire trial. We will make sure to stay and keep the news people on us with a perfectly-scripted rant about the injustices of the court system and how they are sending an innocent woman to jail."

"Are you that certain the verdict is going to come back guilty? I mean, can't you bribe one of the jurors or something?" Kes asked.

"I could, but considering that whoever is behind this has been one step ahead of me, I don't dare do what would seem the most likely. It would be easy to prove that I paid someone off. Most individuals are weak enough to cave under questioning. No, it is better that we keep this as a bag-and-go. Morry will have to take care of the rest once Maeve gets back to her."

"Is that it?" Kes asked, stretching as he stood.

"There is one more thing. Arek, what have you done with Spike? The man has been underground and completely silent for far too long to simply be hiding."

Arek held his arms out, his face the perfect image of shock. "Why are you asking me?"

"Please, Brother. We both know you'd love nothing better than to dig a hole and bury that man in it. Just tell me, is he still alive?"

"I swear I have no idea," Arek grumbled.

Kes couldn't hold it back any longer and laughed. "He didn't make him disappear, Trev. I did." All eyes turned in his direction, and he shrugged. "The guy had no useful information about the Golden Dragons other than the fact they ship the product from Mexico, and he thought that the person pulling the strings here was some rich guy. His phone was full of low-level dealers for the drugs, but he did prove useful for the trafficking hunt I'm on."

"See, it wasn't me. I always get blamed," Arek said, shooting a glare in his direction.

Trev rubbed his eyes. "And you didn't think this would be a good thing to mention to me?"

Kes shrugged again. "As I said, he had no useful information, and now, he's swimming with the fishes," Kes said, putting on his best Godfather impression.

"How did I ever put up with the two of you for so long without killing both of you?" Trev bit out as he glared between him and Arek.

"Why am I getting lumped in with him again?" Arek whined.

Trev lifted a brow at his brother but didn't bother to answer the question. "Let's go. I need dessert and then a little more dessert." Trev's eyes flicked to Cody and there was no denying the heated stare, and that was Kes's cue to get the hell going.

He stood, but a drawing on Trev's desk caught his attention, and he walked forward, picking up the large photograph. "Why do you have this?"

"Do you recognize it? I've been searching all the databases but can't find this spider image."

"Yeah, I do. You guys should as well." Kes turned it around and held it up to Trev and Arek. "You don't see it, do you?"

"If I did, I wouldn't still be looking. Please, just tell us," Trev insisted.

"Give me a marker." Kes held out his hand and accepted the black marker. Popping off the cap, he drew what he could remember around the image until it looked like the tattoo he'd seen more than once. He held the image up again, and it was Arek that recognized it first.

"Well, slap me silly and fuck me twice. How did we not see that?" Arek asked, his eyes wide. Arek looked to Trev, who still didn't seem to recognize the intricate symbol. "Brother, that's Dean's symbol. Well, his family's cartel symbol. Don't you remember the tattoo on his forearm? He said the first thing he was going to do when he got out of the Sandbox alive was to have it colored over and changed into something else, because he never wanted to see it again."

"The question then becomes, why is it not coming up in the database?" Trev asked as he looked to all the eyes in the room.

"Like none of the databases?" Kes asked.

"I have sent it to The Righteous line multiple times and I either don't get a response or they come back saying it doesn't exist."

"Shit," Arek muttered.

"Is this bad?" Cody asked as he looked at their worried faces.

"Yes, unfortunately, this is very bad. I think we have a much bigger problem on our hands. Until further notice, only those in this room, Wolf, and Morry can be trusted, and no one relies on anything they get from HQ."

Kes leaned against the desk and crossed his arms over his chest. "What do you think is going on?"

"I honestly don't know, but...." Trev poked the picture lying on the desk. "Until we find out, it's better to be safe."

# CHAPTER 31

"Hang on," Kes yelled. The alarm continued to scream like a demon in his ear as they spun like a child's toy through the air. The black sky was disorienting, and he couldn't tell what end of his asshole was up. Every muscle strained as he tried to keep the bird from dropping like a stone and blowing them all to smithereens. The spinning would've turned his stomach if he wasn't so focused on them not dying.

With a roar, he pulled on every ounce of strength he had, and by the grace of luck, he slowed the spinning enough to see the sand and a decent spot to crash land. Anywhere on his left side of the window was better than the jagged terrain on the other side.

*"Oh, when they call me home," Ringo sang through the headset. "There's a man in a black coat standing at a crossroads."*

*Kes glanced over at his friend, and although he couldn't see his face behind the visor, he could feel his terror as they continued to drop from the night sky. There was a sudden lurch like the helo just got her tail yanked back, and then they dropped with such force that his teeth slammed together. Without their belts on, they would've been plastered to the roof.*

*There was a moment of stillness where there was no regret and no fear. They weren't falling or spinning, and the alarm wasn't screaming in his ear. In the calm between one breath and the next, he saw Ashley smiling at him. Her blue eyes sparkled in the dark, her blonde hair flowed like a fantasy as she mouthed the words, 'I love you.' She seemed so real, and he had the urge to reach out and touch her. He wanted to draw her in to his body and never let go, and then, with the next blink, she was gone.*

*"Oh fuck," he mumbled as the image of dancing orange flames reflected back at him in the windshield.*

*"We're on fire," Jimmy screamed from the back. Until Jimmy spoke, Kes had assumed the man had been tossed out the open door. "Sit the bitch down, Kes!"*

*"What do you think I'm trying to do?"*

*He braced his legs against the floor of the bird and pulled back as hard as he could to keep the nose up as they tumbled the final however many meters to the waiting sand below.*

*The crash was sudden. One moment, they were dropping, and the next, they just stopped. The jarring motion ripped his hands free from the stick as the windshield exploded in front of him. He became nothing more than a rag doll at God's command. The helo made a sickening, crunching sound like the metal itself was screaming as they skidded along the ground and then flipped and rolled with the momentum. Sand was flying around the cockpit, blinding him further like they were in the middle of a desert sandstorm.*

*And then all went black.*

*He could hear screaming and someone yelling his name, over and over. The words, 'help me, Kes,' were like those of a ghost's whisper inside his fuzzy mind as they combined with the continuous ringing. He blinked as his body jerked, the straps that were holding him released, and then he was moving. A thought crossed his mind that it could be God or the Devil taking him home. He didn't know which one would want his soul, but he had a feeling that the Devil would win out in the end.*

*The screaming was louder now, a high-pitched shriek that broke through the haze and had his eyes darting around to find the source. Ringo's smashed visor and one of his eyes were all he could see of his friend as his brain pieced together the mangled scene in front of him.*

*"No," he yelled and reached for Ringo, who was reaching for him. Their fingertips brushed but once, and then he was pulled further away. "No, Ringo!" Ringo's hands continued to reach for him, his only chance, even as the flames consumed the man's body. The stench of burning flesh was a rancid acid in his nose as the wavering flame claimed its prize. "Ringo," he wailed as he struggled against whatever had a hold of him. His ass thumped hard on the ground, and he winced as the pain registered for the first time. He let out a blood-curdling sound, the horrifying noise echoing inside his helmet.*

*Tears streamed down his face as he was dragged backward on his ass, and with every passing second, his brain registered a little more. The tail rotor being hit, the crash, the mangled bird, the bright flames dancing against the dark night sky. His friend had been screaming for him to save him.*

*"It's going to blow. Get down," a woman's voice yelled, and a moment later, bodies covered him like a shield as a bone-shattering explosion erupted, sending a pillar of black smoke rising into the sky. Tears slid silently down his cheeks and his body shuddered as the guilt gripped him by the throat and squeezed until he was gasping for breath.*

*"Get his helmet off. He can't breathe," Trev's steady voice commanded. The strap under his chin was released and his helmet was yanked free, allowing the cool night air into his lungs. Kes stared up into Trev's and Morry's eyes, both steady even as blood and dirt coated their faces. They were calm. How could they be so calm? He just murdered his best friend.*

*"What do we do about his side?" Morry asked.*

*"We need to find someplace where we can cool it, wrap it, and then...." Trev looked to Morry, whose face was coated in blood, a wide white bandage on her face. "We keep moving, or we all die. He will either make it or he won't, but I'm praying for the latter."*

*He could hear them, but they sounded so far away. Why were they talking about unimportant things when all he could think about was how he killed his Ringo?*

*"I'm sorry, Kes, but this is really going to hurt," Morry said.*

*Nothing could hurt more than the pain in his chest. "I killed him," Kes mumbled.*

*He desperately groped for Morry's hand and squeezed it as she put her hand in his. Unable to look at them any longer, he closed his eyes. "Ringo, I'm so sorry. I'm so, so sorry," he said, then screamed as he was lifted.*

"*K*es, wake up." Someone was shaking him, the voice distant as the twisted body of the helo burned brightly behind his eyelids, Ringo's voice loud in his ears begging for help. "Come on, Kes. Wake up."

Kes's eyes snapped open, and he gasped and jumped from the bed and away from the hands touching him. He stumbled to a window that had a sliver of light shining through and gripped the wall as he tried to control his racing heart, which was pounding dangerously fast.

"Breathe."

Kes glanced over as Ashley crawled off the bed and wrapped her arms around his waist. "Shit, I'm sorry."

"Don't be sorry," her voice soothed as her lips followed with butterfly kisses along his back. He took a slow deep breath and turned in her embrace so he could hold her back. "What happened, Kes? What happened to you over there?"

He buried his nose in her soft hair and held her close—she was the lifeline that he'd always needed. "I love you," he whispered. She shivered against his body.

"I love you too."

"I can't talk about it, not yet." She leaned back, and her thumbs brushed against his cheeks like small windshield wipers as she wiped away the tears. He hadn't realized he was crying.

"Okay, but I'm here when you're ready."

There was nothing sweeter she could have said. It had been years, but the dreams felt like it just happened yesterday. He wanted to push the remnants of the screams and smells from his mind.

Cupping her cheeks, he lowered his lips and savored the feel of her lush lips. Breaking the tender kiss he stared at Ashley's closed eyes and wet lips that were so inviting and wanted a picture of her just like this. "Do we have time before we have to get ready for your appointment? Or, I should ask, is there enough time for me to ravish your body?" He bit his lip as her eyes widened, and a delicious smirk curled the corners of her lips.

She glanced at the clock and then smiled. "We have time." Ashley let out a small squeal as he scooped her up into his arms and marched for the bathroom. They needed to shower anyway, he reasoned as he sat her on the counter, which had her sucking in a sharp breath. "They need to invent counter warmers," she teased and rubbed at her arms.

"I can picture the marketing on that one." He grinned as he turned the water on and made sure it was perfect before he held out his hand for Ashley to take. She took his breath away every time he looked at her. What she saw in him, he'd never understand because she deserved so much better than him.

"Why are you looking at me like that?" Ashley asked. Those eyes like a crystal-clear ocean stared at him with concern, and yet all he felt was peace.

He opened his mouth to say something meaningless, like 'nothing' or 'just because,' but instead, he did something he hadn't done since Ringo's death, and that was sing:

*Behind the clouds, there are always rays, even on the darkest days.*
*Take my hand and take me home, take me where we used to roam.*
*When I look at you, I see a light, one that guides me through the night.*
*Take my hand and take me home. My life is yours and yours alone.*

He barely got the last note out when Ashley nearly knocked him over as she leaped into his arms. Her hands snaked around his neck as her legs followed suit around his waist. Ashley's lips crashed down on his in a rush, stealing the air from his lungs. A waterfall of hair fell around him like a curtain, as if it were closing them in together and telling the rest of the world it could fuck off. He could taste the saltiness of her tears mixed with the sweet flavor of her mouth.

He groaned into her mouth as she nipped his bottom lip, and the realization hit him that no matter how much time they had together, it would never be enough.

"Will you make love to me?" she asked, mumbling against his lips.

"Always. Whatever you want, it's yours." He kissed her lips again, unable to get enough and wanting to savor the softness. Kes sucked on her bottom lip before he let her answer.

"Fast and hard. Make me forget all about this appointment."

"I can do that."

He turned them around so her back was in the water. "Grab the top of the shower and the showerhead." Ashley reached out to do as he asked as she sucked his bottom lip into her mouth. The sensation streaked straight down his body to his cock like a jolt of adrenaline. "Oh, you naughty girl."

"For you? Always."

Gripping her hips, he guided her back and forth like she was on a swing. The soft, wet walls of her pussy felt like she was licking the head of his cock with every pass. Ashley's head fell back, her breasts pushing up into his face and giving him easy access as he thrust into her tight and heated pussy.

"Fuck, you're so wet," Kes said and then sucked a taut nipple into his mouth, drawing a gasp and shudder from her. That was music to his ears. He released the hardened peak just as he gave his hips a hard thrust and sank all the way into her hot pussy.

"Oh fuck, yes," Ashley yelled, not even seeming to notice that he'd driven her body back so she was pressed up against the cool tile.

"Shit, you're so tight and hot," he gasped out as he tried to take a moment to adjust to the pulsing walls that were making him want to blow his load early. The water streamed down his back as he pulled out and drove himself back in with as much force as he could.

"Yes, yes, yes." The serenade in his ear came with every flex of his cheeks and thrust of his hips, of their skin coming together. Ashley's body smacked against the tile, their moans a crescendo together.

Kes's body flexed, a primal sound of desire ripping from his throat as he drove her toward her climax. He could feel her body jerk and twitch, and then she arched her back and yelled his name as if she were trying to yell the building down. He covered her mouth with his, swallowing the scream and muffling the sound.

He claimed her lips as he slowed his pace to give her a breather. His pulse was like a drum in his ears that matched the throbbing of his cock, which desperately wanted to release as her walls continued to tighten like a perfectly-fitting vice around his aching dick.

"Set me down."

Kes stepped away from the wall and reluctantly pulled himself from her body as he placed her on her feet. Unable to help himself, he gripped his cock and gave it a few hard strokes as he tried to reel in the painful need coursing through his body.

He jumped a little in shock as Ashley smacked the hand he was using to service his cock with enough force to make the sound echo in the shower. His hand instantly stilled as his eyes went wide with shock.

"Mine. It's your turn to hang on." Ashley nodded, and lifting her chin to indicate the door where she wanted him to grab.

It took a second to register what she meant until she sank to the floor, her blue eyes hooded with passion as she stared up at him. Holy fuck, it was the hottest thing he'd ever seen. Just when he thought it was impossible for her to be any sexier, she stared at him like that. Releasing his cock, he grabbed for the top of the shower door and showerhead, and not a second too soon. His knees shook as Ashley didn't bother with any teasing, just grasped a firm hold and sank her head down as far as she could go.

"Oh, shit," he said, the sound like a growl as it rumbled from his chest with enough swear words to make his Navy buddies blush. His ass flexed in time to the rhythm of her sucking, her beautiful cheeks hollowing out as she sucked him with enthusiastic abandon.

Ashley pulled back, and he almost cried out as she pulled it from her mouth and teased the head with her tongue. Then, she licked the droplets of pre-come from the tip. Kes's knees shook as his body demanded climax, trying to push over to the other side. Everything drew tight like one of his guitar strings as she trailed a hot line from tip to base with her tongue. The shower creaked as he pulled on the top, his biceps flexing with the force.

"Ashley, please," he begged. He didn't give a fuck if he had to get down on his knees and beg—he needed to fucking come. "I didn't realize you had so much devil in you, woman," he said as she smiled up at him.

"You always knew," she countered as she sucked first one and then the other of his balls into her mouth.

It was a good thing that he was hanging onto the glass door, or he would've been on his knees for sure as his legs turned to jelly. He laid his head back and closed his eyes, allowing every little sensation to flow through his body.

"Oh, fuck. I'm almost there."

A soft growl left his lips as he stared down at his little minx as she stopped once more. His body was right on the edge, and his hands trembled as he forced himself not to finish the job.

With a tantalizingly slow pace, she stood and used her tongue to draw a line across his abs and up to his chest until she could suck one of his nipples into her mouth.

'Fuck' was the only coherent word that tumbled from his mouth over and over as she switched to the other side and gave it the same treatment.

Splaying her hand across his stomach, Ashley ducked under his arm, and like a fucking dog in heat, he turned to follow her. Every sensible and intelligent thought stormed out the door as she bent over in front of him. Ashley's perfectly-shaped apple ass rose in the air toward him, her pussy exposed as she offered herself.

She looked over her shoulder at him, a teasing glint in her eyes. "What are you waiting for?"

The fraying thread to his sanity was severed with those five simple words. He stepped forward, his fingers digging into the soft skin of her hips as he slammed himself home. There was no waiting or adjusting. The animalistic part of his personality shoved the rational part of his brain out the door, slamming it in its wake.

He was mildly aware that Ashley had thrown out her hand to keep from crashing into the wall while his hips worked into her with a ferocity that he hadn't known he had in him. Her walls tightened around him like she was trying to choke him as she came. With a yell, she coated him. That was the final straw, and with a howl that came from the depths of his soul, he came harder than he ever had in his life. The streams seemed never-ending as he drove his cock into her over and over.

He looked to the ceiling with a silent holler as the final jet left his body.

Kes stumbled back, his legs no longer viable, and with a loud thump, he landed ass-first on the tile, taking Ashley down with him. Giving up, he laid his head back to catch his breath. Every limb was weak and useless.

Ashley laughed as she slowly flipped herself over and lay on his chest, peppering his chest with gentle kisses.

"I didn't think it was possible to love someone this much," Ashley whispered as the water fell like a rainstorm down on top of them. "It scares me, Kes, the thought of losing you."

Lifting his head, he stared at the top of hers until she looked up at him. "You're never going to lose me. Not ever again."

"Really?"

"Yes, really."

"So you'll never be hurt or die when you go out on a mission?"

"What?" he asked, swallowing the lump in his throat.

Ashley shrugged. "Zumi mentioned to me that you were not being truthful about what you do, so I did some investigating of my own at dinner last night." His eyes went wide as his racing heart thumped harder in his chest. "I'm guessing by the look on your face you were not planning on telling me what it is you really do?"

He swallowed again, his mind blank as he panicked to think of something to say. "I…I…did, but…."

"That's a no. So, here's the deal, Kes. From now on, you're honest with me, or we're going to have a big problem."

"I'll assume Renee told you?" he asked, his mind still on 'damage control' mode.

"She did. She was reluctant, said it wasn't her place to say. But when I pressed and told her about our history, she began to share. I want the whole truth from you, though, Kes. I deserve that."

He nodded. "Alright, but does this mean you're not going to run away screaming? The only reason I wasn't fully honest was because I was scared of your reaction."

Ashley made a strange little sound with her mouth that reminded him of a horse nickering as she pushed herself up off his body and proceeded to hold out her hand to help him stand. "I'm cooler than you think I am."

He wasn't sure what being cool had to do with it, but at that point, he wasn't going to argue or question. "Come on. Let's get you cleaned up and this appointment out of the way, and then I'll answer all your questions."

"Deal," Ashley said as she wrapped her arms around his neck.

"You really need to stop pressing up against me when you're all naked and wet. I have a one-track mind where you're concerned, and I will take you again."

A wicked grin spread across her face. "Maybe I want you to."

*Oh, hell yeah.*

# CHAPTER 32

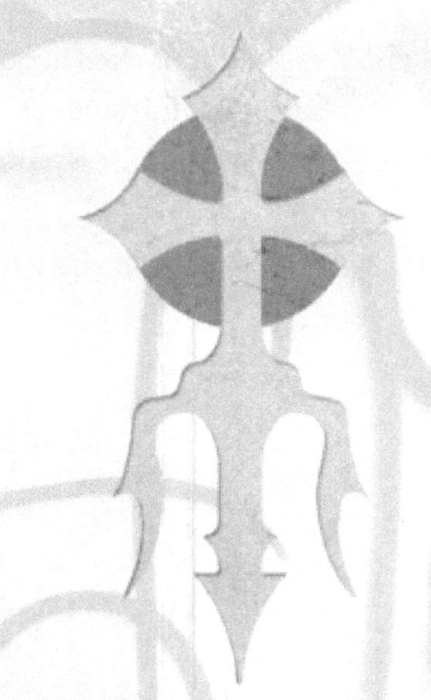

From the second they'd walked into the medical building, Kes had been on edge. He had been to the vending machine twice and paced the waiting area reading the placards under all the artwork, and now that she'd been called into the doctor's office, his knee hadn't stopped bouncing.

"Are you okay?" she asked, but the door opened and the doctor came in before Kes could answer. He nodded and put the worst fake smile on that she'd ever seen.

"Ms. Hartley, thank you for coming in so quickly," he said. A thick folder that was daunting all on its own was placed on his desk as he lowered himself into a large black chair. Dr. Pierce didn't acknowledge Kes, so she opened her mouth to introduce him, but the doctor cut her off as he stared at her paperwork.

"I want to repeat your tests and lab work. Are you able to stay for an MRI? I have an opening today."

"I'm confused. I thought I wasn't supposed to be back for a few months. Is something wrong?" Kes grabbed her hand, and although she was happy he was there, his sweaty palm and nervous energy were not helping.

"I want to switch your medication to a newer one that is having better results, especially for someone of your age. My only concern is how late you were diagnosed. You may already have too much damage to make a switch worthwhile."

"You mean this new medication may stop all the progression?"

"No, but it should slow it down significantly."

"You mean there is no way to cure her?" Kes suddenly asked, and Dr. Pierce looked at him like he hadn't even realized someone else was in the room.

"Unfortunately, no. We do not yet have a cure for MS, but we have made some good strides in giving those with the disease a long and functional life." Dr. Pierce closed the folder and laid his hands on the top cover as he addressed Kes directly.

"You don't have a cure, or you don't want to give her a cure?"

Her mouth fell open as she looked over at Kes, who'd gone from nervous to looking like he was going to kill. His jaw was twitching, his eyes focused on the doctor, reminding her of a dog snarling with its hackles up.

"I'm sorry, but I don't know what you mean?"

Kes made a scoffing sound like he didn't believe what he was hearing. "Don't give me that. You know exactly what I'm talking about—the more tests you run, the more medication you pump into her system, the fatter your paycheck gets. So I'll ask you again, you can't give her a cure, or you don't want to?" Dr. Pierce sat back in his chair, his eyes wide at the accusation.

Kes slid to the front of the seat, and she had the same feeling in her chest that she did last night with him and Arek right before they pounced on each other.

"Hey, Kes. It's okay." He didn't acknowledge she'd spoken even when she gave his hand a squeeze.

"The answer is that there is no cure. Many products will slow the disease, and the sooner Ms. Hartley is on a regiment that is best for her system, the more quality time she will have."

"What kind of time are we talking here?" Kes asked, his eyes narrowing, and she could feel a tremble radiating down to her arm. She'd never seen him like this, and she didn't know what to do to make him relax.

"I cannot give you an exact timeline. Everyone responds differently, and…."

Dr. Pierce didn't get another word out before Kes leaped from his chair. With a mighty roar, he jerked his hand away from hers and jumped to his feet. Ashley could only watch on in terror. A feral sound ripped from his throat as his hands gripped the front of the desk, and with strength she couldn't begin to fathom, he flipped the solid wooden piece upside down. The doctor barely made it up and out of his seat in time to cower against the wall like a frightened animal—his paperwork, laptop, and other items crashed to the floor.

"That's not good enough!" Kes pointed a finger at the doctor, the rage emanating off his body almost tangible. "Do you know who I am? I'll have you fired, and I'll bankrupt this place if you don't do your fucking job and find her a cure."

Kes went to step over the desk, his hands balled into fists, and Ashley quickly ran around the mess and jumped in front of him. "Stop it, Kes. Right now," she bit out angrily.

He blinked and looked down at her as her hand pressed against his chest. "Ashley, he's not doing his job."

"That's enough, I mean it." Keeping a hand on Kes, she turned to look at the doctor. "I'm so sorry, Dr. Pierce. Please excuse Kes. He's a war veteran and suffers from extreme PTSD when he's stressed. This condition of mine is very distressing for him. I will pay for any damages, of course."

The door banged against the wall as it was thrown open, making them all jump. Two large security guards filled the doorway, and Dr. Pierce's secretary was in the hall behind them. Dr. Pierce held up his hand as they took a step into the room. "It's fine. I will be right out," he said, taking a deep breath.

"I can stay for the MRI, and I have a few more questions for you, but can you please give Kes and me a few moments alone?"

"Yes, of course." Dr. Pierce kept his eyes on Kes as he stepped around them, but all the building tension had evaporated like a balloon popping, the air dissipating in the sky. As soon as the door was closed, she turned on Kes.

"What the hell do you think you're doing?" Kes's mouth fell open. "Don't give me that shocked expression. Does this look like a normal reaction to you?" She held her hand out toward the mess.

"But Ashley, you heard him, he's…."

"Don't even say it. I don't know what you have going on in your head, but I'm going to make something very clear. This disease, for better or worse, is mine to deal with. This is my body, and I can't run away from it or flip a table because I'm pissed off. Trust me—I'd fucking love to if I thought it would help. This man is my best chance at having any kind of a future, but more than that, I shouldn't have to deal with your emotions on top of mine." She bent down, picked up a picture of the doctor and his wife off of the floor, and stared at the cracked glass. "If you really want to help me, then you need to keep your shit together or you're not welcome to come with me for support. I don't need this crap, Kes. I don't need to worry what bomb is going to set you off and make you go all Tasmanian Devil tearing everything apart. I'm barely keeping my own shit together. I can't hold you up, too. At least, not here." A tear slipped down her cheek, and she wiped it away to glare at Kes. "I know you have your own demons that you're fighting and I'll always be there to support you, but not in this space. This space is my space to deal with my issue, my disease. Are we clear?"

"Ash, I'm sorry, I…."

"Are we clear?" she asked again.

"Yes, we're clear."

"Good, then we can talk about the 'whys' behind this happening later —this is what's going to happen, and you're going to do exactly as I say. I'm going to tell Dr. Pierce that he can come back in, and in the meantime, you're going to set this desk upright and apologize like a normal human being to the man that is trying to help me."

"But…."

"Ah," she cut in harshly. "I'm not done. You will apologize and tell him exactly what he did that set your PTSD off, and don't you roll your eyes at me, or I will smack that look clean off your face. I'm that angry."

Kes crossed his arms, but the expression he gave her was embarrassed and apologetic. "If you think he's doing a terrible job, then fine, you can search your heart out and find me a new doctor, but you can do that on your own time. Do not ruin this for me, Kes. I mean it. The cost is my life and my treatment with this man. Got it?" She felt like she had to make sure he agreed to everything, or she was leaving a door open for him to act out again.

Ashley made her way to the door and stopped to turn around and face Kes again. "And one more thing. I have questions that I need answered, so if at any time you think you're going to melt down again, find a door and use it."

With that, she opened the office door and stepped out into the hall to apologize to Dr. Pierce again as Kes bent over to pick up the large desk.

Ashley looked over her shoulder at Kes and wanted to hit him and hug him at the same time. Some things never changed.

# CHAPTER 33

Kes sat across from Ashley in her living room and waited for the moment that she stood up, opened the door, and threw his ass out. He'd been as honest as he could be about who he was, what he did, and what had happened to him. The sparkling tree and all of its glittering lights were such a contradiction to the dark conversation between them. Her expressions had shifted between shock and horror, and included a few tears, as the conversation progressed. There was no way to gauge which way she was leaning, and his nerves were making him sweat while his knees shook. He usually always knew what she was thinking, but her face was blank of all emotion, and he swallowed the bowling ball-sized lump in his throat as his heart pounded hard in his chest for the verdict.

She picked up the bottle of wine she'd been pouring into a glass to drink and simply put the thing to her lips. He couldn't stand remaining seated any longer and stood to stare out the window as he let her mull over what he'd dumped on her.

"How does one get involved with this group? The Righteous?"

He shrugged, not turning around to face her. "They didn't get in touch with me. Trev did. Trev, Arek and I all went through the Navy program together, but I wanted to fly and they chose to become SEALs. So for a time we didn't see one another before I got the call about the mission I told you about. He knew that I was still floundering when we got back. I had issues with what happened, and the pain meds I mentioned became a crutch for all the pain not just for my side. A fellow vet from our mission, Morry, helped get me clean. Anyway, Trev called and mentioned the group approaching him and Arek. I said no at first, but I had nothing else to ground me and didn't want to lose myself again. So, after some thought, I decided I could be useful again." He shook his head and watched as a line of cars passed below on the street, some swerving around others in their haste to go to places unknown. "Now, being a part of the group is as natural as breathing. I love my work."

"You love your job of killing people?"

"When you say it like that, it sounds a lot worse."

Ashley slid back on the couch and closed her eyes. "When Renee said you guys hunted down and punished criminals you were after, I never contemplated you were all Mafia-style killers. I mean, how does a lawyer get away with it?"

Turning to lean against the window, Kes stared at Ashley, and he grinned. "You think that's bad. Dean poses as a priest and Wolf is a U.S. Marshal." As her glare found him, he wiped the look away. "Ashley, there is nothing I can say to make this any easier to understand. The people we hunt are those that the law can't lock up or find, so we do it for them. We hide in plain sight and in places that give us access to those that are the worst form of predator."

"Who do you hunt? You said that you all hunt terrible people. Who do you go after?"

He hated this. He wished he could've kept this secret from her. It was a massive weight to bear, and with everything else she had going on, the last thing she needed to be worried about was keeping The Righteous a secret.

Sighing, he answered, "Traffickers, mostly. I find dirtbags that illegally import or steal homeless off the street. I free the girls or boys into a program to give them a real life here in this country if they don't want to go back home. I kill those involved and gain information about other cells working across the country. I've had to help Trev and Arek the odd time, but not often. The only other thing I do is make sure that the pimps in the area only have workers that chose to be with them willingly and are treated with respect. Ironic, right? The bully now protects victims from bullies like I was."

"This is blowing my mind. I don't even know what to think. This goes against everything I believed about what is right."

Kes looked down at his feet. Could he give up what he did? Maybe, but the guilt of knowing what was going on in the streets under his nose would eat at him. "Would you like me to leave for now and give you some space to think?"

The question tasted sour in his mouth, and his heart sped up as he waited to hear her decision.

"That is the most screwed-up thing about all of this. I don't want you to go. I must have something wrong with my head. Scrap that. I 'know' I have something wrong with my head." Ashley stood and walked from the room, the bottle of wine dangling from her fingers.

Kes kept quiet but followed her to the kitchen, leaning against the doorframe. She placed the empty bottle in the recycling bin and pulled another from the fridge. "I feel your judgy glare. I realize I shouldn't drink this much, but I deserve it today. It's not everyday you learn the man you're in love with is some sort of assassin. Meanwhile, I also learned that if I want kids, I have to go off my meds and should do it soon, or I won't have the chance to have them at all," she gasped as she finished her mini-rant. She pulled the new pill bottle out of her purse and sat it on the counter and stared at it like a cat might analyze a new toy.

Her hand clenched into a fist, and she slammed it down with a bang, the vibration rattling the fruit bowl and knocking the pill bottle onto its side. "Shit." Ashley shook her hand, and Kes wandered over to the fridge. Opening up the freezer and finding a bag of corn, he held it out for her to use.

"Thanks." Ashley wrapped the corn up in a dish towel and laid it on her hand. "How do I know you're not going to freak out one day, and it's me that you turn on?"

"That would never happen." Reaching out, he cupped her chin and ran his thumb against her bottom lip.

"You seem so certain."

Kes stepped in close and slipped his arm around Ashley's waist, waiting until she sighed and reciprocated before he spoke. "Because I am. What I do isn't random. The meltdown today aside, I've never freaked out and simply hurt someone."

Laying a kiss on the top of her head, he stepped back and, unable to help himself, placed a chaste kiss on her lips.

"Do you really want kids?" His stomach was in knots over the idea. A dad was supposed to be someone good and decent, and he wasn't sure he was either of those things.

She shook her head back and forth and then lifted her shoulders. He had no idea what that meant and hated it when she leaned away from him to rest against the counter. Kes stared into her eyes, and there was so much emotion swirling around that he couldn't read her like normal.

"I honestly don't know, Kes. I mean, we've been together for all of a minute, and there is all the other stuff to consider. I just wish I had time to make a choice and not be rushed into it." Ashley sat down on a stool and looked exhausted. "I always pictured making that decision because I was in love and wanting a child for the right reasons. I...." She covered her eyes with one hand as tears started to flow.

Stepping in close, he wrapped his arms around her and kissed the top of her head, just letting her know he was there. "I want kids," he said, shocking himself that the words had tumbled out, but he meant it. He didn't want them with just anyone, but he could picture a family with her.

"What?" Ashley leaned back and he cupped her face, kissing away the tears still slipping down her cheeks.

"If you decide you want kids, I'm in. Unless you decide you can't be with me, because of what I do. But, I don't think it's too soon. As far as I'm concerned, we've never been apart. I'd marry you tomorrow if you wanted. If you want to move in together, I will. You want kids, then I want them too. All I wish for is us—you can decide how fast and how much, just know if you choose to go forward and start trying, then I'm all in."

"I...I...."

Kes leaned down and kissed her lips, stopping her from whatever she was going to say. "You don't have to give me an answer right now. I'm actually going to go for tonight. You need time to think, and I should check on Zumi." He reached out and grabbed the pad and pen she had on the counter and scribbled out his number. "If you need to reach me, that's my cell. Call anytime—I don't care if it's to come kill a spider, I'll be here."

She gave a little laugh, and it was good to hear that sweet sound. "I love you, Ashley." He kissed the top of her head and then walked toward the front door.

He was reaching for the handle when Ashley called his name. Looking back, his eyes locked with hers. She bit her lip but didn't say anything more.

"I know," he said. Her eyes were filled with the unspoken emotion. "But I love you more," he teased and smiled. "I want you to know that if you decide we are done, I won't pressure you to change your mind. I won't sneak in here or follow you around. You can live your life without worrying that I will be around the next corner like a nightmare you can't shake."

"I wouldn't think that of you."

"I just wanted you to know."

He waited in the hall until he heard her lock the door and then wandered down the stairs and out into the afternoon sun. He pulled up the hood on his sweatshirt and jogged across the street as his phone rang.

His heart skipped a beat until he saw it was Trev, not Ashley calling him and asking him to come back.

"Hey," he said, after pressing accept.

"I just got the call. The verdict is in."

"I'll be ready," he said and hung up the phone. It was game time, but first, he needed to check on his tent and, of course, on Zumi.

Kes nodded to Momma G, who was sitting near the entrance, her shopping cart by her side as always.

"You fix bad wheel?" She pointed to the wheel on the shopping cart that had been causing her issues.

"Maybe," he said, giving her a smirk.

"You do too much," Momma G called out to his back.

"We're family, Momma G," he said as he wandered past her perch.

Right about now, he would give anything for Ashley to call and tell him that . He couldn't shake the look of shock on her face when he told her exactly what he did for The Righteous, but there was no point in worrying about it. He wanted her more than anything, but he couldn't stop helping those that needed him. Maybe it was a hero complex, or perhaps he'd simply grown to love the hunt and the kill, but whatever it was, it was the one thing he couldn't give up for her. He'd burn the motherfucking world down for her, but he couldn't give up The Righteous. He hated to admit it, and he would never admit it in front of Trev, but the shit kept him sane.

He wandered past Zumi's tent, but she wasn't outside despite the time. He didn't hear anything coming from inside, so he continued to his own tent. He never worried about his stuff, but it was wise not to leave it alone for too long. He unzipped the faded material and looked around at the sparse belongings. The only thing he'd even want to take if he left was his guitar. He hadn't picked it up since Ringo died, but he couldn't leave it behind.

A soft rustling sound had him turning to see Zumi step out of her tent. Kes started to smile but stopped as he spotted the dark purple mark on her cheek and her eye all swollen. His fist balled as the anger flowed through his body. He was going to kill the fucker that hurt her.

He marched out of his tent toward the girl, and her eyes went as wide as saucers as she saw him stomping in her direction, his long strides eating up the distance. She turned like she was going to try and bolt. "Don't even think about it, Kid." She looked down but slowly turned to face him. "Who did this to you?"

"No one."

"So you tripped and fell into a fist? That's a new one." She crossed her arms and gave him a glare before she looked away again. "I mean it, Kid. You tell me who did this."

"No, 'cause you'll hurt them."

"And what the fuck do you care if—," he stopped as the lightbulb clicked on. "Your mother. She did this, didn't she? Why did she hit you, Zumi?" She sucked on her bottom lip and tried hard to delay the inevitable, but he wasn't having any of the silent treatment. "Okay, fine, don't tell me. I have other ways to find out, and I'll start by going straight to the source." He didn't get two strides before Zumi was yanking on his arm.

"No, please don't hurt her."

"Why do you fucking care so much about her? All she does is hurt you and leave you alone. She forces you to take care of her ass when it should be the other way around. I don't get it."

"Because she's still my mother, and she's all I have," Zumi said, letting go of his arm. "She's all I got, and I'm all she has."

"That's not true. You have me."

Zumi's eyes lifted to his, and the pain in them was like a stab to the gut. "No, I don't. Not really. You could leave at any time, and don't lie and tell me you can't. You have this whole new world with Ashley, who I really like for a Dweller, but it's not my life. This is my life." She pointed to her tiny tarp home and the others like it. "You'll choose to leave, and I get it. I'd leave, too, if I could. But when you go, my mother is all that will be here, and besides, she needs me."

"There are so many things wrong with that sentence, but we'll have to talk about it later. I have a job I've got to go do, and I need to get going. Stay in my tent. Keep hidden. If she comes home high again, we'll figure something out." Zumi shuffled her feet back and forth, and he knew she was trying to be tough, which would mean she'd take the beating on principle alone. "I mean it, Kid."

Taking an exaggerated breath, she sighed and nodded. It was as good as he was going to get. The kid was as stubborn as an ox.

"Oh, and there's a knife under the pillow—use it if you have to." He marched out of the tent alley and passed Momma G, who was humming a tune he didn't recognize. Now he just had to convince himself not to kill Chelsea when he saw her again. Regardless of what Zumi said, he was fucking tempted.

There was one thing he hated more than traffickers: a parent who hurt their kid.

# CHAPTER 34

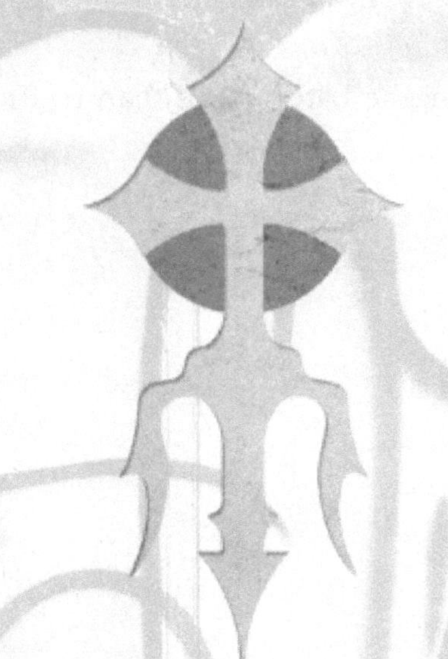

*K*es blended in with the darkening sky, his mask and black fatigues helping him become one with the shadows. Not that he had much to worry about in his current location. It was a part of town that people just didn't seem to go to—he'd often wondered if there were ghosts or something that scared everyone off because people avoided the area. But during the day, it was a lovely spot.

He stuffed the little earpiece into his ear and waited for Arek to say that things were a go. Pulling out his phone, he saw he didn't have any waiting messages. He was tempted to text Ashley, but he had promised to give her space.

"Fuck," he mumbled as he stuffed the phone back in his pants. He hated waiting—he hated a lot of things, but waiting was near the top.

"Alpha One, checking in," Arek said a few moments later.

"Why do you get to be Alpha One?"

"'Cause I'm better looking," came back Arek's reply, making him smirk. Still the arrogant prick, but there were few he'd trust more out there.

"We'll have to agree to disagree on that one. I'm in position." Kes looked up at the old bridge and then along the road as he pictured what was soon to come play out.

"Package is loaded, and party favors are in place. Following now."

"Ten-four."

The idea was simple, not much different than the smash-and-grabs the guys had done a thousand times. This would be his first. Being the exfil point, he always got them the fuck out of Dodge at the end of the line, but this required more than one person, and Trev would have to remain at the courthouse. He was right. He and Cody needed to be on camera front and center, pleading to the hearts of America so that no one could say they might be involved.

"Cargo has been diverted past the second blockade to your direction," Arek relayed. The truck's normal route would bring it near the bridge, but with a few carefully-created diversions, they would have to be rerouted into their trap.

Nothing quite like purposely busting the water mains to flood a street or setting a few cars on fire to make it a productive Thursday. He smirked and shook his head as he pictured Ashley's face. If she only knew what he was up to tonight. Most women worried about their men cheating. She had to worry about whose throat he was slitting. He scratched his chin as he wondered how that would do in a poll of 'worst boyfriends.' He knew he would at least rank a rung about the asshole that hit her. One of these nights, that man was going to find himself strapped to a chair while he had a little chat with him.

He checked the fancy new toy that Trev had given him to make sure the dual chambers were loaded and pulled his hood into place.

"Five minutes out," Arek said into his ear, and he tapped the button on his phone to get Baby Doll to do her part and make sure the light stayed red for cars coming this way. There were no cameras in this area, which made for an added bonus—one less thing to worry about. It always drew attention when they had to black out blocks at a time, not that Arek ever cared about that. He leaned against a column decorated with an assortment of graffiti and stared across the way at a life-like multicolored tongue that had more miniature rainbows than he could count, but it was the equally life-like group of faces that had been mixed into the artwork that made it so unusual and unique. Every time he looked at it, he saw a new face, a new emotion. The large support columns gave him the perfect hiding spot, with dark corners and the poor lighting casting long shadows.

He glanced up and down the road, which had remained dark and empty. This part of the bridge didn't have an access ramp to get on or off, which meant if they stopped the meager amount of traffic that happened to wander in their direction, they wouldn't have to worry about any unsuspecting witnesses.

"Two minutes."

Kes cracked his neck and rolled out his shoulders. A flash of light began to illuminate the far side of the underpass, and he peeked around the edge to see the armored prisoner transport. He was surprised it wasn't a bus. Usually, they reserved those trucks for the guys that would like to eat your face off while you were still breathing.

"Blowing wheels now," Kes said. He hit the button for armed, and then the red button on his phone connected to the small charges Arek had managed to slip into the wheel wells of the truck. The first bang was followed closely by a second one as the charges blew out two of the tires. Kes could make out the driver of the truck frantically trying to keep the armoured vehicle from flipping or hitting the center median as sparks flew in every direction from the bare rims. The loud screeching of metal on the pavement echoed along under the bridge, making a sound like a train was breaking down instead of just a truck.

"Baby Doll, intercept target's transmissions."

"Interception established."

Arek's Hummer roared up behind the armored transport as he stepped out from the shadows of the bridge. The lights of the truck were bright in his eyes as he lifted the gun and took aim at the windshield. The truck jerked and sputtered as it came to a slow stop a few feet away from him. The two guards inside held their hands up. He doubted highly that they would've been nervous about moving this prisoner or having someone try and break out one seemingly lowly girl.

He fired the first round, which punched a hole the size of a pop can into the center of the bulletproof glass. The immense power of the gun slammed his shoulder back with enough kick to knock most people over.

"Damn," he groaned under his breath. That shit was going to leave a mark. The two guards that were manning the front of the armoured truck covered their heads and dove to the sides towards the doors and away from the projectile. As predicted, the canister hit the back wall between them and didn't try to get out until it was too late. Human instinct alone would have them thinking that inside was still better than outside with the gunman.

Kes immediately fired again with round two, which sent a can half the size through the newly-made hole to land between the two occupants. They stared at the can and then began to cough, their hands clawing for the door handles—but the sleeping agent being released into their truck was strong, and neither one ever got their door open before they slumped over.

"Baby Doll, locate tracking device."

Kes could hear Arek working at the truck's back door and the small banging sound as the explosive blew open the lock on the thick metal doors. He slipped under the vehicle as Baby Doll conveyed the information about the hiding spot and then relayed the step-by-step of how to remove the tracking system. He went to work, and as he pulled the final wires free, he rolled back out just as feet walked up beside him.

"Any trouble back there?" Kes asked.

"Nah, Maeve here already had the guy choked out. She took all my damn fun," Arek pouted as Maeve grinned widely like a crazy little clown. This was the first time he'd laid eyes on Maeve, and she had a wild aura to her—he could definitely understand how she was one of Morry's.

"Baby Doll, proceed to pick up." Kes held out the tracking system to Arek. "You good with this?"

"Please, give me something hard to do. I'm sleeping so far."

"Anyone else would say this was a successful mission, and you're complaining you didn't get to kill anyone?"

Arek shrugged. "When you got an itch, you need to scratch it. It's fine, though. I'm sure I can find a piece of trash somewhere on the way home."

"I like you two," Maeve said as she rocked back and forth on her feet. "Morry talks about you guys all the time, but you're even better in person," she said as her eyes roamed over Arek with a heated look that said she was picturing him naked.

Arek cleared his throat and took a step away. The fucking chicken whipped out his phone and looked at it like it had miraculously just rung. "I better get going. Say 'hi' to Morry for me when you get back."

She waved at Arek and sighed as he wandered to the truck, her eyes glued to his ass. "Fuck that is nice." She made a shiver sound and slowly turned to face him. The whole 'prison break' thing was rolling off of Maeve like it was the most normal thing in the world. She seemed to be more interested in finding a date than she did getting her ass back to Arizona. He knew all too well what Morry did to get you clean. He'd found himself addicted to pain meds by the time he was finished with his last surgery. That shit was hard to shake, and he'd seen firsthand the hard line in the sand Morry drew, but he'd been clean since and hadn't looked back, so he owed her his life twice now.

Arek turned his Hummer around and drove away just as Baby Doll pulled up. "Hop in the back and lay on the seat."

"You planning on joining me?" There was no denying the suggestive tone in her voice, but he had less than zero interest in whatever she was thinking.

"No," Kes said, closing the door as Maeve laid down. He marched around to the driver side door of Baby Doll and jumped up into the seat.

Kes hopped in behind the wheel of his girl and turned her around, heading in the opposite direction of Arek. He pulled off his mask but kept the hood in place as they drove, leaving the city and the lights of Los Angeles behind.

"It should be safe for you to sit up here now," he said over his shoulder some time later. The outskirts of the city were dark, with open land and limited lighting or vehicles. He'd purposely chosen a more back-road route to his destination over the busy freeways that left him more exposed.

Maeve sat up and crawled into the front seat. "You taking me to Morry?" Her unusual light caramel-colored eyes turned to him.

"No. We figure that whoever set this up will be expecting that move as soon as they discover you have escaped. I'm going to drop you in Las Vegas, and you'll have to make your way from there."

"Hmm, Vegas and I are not friends."

He glanced over at her. "Lucky for you, you don't have to stay long."

Maeve rubbed at her eyes and crossed her arms as she looked out the passenger window. "I didn't think Trev would find a way. I mean, Morry always talked about him like he was the best, but I thought for sure once that verdict came down, that all was lost, and I was spending the rest of my life in jail for something I didn't do."

"Do you have any idea why someone would go to this much trouble to frame you?" A lone car passed them, and for a moment, the headlights lit up the interior of the cab and Maeve looked over at him. A sad expression stared back at him before they were plunged into darkness once more.

"No fucking clue. I'm a group home kid, and other than getting into trouble with stupid shit like painting walls, getting drunk, and trespassing, I can't think of a single reason. I'm a nobody." The last part of the sentence was weighted, and he could almost feel the weight of her sadness.

A hand landed on his leg and made him jerk, his head swinging to the right to look at Maeve. She was leaning across the center console, her eyes were suddenly full of lust and were trained on his crotch like she wanted to take a bite. "What are you doing?"

"You're really sexy, and I've been locked up for months. How about we make a detour on our way?"

He grabbed her hand before she could finish sliding it up his leg towards his dick and held her arm away from him. "Taken, and my girlfriend doesn't like to share," he bit out. "Don't touch me again."

"And what will happen if I try?" she said and laughed as her other hand found his leg.

Kes slammed on the breaks, thankful that no one was on the road. Maeve, who'd yet to put on her seatbelt, slammed into the dash, her head bumping into the glass. "You'll get out and fucking walk."

The Hummer rumbled steadily, but there was no other sound as the two of them stared at one another. "Wow, I'm impressed. Most men aren't that loyal. They'd happily take me up on a quickie in the back on a dark road where no one would ever know."

He cocked a brow at her as she rubbed at the spot that was certainly going to have a bump. "Then you're obviously fucking the wrong men. Are we going to continue to have an issue?"

"No, I'm good. Still horny, but good. Whoever your girlfriend is, she's one lucky woman."

Kes wasn't sure Ashley would agree with Maeve on that one. Releasing the brake, he floored the truck, the engine revving to life. He picked up his phone and stared at the screen for what felt like the millionth time, but there were still no messages. His heart sank. Maybe it really was going to be too much for her.

# CHAPTER 35

Shit, he was fucking tired. It had been a long-ass time since he'd had to stay awake that long, and at one point, it used to be second nature. Kes rubbed his eyes. Everything was blurry as he pulled back into Los Angeles, and he had to smack himself a few times to stay awake. A freaking five-hour drive with the chatterbox from hell. Maeve was fine once she settled in and stopped staring at him like he might change his mind and fuck her. He thought for sure they were going to have to have another chat about it when they stopped for gas, and mentioned he needed to take a piss and change out of the black fatigues. For all his trouble, he ended up with an energy drink, a bag of chips, and a day-by-day account of what it was like in prison and who she had to watch out for—it was official, he was getting old.

By the time he arrived back home, he was too tired to park Baby Doll in her normal spot and instead pulled up outside the fence closest to his tented home. The sun was already bright in the sky, but he didn't care as he stepped out and yawned. He planned on sleeping until it was dark again. Kes could see Momma G pacing in front of the chain link fence, her uneven gait exaggerated with the short, fast strides. She randomly waved her hands in the air as her mouth moved, but if she was saying something, he couldn't hear it.

He was tempted to turn around before she noticed him and sleep in the truck instead. When Momma G was in a fit, she could rant for hours or ignore you completely, and it was a coin flip as to which this was. Before he could make a great escape, Momma G's eyes lifted from the line she was pacing. As soon as she saw him, she shuffled in his direction like she was trying to run. He stopped walking and glanced around, looking for any impending threat, his body instantly awake.

Momma G grabbed the front of his sweater in her fists. "You go. You help. You go, now, go, go, go." Kes had no idea what she was talking about—he gripped her arms, trying to steady her as she trembled like she was about to fall over.

"Momma G, slow down, I don't understand. Go where?"

Tears trickled down her weathered and dirty features, causing his body to shiver in response. He'd never known Momma G to cry. Despite all her pain and her head injury, the insulting comments from the Dwellers, she remained unaffected with emotions like sadness. To see her cry had his pulse pounding in his veins like the hoofbeats of a thousand horses thundering under his skin.

"They took her. She gone. You go!" Momma G yelled frantically and pushed him in the chest, pointing for him to leave.

"Who took who?"

Momma G reached into her long coat and pulled out the knife he'd left in his tent. His heart hammered as she held it out, the end stained with dried blood. "Zumi. They took her."

Kes took the knife from her hands and wrapped his arms around Momma G as she began to sink to her knees. "Who took Zumi?" he asked, trying to decipher her cryptic mind.

"Men came. Took dem both."

He assumed 'them' was both Chelsea and Zumi. "Did the men have guns?" Momma G nodded. "Did they drive a fancy car?" She nodded again. "Did Chelsea seem to know the men?" Momma G's eyes went wide as she nodded furiously this time.

"Go, you go help."

Kes jumped to his feet and ran for the Hummer, the weariness forgotten. Adrenaline coursed through his veins as he pulled the Hummer out onto the street and pressed his foot to the floor. He didn't need to change the lights to green. He knew every back alley and shortcut in this city to get where he needed to go faster than any digital tricks Baby Doll could accomplish. He was particularly familiar with the routes leading to the lairs of those that controlled the darker side of the city. There was only one person Chelsea could've pissed off enough to send people with guns to collect her, and that was her pimp.

"What the hell have you done now?" he wondered aloud.

Kes swerved around a series of dumpsters like he was doing a fucking obstacle course and had multiple horns blow at him as he flew across a street, narrowly avoiding getting hit. Baby Doll's wheels screeched, smoke rising into the air as he braked and drifted around the next corner onto a side street of Dead Man's Lane. It was the nickname among all those that lived in and worked the streets because the strip held one illegal business after another.

The bar he was after had a back entrance for the clients that were not just there to purchase a drink. The front would be closed, but he knew for a fact that the dick that held Chelsea's leash lived above the bar. He tucked the Hummer off to the side of the street and hopped out with his hoodie up. Opening the back door, he grabbed his throwing knives and made sure the one on his back moved freely in its sheath. He grabbed two hand guns and put one in the waist of his jeans at his back and the other in the front. There was no time to do a fancy gear up.

"Baby Doll, lock down all cameras in the vicinity," he said as he closed the door and marched for his destination. Kes slipped one of the small throwing knives from the sheath on his chest, carrying it in his hand with the blade pointing up his wrist.

The guard leaning against the wall having a smoke stood up straight, his hand slipping into his jacket. As Kes closed in, he wasn't wasting time, he had no idea when Chelsea and Zumi had been taken, but every minute they were in the fucker's grasp was a minute too long.

One thing that you can always count on is human stupidity. He turned to look down the alley and nodded as if he was saying 'hi.' The guard instantly turned his head to look in the same direction.

That mistake cost him his life. With a quick flick of his wrist, he turned the blade around and took aim, letting the lightweight weapon fly. The blade glistened in the morning light as it spun, finding its target. Kes's aim was perfection as the blade sank home in the man's temple. There was a moment of shock that registered on his face before everything went slack and he fell sideways, his body hitting a few empty beer cases that had been set out for collection. Without missing a beat, he grabbed the knife and pulled it free from the man's leaking temple as he drew his gun and shot the lock. The muffled sound was camouflaged by the noise of the nearby main street. Lifting his leg, he kicked out with all his strength, his boot finding the middle of the door a second after the shot.

The door banged hard into someone and bounced shut. Kes gave it another kick, and it slammed open with force this time. The guard was on his knees, hands covering his nose, which was gushing blood all over the hallway. With a hard thrust and a twist, he sank the throwing blade into the guard's eye socket. Yanking it free, he kept walking as the rage continued to build. It coiled in his system like a once-slumbering great dragon now awakened to find that its dearest treasure had been taken. Zumi was his family, and no one fucked with his family.

He rounded the corner at the end of the hall. There was a doorless entrance to the bar. Music loud enough to mask his entry thrummed and echoed, explaining why no one was running into the hallway to greet him. He could see the man of the hour sitting at the bar with a naked brunette on his lap. She looked more interested in the glass of whatever she was drinking than in the man beneath her. Kes had endured a conversation with Vance once before. It had gone a little along the lines of, 'If you mess up your girls, you rip them off, or you bring in anyone underage to work for you, I'll fucking cut your dick off and make you eat it.' Either he'd forgotten the little conversation, or Chelsea had done something to warrant punishment. The question was, why take Zumi?

He could make out the edge of an arm on either side of the door, which had to be a set of guards. Kes stuffed the gun into his jeans and opted for a second throwing knife. He twirled the special blades that he'd designed for himself until they sat comfortably in his two palms like a deadly spike sticking out either side.

Kes had no idea how many people were on the other side of that door, but it didn't matter. He'd kill every last one of them to get the answers he was after.

His jaw clenched tight and his lips pressed together in a hard line as his body coiled, and then, with a burst of speed, he bolted for the opening. With the precision that comes from slitting too many throats, he cut straight through the carotid artery on both men in one swift slice as he ran past like the devil himself was on his heels. Inside the guarded room, a couple of booths were occupied with guards relaxing while being entertained by girls that worked for that piece of shit.

Screams filled the room as he released his two blades, each one a killing blow finding its mark in a man struggling to his feet from the booths. He was fast, and he was deadly accurate. This was an art he'd perfected overseas and kept practicing like a ritual.

"What the fuck," Chelsea's pimp, Vance, yelled and jumped up, depositing the girl on his lap on her ass with a thud. She crawled away and rounded the bar out of sight.

Four guards ran in from two different directions as girls ducked and bolted for the exits. Kes pulled one of his guns and fired at the two rushing at him from the front. Confident in his aim, he spun while pulling free his longer blade from his back sheath.

"Stop, don't go near him," Vance yelled, and the remaining two guards' faces morphed into confusion as they looked between their boss and the threat that had a gun on them. "Put your guns down and back up."

Kes looked over at Vance, suspicious as to what he was trying to do. He was tempted to squeeze the trigger anyway and kill them both guards, but one of the men in the place may have taken Chelsea and Zumi, and if all the men were dead, then his fastest way to find them might die with them.

The two guards placed their guns on the floor and did as their boss asked, backing away until their backs were against the wall.

"Have you come to kill me?" Vance asked.

"Most likely," he said, his voice as threatening as the rest of his appearance. "Where are Chelsea and her daughter?"

"That's what this is about?"

"Answer the fucking question." Kes's voice came out deep and rough with the strain of his control.

"The bitch had it comin'. I sent two of my men to pick her ass up and teach her a lesson. She stole over five grand in cash and some party products. I have her on camera, and this is a business. I can't have her or any of the others making a fool of me."

"Why take the girl?"

"I know nothing about that."

Kes ground his teeth. "Where did they take Chelsea?"

"I don't know."

Kes marched across the space, his hand squeezing the large blade tight as he pictured thrusting it up into the man's jaw and not stopping until he hit his brain. "Call them now, or I will kill you."

One of the guards thought he'd be smart and dive for his gun while Kes's attention was elsewhere, or at least the guy thought it was elsewhere. Kes could clearly see the motion out of the corner of his eye, and as soon as the guy made the dive for the gun, Kes swung his gun around and fired. The man dropped dead, his hand lying on the gun.

"Jesus Christ," Vance jumped back, his back hitting the tall bar blocking his retreat.

"I'm pretty sure he's not coming to save you. Your men seem to have an issue with listening to orders. Maybe it's the men in this dump that you needed to teach a lesson to and not the girls." Kes knew he hit a nerve when Vance's eyes flared, and his lip twitched up in response. "Make the fucking call!"

Kes glanced outside to the front of the bar and the people strolling by on the sidewalk—the mirrored finish made it so no one could see the drama taking place a few feet away. The man dug around in his pocket and pulled out his phone. As soon as the pimp had the phone unlocked, Kes snatched it away from his hand. He'd never had any intention of letting Vance use his phone.

"What are their names?"

"Igor and Ricardo."

Kes glanced over his shoulder to the one girl still on a booth as he thumbed through the apps. "Be a dear and pull those knives out for me and bring them over."

He was shocked when she jumped up and, with minimal squealing, pulled the two knives from the men's skulls before holding them out like they might bite as she brought them over. Kes slipped the long knife home into the sheath along his back. "Thanks, you can go sit back down," he said, taking the two blades and wiping them off on his pants before sheathing them on his chest. He found what he was looking for, and his eyes found Vance. "I'm keeping this, and you better pray that the girl is not dead. I don't give a fuck about the mother, but if one hair is harmed on the daughter's head…." Kes stepped in close, his nose almost touching the other man's nose as their eyes locked. Fear wavered in Vance's eyes as Kes's enraged ones said more than even his words could. "I will be back, and I will hold you accountable for what they've done." Vance sucked in a sharp breath as the tip of the knife pressed into this stomach. "I will make sure you suffer. You will beg me to kill you, that much I can promise. There will be nowhere you can hide that I won't find you."

Spinning back the way he'd come, he saw a subtle flinch in the guard that was by the wall as his eyes stared at the gun.

"I wouldn't try it. Not unless you want to end up as dead as your buddy," Kes said, never slowing his stride as he stormed out the way he'd arrived. If Zumi were dead, he'd burn the whole fucking place down around them, and he'd dance on their motherfucking graves.

# CHAPTER 36

*K*es turned off the side street and onto the main drag when Baby Doll posted the route the men had taken. The beauty of a pimp—they were as paranoid about what their people were up to as the drug dealers. They always installed tracking systems on all of their employees' phones.

He flew across town, weaving his way through dark alleys and main roads to get to the new location. Each time the men he was tracking had stopped, there was a time tracker attached to the location—everything from a few seconds to a few minutes. The one he was after was the spot near part of the beach where people rarely went. It was a spot he'd ventured to from time to time, and it didn't have great access. The only reason the men would've gone there was for privacy. The thought had a cold dread filling his body.

The time stamp showed the men had already left the location, but they'd stayed there for over an hour. His heart hammered hard in his chest as his panic notched higher, replacing the fiery rage. He preferred the rage—it allowed him to think straight. The fear that was bubbling inside him threatened to break him, and he couldn't have that. He needed to stay focused. The world was a blur as he flew past, everything melting away and leaving him with Zumi's smiling face hovering in his mind.

"God, please let her be alive. You fucking owe me one. Give me this."

He pulled off the main drag onto an access road that made its way toward the private beach. Only a couple of homes were built along this stretch of road, and as he turned onto the remote access driveway, the anxiety over what he was going to find was making him sick to his stomach. The Hummer bounced wildly over the rough rocks and mogul-like mounds, but he never let up, the engine growling as it reached the mouth of the secluded beach.

His eyes scanned the short stretch of beach, and as they landed on Chelsea's crumpled form, his heart sank through the floor. Chelsea was naked, blood painting her body as it lay splayed facedown in the ocean. Her legs were still on the beach, but there was no movement, no sign of life. He'd thought about killing the woman himself so many times, and if she wasn't already dead, he might have finished the job for dragging Zumi into her mess. Off to the side, he glimpsed something dark in the sand.

"No, no, no."

Kes barely got the Hummer into park before he leaped out the door and ran for a small rise he couldn't quite see over, and his steps faltered as he took in Zumi's battered and broken body in the sand. Kes pulled his sweater off as he ran the rest of the distance and skidded to his knees in the moist sand beside her small body. Her one leg was possibly broken, and bruises lined either side of her body, her skin so pale around the dark marks.

"No, no, please no," he begged to no one and everyone at the same time.

He gripped her small shoulder and slowly rolled her over. He immediately covered her exposed body with his sweater. He was unable to look at her any closer or process what had happened to her or he was going to lose his mind. His hands shook as he placed two fingers on her throat. A large handprint from one of the men that did this marred the skin there. His fear was off the charts he could barely feel his own fingers through the shock and adrenalin, making it difficult to feel for a pulse.

"Zumi, come on, Kid. Show me you're alive."

He lowered his ear to her mouth and held his breath as he listened for any sound, his eyes watching the sweater for any sign of her chest lifting to breathe.

Swollen lips cracked and caked with sand moved slightly. His heart surged as she breathed his name. It was small, but it was enough. He wrapped her delicate frame up in his large sweater and scooped her tiny body into his arms.

Kes ran for the Hummer and slammed the front door closed, opting to hop in the back with Zumi still in his arms. "Baby Doll, destination nearest hospital, and take the fastest route," he ordered.

The light on the dash for auto-drive flicked on as the Hummer's tires spun in the soft sand, the beast of a machine spinning them in a circle and flying back out the way they'd come.

Tears filled his eyes as he cuddled the limp body to his chest. "Come on, Zumi. Please fight. You're so strong, so much stronger than I was at your age." He smoothed her dark hair away from her face as his tears dripped onto her skin.

"Baby Doll, call Ashley."

The phone began to ring, and as Ashley's sweet voice came onto the line, he lost his remaining control. "Kes? Kes, is that you?"

He tried to speak, but was only able to say half of her name before he yelled. The sound was like a roar from a wild beast as emotion gripped him by the throat. Images of Ringo screaming and reaching for him flashed through his mind like a horror movie. The scent of burning flesh was overpowering even though there was no fire. The same useless feeling blanketed him with its suffocating presence as he wailed, rocking Zumi's still form.

"Oh my god, Kes. What's wrong?" Ashley's voice was frantic—he could hear the fear, and still, he couldn't get out the words. "Baby Doll, are you there?"

"Hello, Ms. Ashley. How may I assist you?"

"Baby Doll, where are you?"

"On route to St. Jude's Hospital, time to destination is twelve minutes and thirty-three seconds."

"Baby Doll, is Kes okay?"

"I do not understand the question."

"Is Kes physically unharmed?"

"Vital signs are all stable."

"Kes, I don't know if you can hear me or what's happening, but I'll meet you at St. Jude's. I love you." The line went dead.

Zumi's body shivered in his arms, and a glimmer of hope sped through his system. He tucked the sweater in tighter around her, reached into the back hatch area to grab his jacket, and quickly wrapped her up more. He gently wiped away flecks of sand from her cheeks, avoiding the bleeding cuts and darkening bruises. One swollen eye fluttered, her dark lashes parting just enough that he could see her eyes.

"Hey, Kid. I've got you." He tried to give her a reassuring smile but knew it wouldn't reach his eyes.

"Kes," she said, her voice as gravely as the sand on her face. The corner of her mouth twitched before she winced. "I didn't stop fighting," she whispered "I used the knife." She took a wheezing breath that he didn't like the sound of. "I bit him." A small smile lifted the corners of her mouth before her eyes fluttered closed again. "I knew you'd come," she said before she passed out again.

He raised her body so he could lay a kiss on the top of her head. "I'm going to kill them, Kid. Now, you continue to fight your ass off," he whispered as the Hummer pulled into the emergency area. People stared as it came to a skidding stop. He pushed open the door with his foot and jumped out, running through the emergency doors.

"Help!" he yelled as he ran for the triage nurse. "She's barely breathing." The nurse tried to get him to calm down, but he wasn't hearing her. All he could say was 'help her' over and over as his mind continued to fry out. Boom—the sound of the helicopter exploding with Ringo inside, pillars of smoke rising into the night sky, the sound of screaming and pain, it all mixed with the present. He shook his head, trying to clear it to get out what he needed to.

A hand gripped his shoulder hard, and he looked at the hand and then into the eyes of Trev. Was this really happening, or was he a figment of his imagination, too? He blinked as Trev spoke to the nurse, and he must have been real because soon he was following along as they placed Zumi onto a stretcher and ran her down a long hall.

"Zip up your jacket," Trev said, standing in front of him. He looked down confused but realized he was still strapped with weapons. Hands shaking he did as he was told. "Does she have any health conditions?" Trev asked, and he nodded.

"Heart, something with her heart. I don't know what, she had an appointment tomorrow with a doctor."

"What's the doctor's name?"

Kes smacked at his head, wishing he could get the fucking thing to work right. "I...I can't remember."

"Come on, Brother. Come sit down." Trev led him to a small sitting area that didn't have anyone around, but he couldn't sit and instead paced the space as the image of her abused body kept running on a loop in his mind. "Stay here. I'll be right back."

"Kes?"

He turned at the sound of Ashley's voice and opened his arms as she ran to him. They clung to one another, tears falling again. "What happened?"

"They hurt her," was all he could get out before he needed to sit down and stumbled backward, his ass landing hard on the ground as his body and mind began to shut down. He looked up at Ashley as she squatted beside him and wrapped her arms around him. "I killed him," he said. "I failed her. I failed them both."

"Shhh, it's going to be okay."

A long shadow fell over Ashley and Kes, and she looked up to see Trev as he walked into the small waiting area.

"Thank you for coming. I was so scared. I didn't know who else to call other than Renee." She held Kes's head to her chest, but he seemed to have slipped into a catatonic state and hadn't said a word or moved since.

"You did the right thing. I was at the courthouse and got here not long after Kes," Trev said as he knelt beside her and reached out to lift Kes's chin in his hand. She could see him analyzing Kes's face and those eyes that remained unfocused. Trev's entire persona shifted. Gone was the mild-mannered lawyer, his face hardening and jaw setting into a firm line. "Look at me, Soldier," he practically growled, so commanding that Ashley sat up a little straighter. Kes's head lifted slightly and his eyes slowly found Trev's. "You have work to do, so I'm going to give you a few to work through your shit, but then you're getting your ass up off the floor and keep moving. Do you understand, Soldier?"

"Yes, Sir," Kes mumbled softly.

"I didn't hear you," Trev barked out, his voice taunting and on the edge of anger. His fingers squeezed Kes's chin hard enough to depress the skin and turn the area white. "What do you say?"

Ashley shivered with the tone and wanted to cower away. She wasn't sure this was the best form of therapy for someone in an obvious state of shock, but Kes stirred in her arms. "Sir, yes, Sir," he yelled, shocking her and making her body jolt.

"That's better." Trev let go of Kes's chin and signaled for her to follow him out of the room.

"I'll be right back," she said. She went to stand, but Kes wouldn't let go of her hand. "I'll be right over there. I promise I'm not leaving." She kissed his temple as his hand slowly released her own.

Trev was waiting out in the hall, his calm demeanor already back in place. She had no idea how he managed to do that, but it helped to steady her own nerves. "Do you know what happened?" she asked.

"Not much. I will need to go download the information from the AI, and then I should be able to piece it together. I do know that someone attacked Zumi, and she's not doing well." Her hands flew to her mouth as tears pricked her eyes. "Her leg is broken, she has internal injuries, and from what I was able to get from bribing the nurse, she was sexually assaulted. I'm making sure they keep me posted on every aspect of her exam, but she is going to need surgery and support. Do you know if she has any family?"

Ashley wracked her brain trying to think. "A mother, she mentioned she had a mother."

Trev sighed. "Yeah, that's not going to work. Kes filled me in once I got him in the waiting room about what happened. Zumi's mother is already dead."

"Oh my god. Well, put me down. Can you do that? I'll act as her guardian."

"No, but I will figure something out. Keep an eye on him, he is going to come out of this, and when he does, he's going to need you." Ashley nodded as she wrapped her arms around herself, the tears seeping from her eyes in a slow, steady stream. "Arek will be here shortly."

"Is that a good idea?"

"They are closer than you think, and Arek understands him. It will be fine," Trev reassured her as he laid a hand on her shoulder.

Giving her a smile, he turned to walk away and then stopped to look back over his shoulder at her. "If you have any reservations about what we do…this is the time to leave or be all-in." Trev peered through the glass at Kes and then back to her.

"He's going to go after whoever did this, isn't he?" she asked, already knowing the answer.

"I would be shocked if he didn't." Trev continued on his way, and she took a deep breath as she stepped into the small waiting room once more.

She slowly made her way over to the man that had owned her heart for as long as she'd known him. Sitting herself down beside him, she entwined their fingers and laid her head on his shoulder. No matter what her ethical compass warned her about, she already knew she was all-in the moment she found him in her home. She'd follow him through whatever hell he dragged her through willingly because he was the other half of her soul.

She'd never believed the fairytale stories about once-in-a-lifetime soulmates, but she was now a converted believer. He was hers, and she would die before she turned her back on him.

What did that say about her? She didn't know, but she was getting to the point that she didn't give a fuck.

# CHAPTER 37

*K* es glanced toward the door, but it was only Vanessa, his on-again, off-again girlfriend, that came strolling in. Ashley's chair had remained empty all week since the locker incident.

"We did it," his girlfriend said. Her voice annoyed him with just those three words. Why was he still with her? Because his father and her father were good friends, and dumping her would make his father look bad.

"Did what?" he asked, the rest of the group they were hanging around with turning in their seats to listen.

"Your pet is leaving." She smiled wide and clasped her hands together like it was fucking Christmas.

"What do you mean, she's leaving?" A pain formed in his chest, making it hard to take a deep breath.

"I heard from Stephanie, who was in the main office, that she overheard the principal and your Pet talking." Vanessa paused and bit her lip like she was keeping the juiciest secret in the world, which at the moment, she was. He was on the edge of his seat, but not for the reason they all thought. "Apparently, she decided to do the right thing and switch to a school more suitable for someone like her."

"This can't be true," he said, mostly to himself, but Vanessa answered anyway.

"Oh, it is, and it gets better. She's cleaning out her locker right now. I had to go and check for myself, and there she was, box in hand. Isn't this, like, the best news?" Vanessa gave the rest of the group a high-five, but he needed to go. He couldn't sit there and let this happen.

Jumping up, he rushed to the door as his chair slammed to the floor.

"Where are you going?" both the teacher and Vanessa chorused at the same time.

"Give me detention, I don't care, but I've got to go." He stopped with his hand on the door and looked at Vanessa. "And we're through. Consider this our final breakup."

Kes didn't bother waiting for a response—instead, he ran like a fucking track star through the empty halls. He was annoyed that he had to slow down to push through the double doors leading to the stairs. Three at a time, he stormed up the stairs to the second floor. He burst through the doors at the top and turned right. There she was, just as Vanessa had said, a box on the floor as she piled her binders and whatever else into it.

His feet loudly echoed as he ran past the long line of lockers and closed classroom doors. Ashley glanced his way and her eyes went wide, but she turned her head away and resumed what she had been doing.

He halted, panting, leaning a hand on a locker a few down from hers to catch his breath.

"You come to do your victory dance?" Her eyes found his, and there was so *much hate in them. "Or maybe lock me in a locker again?" Ashley tore pictures off of the inside of her locker and let them fall into the box.*

*He'd never paid much attention to them before, but as the last one fluttered down, he grabbed the small pile and lifted them to leaf through. The first was a news article with a black and white photo of Ashley smiling as her old principal held out a plaque. He scanned the article, which said she had a perfect school average and that it was the first time in the school's history—they were awarding her a special grant to go to any school of her choosing. The next was a family photo—they were camping, or at least he assumed they were, tents in the background with a bonfire they were all sitting around, smiling.*

*"Can you put that back in the box when you're done? Unless you plan on burning them or posting them all over the school or whatever else you come up with," she shot at him.*

*Ironically, he hated the sound of her voice all bitter. He'd done nothing but pick on her for almost two full years. What else could he expect?*

*"No, I didn't, I swear."*

*"What are you talking about?" She clutched a school sweatshirt to her chest as she peeked around the edge of her open locker door to stare at him.*

*"I didn't come here to...." Kes paused, the words frozen on his tongue.*

*"Bully me? Pick on me? Torture me? Choose a word. There are so many options." Ashley dropped the sweatshirt into the box and grabbed her backpack before closing the door. She swung the backpack over her shoulders, and his panic tripled alongside his mounting heart rate.*

*"Don't go."*

*Her face twisted into a look of pure confusion.*

*"Please, Ashley. Don't go."*

*"Kes, you're crazier than I thought. This is what you wanted all along. What you and your friends and now the entire school seems to want—for me to leave because I don't belong. Well, your wish is coming true. You won, I lost. I can't do it anymore, even I have my limits." Her eyes filled with tears, but she blinked and looked away from him.*

*"It's not like that. I want you to stay. I'm sorry," he said, and as the words*

left his mouth, he realized how insignificant they were in comparison to what he'd done.

Ashley leaned to the side and looked around him, her eyes scanning the empty hall. "What is this? Your last chance to make an idiot out of me? Make me think that you've had this magical change of heart and then have everyone come out of the classroom laughing at me for falling for the act again?"

"I promise it's not like that. I really am sorry that I've been a douche. I won't, um...I won't treat you like crap anymore, and I'll get everyone else to stop."

"It's called bullying, Kes. That's what you are, a bully. You should at least own the word. You do it well enough." Ashley's eyes looked him up and down. "Nope, I'm not buying it." Bending over, she grabbed her box and turned, marching away from him.

"Please, I'm begging you not to go." He jogged around her and blocked her path, and in the most dramatic action he could think of, he got down on his knees, clasping his hands together like he was praying.

"What the—?"

"I feel terrible for what I've been doing. Just give me a chance to prove it."

"Kes, it's not my responsibility to absolve you of your guilt."

She went to step around him, and he crawled in front of her again. He knew he looked ridiculous, and if anyone saw him, they'd think he had lost his fucking mind, but he didn't care. "That's not why I'm asking. You deserve to be here. Just please, stay."

"You actually expect me to believe you woke up with this huge change of heart?" She cocked her hip and glared at him as she dared him with her eyes to try and prove her wrong.

His stomach flipped and tumbled as he stared into her blue eyes. He wanted to say that he loved her, that they may be young, but he had loved her from the moment he first saw her, but that would probably have her running for the hills.

Standing, he grabbed onto the box in her hands and held on to it tight, not letting her move. He smiled widely, which narrowed her eyes further. "Let me prove it to you. We'll go to the principal's office right now, and I'll tell him what

*I've been doing. How it's all my fault that you keep ending up in detention and everything else."*

*"Kes, he's not going to let me stay. I think he was relieved that I was leaving."*

*He tugged on the box again, and this time, she let go. "Come on, let me do this."*

*A guy came out of the classroom nearby, and he stopped walking and smirked when he saw them, his eyes lighting up like he was going to get a show. "What the fuck are you looking at?" Kes snarled at him.*

*"Uh, nothing," the guy said.*

*"Good, then get the fuck out of here. There is nothing to see here—and spread the word. If anyone picks on Ashley Hartley, they will have to deal with me. She is under my protection. You got that?"*

*The guy's mouth fell open, but he closed it and nodded as he turned and jogged the opposite way. His eyes skimmed over Ashley's face, and she had the same shocked expression as the guy that he had just chased off. Her mouth was hanging open, her eyes wide.*

*"I told you, I'm sorry, and I'm going to prove it. Now, come on." He marched off and then looked over his shoulder. Ashley was still in the same spot with the same expression. "Ashley?"*

*Her eyes flicked up to his.*

*"Come on. I want to catch Principal Sharpe and sort this out now."*

*Ashley followed him tentatively as they made their way down the stairs and along the hall to the main office. She kept looking over at him like he was about to yell, 'just joking.' He held his head up high as they walked, drawing stares and whispers from everyone that saw them.*

*"Mr. Reynolds, what can I do for you?" the secretary behind the counter asked as he sat the box down on the counter.*

*"I need to speak to the principal," he said, giving the woman his best smile.*

*She looked in the direction of the office and then back up at him. "I'm sorry, but he's on a conference call right now. Can I schedule you in for tomorrow?"*

*Kes glanced down and saw the pile of paperwork on her desk, and right on top was Ashley's transfer papers. Reaching over, he grabbed the papers. "Hey! Mr. Reynolds, give that back."*

*"Kes, it's okay," Ashley whispered quietly.*

*"No, it's not, and I'm fixing this now." He strode toward the principal's office as the secretary jumped up and chased after him.*

*"You can't go in there," she said, but he grabbed the handle and threw the door open wide with a bang. Principal Sharpe jumped and turned away from the window.*

*"Give me a moment," Sharpe said before covering the bottom of his cell. "What's going on?"*

*"I'm sorry, I told him he can't come in here, but he just stormed in."*

*"I need to speak to you now and it can't wait," Kes said, and then he grabbed Ashley's hand to pull her over to the chairs before sitting down. She slowly followed suit and gave him a glare, but didn't say anything.*

*"I'm going to have to call you back, I have a situation I need to take care of." Sharpe hung up the phone and looked at the secretary. "It's fine, I'll take care of this, please close the door."*

*She grumbled something under her breath but left the three of them alone. Principal Sharpe took a moment to look between the two of them. "Do I even want to know?"*

*Kes placed the paperwork on the desk. "I need you to undo this, now. Ashley is not transferring, and you will remove all flags and black marks that you have in your folder about her."*

*"Kestrel, Ms. Hartley here made it quite clear that she wanted to leave."*

*"Well, she doesn't any longer."*

*The principal sat down and placed his hands on the desk. "What is this?"*

*"All the issues that have come to you about Ashley have all been because of me. I have orchestrated every single one. Look, all you need to do is reinstate her and remove all the shit in your file that says she's a troublemaker, that's it."*

*"That's it?" Sharpe mocked. "Is this true, Ashley, has he been causing all the issues?"*

*Ashley sighed. "I've tried to tell you that over and over, but no one would listen to me. Yes, what he says is correct." Even though Ashley didn't say it, he could feel her wanting to add Dumbass to the end of the sentence.*

*Principal Sharpe leaned back in the high back leather chair and shook his head. "I don't know what to do with this information. You've put me in a very difficult position, Kestrel."*

*"Just fix the paperwork. I don't care how you have to do it, just make this right."*

*Principal Sharpe looked at Ashley. "Do you want him expelled?"*

*Ashley looked over and their eyes locked—this was her opportunity to get him in the trouble he deserved. "No, I don't, and even if I wanted you to, I'm not stupid. I know his father is a major contributor to the school, so it would only hurt the school I love to try. I would like to stay, though, if Kes promises the bullying will stop for good."*

*"I promise."*

*"Oh, for the love of god. Fine, I will find a way to fix Ashley's transcripts and I'll tear up the transfer, but Kestrel, this is your one and only warning. If I find out you're harassing or bullying anyone else then you will be tossed out and we will suffer the loss of your father's money. Now the pair of you, get out of my office. I'm so sick of teenage drama."*

*Smiling wide, he jumped up and held open the door for Ashley to walk through. The secretary gave him a dirty look as he grabbed the box off of her desk and continued on, but he didn't care. His heart was literally soaring. It was the first right thing he'd done in a very long time.*

*Ashley touched his arm and he stopped walking to look down at her. "Thanks, Kes. I really hope you mean this and you're not just screwing with me, though."*

*"I'm not, and I'm not done proving myself to you yet. Come on, let's get this stuff back into your locker."*

.   .   .

*K*es jerked awake and sucked in a deep breath like he was coming up for air. He sat up straight and stared at Arek sitting in a chair across the way, while Ashley was curled up on the pair of seats beside him. He laid his hand on her shoulder and rubbed his thumb back and forth, just needing the contact.

"You good?" Arek asked. His body was stretched out, head against the glass wall of the small room with his eyes closed and hands folded in his lap. One eye opened enough for Kes to see the soft blue gaze shining back at him.

"Yeah, I'll be alright."

"You sure? I've been down that rabbit hole if you need someone to talk to?"

He shook his head slowly. "I'm alright. I had an episode, but I'll be fine now. Why are you here?"

Arek's shoulders shrugged up. "Where else would I be when one of my brothers needs me?"

"This 'nice guy' routine—it's not going to make me like you," Kes warned while Arek smiled widely, their stares locked. "Fine, it may make me like you a little more."

Before he could say any more, Ashley stirred beside him. Yawning, she pushed herself up and rubbed at her eyes. "Hey, you're awake. Did I miss anything?" she asked. Cupping her face, Kes kissed her forehead and then the tip of her nose.

"No, I just woke up. Has there been any news about Zumi?" he asked, afraid of the answer.

"Last I heard, she was still in surgery. No one has come by since to announce her status. Trev has been keeping me posted while you two sleeping beauties rested," Arek said through a yawn.

Kes searched Ashley's face and couldn't understand how he'd

managed to get so lucky as to have a second chance with such a woman. "Can I ask you something?"

"If you're going to ask her to have sex in here, let me know so I can leave and warn the nurses to stay away," Arek piped up, and Kes shot the guy a glare that rolled off him like water off a duck's back.

"Ignore him. What do you want to ask?" Ashley asked, bringing his attention back to her.

"Why did you forgive me? After all the shit I did, why did you decide to go to prom with me?"

"You mean other than the fact I was hopelessly in love with you?" She blushed, and while he would normally ravish her for saying that, he was too worried about Zumi, and he needed to know what exactly it was that he did to get her to give him a chance. It was gnawing at him.

"There were a lot of reasons, Kes. There wasn't just one thing you did the rest of the year, it was all the little things that proved you'd changed. I guess it basically all came down to you redeeming yourself." Kes leaned in and gave her lips a soft kiss before standing. "Where are you going?"

He didn't know if she'd understand, but this was something he had to do. "I'm going to go redeem myself."

"Not without me, you're not. You don't get to have all the fun," Arek said, jumping to his feet.

Ashley grabbed his arm and stood. He stared into her eyes and never wanted to let her go, but he had to do this. Her hand tightened on his forearm, her normally sweet features transforming into a look that would scare the most hardened criminal.

"Make sure none of them are left breathing. What they did to her—," Ashley paused and shook her head. "I'll look after her until you get back."

Grabbing her face, he crashed his lips to hers. There was nothing she could've said that meant more. "I love you."

"I love you, too."

He turned to face Arek, who already looked like he was ready to eat bones for dinner. "You ready to party?"

Arek scoffed at the question. "That's like asking me if I love sex, man. Let's get the fuck out of here."

Shadows of death danced around him like a ritual in his mind as he stomped out of the hospital. Those demons would get their taste of blood tonight.

# CHAPTER 38

Kes had stealth mode on as he rolled up to the end of the driveway that led to the rundown country home. The pieces of shit he was after were hiding inside and apparently shitting their pants, which they should be. He'd known that Vance would warn them, but at the time, it had been more important to find Zumi. Vance thought he was safe hiding in his fallback location, but he'd taken it upon himself to mark off every spot these guys owned or frequented.

In the end, he'd killed Vance and found out where the men that hurt Zumi were hiding. To be fair, he did warn Vance that if Zumi were hurt, he'd come back for him. Kes glanced at Arek as he hummed a song they all used to sing around the fire from time to time. He'd remember Vance's screams for the rest of his days. The image of him tied to his desk as Arek ripped his bowels out inch by inch was a sight you just don't forget.

He peered around and then stared at the map Baby Doll had across the screen. The place was spectacularly off the beaten path, with only a smattering of farms around for miles. It was smart on their part to get out of the city limits, but too bad for them that there wasn't a place on this rock to hide that he wouldn't find them. A shiver of anticipation spread throughout his body. He seriously couldn't have dreamed up a better place to kill these fuckers.

They'd started with the trafficker's houses that he'd already been planning on slowly hitting over the next few months. He'd forgotten how fun it was to kill shit with Arek. He'd left the burning down of the five houses to ash for Arek to do. That much fire was too much for his brain to handle, but he did find it amusing to picture the cops' faces when they found the dead men left inside. They'd had a jam-packed night running from one end of the city to the other, but they weren't done yet.

Wolf had a meltdown when Kes called and said how many kids needed to be picked up. That was a dilemma for Wolf to figure out. His goal was to kill off as many of the parasites as he could before the sun was up. He wanted to get back to the hospital as soon as he could. Every second he was out here, the worse he felt about leaving Zumi's side. He picked up his cell to see if there was any news, but no messages had been received from Ashley or Trev.

"Any word?" Arek asked.

"No, but I'm going to assume no news is good news." He put his phone away and looked over at Arek. "How do you do it? How do you handle being a dad? I mean, Zumi isn't even my kid and this feeling…." His hand hovered over his chest as he tried to explain what it was like and yet found no words.

Arek looked at him and shook his head. "Renee, she keeps me sane. I'm fucking terrified twenty-five out of twenty-four hours in the motherfucking day, but I wouldn't change a single moment. Between J.J. and Levi, I have my hands full, and yet I've never felt more whole than when I am curled up on the couch with my two boys."

"I wanted to ask you, wasn't Scooter's real name 'Levi'?" Kes looked over at Arek, and a ghost of a smile played across his features.

"He saved my life. Scooter was a hero that no one will ever remember because the mission was classified, so it's like his life and sacrifice of death never fucking happened." Arek's stare locked with his own, and he knew what he was thinking, what he was feeling. "My son deserved to have a hero's name, and I couldn't think of anyone better to name him after"

"Damn, that is the most beautiful fucking thing. I didn't know you had it in you."

"I have the odd moment. It's how I keep Renee from running for the hills, because I punched way above my weight class landing her."

Kes laughed hard, his hand hitting the steering wheel as the image crossed his mind. "See, now that I believe." He nodded toward the house. "You good for one more?"

Arek held out his fist, and Kes looked at the fist and then at Arek. "Come on, don't leave me hangin' out here like a fucktard."

"And then you wonder why I never took you to party on the yacht," Kes said, but indulged him by tapping his knuckles.

"That's hurtful. There is no need to leave me out like that," Arek pouted and then smiled widely.

"Oh, fuck off, and get out of my Hummer." Kes jumped out before he changed his mind about taking Arek with him. He was going to need him, though. He was concerned he may lose himself to what was inside him in that house—not that he'd ever admitted that shit to Arek. You knew you were in deep when Arek was your life preserver.

They quickly geared up and faded into the shadows of the

surrounding shrubs. Someone was smoking outside. The red tip glowed brightly and then went dull again. They snuck up onto the dark front porch, and with a quick, coordinated attack, the man crumpled to the ground with a soft thud. Arek's gun barely made a noise, the gun's sound quickly whisked away by the breeze.

"Heat signatures. Two on the main level near the back of the house and two upstairs. Four in total," Arek said. "I really wish you'd wear the fucking tech, man."

"Get over it. It's not happening." He couldn't put the night vision eye piece on. It was an instant trip down the path to mind-fuckery as he was instantly transported back in time to the crash. He'd have to get over it at some point, but it wasn't happening tonight. "Remember not to kill the two I'm after."

"What if they force me to?"

Kes rolled his eyes. "You can break their kneecaps. Just don't kill them."

"Can I also break all their fingers?"

"I'm going to break your fingers if you don't shut up."

"Shit, Kes, you're too much fun. I need to do this more often." He could hear Arek's snicker from across the yard as they moved in on the house. "You want this quiet or hard and dirty?"

"Let's go hard. You take the back, and I'll take the front door."

"I love it when you talk dirty."

Kes bit his lip and shook his head—he couldn't even be bothered to tell Arek off. It would only encourage him more. The blinds were pulled shut, but the internal lights gave an eerie glow to the dilapidated place. The old molding was chipped and faded, while the wooden pillars looked like they could be pushed over with a strong wind.

He stayed close to the house and peeked through the windows along the front. The thin line that the blinds couldn't completely cover gave him just enough of a sightline inside the house. He stepped over the puddle of blood from the dead guard lying near the front door, making sure not to get any of the slippery substance on his boots.

"Ready?" he asked as they got into position to make their entry.

"All systems are go."

"Then let's do this."

The resounding crack and bang would have woken the dead as the two doors splintered and broke away from their shitty frames to slam against the walls. Instantaneously, yelling erupted inside the house, along with the sound of running feet. He could just make out Arek down the narrow hall and awaited his prey. Sure enough, like a deer being 'dogged' through a bush, Arek drove the second guy from the back of the house toward him. He was running blind, his turned slightly looking over his shoulder—fear apparent in every stride.

The guy looked forward and caught sight of him. He tried to stop but ended up falling on his ass. Kes raised the gun and fired. The man was dead before his skidding body came to a halt.

Arek walked his way through the rest of the lower level before meeting him at the front door, which was near the stairs to go up. "Where are they?" he asked as he kept his focus on the stairs.

"Huh. It's kinda like they're flying around inside of the walls, but I'm pretty sure they aren't loaded up on pixie dust and happy thoughts like Peter Pan, so there must be a hiding space built in."

"You want to lead the way?"

"Sure. I knew I brought these along for a reason." Arek tapped at the canisters of tear gas he had at the ready hanging from his chest.

There was no point in being quiet. The occupants already knew they were in the house, and there was a sick joy associated with letting them know that they were going to die shortly. The earlier rage that had dissipated from one slit throat to the next returned with each step they took. The image of Zumi back on that beach had his jaw clenching as his hand gripped the knife so tightly that the small ridges along the handle were going to leave indentations.

Arek signaled for him to get down, and he got on his stomach as Arek swung his automatic rifle around and lay down beside him. He pointed out where he was going to shoot and what he was planning.

The gun echoed like a thousand balloons bursting beside his ear as the bullets flew from the weapon. Bits of wallpaper, drywall, wood, and dust were released into the room as they went flying. He could make out some yelling from the men as they more than likely shit their pants.

A hole the size of a beach ball quickly ripped open in the wall as Arek unloaded the gun. As the bullets continued to fly, Kes dug around in the pack and handed over a gas mask as Arek laid the gun down. Arek grabbed a canister off his chest, pulled the pin, and let it fly. It missed the hole and bounced harmlessly off the wall to roll into the center of the room instead.

"Great throw," Kes said sarcastically.

"Think you can do better? Here," Arek held out another canister.

Reaching back, he aimed and let his arm fly. The canister flipped through the air before it sailed through the hole and bounced around.

The coughing was instantaneous. A moment later, like a bloody magic trick, the men pushed through a hidden door that blended into the rest of the wall. Both of the men fleeing the compartment were holding guns, but them being blinded by debris and tears and coughing up a lung made disarming them a simple task without even having to blow anybody's hand off.

Grabbing one of the pieces of shit by the neck, he cracked the man across the face until blood poured from his nose. He wanted to take his mask off, but the two canisters of that shit still lingered, so he fisted a handful of the man's T-shirt and dragged his ass along the floor to the bedroom across the hall.

As he threw the man on the old bed, the springs squeaked, like something wailing out of a haunted house, before Dickhead joined in with his groans as Kes kneeled on his back. He yanked the mask of his head and tossed it to the side.

"Get…off…me," the man he was pretty sure was Igor said. He looked like an Igor. The words came out in a gasp in between his coughing. His face was bright red as tears ran down those reddened cheeks like a waterfall.

"That's funny," he mumbled. "Is that what you did when Zumi screamed to get off her?" The fury in his chest was an inferno once more, and he grabbed one of the knives out of his chest holster and lifted it up to stab the man, but then took a steadying breath to calm himself. He wanted them to die slowly. For that, he needed control.

Putting the knife away, he unhooked the tightly-wound coil of rope attached to his belt. The thing didn't look like much, but it could hold both Arek and him while dangling from a helicopter, so looks were deceiving. He pulled the tie on the knot and wrapped first one hand and then the second so they were tied together and then to the top of the bed frame. Kes did the same method to the mans feet, just as Arek tossed a limp Ricardo through the door.

"Sorry, I got a little over zealous, but he's still breathing."

Kes looked at the blood coating his face and chest and was surprised to see that Ricardo was indeed still alive, even if his face was a mess. "Can you string him up over there?"

"On it."

Kes focused on his own prey as Arek went to work, hanging Ricardo from the bare rafters where part of the vaulted ceiling had caved in, leaving the beams accessible. As soon as Igor was secured, he leaned over the dazed man, and that time, when he pulled the knife, he stabbed it through one open palm like he was auditioning for the part of Jesus's executioner.

A pained scream echoed through the house and made him smile. He forced open the guy's other hand and did the same thing to the second palm. Igor's back arched, lifting his weight slightly off the bed.

"Had to even things up," he offered by way of an explanation. Now every time the man tried to move or thrash around he'd hurt himself more as the sharp blade cut through his hands.

Kes slid off the bed and stood to his full height as he stared down at the man that may or may not have hurt Zumi. It didn't really matter which of them did the physical work—the other was there. The other watched and did nothing. They would both die, and he would dance in their blood before he was through.

"I need to do this one alone," he said, turning to look at Arek as he finished securing the knot holding Ricardo.

"I figured." Arek wandered over to the pack he had left on the floor. He dug around inside until he pulled something strangely shaped and metallic from inside. "Here, take this."

"What the hell is that?" Kes asked, taking the strange spiked contraption. He rolled it over in his hand, and it reminded him of a cross between a long, narrow pear and a flower, but with an unusual key-like crank device on the end.

"That, my friend, is a pear of anguish, otherwise known as a paravenous." Arek's smile faltered. "Do you not know what it does?"

"No."

"Man, you've been missing out. This was designed in the Medieval era—you shove the blunt pear-shaped end up their ass or down their throat and then crank this part, and it opens up. Very painful. Lots of screaming. You'll love it."

"And you just happen to carry this around with you?"

"You can never be too prepared." Arek looked at his phone. "You have an hour, and then we need to leave."

Kes stared at the thing Arek had given him and then looked between the two men. "That's all I'll need, but if I'm not out in an hour…."

"I'll come to get you." Arek laid his hand on his shoulder. Although he meant physically, the look in his eyes said he'd mentally pull him back too if needed.

"Thank you."

Arek marched from the room, his boots loud on the wooden stairs as he jogged down. Kes glanced between the two men, both of which were groaning in different degrees of pain.

"Alright, let's start with the only important question. Who touched Zumi?"

# CHAPTER 39

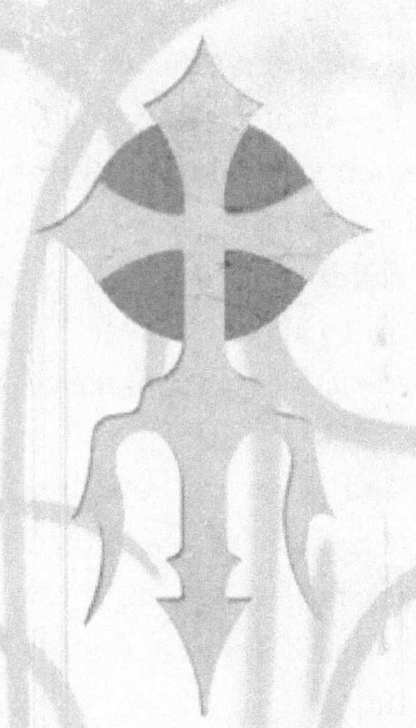

Kes leaned his head back on the chair, his eyes closed but his senses on full alert. How many hours had it been since he slept? He had to be rounding on seventy-two, but he couldn't shut his mind off, and he was terrified he was going to miss Zumi waking up.

"How is she doing?" Ashley asked as she walked into the hospital room.

"No change."

He winced as he shifted himself into a more upright position and smiled as his eyes fell on the angel in the doorway. She'd gone home to shower and take her meds, which he'd had to order her to do. Fuck, she was beautiful. Her blonde hair fell around her shoulders in soft waves, and although the loose-fitting sweater that fell off one shoulder was meant to be warm and comfortable, it made her look like walking sex to him.

Kes held out his hand, and she came around to his side of the bed. He guided her onto his lap, wrapping his arms around her. She sank into him and the chair, molding to his body perfectly.

"Did you mean it when you said you wanted some?" Ashley's voice was soft and timid as she asked the question.

"You mean, to have children?"

She snuggled deeper into his hold. "Yeah."

"I'm not exactly dad-of-the-year material, but yes, I meant every word."

She lifted her head, and as her eyes met his, he knew he'd agree to as many as she wanted. "You're a better man than you think you are, and I think you'd be an amazing father."

"I don't know about that." His eyes flicked to Zumi. "I failed her. I promised to keep her safe."

"Kes?" Zumi's lips moved and then she smacked her lips like her tongue was heavy. That one word seizing his heart. Ashley stood, and he immediately pulled his chair closer to grab Zumi's hand.

"Hey, Kid. Yeah, I'm here."

A wisp of a smile graced her features as she turned her head to look at him. "I knew you'd come," she whispered, her voice harsh from the damage to her vocal cords. If he could, he'd bring the men back to life just to hear them scream again for what they did to her. "I knew you'd save us."

His face fell, and he looked away from her eyes. "I...um...."

"What is it?"

He gave her hand a gentle squeeze. "I'm sorry, Zumi. I didn't get there in time to save your mom. She had already passed when I arrived."

She rolled her head to look up at the ceiling. "Oh."

"I'm sorry, I—."

"It's okay, she was a shitty mom," Zumi said, her words a stark contrast to the tears leaking down her cheeks. "I'll figure something out."

"Listen, you don't need to worry about that. I've got you, Kid. You will come home with me to my boat, and we can figure out our next move."

Zumi nodded but closed her eyes. "Can I be alone?" she asked, and her voice was so firm. He knew she had to be breaking inside, which killed him.

"Sure, Kid. I'll be out in the hall. Just yell or push a button or something if you need me."

He stood and walked out with Ashley by his side. They closed the door softly, but before it clicked shut, he could hear the first heart-wrenching cry as she let her emotions out.

"Kes, we need to talk," Ashley said and pointed to the door.

*Oh, shit. This can't be good.*

"What's wrong?" he asked as they stepped out into the hall. Ashley didn't speak and kept walking until he followed her out of the hospital into the warm sun.

"You mind telling me what you meant by your 'boat'?" She crossed her arms over her chest, and he swallowed hard.

"Well, it's my father's boat, but I use it whenever I want. He never uses it, so it's just kind of sitting there."

She turned her head like she was inspecting him, and the look made him want to run. "Are you really homeless, Kes? Be honest with me. Do you choose to live on the streets because you have to, or because you decided one day that you wanted to?"

He stuffed his hands in his pockets, unsure of what answer she wanted to hear. "I felt more comfortable with the people on the streets."

"But you still have your money?"

He looked away and then down to the ground, suddenly knowing exactly what it felt like when he scolded Zumi. "Yeah, I have all of what was in my trust."

Ashley took a step back and shook her head. "I don't believe this."

"I don't understand why you're so angry. I'm no different than anyone else that chooses to live on the streets. There are plenty of people that don't like the day-to-day grind of the Dweller lifestyle."

Ashley lifted her hands in the air and then let them drop. "Kes, for shit's sake. First, I told you no more secrets. Did it happen to slip your mind that you have millions of dollars?" she seethed, but it felt like she was yelling at the top of her lungs. "Second, you claim you want to help those on the streets. Zumi said that you protect them. This is how you protect them? Do you have any idea what having that kind of money can do? How many lives you could save?"

"Of course I do. That's why I bought Salvation Place." As soon as the words left his mouth, he wanted to smack himself.

"I knew it, deep down I knew it. Just one more thing you've kept from me. Tell me, Kes. Why did you have this sudden change of heart at the last possible hour and decide to save the shelter?" This was worse than being tortured and held for questioning. Sweat trickled down his back as he swallowed—it felt like rocks were lodged in his throat and scraping their way down. She held up her finger. "I want the truth."

"Would this be a really bad time to say you can't handle the truth?" There are those moments in your life where you think, 'why the fuck did that come out of my mouth?' and that right there was one of those times. Ashley's eyes widened, her lips pressing together in a hard line as she stormed past him.

He grabbed her arm and quickly diverted her path to leave. "I'm sorry, bad joke, bad timing. I purchased the church because I knew it was a spot you liked to go and I would find you there."

Ashley sighed and pinched the bridge of her nose. He was dying to make a comment about how adorable she was but was very invested in not making this worse so kept his mouth shut.

"So, let me recap. You claim that you don't want to be like your father or live under his thumb, yet you still take liberties with your money and his yacht that a normal person couldn't dream of, all the while hiding on the streets from him and pretending to be someone else. Do I have that right?"

"Um…when you put it that way, it sounds a lot worse than in my head."

Ashley poked him in the chest. "That's because it is. If you really wanted to make a difference and help those you claim to care for, including your fellow veterans, then if I were you, I'd find a way to make better use of my money. And I don't mean lavish half-hearted gestures to get near me. I mean something that will make a real difference, Kes," she fumed. She strode away a few feet and then back again. "You're being a hypocrite, and you're being one because you're scared. Neither one of those things looks sexy on you. I'm going home because I can't look at you right now."

"Ashley," he started to beg, but she stopped and held up her hand to ward him off.

"No, don't touch me. I'm so angry I could smack you. Don't you see? You were always brilliant. Not only are you letting that go to waste, but on top of that, you're letting your father win, and—." She paused and looked away before scrubbing a tear off her cheek. "You could be doing more with your life. Build a school for the unfortunate, fund research for diseases, or help veterans with programs that our government won't provide to help get them back on their feet. I don't care what you decide to do, but sitting around and offering the occasional meal to a little homeless girl that you claim to love while you run around like some version of Batman in the dark…I thought you were better than that." She looked him up and down, and he'd never felt so ashamed. "Maybe I never really knew you at all."

She marched away, and he let her go. There was nothing he could say right then to make it right. Ashley was right, of course—he'd been weak and not facing what he was so afraid of all this time, and that was his father.

Kes wandered back into the hospital and spotted Trev leaning against the nurse's station like he owned the place. It was irritating how he fit in like a fucking chameleon wherever he happened to be. Put him in fatigues, and he was a soldier. Put him in a suit, and he would tear your ass out in court. He wouldn't be surprised to see him in scrubs with a stethoscope around his neck looking just as much at home.

"Is everything alright?" Trev asked. He shook his head no but didn't elaborate. "Well, you have some paperwork to sign for Zumi to be released."

"Already? Shouldn't she stay longer?"

"She is fine to go home and be looked after. But the doctor did mention when he was through that she would need a heart transplant in the next couple of years. He spoke to me like I should know what he was talking about, so you will need to speak to him further." Trev held out a clipboard, and he grabbed it, giving it a quick read-over and noticing that he'd managed to put Zumi's last name down as Reynolds. That was smart.

Kes scribbled out his John Hancock on the bottom of the sheet and handed it over the counter to the nurse.

Heading back to Zumi's room, he looked over at Trev. He was uncharacteristically quiet, never a good sign. This was the day for shit, apparently.

"That was smart thinking, putting my last name on her records. How did you manage that?"

"It wasn't that difficult," Trev drawled sarcastically. "Considering it was already her last name." Trev lifted and eye brow at him.

Kes smiled and then laughed, but he stopped when Trev didn't laugh with him. "You don't think…? You do. You think she's my kid. Like actually mine?" Trev remained quiet the same expression never leaving his face, which was the worst form of interrogation. "It's impossible. I wasn't even in the country when she would've been conceived, so unless I'm fucking God or I have super sperm that flew across the pond, I did not impregnate—." He froze, his next words failing as his mind came up with an alternative possibility. "Oh shit." Trev gripped his shoulder and helped him to the small chair outside Zumi's room.

"I'm afraid so, my friend. She's your sister. I had a DNA comparison run to confirm it."

"I'd always wondered how Chelsea found this amazing anonymous donor for Zumi's surgeries. It was fucking hush money wasn't it?" Trev didn't answer, but his face said it all. Kes put his head in his hands as he leaned on his knees. "I'm going to kill him. I'm going to fucking kill him."

"I think there are better ways to express your anger, that will have a much longer lasting and affect," Trev said.

Kes lifted his head and stared into Trev's eyes. The evil glint shining back at him calmed the angry beast in his chest. "I want to tear him apart."

Trev leaned back in the chair beside his. "And so we will."

Reaching out, his hand hovered over Trev's arm, drawing a confused look from the man himself. Raw emotion clogged his throat as he finally gripped Trev's forearm and took a deep breath.

"Thank you. I've never said how much you always being there for me, even when I make it difficult, has meant to me."

Trev laid his free hand on top of his own. "Brother, we stand together."

"Apart we fall," Kes finished.

# CHAPTER 40

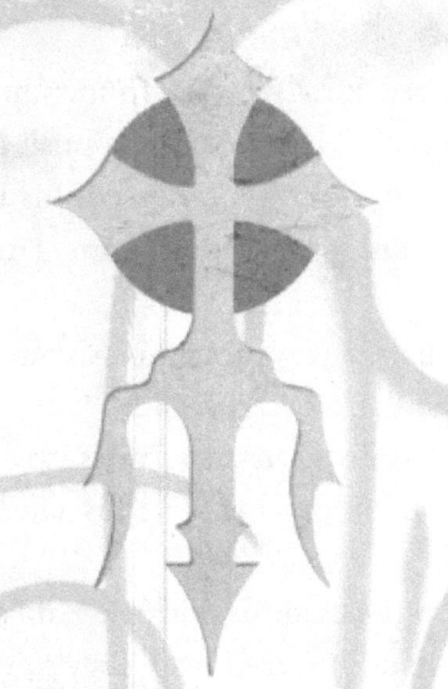

$K$es rolled out his shoulder, the stiffness setting in from the rigorous workout he'd received last night. He really needed to stop hanging around Arek so much—he was a bad fucking influence. Arek had managed to talk him into taking him along to pay a visit to the prick that Ashley had dated, the one who decided it was a good idea to hit her.

He'd planned on letting it go, as Ashley had said she just wanted to put it in the past and keep it there, but he'd made the mistake of mentioning it to Arek, and the man was having none of it. Besides, *gave me the push I'd been looking for to go after the piece of shit.*

There were moments where he genuinely worried about his own sanity, but you only needed to spend an evening with Arek as you pummeled the shit out of a man to know that Arek had him beat by a mile. His mouth pulled up in a lopsided smile as he thought about the look on Kevin Matthews' face when he'd opened his door and the two of them in all of their black combat gear had greeted him. Arek was like a man possessed by a demon as he made sure that Kevin wouldn't walk again for a while. He shook his head. If he had to be the voice of reason, it was one motherfucking scary scene.

Kes stepped out onto the sunny deck of the yacht and couldn't help but smile as he took in Zumi lying on one of the deck chairs and reading a book. Leave it to his father to put a small pool on a fucking boat. Zumi seemed to love it and, her damp hair showed that she had obviously just used it.

The dark bruises were long gone, and for the most part, she had physically healed. Mentally, that was another story. She woke up most nights screaming and wouldn't fall back to sleep unless he sat in the room, but he hoped that would fade with time and therapy. Something that he should've gone to long ago. She was still going to need a new heart, so her activities had been restricted to online school and lounging on the yacht while he got his shit in order. Not that he should've worried. She was like a sponge, and she was flying through the schoolwork and taking any extra classes she could find.

"Hey, Kid," he said as he stepped closer until he was under the shade of the retractable canopy.

Zumi put her tablet down and looked him up and down. "Wow, where are you going dressed like that? I didn't even know you owned an outfit that fancy."

He looked down at the monkey suit he was wearing and still couldn't believe that Trev had talked him into one. The tailored suit fit perfectly, and yet, he'd take his fatigues over this thing any day.

"I have a meeting that I need to get to. Do you think you'll be fine alone for a little while?"

"Kes, it's only been like a couple of months since I was literally living on the streets pretty much alone. I think I can handle lounging on a luxury yacht for a few hours by myself. You don't have to be so overprotective. I think you've killed off every bad guy in the state."

"I should've had the doctor remove your sarcastic tongue while you were under the knife," he teased as he stepped a little closer and nervously tapped the manila envelope against his leg.

"And your jokes haven't gotten any better. Anyway, Momma G is planning on stopping by. I finally talked her into sitting on the boat rather than yelling at me from the dock." She giggled.

He smirked and then cleared his throat. "Do you like it here, Zumi?"

"Yeah, of course. Why? Did I do something wrong? Do you want me to go?" She pulled down her sunglasses, and he shook his head and smiled.

"No, it's nothing like that. Never anything like that." He sat on the chair next to hers, and Zumi spun so she was facing him with her legs crossed. The long scar that stretched from her chest down to her belly button always made his heart ache for her. For what she'd endured, and he wished he could take the terrifying memories and pain away.

He smirked as she took a few extra moments to get into the lotus position and straightened her back. He'd been teaching her yoga along with her fighting techniques, which had become more theory than practice until her surgery. "What I mean is, we haven't really talked about your mom, or if you blame me for not...." He looked away and then down. "I guess I just assumed you'd want to stay with me, but I should've asked you if this is what you wanted."

"Of course I want to. Does this have to do with Ashley not coming around much? No offense, but you guys are acting weird."

"Ah, well, she's pissed with me. Long story, but I'm hoping to correct that today. But that's beside the point. What Ashley and I have going on has nothing to do with me asking you this." He hadn't told her that he was her brother. So many times, he'd wanted to, but that could lead to her wanting to meet their father, and that would only happen over his cold dead body.

Her big dark eyes studied his face. "Okay then, what's this about? You're acting really weird."

"Fuck it, I had this whole speech in my head, but I can't seem to get the words out." He held out the envelope for her to take.

"What's this?"

"Open it and find out." His heart hammered like a rabbit running in his chest. The pitter-patter made him nervous as fuck, so he stood to wander away a few steps as she pulled out the paperwork.

"Oh my god." He couldn't look away from her face, hoping he'd see a happy look and not anger. Her mouth had dropped open, her eyes wide as she stared at the legal document. "Is this for real? Did you adopt me? Like, full-on adopted? You can't give me back when I'm a pain in your ass?"

He laughed as he pictured returning her to a store. "It's very real. And I know I'm not your mom or dad, but Kid, you're my family, and I wouldn't have it any other way. I want you to stay with me. Unless you hate the idea, of course."

Zumi jumped from the chair and ran the few strides separating them to hug him. He'd promised himself he'd keep his shit together and not cry, but he could feel the emotion bubbling up. It was the first time she hadn't flinched while touching someone male since the attack, and he slowly gripped her small frame to return the gesture.

"I love you, Kid. You know that, right?"

She nodded and then backed away, wiping her own tears away from her face. "I know. I love you, too. I'm not sad, really. I'm crying cause I'm happy."

"Well, let's see if I can go make shit right with Ashley, and then maybe you'll have both of us around."

"A Dweller?" She drawled out dramatically. "I guess she's pretty cool. I mean, she puts up with you, so I guess we can keep her." A wide smile spread across her face.

"You'd better be careful. You're one of those disgusting Dwellers now."

"Touché."

"And all fancy-pants learning French. What's next on the list? German?"

"Actually, I'm thinking of going with Portuguese next since there are similarities to the Spanish and French, so I think I'll pick that up quickly, and then I want to tackle Mandarin."

His smile dropped, and he gave her a steady look as he studied her face. "I'm really proud of you, Zumi."

She blushed and held the envelope to her chest. "On that note, I better go. That was way too much sweet, mushy shit out of this mouth."

Zumi laughed as he walked away to embark on step two of his three-step plan.

He pulled at the top of his shirt as he stepped out of the elevator. He didn't even remember being this hot in the desert, but a few emotional conversations and his body temperature was rising off the charts. Ashley hadn't been ignoring him since their conversation at the hospital, but there had been a cool edge around them ever since, like a void had been wedged between them that he couldn't fix with his normal tactics.

"You can do this," he mumbled. Raising his hand, he knocked on the door, and felt like it took a year for him standing there, waiting for her to answer, before he finally heard faint shuffling from the other side of the door. Just like every time he saw her, when the door opened, his breath was stolen from his chest.

"Kes, I wasn't expecting you." Her eyes raked over his suit, and the heated look she tried to cover made him smile.

"May I come in for a minute?"

"Yeah, of course." She stepped back to greet him in, it felt like only yesterday that he'd crawled through her window for the first time. "You look…."

"Dashing? Debonair?"

The sound of Ashley's laugh had him half hard and ready for more, but he forced the urge down. "I was thinking handsome, but those words work. What's going on?"

"It took me a little longer than I thought to get what I needed to organized, so I didn't want to say anything to you until I was ready." He held his hand out toward her living room. "Did you want to sit down?"

"The suit comes with high-class manners? Now I am suspicious."

"No, that's a total act, but it does come with an apology." He followed her into the living room and proceeded to pace a small line from one end to the other, all too aware of her eyes following him.

"Kes…."

"No, please. Let me get this out. I just need to have it right in my head." Taking a shuddering breath, his nerves went off the charts as he approached her. Kes lowered himself down onto one knee, and Ashley gasped, her face frozen with the shock. "Breathe, Baby Doll."

He waited until she laughed and started to breathe normally before continuing. "Ashley, I have not always been a good man, and I regret many things, but none as much as the time together we have lost." He held out his hand for her to place hers into his. He leaned forward and kissed the back of her shaking knuckles. "I'm sorry that I wasn't honest with you, and I'm sorry that it took you calling me out again on my bull-shit to see the scared jerk I had become. You were right when we were teens, and you told me that I was scared of being seen for who I really was. And you were right again at the hospital. You, Ashley, make me a better man simply by being the beautiful and honest soul you are." He paused, reached into his pocket, and then held out his closed fist to Ashley, but didn't open his hand. "Today, I'm going to do two things that I should've found a way to do years ago. The first starts right now." Opening his hand, he held out the little paper lotus he'd made, but this time, it had a diamond ring nestled in the center. "You are my world. I forgot what it was like to feel my heartbeat until I found you again, and I can't picture a future that doesn't have you by my side. Whether we have a month, a year, or a hundred, you'll always be the woman I want to be married to." Tears traveled in two streams down her face, but the smile and light in her eyes made him smile back. "Will you do me the honor of being my wife?"

Ashley opened her mouth, and a soft sob was the only sound that came out, but her head nodded furiously up and down.

"Is that a yes? Or should I leave and try again?" he teased.

"Oh, shut up. Of course I'll marry you!"

Leaning in, she cupped his face, and he groaned at the feeling of her lips. She was perfect, but he had to back away or he was going to push her down on the couch and screw up the rest of his plans. It was so very tempting, and his willpower almost caved as she nipped his bottom lip.

"Fuck, I want you so bad."

"Now, that's the Kes I know and love."

Grinning stupidly, he lifted the ring from the lotus's center and slid the exotic marquee-cut diamond on her finger.

"It's stunning, Kes. This is too much."

"It's not even close to being too much, but I knew you wouldn't wear anything bigger. I do have a couple more surprises, but I need you to go get changed for me."

The suspicious look was back in her eye. "Where are we going?"

"I'll tell you on the way, but I would dress business professional."

He smirked as she stood and slowly made her way out of the room while continuing to eye him like if she stared long enough, the answer would appear.

While he waited, Kes walked over to the small picture stand that now held a picture of himself, Zumi, and Ashley sitting together on the boat. Ashley had insisted on the selfie photo even as Zumi and he had made faces at the camera. He sat the paper lotus down with the frame.

Two missions down. One to go.

# CHAPTER 41

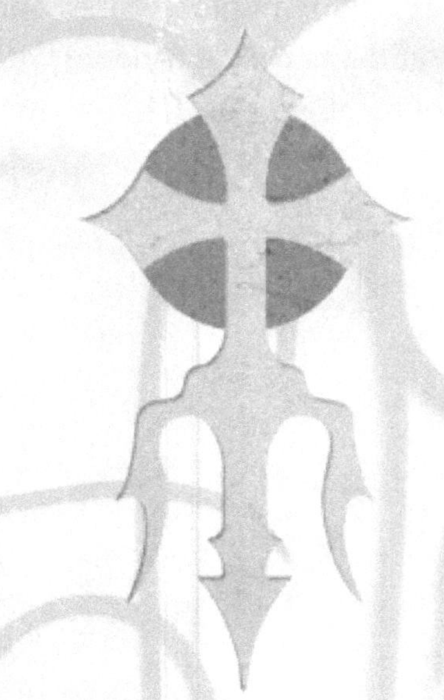

Kes glanced over at Ashley as she stared at the DNA test, her mouth hanging open. The red light he was at turned green, and he pulled away from the light as he continued toward downtown.

"This is real? Zumi is your sister?"

"What are the chances, right? Of all the areas Chelsea could've chosen to live in, I chose the same spot. I've always felt drawn to Zumi. Do you think I could've unconsciously known?"

"I don't know, Kes, but the world works in mysterious ways. Does she know yet?"

Kes looked over at Ashley and sighed as he shook his head. "She knows that I have adopted her. I gave her the paperwork before coming to see you. Trev has friends in family law, and they were able to finalize the adoption quickly since my father signed away all parental rights after her second surgery. The thing is, I don't want her reaching out to my father—our father. Seems strange to say that."

"She has a right to know who her dad is, Kes. At some point, you're going to have to tell her."

"I know, and I will sit her down and tell her all I know when she's a little older and she's healthy and has her feet on solid ground." He flicked the radio off, the bit of background music not soothing his nervous energy. "The kid has been through a lot. I don't want to shake her world up only for my father to rip the rug out from under her. I mean, the man signed away all his rights, Ash. From what I can figure out, he paid for the surgeries to keep Chelsea quiet and then ran, wiping his hands of the two of them." His hands clenched into a white-knuckle hold on the steering wheel. "I didn't like the woman, but I can't imagine what it cost her to have to go to him and beg to save Zumi."

Ashley stuffed the paperwork back into the file and gave him a small grin. "You're right. This is heavy for anyone to deal with, and waiting until she has a new heart might be smart."

They pulled up in front of a shiny building, and Kes stepped out and handed the keys to the valet before walking around and helping Ashley out the other side.

"You ready to do this?"

"At some point, you just have to decide to be brave, and this is that moment." He looked up at the building that he hated almost as much as the man that ran it. "It should've been done years ago."

Ashley hooked her arm into his as they made their way up to the front doors and to the man that was waiting out front. "Is everything ready?" Kes asked.

Trev smiled wide. "All the paperwork is ready to go."

"Excellent. Let's go cut the head off a snake."

They drew stares from everyone scurrying around the lobby. Things hadn't changed much. The people there always ran like they were being chased, and in some ways, they probably were, working there. He walked straight to the private elevator, and the guard manning it held up his hand to stop him.

"Name is Kes Reynolds. I'd advise you to step aside." He held up the key that unlocked the elevator, and the man all but leaped away to give them access. His name carried weight whether he wanted it to or not, and it was time he accepted that—but if he were going to accept it, then it would be on his own terms.

The elevator dinged as they reached the top floor. Kes had already done his homework and knew exactly where his father would be. Today was a boardroom meeting day with the rest of the executives. Trev walked on this left side while Ashley was on his right side, and a calm washed over him with their unwavering support.

The large boardroom was at the opposite end of the building from his father's office and stretched the entire width of the building. It was obscene and ridiculously large, with floor-to-ceiling windows that you could only see out of with the mirrored glass, while the inside had a full bar, televisions, and catered food. He wouldn't have been surprised if his father had installed a stage with poles for girls to dance on. Then again, his father preferred to keep those extracurricular activities secret.

The décor had changed to a sleek, silver and black modern look with splashes of brightly-colored abstract art on the walls, but it didn't matter how you dressed up a pig—it was still a pig.

Very little gave him as much satisfaction as marching through the boardroom doors like he owned the place. The doors flew open with a hard shove and drew everyone's attention, including his father's, who was standing at the head of the table with a large monitor showing pie charts and bar graphs behind him.

Kes came to a stop at the opposite end of the long table, staring at the man who seemed shocked for the first time in his recorded memory. Those lining either side of the table looked like they were at a tennis match, their heads turning to stare at him and then back to his father. It had been over fifteen years since he'd laid eyes on him, and the man was not how he remembered.

Facing the dragon of his childhood memories Kes wiped his heart clean of the fear that had always gripped his soul. The desire to prove himself to the man or to do as he wished to stay in his favor was gone.

As he stared at the older version of the man he knew, with greying hair and a potbelly that announced he ate and drank too much without exercise, he felt nothing but free.

"Son?" his father asked, breaking the silence first.

"It is I, the prodigal son has returned," he sarcastically said as he smiled.

The anger and hatred coated him like a second skin as he thought about what this man had cost him.

"Well, isn't this a great day? The son that will eventually take over the family business has returned," his father said like the whole thing was entirely his idea. The people sitting around the table tentatively clapped.

"I plan on taking over, but not eventually. I mean to take over today."

His father nervously laughed. "Such a kidder, my son is. Always making jokes. I see that hasn't changed."

Kes stared at the man lying through his teeth and shook his head in wonder. What had he ever seen in the man to make him think he needed his approval? He looked to Trev, who pulled a handful of images of Zumi and Chelsea from a folder and tossed the eight-by-ten printouts on the table, the pile skidding across the surface and showing off mother and daughter.

His father's face paled, the blood draining out as his eyes recognized the faces staring back at him from the photos. "Father, I think this would be a good time for us to have the room."

"Could everyone give my son and I the room? We need to have a family conversation."

The people jumped and scattered like they couldn't get the hell out of there fast enough. Chairs rolled back, briefcases were grabbed, and the sound of feet thundered toward the door. Kes was pretty sure every single person in the room knew about his father's escapades. Shit like that just didn't stay hidden, and they saw an explosion about to erupt.

"What the fuck is this, Kestrel?" His father picked up a picture and shook it for him to see Zumi's smiling face. "And who are these people with you?"

"Sorry, where are my manners? This is Trevor Anderson. He is my attorney. You may have heard of him—he's pretty famous." His father swallowed hard, his eyes wide as they settled on Trev's calm face. "And you should remember Ashley—well then again, why would you? She was nothing more than an inconvenience to you, a blemish that needed to be removed before it damaged the family image. You will be happy to know that your efforts failed, and we are engaged." Kes linked his hand with Ashley's, and she gave his hand a little squeeze.

"If you want to waste your life with a woman that will never better you, then that is your business. But I didn't approve of it then and I don't have to approve of it now."

Looking down at Ashley, Kes leaned in and gave her temple a gentle kiss. Letting go of her hand, he trailed his fingertips along the long table as he approached his father. "Here is the problem with that sentence, you wouldn't know the true meaning of bettering someone if it bit you in the ass, and I don't care about your approval, not anymore."

His father narrowed his eyes at him. It was the look that used to make him shit his pants and run for his bedroom, but now he felt like laughing.

"What do you want? Money? Is that what this is about? You're angry that I said I wouldn't give you any more than your trust fund?"

"I thought you would know what I've been up to and what I want. I mean, isn't that what you said to me? That you know everything?" Kes watched his father's face redden and his nostrils flare as he tried to maintain his composure. "I guess your P.I. didn't tell you that I found him, paid him more than you, and then convinced him that it would be in his best interest to stop following me around. I'm also guessing you haven't noticed that I disabled the tracking device on the yacht, or you'd know that I've been living on it for the last couple of months."

"I'll ask again. What do you want, Son?" His father sat down with a huff like he was wasting his time and had better places to be.

"You used to be my hero," Kes said. His father's brows twitched slightly, but he didn't show any emotion other than that. "I think you hurt me so badly when I realized what type of person you really were because I genuinely thought you could do no wrong."

"Does this story have a point to it?"

"No, not really. I just wanted you to know that what is about to happen is of your own making." Kes waved Trev over. Trev marched up the other side of the table and laid his leather briefcase down, the click of the locks coming undone loud in the quiet room.

"This is the contract for you to sign over all of your shares and rights in the company to Kestrel," Trev said, laying the thick sheath of papers down. "The pages that need to be signed or initialed are marked with small tabs."

His father pushed the contract away, a bitter laugh escaping his lips. "I'm not signing that, not now, not ever."

"Oh? I wouldn't be too hasty if I were you."

"Why are you doing this? You hate the company, and you never wanted to have anything to do with it before."

Kes crossed his arms over his chest. "I realized that it wasn't the company I didn't like. It was you that I didn't want to be around. I have plans for the company, plans to make it better and take it in exciting new directions, but to achieve that, the old regime must go."

"You always thought you knew better, but you're still the same ungrateful, sniveling brat that you always were. You were lucky I didn't press charges against you the night you attacked me like a savage animal. Instead of showing gratitude for my generosity, you ran off like the spoiled child you are and joined the Navy." His voice was laced with disdain, as if the word 'Navy' was disgusting.

"You didn't have me charged because you thought it would teach me a lesson, and that I'd come running to you and begging for your forgiveness. It also meant I wouldn't have a record, like I would if I were carted away by the police. That, of course, would hurt the family image—couldn't have that. I was never going to let you control me like that again."

His father shook his head and stood in a rush, his fingers fixing the bottom button on his suit jacket. "I don't have to put up with this. I will be calling security to have you, your lawyer, and—," his father stopped and looked at Ashley. "'Her' removed."

His temper flared, and Trev must have sensed it because he gave him a hard glare and shook his head no. Kes waited until his father was a few strides away and then spoke. "Nezumi is not the only illegitimate child I know about." His father paused mid-stride. "I know that Chelsea used to work here as your secretary, and that she was mysteriously fired. Nine months later, Nezumi was born. I also know that you'd had Chelsea shipped in special from Japan, a real beauty before she got hooked on drugs and forced out onto the streets. You left her pregnant, jobless and without immigration papers." His father slowly turned to face him. "I know that you paid for both of Zumi's heart surgeries, but signed away all rights to being her father and left her and her mother penniless and homeless on the street. Smart thinking on Chelsea's part to put our family last name down on Zumi's birth certificate. I didn't think she had it in her to actually care about Zumi but looks like at one time she had at least thought she may need the insurance policy of what that name brings." Kes took a step toward his father. "And do you know what else I found out? That there have been more than a dozen women from your company with similar tales. Huh, my father, the breeder of bastards."

"Shut up. This is all speculation. You don't have any proof."

"Do you really think I would march in here like this if I didn't have proof? I don't play poker, so I never learned to bluff. Now, I do realize that almost all of those women took a sum of money and signed an NDA in return, but there were a few you missed before you got smart, and my brilliant lawyer here says that the NDA's wouldn't hold up in court because they were all signed under duress. A forced signature is not a real contract."

"You son of a bitch," his father said, his voice a mix of fear and anger.

"Since you brought Mother up, it's amazing what Mom told me once she realized I was going to help her get away from you." Trev laid another sheath down on the table. "You'll find her divorce papers in there, and yes, they need to be signed today, too. It really would be a shame for all of this to become public. The board members would be forced to remove you, and the public ridicule, as well as the lawsuits I'm certain would start rolling in, would indeed bankrupt you and ruin this company within a year."

His father was shaking from head to toe. The arrogant mask that he always wore had slipped, revealing the real man underneath—the man that was cruel and vindictive. The man who was a control freak and a narcissist.

"Now, before you freak out and start demanding that I get out again, you should also know that I already own forty-five percent of the company."

"That's impossible."

Kes smirked. "But is it? Over the last two months, I've purchased large shares of the company from multiple shareholders under multiple shell companies. Now I, of course, didn't personally have the money for all of that on my own, so it is a really good thing that I have a lawyer that not only has deep pockets but also sees the value in having this company under new leadership."

Kes slowly made his way back to Ashley and wrapped his arm around her waist. The slight smile she gave him warmed his heart as her eyes told him how much she loved him. "So, Father, this is what's going to happen, and I assure you, this deal is a better one than you would offer anyone else, but I'm a generous man that way. You're going to sign the divorce papers and free Mom from you, and you will never reach out to her again for anything. You're also going to sign the company over to me and hold an emergency press conference to announce the exciting news. And what truly exciting news it is, you handing over your company—its' the best thing that has happened to you in a long time, even. I'd recommend a tear for effect. I mean your son is taking the reins of the company so you can finally retire. Don't worry, though. In return, your disgusting infidelities will remain secret. I've also built into the contract a retirement package that will allow you to retain a reasonably comfortable lifestyle until you die. Won't be what you're used to, but such is life."

He took a moment to stare at his father's face and felt no remorse for what he was doing. He most certainly deserved worse, and if the man weren't his father, he would already be bleeding out somewhere, but he'd let the Devil take care of that man's soul.

"I hate you," his father said through gritted teeth.

"I've hated you far longer. You owned my life, but I'm taking it back. You can consider this a hostile takeover." He gave his father a cold smile. "I'll leave Mr. Anderson here to speak with you and get the documents signed. Don't take too long. I've already got the news stations on the way and a party planned in the lobby for the celebratory event."

Not wanting to spend a minute longer in the same room as that man, he held Ashley close to his side and marched out the door he'd entered.

"That was the single sexiest thing I've ever seen in my life, and I couldn't be more proud of you." Ashley stood on her tiptoes and kissed his lips. It was a feather-light touch, but it sent a surge of desire through his body. And just like that, all the shit with his father was gone, and all that existed was her and how to get her laid out on a desk as soon as possible.

"Sexy enough to forgive me for being an ass?"

"So sexy that not only are you forgiven, but all I can think about is getting you home and out of this suit," Ashley whispered a little lower, and his body instantly responded.

"How would you like to have some dirty sex on an office desk?"

"Lead the way," she said, and he groaned softly as she teasingly bit her lip.

Grabbing Ashley's hand, he led her down the hall. "Have I told you today that I love you?"

"A couple of times, but tell me again. I like hearing it."

The smile on his face couldn't get any wider as he glanced down at his beautiful fiancée. "I love you."

# EPILOGUE

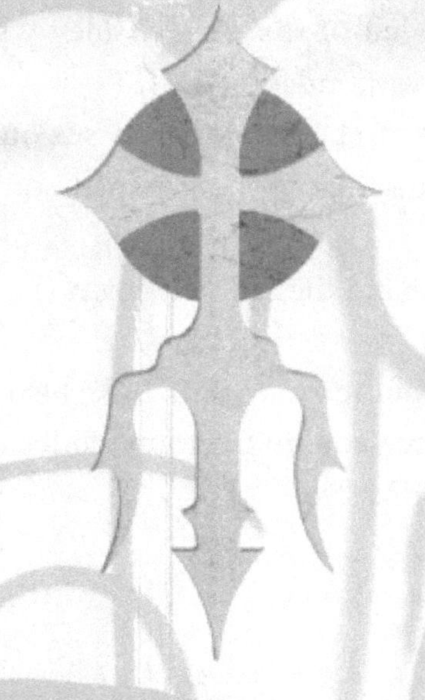

shley was currently doing her best to remain unnoticed and out of the way as Kes, Trev, Arek, and herself all stared at the heated sibling argument.

"Do you think we'll actually get married today?" Arek asked, nudging Trev's arm.

"It would be a waste if we didn't, but at this point, I'm not sure," Trev responded as Renee took the beautiful bouquet in her hands and began smacking it off her brother's chest. Cody was fuming and pointing at his sister and saying that she was forcing a sneak attack on him.

"Mom will be upset if this double wedding doesn't happen." Arek gave his brother a pout, making Trev roll his eyes.

"If you're insinuating I should be playing negotiator, I don't know if even my skills can handle this one. Cody is pretty determined not to speak to his father."

"And Renee won't get married without him here. Come on, man, you have to try. My skills are better directed at killing shit. I will only make this worse," Arek pleaded.

Ashley wrapped her arm around Kes's neck as she sat on his lap. "You're awfully quiet. Is everything okay?" she asked, whispering in his ear.

"Honestly, this is the most entertaining shit I've ever seen. It's like *Monster Brides* clashed with *Survivor* to give you this." He held out his hand toward the action that Trev was slowly inching his way toward nervously. Smiling widely, he popped a strawberry in his mouth and held one out to her.

"You're terrible," she said, but then snickered softly as she took a bite of the fruit.

"And you love it." He kissed her, and it was no sweet little public kiss' as his tongue explored her mouth, his hand going to the back of her head and making her squirm. She couldn't deny his claim, though, so she kept quiet and kissed him back. "I will always think of you with the smell and taste of a strawberry."

"Will strawberries make you think of other things?" She wiggled a little on his lap, already able to feel him hardening under her perched butt.

"Oh, definitely that. How are you feeling?" Kes asked before moving a piece of her fancy curled updo away from her neck to lay a kiss on her jumping pulse.

"Better. The new mix of herbs is helping." It had been a bit of a trial-and-error the last couple of months to manage her symptoms while off her medication. Her mother was, of course, ecstatic that they were going to try and have children right away, but her father had surprised her by telling her he didn't approve and wanted her to go back on her meds. It seemed that everyone had been having some family drama lately.

"Well then, I think we should celebrate." Kes's eyes lit up with child-like mischief. The corner of his mouth pulled up with a special little grin he only gave her, and only when he was thinking of something devious.

"What do you have in mind?"

Instead of answering, Kes stood and placed her on her feet before grabbing her hand. They made it around Arek, who stood like a terrified statue as Renee began to cry.

"You can't leave me here alone." Arek grabbed Kes's arm, a desperate look in his eyes, making Kes laugh.

"You've got this. Besides, I don't think Trev can settle this on his own. Time to tag team, Brother."

Arek nodded, although his facial expression didn't seem as confident. "You're right. It's time I jumped in and helped. I just wish a gun could solve this."

"I wouldn't suggest that," Kes laughed as he gave Ashley's hand a tug, breaking them out of Trev's large office area.

As they passed the bay windows that looked out toward Arek and Trev's backyard, his eyes scanned everyone standing outside waiting for the ceremony to begin. She knew without having to ask that he was searching for Zumi. She could feel his body relax as he spotted her laughing and eating from the large buffet table with Simone and J.J.

"She's fine." Ashley gave Kes's hand a squeeze, and he sighed in response.

"I know. I just worry all the time."

"You want us to double that by getting pregnant? If you think you're worrying now, you just wait until a tiny little baby is placed in your arms."

"How can something be the single best and yet most terrifying thing you've ever heard?" Kes smirked at her. "Have you changed your mind?"

She shook her head no. The smile on her face couldn't be wiped away, not when it was buoyed up with the thought of having a baby in their home. She loved Zumi and doted on her every chance she got, but she wanted to have the sleepless nights and the disgusting poopy diapers and the first steps that Zumi was well past. She also couldn't imagine anything cuter than holding a small bundle that looked like a miniature version of Kes.

"Good, because I thought we could continue our mission to get you knocked up right now."

"Such a way with words you have," she said, laughing as Kes poked his head into a vacant bedroom and closed the door. The soft click seemed loud as he flipped the lock into place. "You're serious?"

"I'm very serious." Kes pulled off the leather strap of his belt, and that one move made her stomach clench.

"But what if they start the wedding? We're both supposed to be standing up there with them," she said half-heartedly as the button and fly were released, giving her greedy eyes an unobstructed view of his hard cock. She ran her tongue along her lips, eyes fixated on his hand and how sexy he looked slowly stroking himself.

"We'll make it quick," he said, and her body flushed like she'd been standing outside in the sun all day with the look he was giving her. She'd always enjoyed sex, but not like this. Maybe it was because of the bond between them, maybe he just fit her better, but whatever it was, her panties were damp, and she was ready before he even wrapped an arm around her waist.

"I think we can squeeze in a quickie," she agreed, hungrily accepting his mouth like it was her last meal. Kes worked fast. His hands balled the sundress up, and he groaned into her mouth as his fingers ran across the damp material, pushing it up delightfully between her pussy lips.

Everything zeroed in on the sensation of his fingers rubbing the worked-up and sensitive area, making her forget where they were or why. After gripping the edge of the simple lace panties, Kes pulled them down her legs, and she braced herself on his shoulders as she stepped out of the delicate material.

"I wish we had more time. I want to lay you out on that bed and service this pussy the way it deserves to be treated." Ashley gasped as a finger slid into her core as his tongue swirled around her clit. "You taste like heaven," Kes mumbled between licks. She wanted to grip his hair but held on to his shoulders instead so she didn't mess up his hair. "I have to stop, or we're going to be here for a very long time."

She was drunk on the heated desire that was coursing through her veins as Kes stood and picked her up so her legs could wrap around his waist. There was no fumbling as he slid home and captured her lips to contain the scream he knew from experience would escape her.

Bliss. There was no other word for what she felt as he moved inside of her as perfectly as if they'd been together years rather than months.

The door suddenly rattled and made a soft thud as it tried to open but failed with the lock in place. She gasped, but Kes wasn't stopping. In fact, he didn't seem to hear whoever was out in the hall.

"Why is this door locked?" an unknown voice asked.

"I don't know. I'll go get the key," Arek responded.

"Kes," she moaned as his movements quickened. "People," she managed and then sucked in her lower lip as his hands gripped her ass harder. The slightly different angle had him pressing against her G-spot, and she bit down on her fist hard to try and keep from screaming out.

The sound of a key in the lock had him moving. Kes reached out and grabbed the door handle to the closet. He stepped them both inside the large space, closing the door behind him. It was dark in the closet, but the move wasn't a moment too soon, as shadows could be seen moving out in the bedroom.

"All the extra gifts can go in here. We don't use it for anything," Arek said as Kes pushed her back up against the wall.

She'd never been into daring exhibitionism, yet there was something about being so close to getting caught like this that cranked up the already intoxicating need that was bringing her dangerously close to screaming Kes's name—whoever was in the room be damned.

Her ass was bounced up and down harder with the added leverage of the wall. With the erratic thrusts came the murmuring for her to come as Kes pressed his lips against her ear. She could hear the strain in his voice and knew he was close, and that final thought pushed her over the edge. Her head pressed back against the wall as she opened her mouth in a silent scream. Her body spasmed around his cock as his desperate moans only heightened the release with the vibrating along the sensitive skin of her neck. Ke's teeth locked on to her earlobe and sucked. He knew she loved it when he did that. It always drew out her orgasm, and sure enough, she gasped as the wave she was riding surged.

More shadows came along with the sound of boxes and paper as person after person arrived to set down items in the room. "Yes, put them over there," the voice of a woman she didn't know said. "Okay everyone, back to your other positions. That should be good." The room fell silent, and she slumped in Kes's arms as he continued to pant quietly against her neck.

Embarrassment washed over her as Arek spoke aloud, "I'm all for fucking at my wedding, but next time, don't leave your underwear in the middle of the room if you're gonna try and hide. Rookie move, Brother."

She placed a hand over her mouth to keep from laughing as she flushed for a whole new reason.

"Yeah, yeah," Kes grumbled.

Arek's laugh was loud and infectious. She could almost see him bent over as he smacked his knee. "They're currently hanging on the closet door handle. Don't worry, I don't think the wedding planner saw them, and I won't tell Trev. Oh, and the wedding is going to start in ten minutes. Would be good to have the best man there." Arek moved away from the door. "Balls, Brother. That took balls. I'm so proud of you."

"Get the fuck out," Kes said, but she could tell even he was having a hard time holding back a smile.

Arek's laugh could be heard from all the way down the hall after he left the bedroom, closing the door behind him. Kes stepped away from the closet wall and lowered her to her feet. "You good?"

"Steady as a rock."

"I meant to face him. 'Cause he is not going to let this go." Kes pushed open the door and reached around to grab her underwear, and this time he helped her step into them.

"Sure he will. I have a secret weapon. It's called Renee." She smiled wide as Kes stuffed himself, and his shirt, back into his pants.

"You're beautiful when you're being devious." Kes held out his hand for her to take, and she'd never felt more alive. No matter what they might face, as long as they were together, she knew they'd be able to overcome any battle.

"And here I thought I was beautiful all the time." Ashley nudged his arm and his face grew serious, but his eyes were filled with so much emotion that they held her and made her feel as warm as if she were wearing a well-worn sweater. "I was teasing."

"I know, but I just wanted to admire this 'I've been fucked hard in a closet' look. It's hot on you."

She smacked his arm as she laughed. He'd totally set her up for his usual sweet praise. "Come on, Doll. We have a wedding to attend, and then I may find another dark corner in this massive place to take you again."

As they wandered down the hall hand in hand, she stared up at the man that she'd never thought she would have. She'd told herself over and over how stupid she was to hope he could ever belong to her. Apparently, hope had a lesson for her.

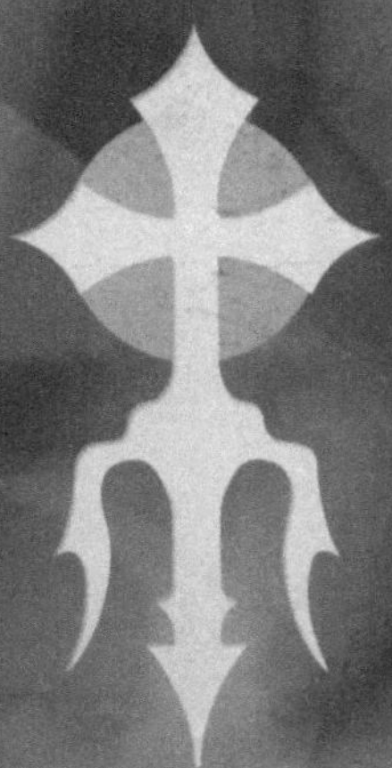
COMING
SOON
REDEMPTION
IN THE
DARK

# REDEMPTION IN THE DARK

## BOOK 5 - CHAPTER 1 - THE RIGHTEOUS SERIES - BY: BROOKLYN CROSS

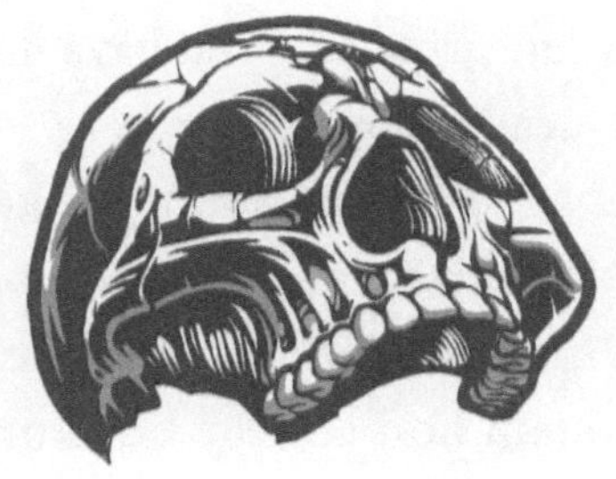

Wolf knew this job was going sideways the moment he was handed the damn order. You don't just stroll into a notorious biker bar, take out their leader, and think you're walking back out again like it's a fucking coffee shop.

Luckily, he'd been provided with some backup, but the place had quickly turned into the Wild West. The leader of the motorcycle club, Hammer, gave the order to 'fuck shit up.' The guy seemed more like a box of loose screws than a hammer, but that was a personal opinion.

Wolf ducked away from a fist coming for his face just in time for a chair to collide with Hammer's head. He had no idea who threw it, but he owed them a beer. The big man stumbled to the side and grabbed the bar for support. Seizing the opportunity, he grabbed the leader of the biker crew by his cut, and with a good old heave-ho, threw him over the bar. Half-drunk beer mugs smashed to the floor as the large man kicked out wildly.

Grabbing the faded brass rail like it was a hurdle, Wolf leaped over the bar and landed beside the dazed man.

"Look out," someone yelled.

Wolf covered his head as he dropped low behind the bar. The mirror on the wall behind the bar smashed into a million tiny shards, raining down on himself and Hammer. The man groaned and shielded his head, but they were both going to have cuts and abrasions from the onslaught.

Glancing at Hammer, Wolf caught the glimmer of a shiny blade and managed to snatch Hammer's arm before the switchblade could slice into his calf.

"Just give up already," he growled. "You have nowhere to go."

"Only over my cold, dead corpse."

"Don't fucking tempt me," Wolf said, teeth gritted as they wrestled over the weapon. Fighting this man was like trying to fight a bear. Or at least what he assumed it would be like since he hadn't tussled with a bear…yet. Sure, a mountain lion and an alligator, he'd wrestled both a time or two, but not a bear.

"Oh, fuck it." Bringing his knee in toward Hammer, he hit the man in the crown jewels as hard as possible. It wasn't a great shot from the odd angle, but it did the trick.

Hammer's eyes bugged out, and his cheeks filled with air as the pain registered. Hammer's arms weakened, and he was able to disarm the man and roll the guy over onto his stomach to put the zip ties on his wrists. Besides, he really loathed the idea of getting stabbed again. The last time he'd been knifed, it cost him over a month of work, and they'd had him riding a desk until he was able to get back out into the field.

He flopped back on his ass, breathing hard. Sweat streamed down his face in the unairconditioned, unseasonably hot bar. Wolf's eyes scanned over him as he continued to groan in pain. It wasn't his finest fighting moment, but he was more than done with this Hammer and his biker buddies.

His patience had disappeared a while ago. After sleeping in his car for weeks while he kept surveillance on this clubhouse, waiting for the okay to storm it and take Hammer. There were only so many times you could piss in a bottle and eat bags of junk food for meals before all you craved was a hot shower, a half-decent meal, and your bed.

Hammer had been important enough to sacrifice the hours for—the man was wanted on multiple charges, including four counts of murder they could prove and who knew how many more they couldn't. He wanted to ensure the evidence was airtight before handing the case over to his higher ups for the prosecution.

Hammer was regaining his wits and was pushing himself along the floor like a massive worm as he tried to get his feet under his body to stand.

"Come on, man. You're just annoying me now," Wolf said as he stood and followed. Reaching down took some effort, but he managed to roll the man over onto his back and cracked him as hard as he could across the face a couple of times. The blow only seemed to antagonize Hammer rather than have any real effect. "Are you fucking high?"

"Give me the pain. I like it." Hammer spit a little blood onto the floor.

"You're going to love prison then." Wolf grabbed the man by the front of his cut and hauled him onto his feet.

The room had been reduced to shambles. Broken tables and smashed glasses crunched under his boots. Pictures hung at odd angles or were off the wall and had been used as weapons. Wolf cringed as he stared at the rookie he'd brought with him for backup. He was unconscious on the pool table, but his pants were pulled down to show off his ass and the long pool cue sticking out of it. Wolf shook his head. That was going to be a story the guy never lived down.

"Marcus, can you go help the new guy?" Wolf pointed to the pool table, and Marcus's face twisted in horror. He then proceeded to laugh and shake his head no. "At least make sure he's still breathing, you fucker."

Marcus continued to laugh like a braying donkey as he pulled a phone from his pocket. I knew what he was planning and there was simply no point trying to stop him, Marcus always did what he wanted.

Wolf pushed Hammer through the shattered bar door and out into the bright sunlight. It was going to be another scorcher of a day, and he was looking forward to a cold beer and an even colder shower.

"Here," he said as he handed Hammer over to the men loading the prisoner van.

As he walked away, he assessed his injuries. Nothing major. A few cuts and bruises, but nothing life-threatening. He limped his way toward his car and took a deep breath as he undid the Velcro sides of the bullet-proof vest and pulled the heavy thing off. He quickly brushed off some mirror shards from the front of the kevlar that had stuck to the U.S. Marshal symbol before tossing it into the back seat.

He slipped behind the wheel with a sigh and turned the key in the ignition. As soon as he did, his phone rang, and his special phone binged a text.

"Really, people? You can't let a guy have one night's rest before you go harassing him?" he mumbled, picking up his work phone first. "Wolf, here."

"Executive of Special Operations, Wigfield here."

He sat up a little straighter even though the man couldn't see him. "Executive, this is a surprise."

"I wanted first to commend you on your operation today. I heard it was a success."

News certainly traveled fast. He shouldn't be shocked by now, but it was a little creepy how quickly they always found out how well a mission did or didn't go. "Thank you. We apprehended Hammer as well as a number of others that were on lists to be picked up for lesser charges. They are all in custody now."

"Very good work. The reason for my call is we have a new fugitive that needs to be apprehended as quickly as possible, and I have it on good authority that you're the best."

His chest puffed out a little with the compliment. "I'd like to think I am."

"Good. I will send a package to your phone for you to review. Time is of the essence. We don't want this individual slipping out of the country."

"Understood. But is there a reason you're the one calling?" he had to ask.

The Executive hadn't spoken to him once since he'd joined the U.S. Marshal's office, unless he was forced to and to the best of Wolf's knowledge, never called any of those that were not top brass to assign a job. The only reason could be that whoever the mark was, was important, and it also meant that he wouldn't be read in unless it became a must-know situation. The white shirts liked their secrets.

"This one is important to me. I'd consider it a huge, personal favor and one that could hold a promotion at the end if you can complete it," Wigfield said, confirming his suspicions.

Wolf looked at the phone, not believing his ears.

"Yes, Sir. I will get right on this for you," he said as his phone dinged, signaling that the package had arrived.

"I'll await an update."

The line went dead, and he tapped on the new file and scrolled through the details. His eyes finally landed on the girl. It might have been sexist of him, but he was expecting another Hammer, not a girl smiling for the camera like it was a school photo rather than a mug shot.

He placed his work phone in the holder when his off-the-books phone buzzed again, reminding him he still needed to look at it. He was pretty sure all Righteous members had two phones. It was a part of the life. As a member, everyone was required to keep communication and identity completely separate from everything else. It was an encrypted email, as was the norm with a new manhunt. The Righteous knew he preferred to arrest first and only kill those they assigned directly.

He quickly typed in the fifteen-digit password, a series of random letters and numbers, and opened the file.

"What the fuck?" His eyes scanned over the image of the same woman. He picked up his other phone and compared the two images. She looked different than in the image that Wigfield had sent. The picture from The Righteous contact looked like she'd taken a beating and managed to live to tell the tale. The sight of the bruised face with her eye almost closed tight from swelling didn't ruin her beauty, but it did make his blood boil. No matter what she'd done, she didn't deserve to be beaten.

"What did you do to warrant all this attention, Maeve?"

*It didn't matter.*

As a U.S Marshal, his job was to apprehend, but now with the new orders from the Righteous, dead or alive was an option.

# Thank You

for reading
Hiding in the Dark
If you enjoyed this book
please consider leaving a
review. Reviews are the best
way to show your love and
are always appreciated.
If you would like to be
among the first to know
about new releases in The
Righteous Series then join my
Facebook Group Crossfire - A
Brooklyn Cross Reader
Group
Look for more books in
The Righteous Series

# BROOKLYN

If you like it dark and edgy then look no further. Brooklyn Cross has always had a deep passion for writing that stemmed from a wild imagination. When she is not busy typing away about the next character you will fall in love with, you can find her walking with her dogs on the farm and sipping a hot cup of coffee.

In addition to getting her degree in business she was highly competitive in the equestrian sport of dressage, with aspirations of an Olympic dream. She is an entrepreneur at heart and has coached and trained many of a riding enthusiast or their wonderful mounts, but always found herself drawn to writing full-time.

"Writing is what I love. I just want to be authentic with my characters. To tell a story that others can immerse themselves in and enjoy, but also relate too. If I can make you smile, laugh, cry, or your heart pound then I have done my job. To drop people into my worlds and for a short time have you live alongside my characters, is what I have always wanted."

# CROSS

Below are the links that you can use to find me if you'd like to follow me on my social media platforms.

Goodreads: <u>Brooklyn Cross (Author of Dark Side of the Cloth) | Goodreads</u>
TikTok: <u>Author Brooklyn Cross (@authorbrooklyncross) TikTok | Watch Author Brooklyn Cross's Newest TikTok Videos</u>
IG: <u>Brooklyn Cross (@author_brooklyncross) • Instagram photos and videos</u>
FB Group: <u>Crossfire - A Brooklyn Cross Reader Group | Facebook</u>